CLAIMED BY THE DRAGON KING

JESSICA GRAYSON

Purple Fall
Publishing

Identifiers:

ISBN: ebook 978-1-64253-375-0

paperback 978-1-64253-112-1

Cover Design by Kim Cunningham of Atlantis Book Design

PRINTED IN THE UNITED STATES OF AMERICA

DEDICATION

To my husband: You are not just my husband, you are my best friend and my rock. Thank you for all your love and support. I love you more than words can ever say.

-Jessica Grayson

CHAPTER 1

FREYJA

I *dream of fire and ruin. Destruction and flame. A strange man shrouded in darkness, with emerald eyes that burn into mine, their vertically slit pupils expanding as he studies me with a piercing gaze. "T'kara," his deep voice echoes in my head, and although I do not know this word, I can feel the possession that seeps into his tone.*

He is the man who haunts me both night and day, the future that rushes toward me. I know not if he is my salvation or my end; I only know that fate is the hunter I cannot escape.

RUSTED HINGES CREAK LOUDLY, startling me awake. Two guards stalk toward me and jerk me up from the pitiful straw palette that has been my bed these past few weeks. My breath quickens as I recognize the one that gave me a lashing three days ago, attempting to secure my confession of witchcraft.

I clench my jaw, determined not to break. If he's come to whip a confession out of me again, the only answers he'll get

1

are the muffled cries I cannot bite back. I will never admit to the crimes they've accused me of because they are not mine to claim.

I squint my eyes against the harsh rays of the sun as their rough hands pull me from the castle dungeon and into the courtyard. It feels like forever since I've been outside, and the light is so bright it's nearly blinding.

The guards grasp my arms in a bruising grip as they drag me through the maddened crowd. It seems they have gathered here today to witness my execution, shouting and calling for the death of the witch.

Witch. The word settles in my gut like a heavy stone. I am a princess and a shield-maiden of Ruhaen. I've never conjured a spell or cast an enchantment, but I've had dreams of things before they have happened. Only a handful, but enough to recognize the truth.

I have inherited the curse of my mother's bloodline.

The Order of Mages has forbidden all magic—even that of seers—and considers it witchcraft, punishable by death.

I would have taken this secret to my grave, if not for my nightmare, less than a fortnight ago. Closing my eyes, the memory of the Wraith invading our kingdom, a trail of death and devastation left in their wake, returns in vivid detail.

When I awakened, I knew I had to tell my uncle—the king. I confided my truth to him and his betrothed, Luria. Only seven years older, she had befriended me and become my closest confidante. I felt compelled to warn them so we could make plans to defend the kingdom. How could I remain silent if it meant others might die? I believed I could trust them, but I was wrong.

Luria turned on me first, convincing my uncle in less than a heartbeat that I had to be imprisoned. Her betrayal and his complacency cut deeper than any knife ever could. My uncle has never trusted the Mages; he and the council cast out the last High Mage over a year ago. And yet he reported me to their order as if I meant nothing to him.

My heart stops at the sight of the large, raised platform with a wooden stake in the middle. Thick stacks of wood surround the base for the fire that will be lit to burn my body to ash.

As the guards drag me up the steps, I thrash against their hold, but they grip me in an iron vise and slam my back against the pole. Forcing my arms overhead, they bind my wrists with rope. Several strands of my long red hair fall loose from my braid as I struggle against the rough twine digging into my flesh.

"Please!" I cry out. "Do not do this!"

"Silence, witch!" one guard hisses as he wraps another rope tight around my ankles to keep me in place.

Frantic, I turn my head toward the raised dais off to the side and lock eyes with the King. "Uncle Harald, please! Let me go!"

Dressed in his full regalia, his red hair, peppered with gray, is perfectly coiffed beneath his heavy gold crown. His pale blue eyes are dull with disinterest as he gazes at me while his soon-to-be wife, Luria, leans close and whispers in his ear.

"Silence her!" he calls out. "Before she bewitches you all!"

Without hesitation, the guards cinch a leather belt tightly over my mouth while Luria watches with a sneer on her otherwise perfect face.

Her long blonde hair shines like gold in the sunlight, matching the lavish gold chains and rings gifted to her by the king. Her green eyes meet mine and a glowing light flashes behind them, turning them raven black for a moment.

Heat floods my veins as the pieces all fall into place. Luria is not human. She's a Mage. A spy sent by the Order to influence our king and bring our lands back under their dark and twisted rule.

With my uncle under her spell, the entire kingdom will be laid bare at her feet when they marry. The King will be little more than a figurehead, while the Mages control everything.

Harald has been a father to me since my parents' death, and his betrayal is a mortal wound. But as my gaze sweeps over the frenzied crowd, it seems no one is immune to Luria's powerful magic. My uncle loved me. I know he did. Tears blur my vision and sting my eyes as I regard him once more. Only now do I understand that he is under her spell and knows not what he does.

Satisfied that my bindings are secure and that I cannot speak, the guards leave the platform and light their torches while the crowd screams for my death and gathers small stones from the courtyard to throw at me.

Each impact of the rocks against my flesh is agony, and I lower my head to shield my face from the assault. My heart hammers and tears spill down my cheeks as the wood surrounding the platform catches fire.

Flames lick at my feet, and I scream beneath my gag as the heat sears my flesh. Smoke billows up from beneath me, stinging my eyes and my nostrils with each inhalation. The world tilts and spins around me as the fumes make it difficult to breathe, shrouding my mind in a fog-like haze.

With the last of my strength, I lift my gaze to the sky and send a silent prayer to the gods, pleading for this not to be the end. I'm not ready to die and meet them today.

A dark shadow moves overhead, blocking the light of the sun. The massive form is vaguely familiar, as my mind struggles to make sense of what I'm seeing.

A deafening roar fills the air.

"Dragon!" someone shrieks. "Take cover!"

Panicked cries ring out as a great silver-white Dragon

circles the crowd. My heart leaps into my throat as he flies straight toward the platform. Black smoke whirls around him with the heavy beat of his massive wings. His scales shimmer iridescent, reflecting the glow of the flames, unscathed by the fire that encircles his terrifying form.

Piercing emerald eyes meet mine, their reptilian pupils contracting and then expanding wide.

"Mine," a deep voice whispers in my mind, fierce and possessive.

Lightning fast, the Dragon extends his sharp claws, slicing away my bindings and pulling me free from the wooden stake. Wrapping his massive front paw around my form, he shields me from the inferno as he pulls me to his chest.

My throat is raw and swollen, and pain stabs through me as I struggle to draw in a deep breath. Darkness closes in around the edge of my vision as my eyelids blink open and closed.

Lethal black claws as big as spears dig into my skin but do not break it as his green eyes travel over me. Rage fills my chest, and somehow, I know it is not mine. It's his.

He releases a thunderous roar as he turns to the crowd. His dark voice, full of unbridled anger, echoes in my mind. *"I will raze their kingdom to the ground. All of them will burn for daring to harm what is mine."*

The silver scales across his chest glow as fire builds deep within. He opens his mouth, and a devastating stream of flame erupts from his throat and into the crowd.

The world tilts and spins, fading away, and my vision narrows as I slowly lose the fight to remain conscious. My head falls back, and I tumble away into the dark and beckoning void.

CHAPTER 2

AURDYN

My *T'kara—my treasure. My Fated One. My mate. Mine.*

The sacred words echo in my mind as the mate bond snaps firmly into place.

My T'kara is human: with hair the color of flame and pale blue eyes that seem to stare straight through me. Her small form shudders in my grip, and rage blisters through my veins as I turn to the ones who wished to end her.

All of them will burn for daring to harm what is mine. I swear it to *Draegar*—the ancient god of fire and destruction.

Fire builds deep in my chest and I open my mouth, releasing the flames of my anger. I will incinerate them all and raze their entire kingdom for what they've done. The crowd scatters, desperate to escape my wrath. But there will be no escape. Only vengeance this day.

It has been many years since I dealt with the humans, and our tentative treaty is at an end. I prayed to the gods and received a vision, instructing me to come here. Alone. I knew not what I'd find, only that it would be important. I never expected my Fated One would be here, nor that she'd be human.

Holding my T'kara securely to my chest, I level a dark glare at King Harald. Fire gathers at the back of my throat, and black smoke trickles from my nostrils as I speak through my fangs. "What is the meaning of this?"

"She was caught practicing witchcraft," the king replies firmly. "The penalty for this crime is death."

Fire licks the back of my throat with want to roast him where he stands. "How dare you harm what is mine," I growl. "I will end you for hurting my T'kara!"

"Your T'kara?" The woman beside him gasps. A flicker of magic moves across her face, revealing her true form beneath. Her pale skin fades to light gray, her long blond hair turning silver as her eyes shift from green into twin pools of pitch-black darkness. She is a Mage—an old one judging from the state of her haggard appearance.

Her gaze locks onto my mate. "A *sanishon*," she rasps through sharp, white fangs.

Sanishon. Wisps of a long-buried memory unfurl within my mind. This word means *Outsider* in the archaic tongue, originating in a prophecy in the Ancient Tomes of the Lythyrian.

"Guards!" The Mage raises her hands, red bolts of energy crackling across her fingers like lightning. "Kill her! Kill them both!"

As one, the guards turn, raising their swords. Their eyes are glazed under the effect of her enslavement spell. Even the king's expression is fixed and unfocused as he stares dully at me.

Something whistles through the air, and I turn in time to see an arrow bounce harmlessly off my scales, followed by several more.

Foolish humans. The pitiful weapons of man cannot harm me, but I realize they can very easily kill my mate if I do not protect her.

Opening my mouth, I spew a torrent of flame at the Mage. She conjures a shield to protect her and the king, deflecting the devastation that would melt their skin and char their bones.

"Use the black arrows you fools!" she screeches to the king's guards.

A flash of metal glints in the light and I turn as an archer in the nearby tower nocks a black arrow in the large bow mounted atop the battlement.

These arrows are tipped with obsidian stone—a rare and expensive ore from the *Cragyr* mountains. They are the only thing that can pierce a Dragon's scales. Six more archers appear along the walls, each of them drawing back their bows to fire their black arrows.

Inwardly, I curse myself for having come here, unprepared. My advisor suggested I bring three guards, but I ignored him. My vision had stated I must come alone.

I am the Dragon King of the Ice Mountains. I'd believed I could handle a kingdom of pitiful humans if things went wrong. I had not counted upon them having so many black arrows.

The first archer lets loose his deadly arrow and time slows as it spirals toward me. I twist to one side, but not fast enough. A pained cry rips from my throat as it sinks deep into my hind leg.

Taking advantage of my momentary distraction, the other guards send a volley of arrows, directed at my mate.

My chest tightens. I must get her to safety.

Extending my wings, I flap them furiously, catching the wind in the great sails, and lifting into the air. Another black arrow rushes toward me from the far tower and I barely avoid the hit as we ascend.

I expel another wave of fire at the castle turrets, sending several of the guards diving down the stairwells as we spiral up toward the clouds and disappear into their cover.

As I turn back toward the Ice Mountains, my wings feel heavy and sluggish to respond. A strange sensation suffuses my body, and my mind floats in a dream-like haze. I shake my head to clear it, but the world tilts to one side.

I flap my wings to correct, but they barely move as a dense fog wraps tight around my mind. My eyelids blink open and closed as sleep tries to claim me.

I do not understand what is happening, but when pain arcs through my leg from the black arrow still embedded in my flesh, a moment of clarity pierces the darkness, and I growl low in my throat.

Curse the humans. The arrow was tipped with poison.

Panic grips me in an iron vise as I glance down at the female in my front paw and find her unconscious. I must locate a place to land and get her to safety before the poison renders me senseless.

Mustering my strength, I dip my left wing, catching the current. I spread them wide, allowing the great sails to ride the wind and carry us over the snow-covered forest and toward the Ice Mountains that my people call home.

I fight the poison's effects and struggle to remain conscious. I just need to make it to the mountains and find a cave or someplace to shelter until it wears off. But as I scan the terrain, my vision begins to blur, and I know I won't make it much farther.

A small cottage in the distance catches my eye. Nestled in the center of the forest, it's far enough away from everything that it should be safe. Despite the snow that blankets the woods, there is no smoke rising from the chimney, suggesting this place must be abandoned. Humans cannot survive in these cold conditions without the warmth of fire. At least, not very long.

Clenching my jaw, I make my way toward it. If I can just get us there, we have a chance. If not, my mate is as good as dead. Sending a silent prayer to the gods, I ask for the strength to reach the shelter.

We glide low over the trees, their snowy tops brushing my scales and exploding in puffs of white powder as I beat my wings awkwardly, struggling to land. We crash and tumble through the thick branches. Holding my mate close to my chest, I twist onto my back at the last second, shielding her from injury as we slam to the ground. A sharp crack slices the air and pain arcs through my left wing like fire.

An agonized roar rips from my throat, and I shift into my two-legged form as we skid across the ice and snow, banging into the cottage door. Fighting the sedative effects of the poison, I blink several times and force myself to stand.

I hoist my mate into my arms and kick open the door, slamming it shut behind us. My nostrils flare. Whoever lived here is gone and has been for a while. Barely able to remain upright, I stumble toward the fireplace. Drawing in a deep breath, I gather my fire and then release a stream of flame to the stacked wood on the hearth.

Relief fills me as it catches immediately, but it is short-lived as I glance over my shoulder. My left wing hangs at an odd angle by my side, the support joint dislocated and swollen. I suffered this injury many times in my youth; fortunately, I know how to correct it.

Gritting my teeth, I fully extend it. Sharp pain arcs across my wing, and I bite back a roar as it snaps firmly into place.

Fierce protectiveness floods my veins as I glance down at my T'kara, lying unresponsive in my grasp. She needs warmth or she will not survive the night. Pushing through my agony, I wrap my arms and wings solidly around her smaller form.

Unable to stand any longer, I drop to my knees and lie down by the fire. Holding my mate tight to my chest, I close my eyes and fall away into the dark and beckoning void.

CHAPTER 3

FREYJA

When I wake, warmth completely surrounds me. I cannot remember the last time I slept so soundly. My eyes snap open and my breath catches when I realize I'm in an unfamiliar room.

Bright sunlight spills in from two small windows on the other side of the room, gilding the cobwebs that cross the ceiling and the corners of the glass windowpanes. This looks to be some sort of cottage, but I have no idea where I am. The wooden floor is worn with use but surprisingly clean. A small mound of dirt near the door tells me that someone must have recently swept.

The crackling wood of a fire draws my attention and I turn toward it. Alarm ripples down my spine. Orange firelight casts sinister shadows over a large figure crouched before the hearth—a man. Ice freezes my veins as large, leathery wings extend from his back, and he flicks his long tail behind him.

This is no man. It's a Dragon.

Myriad images flood my mind as the memory of the Dragon pulling me from the flames returns.

He goes completely still, as if sensing my observation. In one fluid motion he stands, turning to face me. He's dressed in black pants, leaving his torso completely bare. Instead of skin, silver-white scales cover him. Broad shoulders taper to a chiseled, muscular waist. Light and shadow sculpt the hard planes of muscle that line his abdomen and chest. Dagger-sharp black claws tip his hands and feet. Two small black horns on either side of his forehead jut up through shoulder-length, silver-white hair.

His face is set in a stern expression, accentuating his masculine square jaw, proud nose, and ridged brow. Emerald eyes study me, their vertically slit pupils expanding as his nostrils flare.

"Your scent was soft and warm only a moment ago, but it is now soured with fear." His voice is low and rumbling. "Why?"

I stare at him in shock. Those are the same eyes that haunt my dreams.

His long tail flicks agitatedly behind him. "Are you in pain?"

I open my mouth to speak, but the words die in my throat as he crosses the room in three steps and drops to his knees at my side. "Speak, human," he demands, flashing two rows of sharp white fangs. "I am King Aurdyn of the Ice Mountains, and I command you to answer my question, female."

Indignation fills me, overriding my fear. "I am *not* one of your subjects to command, and my name is Princess Freyja." I keep my eyes locked on his. "Not 'human.' Not 'female.' Do you understand?"

He clenches his jaw. A wisp of black smoke curls out from his nostrils, and I regret my words immediately. I've heard enough stories of his kind to know that it is never wise to mouth off to a Dragon. Fire burns in his eyes as he glares at me, and I fight the urge to bolt. Dragons respect strength, so I must not show any fear.

I push up to my feet, meaning to stand tall, but stabbing pain shoots through my legs, and I fall forward.

Strong hands wrap around my waist before I hit the ground, and then lift me from the floor as if I weigh nothing. My heart rate spikes and I flail wildly before he pulls me to his chest, holding me still in a vise-like grip. "Do not struggle," he grinds out. "You will only hurt yourself."

"Let me go!" I punch at his chest, only to be met with unyielding firm muscle.

"And just where do you think you would go?" he asks, arching a condescending brow. "Your own kind tried to kill you, human. If not for me, you'd have been burned at the stake."

Anger flares brightly. "I already told you. My name is not —" Pain arcs up my legs, stealing the breath from my lungs. I focus on them, only now noticing the strips of fabric wrapped from my calves to my feet.

"I made a salve for your burns, *Princess Freyja*." He answers my unspoken question, emphasizing my proper name and title. "Your skin should be healed either tomorrow or the next day."

I blink several times. He saved me from the fire, *and* he treated my burns. "Thank you." The words leave my mouth automatically.

Tipping up his chin, he stares down at me imperiously. "Does this mean you will not try to run away now?"

"I was *not* trying to run away," I state firmly. I look down at my legs again. "Even if I wanted to, I cannot."

He narrows his eyes, gauging the truth of my words, and I shiver slightly. Not so much from the chill in the air but from the hard expression on his face. My gaze travels over the room again and I wonder what he plans to do with me.

The Dragon King walks toward the fireplace and sets me down before the hearth. He turns his back to me as he stokes the fire.

I've always been one to face the truth head on, no matter how hard. It is common knowledge that Dragons hate humans, and yet, he saved me and treated my wounds, but I know not for what purpose. "What are you going to do with me?"

He flexes his massive wings, tucking them tightly against his back, flicking his tail once again as if in irritation. "I have not decided yet."

His answer is only mildly reassuring. "You're not going to… eat me, right?"

Aurdyn looks at me as if I've lost my mind. "What do you think I am?" he asks incredulously.

Is this a trick question? "You're a Dragon."

"Do you truly believe that I just fly over the land, eating anyone that crosses my path?" He huffs. "My kind do not eat yours, nor any other sentient creatures." He lifts a condescending brow as he studies me. "And if we did, you'd have nothing to worry about anyway. There is barely any meat on your bones."

Oddly, I'm both relieved and mildly insulted by his answer. "Is this your… lair?" I'd always heard that Dragons live in caves in the Ice Mountains, not in cottages or homes.

"My lair?" He scoffs. "As if a Dragon would live in a hovel like this." He scans the room with a look of disdain, his gaze dropping to the pile of dirt near the door. "I did what I could to clean this nest while you slept." He looks up at the ceiling and the cobwebs spanning the rafters. "But there is still much to be done."

That was… rather thoughtful of him. Despite his somewhat abrasive manner, my fears are rapidly disappearing with each question he answers. He saved me and as I look at the fire burning in the hearth and the furs draped over my body to protect against the chill, I think he's trying to take care of me, but I do not understand why. I'd always heard that Dragons have little love for my kind.

He turns his attention back to the fireplace, adding more wood to the flames.

I open my mouth to ask another question, but my stomach growls loudly.

His head whips to me, and my cheeks flush in embarrassment. "You are hungry." He shifts his gaze to the entrance. "I must go hunt. I will return with food shortly."

Before I can say anything, he crosses the room and opens the door. A gust of wind blows into the cottage, nearly smothering the flames in the hearth. Snow falls heavily outside in sheets so thick I can barely see anything beyond his crowded figure in the doorway. "Wait!" I call out, and he halts, turning back to me. "You cannot go out in that weather."

"I am a Dragon of the Ice Mountains." He sneers and gestures outside. "This is nothing to me. You will see when we reach my home."

He's taking me to the Ice Mountains? "Why did you save me?" I blurt without thinking.

His emerald-green eyes study me with a piercing gaze. "Because you are mine."

My heart seizes in my chest. *Oh gods above, he's taken me as his slave.*

Before I can say anything else, he steps out the door and closes it behind him, disappearing into the storm outside.

CHAPTER 4

AURDYN

Frustration boils as I move across the ice and snow, searching for prey. Curling my hands into fists at my side, I curse the humans once more. If not for their poisoned arrow, I'd never have injured my wing. It will take at least a week to heal enough that I can fly again, which means we will have to travel to my kingdom on foot.

My thoughts turn to my Fated One—my T'kara—the Princess Freyja. If I were alone, travel would be no issue. But I wonder how she will fare in these conditions. She is human, and as such, her body is fragile and intolerant of the cold. My grandfather knew this about their kind. It is the reason he moved our people to the Ice Mountains. After the last Great War with the humans, he believed it was the only place they would not dare to attack.

Puffing out a breath, I lift my gaze to the sky, seeking answers. Why did the gods choose for my mate to be human instead of Dragon? Her kind have a long history of animosity with mine and they are weak. They have no wings nor any natural defenses that I am aware of. Instead of fangs, she has flat, white teeth, and her claws are short and blunt.

I glance down at my own claws which could so easily shred her petal-soft skin. What purpose does it serve for the gods to have created my T'kara in this soft and delicate form? Why could she not at least have been born with some sort of protective scales?

Despite all of her disadvantages, she faced me, unafraid. Most humans cower in fear when I approach, but not her. There is a fire in her eyes that speaks of a fierce heart. She kept her gaze locked onto mine, brave and determined—all traces of her fear scent gone as she demanded that I acknowledge her as an equal.

A low growl rumbles deep in my chest. If she were a Dragon female, I would have thought her ready to challenge me to the mating battle. But she is not, and I know nothing of her people's courtship and mating rituals. Given how soft humans are in general, I doubt it involves any sort of fighting between potential mates.

Even though she is human, I cannot deny that she is attractive. Her face is heart-shaped and her features refined. Her cheekbones are high enough that, if not for her curved ears, she could easily be mistaken for a High Elf.

My thoughts keep returning to the plush bow of her pink lips. I wonder if they are soft and warm, or as hard and unyielding as her brave spirit.

Although I've not seen her undressed, she appears rather thin, and I wonder how long she was mistreated by her people before being tied to the stake for execution.

I've seen enough of her kind to know she is rare. Her hair is the color of flame and soft as the finest of silks. Her blue eyes remind me of pale blue skies, and I am fascinated by the tiny spotted markings that cover her flesh. Spread out in irregular patterns, they are just a shade darker than her otherwise pale skin.

Very few among my race are blessed with the fated bond, and I have heard that it is intense, but I never expected it to pull at me so strongly. The very thought of her heightens my possessive instincts. The need to protect and provide for her is all-consuming.

Molten rage flows through me as I think of her raw and angry wounds. Her skin is red and blistered from her feet to her calves. I can only thank the gods that I was able to rescue her when I did.

Yet, despite that I saved her, she does not trust me. And from the questions she asked, I suspect she feels nothing of the bond that exists between us. If she did, she would already know the power she has over me.

I have always considered myself a strong male. Among my kind, I am respected and revered for my strength. And yet... this bond could undo me entirely. If she but asked, I would burn the entire world for her and lay the ashes at her feet.

Is this truly how others experience the bond, or have I fallen under some sort of spell?

Her people claim she is a witch. If this is true, whatever magic she possesses must not be dangerous, else she would have used it upon me already. Unless her skills are in the art of manipulation. If so, I am already bewitched.

I've heard the human kingdoms burn those practicing witchcraft, but I thought it only pertained to those that delved into the dark arts. If there was such a darkness around my mate, I would surely have sensed it through our bond.

Movement catches my eye, and I turn to find a stag grazing on a few green springs jutting up from beneath the snow. It lifts its head at the last second of my approach, but too late, and I end him with a quick swipe of my claws.

Despite the presence of the bond, I still have to prove myself. Dragon females only choose the strongest males for their mates—the ones they know for certain will be able to protect and provide for them when they are vulnerable during their nesting period. Carrying my prey back to the cottage, pride swells in my chest. Surely such a fine kill will impress my T'kara.

Even so, I am torn between wanting to prove myself to her as a worthy mate and troubled that the gods have bound us together. Humans are nothing like Dragons, and I worry that our pairing will be difficult. For her and for me.

When I reach the cabin, I quickly slip inside the door. My T'kara is asleep before the fire, wrapped in the blanket I found for her. Quietly, I approach, not wanting to startle her.

I lower my kill to the floor, laying it before the hearth for her appraisal. I move to stoke the fire and hear her sharp inhalation behind me. I turn to find her eyes wide open, blinking up at me in a look somewhere between worry and bewilderment. "I have brought this for you." I gesture proudly to my kill.

Extending my dark claws, I slice a line through the carcass and extract the heart. It is the most coveted part—a delicacy among my people—and I present it to her proudly.

She is so impressed her jaw drops as she stares at my offering. "Eat," I tell her. "This is—"

I stop abruptly as all the color drains from her face, followed by a light verdant tinge. I lean in, studying her curiously. I've seen humans pale before, but I've never seen them turn green. "Is it normal for your skin to turn green?"

Instead of answering the question, she points to my offering. "Wha—what is that?"

"It's the heart. It is a delicacy." I lift my chin and puff out my chest, waiting for her adoration and praise.

"You cannot expect me to eat that," she says in horror.

My chest deflates. This is not the answer I expected. I thought she'd be pleased. "Why not?"

"It's raw."

I do not understand the problem. "It is fresh," I point out.

"If I eat meat that is not cooked, I'll get sick."

"Cooked? You mean... flamed?"

She nods, and my lips curl back slightly in disgust.

Scorching the meat will ruin the taste. No Dragon would ever think to do this to such a glorious meal. Then again, she is not Dragon. Her human body apparently cannot digest raw meat, nor is it equipped to survive in the ice and snow, I think grimly.

Perhaps this is why the gods paired us—they want me to help keep her alive. As her mate, it is my duty to provide for her.

Extending my sharp claws, I proceed to skin my kill. Her eyes are wide as she observes while I cut several chunks of meat. Recalling her flat, white teeth, I make certain to choose the softest, juiciest bits for her while setting the tougher pieces aside for myself.

When I am finished, I gather the meat I've reserved for her and place it upon the hearth. Opening my mouth, I release a stream of flame, cooking it thoroughly. I spear several chunks with my claws and offer them to her. "Here. This is for you, female."

Anger flashes across her face. "My name is—"

"Freyja," I correct. "This is yours."

The fire leaves her eyes, and she glances at the meat. "It's too hot."

"You wanted it flamed, did you not?" It is well-known that humans are fickle, but this is rather extreme.

"Yes, but it needs to cool a bit before I eat it, or else I'll burn my mouth."

Ah, yes. How could I forget her soft and delicate flesh? Sighing heavily, I wonder once more why the gods could not at least have granted her a layer of protective scales. Even fledglings hatch more equipped to face the world and its dangers compared to fully adult humans.

Running a hand through my hair, I study the door and the snowstorm outside. We must leave here for my kingdom as soon as possible because the Mage will search for us. Of this, I am certain. She wants us dead. But in order to depart, my T'kara needs to heal. And to heal, she must be well-fed and hydrated.

Walking to the small alcove that must have once served as a kitchen, I retrieve a small bowl and place the chunks of meat inside it. A pitcher of snow I melted earlier sits on the counter and I pour a cup of water for her as well. I offer her the cup of water and bowl of meat. Cautiously, she takes it, her gaze holding mine.

If she is indeed a witch, she must not be a very powerful one. The acrid scent of her fear permeates the air, yet her expression betrays nothing.

My mate is brave, and this pleases me immensely. Perhaps our union will not be as difficult as I thought. I want to know, however, if she truly has any powers. I'd prefer not to have to sleep with one eye open every night. "Your people accused you of witchcraft. Why?"

She looks down at her hands. "I'm not a witch."

I wait for her to continue, but she does not. The Order of Mages controls the human kingdoms and the punishment for any caught practicing witchcraft is death. I understand her hesitance, but I want answers. So, I move to reassure her. "Dragons do not forbid magic."

Her head snaps up to mine. "I have no magic."

Something about her answer bothers me. Through our connection, I can sense a falsehood that underlines her words. "Something else then." I rub my chin thoughtfully. "But what?"

Freyja's eyes widen slightly. It seems my words ring with truth. Humans are generally more expressive than Dragons, and I study her in fascination as a dozen emotions flit briefly across her features. Still, she admits nothing.

Seer. The word comes to me as if whispered in my mind and I wonder if it is the bond allowing me to sense some of her thoughts. If this is true, our connection is stronger than most. Fated mates are usually only able to hear each other's thoughts when in their four-legged *Draken* form. Only one way to know for sure if I am right. "You have the gift of foresight."

Her mouth drifts open. "How did you know?"

"It is true, then." I lean forward, avoiding her question. I will not speak of the bond until I learn more. "Tell me: what did you see?"

"Wraiths." She swallows hard. "I had a nightmare that they invaded the kingdom, and I told my uncle—the King. He turned me over to the Mages immediately." Her gaze drifts to the wall behind me with a faraway look, and I recognize it well. The sting of betrayal is a terrible thing, made all the more painful when it comes from those who are supposed to be family. "I-I had to say something," she says, fighting back tears.

My brow furrows deeply. "Even knowing it could mean your death?"

Her eyes search mine, full of fire. "How could I hold my tongue when so many could be hurt or killed by my silence?"

"But only *if* you were right," I point out. "You could be wrong. It may only have been a nightmare, and you risked your life for nothing."

"I considered this." She gives a curt nod. "But I decided it was worth the risk, if it meant the lives of others could be saved."

My respect for her grows. She is both brave *and* selfless. Something I'd not thought her kind capable of. Perhaps the gods have matched me well, after all.

When we're finished eating, I inspect her legs. "I must apply more salve to your wounds." I reach for her ankle, but she snatches it away before I touch her. It seems she is still hesitant to trust me. "I will not harm you, human."

"It's Freyja," she replies firmly. "Or are we to call each other 'human' and 'Dragon,' because that will get old rather quickly, don't you agree?"

She is possessed of both fire *and* wit. I let out a loud breath even as a hint of a smile tugs at my lips. My human is brave indeed to speak to a Dragon this way. "Freyja," I repeat her name and am surprised by the low growl that rumbles along with the word. The primal part of me intrigued by she who would be my mate.

CHAPTER 5

FREYJA

His emerald eyes hold mine as if in some sort of silent challenge, but I do not back down. Although I am well aware that he's a Dragon and could kill me easily, I do not think that's his intent. He has already gone to great lengths to prove he will not harm me, but I do get the distinct impression that he is used to having his way. I suppose that is true of most kings, but I will not be intimidated or beaten into submission.

"Will you allow me to treat your wounds?" he asks.

I give him a reluctant nod and brace myself. If the agony I experienced when I tried to stand earlier is any indication of the extent of my injuries, I am loath to see my wounds.

King Aurdyn is careful to retract his sharp, black claws as he unwraps my bandages. Despite my attempts to hold it in, a small whimper of pain escapes my lips.

He stills, and his gaze snaps to mine, full of concern. Before he can speak, I gesture for him to continue. "Best to just get it over with as quickly as possible, don't you agree?"

He nods and then removes the last of the fabric. I gasp at the sight of my ruined flesh. I feared it would be bad, but I did not expect this. Tears gather at the corner of my eyes, but I blink them back. Crying will not change what is done, and I learned during my time in the dungeon that no one cares about my pain but me.

I'm surprised by how gently he rubs the salve over my lower legs and feet, taking great care to apply it thoroughly. The burning pain begins to ebb as it seeps into my skin, and I notice light scar tissue already starting to form along the edges. "What is that exactly? It's healing my skin faster than anything I've ever seen before."

"It is *kavo* root. It works rapidly. You should be completely healed either tomorrow or the next day. We use it to treat burns on fledglings."

As shocked as I am about how soon I'll be healed, I'm even more astonished by what he said about their young. It is common knowledge that all Dragons are immune to the effects of fire. "I thought Dragons could not burn."

"Until their mature scales come in, fledglings are vulnerable to fire," he explains, carefully redressing my wounds. When he is done, he arches a brow. "And unfortunately, their ability to breathe flame develops before their scales harden."

The topic of children makes me curious about his life. I wonder if he has any family. "Do you have any… fledglings?" I ask, making sure to use the same word he did.

"No."

"A wife?"

Something flashes behind his eyes, but it's gone too quickly for me to know what it was. "I have not yet taken a mate."

I glance down at my bandaged lower legs and feet, pondering my own future. My freckles were already considered unattractive by two of the suitors my uncle tried to match me with, but now I have these scars.

I know vanity is foolish. It is not uncommon for warriors to bear scars, many of which they wear proudly. But mine were not received in battle. Mine were the product of betrayal of the worst kind, by someone who was supposed to love me. I bunch my fists in the fabric of my skirt.

Aurdyn frowns. "Does it still pain you?"

It does, but not in the way that he imagines. The memory of my uncle's cold indifference when I begged for my life is a wound so deep, I wonder if it will ever stop hurting. "No," I lie. "It is fine."

When he shifts, I note the slight wince he makes as he flexes his wings. "You are hurt."

"I will heal."

The last thing I remember is him pulling me free of the flames, and then waking up here. "What happened? Where are you injured?"

"A poisoned black arrow hit me when we escaped. It impaired my ability to fly, and when we landed, I injured my left wing." His hands curl into fists at his side. "My wound is already closed, and my wing will heal, but it will take at least a week before I can fly. We cannot afford to wait that long."

"Why?"

"The female who stood with your king, she was a Mage. She will be hunting us."

Emotions tighten my chest as I think of Luria, remembering the shimmer of magic on her skin. "She bewitched my uncle—the king." Bitter acid rises in my throat, but I swallow it back down. "I trusted her. We both did, and she betrayed us." And now, she wants me dead.

Aurdyn looks to the window and the snowstorm outside, his brow furrowed deeply. "This storm has not let up since we arrived. It is unusual for this time of year. I suspect it is her doing. She is trying to delay us from reaching my kingdom. Which is why we must leave here as soon as your wounds have healed."

"That could take days."

"As I explained," he says, a hint of irritation in his tone. "The salve works quickly."

"You've used it on humans before?" I challenge.

"No," he grumbles. "But you saw with your own eyes that you are already beginning to heal."

I study my legs and sigh heavily. "But until they do, we're trapped." His gaze snaps to mine, and I huff out a laugh. "What a fine pair we are. A human who cannot walk, and a Dragon who cannot fly."

"Indeed," he rumbles, even as a hint of a smile tugs at his lips.

"These were left behind by the previous occupants." He gestures to a pile of folded leather clothes and a pair of fur-lined boots by the fire. "Change into them while I am gone."

It will be nice to change into something relatively fresh. I glance down at my tattered dress, the fabric singed along the hemline and black from the smoke.

He stands, and starts for the door. "Where are you going?"

"To check the perimeter."

"King Aurdyn?" He halts abruptly with his hand on the latch. "Be careful."

"I am a Dragon," he growls low in his chest. "My kind are not easily killed."

It's easy to see I've insulted him. At first, I'm confused, but then I remember I've heard many times that Dragons revere strength. "I just... no one is invincible and I—"

"I am a Dragon of the Ice Mountains. You'd do well to remember that." He tips up his chin to stare down at me imperiously. "I am not a weak and pitiful human."

My jaw drops, but then my blood begins to boil at his arrogance. "I'll have you know that humans are not—"

Before I can finish, he stalks out into the storm, slamming the door shut behind him.

Did he really just cut me off like that? And then leave?

Squeezing my eyes shut, I draw in a deep breath and rub at my temples, trying to calm the anger swirling inside me. I throw my head back, and look up at the ceiling as I send a silent prayer to the gods. It seems they've decided to pair me with King Aurdyn to teach me about patience.

While I wait for my grumpy Dragon caretaker to return, I change into a pair of dusty, but otherwise warm and comfortable pair of leggings and a tunic before curling up next to the fire. I still do not understand why he's helping me. He said I was his, but we still haven't discussed exactly what that means. If he thinks I'm going to be his servant, he is sorely mistaken.

Frustration and anger swirl deep within as I study the dancing flames on the hearth. I have several imagined conversations with him in my head: each of them spelling out in no uncertain terms that I refuse to serve him.

But as time ticks on, my eyelids grow heavy, and I struggle to stay awake. Eventually, I allow myself to drift off, hovering in the place between sleep and wakefulness before finally succumbing to the beckoning oblivion.

* * *

I AWAKEN from a deep sleep as an uncomfortable twinge in my lower abdomen tells me I need to empty my bladder. This is a one-room cottage. There is no cleansing room here. I only hope there is at least an outhouse somewhere nearby.

I glance out the window, watching the heavy snowfall that blankets the landscape. When I look down at my feet, I grimace at the thought of having to walk. It was painful to even stand up earlier, and I doubt I'd make it very far in this condition. Sighing heavily, I look toward the door. It's either wait for Aurdyn to come back and help me or try my best and figure it out myself. To be honest, I'm not sure which one I dread most.

Another pinch of urgency in my bladder makes the decision for me, and I cautiously push myself up to standing. It hurts, but not as much as it did earlier. Aurdyn is right. The salve is doing its job. My lower legs and feet still ache, but at least I can walk a bit now.

I grab the overly large fur boots by the fireplace and carefully slide my bandaged feet into them. Wrapping a blanket and fur tightly around me, I push open the door.

An icy blast of wind hits me immediately, robbing me of breath. As much as I want to go back and sit near the fire, I have to take care of this. I force myself to step out into the frigid wasteland. Snow falls steadily all around me, but I'm able to make out a structure off to the left that I pray is an outhouse.

As soon as I reach it, I make my way inside and quickly relieve myself. With that done, I tug the fur cloak tight around my body and step back outside. My boots crunch over the ice and snow as I make my way back to the cottage. I cannot believe the Dragon king went out in this weather, and with no clothes save his dark pants.

Dragons are creatures of fire, but I had no idea they were so immune to the effects of this sort of cold. I suppose that's why they are able to make their home in the Ice Mountains.

Movement catches the corner of my eye and I turn toward it, peering through the heavy snowfall as I search for the source. The forest is thick all around the cottage, the tree branches bowed and heavily laden with snow, the entire landscape blanketed in a thick layer of white.

The sun is low on the horizon. Scattered beams of orange and gold reflect brightly off the snow and ice, making it difficult to see. Something tall and dark moves in the distance before disappearing behind a tree, and I still.

Goosebumps pebble my flesh as primitive instinct flares deep within. The compulsion to run is a fire in my veins, but I cannot move. Long tendrils of fear unfurl and wrap tight around my spine as a large shadow peels away from the trees and stalks toward me.

Its glowing red eyes blink in the distance, and my heart hammers in my chest. Whatever this is, it isn't human. Alarm rushes through me, all-consuming fear overriding the pain in my legs and feet as I break into a run, heading for the safety of the cottage.

The shadowy figure races forward with inhuman speed and slams into my side, throwing me against the outer wall of the cottage. The back of my head strikes the stone and the world tilts and spins as darkness dances at the edge of my vision.

A heavily muscled body pins me against the structure. Blood-red eyes glare at me from a sinister gray face. The cheeks and brows too sharp to be human. Dark lips pull back in a feral grin, revealing sharp yellow fangs as pale fingers tipped with ebony talons skim across my cheek. "I have been searching everywhere for you, Princess Freyja," he says darkly. "Luria sent me. The Mage is desperate to have you returned to her." His gaze drops to my chest. "Your heart anyway." A sinister smile curves his lips. "That is the only bit she and her kind are interested in."

"Please," I say shakily. "You don't have to do this."

He cocks his head to the side, studying me like a wolf that has cornered its prey. "I know. But it's been several hours since I've eaten, and you look like an excellent meal." Horror floods my veins. "Now, tell me: where is the Dragon?"

My first instinct is to look toward the forest, but fortunately my mind is working well enough that I force my gaze to remain locked on his. I will not give away Aurdyn's location. "He's gone."

"You lie." He leans in and sniffs at my collar. "His scent is still fresh."

Dressed all in black, power radiates from this creature despite his tall and wiry form. His grip is bruising as he holds me in place. Whatever he is, he has no fear of Dragons, which means he's extremely dangerous.

He blinks and his eyes turn pitch black. "Tell me where he is." He wraps a hand around my throat. "Now."

Sharp claws prick my flesh as fathomless pools of darkness stare down at me with a murderous gaze. Whatever my answer, he'll kill me anyway.

I am a shield-maiden of Ruhaen, trained in the art of combat. I will not die without a fight worthy of earning me a place in the halls of my ancestors.

Without warning, I jerk my knee up, hitting his groin. He cries out and releases my neck, doubling over and howling in agony. Taking advantage of his injury, I push past him to run, but his long fingers wrap around my ankle, causing me to stumble face first into the snow.

"Bloody witch," he snarls, dragging me back to him.

Desperate for a weapon, I grip a fallen branch the width of my wrist. Lightning fast, I twist onto my back and swing it with all of my might. A loud crack slices the air as it makes contact with his head, and he falls to the side.

A menacing growl rips from his throat as he pushes himself up onto his hands and knees. Blood trails down his scalp, staining the snow black beneath him. Gripping the branch with one hand, he wrestles it from my grasp, and backhands me with the other.

My head whips to one side, and the sharp taste of iron

fills my mouth as pain blooms across my cheek. Mustering my strength, I knee him again. A pained grunt escapes his clenched jaw at the impact.

"You'll die for that." He seethes, wrapping his hands around my throat.

Raw panic fills me as I claw at his hands, thrashing wildly beneath him as he tightens his grip. Darkness gathers at the edge of my vision as I struggle, gasping for air.

A thunderous roar echoes through the forest behind him. Silver-white scales flash through the trees as Aurdyn races toward us. In a blur of movement, he rips the creature away from me, slamming him into a nearby trunk with a sickening thud.

My lungs burn as I cough and gasp, drawing in several gulping breaths.

Aurdyn positions himself in front of me, spreading his wings wide to shield me from my attacker as the creature pushes himself back up to standing.

The creature's lips curl up in a snarl as he glares at us both. Blood soaks his now shredded tunic, the deep gouges on his shoulders left by Aurdyn's claws bleeding profusely.

Thick cords of muscle ripple beneath Aurdyn's scales, and a deep growl rises in his throat as he faces down the assassin.

Lightning fast, the beast charges forward. Aurdyn ducks at the last moment, gripping the creature's arm with one hand and impaling his chest with the claws of the other. The sharp talons sink deep into his pale gray flesh with a sickening squelch. Blood pours down his front from the gaping wound as Aurdyn retracts his hand.

The assassin's eyes swirl red and black, his chest rattling as he struggles to draw breath. "My makers will not stop, Dragon king," he rasps. "Not until she is dead." His body slumps forward and crumples to the snow, falling still.

Aurdyn spins to me and drops to his knees. "Are you all right?"

Shakily, I nod. "What was he?" I ask, my eyes fixed on his twisted and sinister form. "I've never seen—"

"A shadow assassin." He takes my hands, drawing my attention back to him. "They are a ruined form of life, created by the Mages to do their bidding." His gaze flicks to the dead body. "What he was before he was turned, I cannot tell. But if he found us, there will be others. We must go." His voice is an urgent whisper. "Now."

CHAPTER 6

FREYJA

"Go where?" Nervous energy courses through my veins, but I force myself to push it back down. "Do you know where we are?"

"No, but we cannot stay here," he replies in a low voice, his eyes already scanning the forest as if expecting another attacker to step out of the shadows. "That assassin will not be the only one the Mages have sent. We must leave. Now."

I know he's right, but now that the immediate danger is gone, pain flares again in my lower legs and I can barely walk. As if reading my thoughts, his gaze drops to my feet. "I will carry you."

"What?" My head jerks back. "I'm too heavy. I'll slow you down and—"

A wisp of black smoke curls from his nostrils as he huffs. "Even though I am unable to shift forms right now, I am not weak," he practically growls, and I know I've insulted him yet again.

"I *know* that," I stop short of rolling my eyes. "I just—"

The air leaves my lungs as he hoists me up. His emerald-green eyes meet mine, as if challenging me to question his strength again.

"All right. I get it. You're a very strong Dragon," I concede.

He tips up his chin but then looks to the cottage. "We must take a few supplies for our journey."

As soon as we walk inside, he sets me down while he gathers some of the meat in a bowl and then wraps it in a fur to carry like a sling over his shoulder. He stops abruptly and his nostrils flare. "The assassin's scent is not in this space." His tone is accusatory as he turns his sharp gaze to me. "I *thought* I told you to remain *here*"—he points firmly to the floor—"while I was gone."

"Yes, but I had to—"

"It was a *simple* command," he growls. "One meant to keep you alive."

How dare he speak to me like this? I stab a finger at him. "First of all, I am not your subject to command," I snap. "Second, I did not have a choice. I needed to relieve myself."

"You should have waited for my return." He clenches his jaw. "It would have been safer for you."

"You left in a huff," I point out. "And I did not know when you'd be back."

"I did *not* leave in a huff."

"Yes, you did," I counter. "After you offended my entire race, calling us pitiful and weak."

His brow furrows deeply. "How is it offense if it is truth?"

I roll my eyes. Aurdyn may be handsome, but *charming*, he is not. "Have you ever heard of tact?"

He purses his lips. "We do not have time for this. We must go." He gathers me in his arms again, holding me to his chest. I sigh heavily. This will not exactly make it easy for him to traverse the snowy terrain, but I'm not sure how to say this without offending him again. I certainly do not want our conversation to devolve into another argument about strength. So, I make my statement as neutral as possible. "Maybe we should do this in a way that you can have your arms free if you need to."

He arches a brow, but I continue. "What about if I hold onto your back? Do you think that would agitate your injury?"

He frowns, considering, before he sets me on my feet. "Let us try." He turns his back and kneels for me to climb on.

I study his left wing, noting the slight swelling where it connects to his back. I'm careful not to touch that area as I climb up. I loop my arms around his neck and wrap my legs around his waist. His strong arms loop up under my legs and his large hands grip beneath my knees. In one fluid motion, he stands as if I weigh nothing.

Pressed against him like this, I'm surrounded by his masculine scent—a delicious mix of warm spice and ginger. His muscles flex and bunch beneath me with each move-ment. My stomach twists into an uncomfortable knot and my entire body flushes with warmth. I've never been this close to a man before.

His grip tightens on my legs, and I worry that I'm already a burden to him. "Are you sure your wing is all right, and I'm not too heavy?" Inwardly, I wince, realizing that I've just questioned his strength again, but I cannot take it back.

"My wing is fine." He turns back to me and smirks. "And you are lighter than an Elf."

"Carried many Elves, have you?" I ask, unable to stop myself from teasing him.

Aurdyn arches a brow. "Only the ones I have eaten."

My jaw drops, but I immediately snap it shut when I

notice the hint of a wicked smile curving his lips. "You're joking."

A laugh rumbles up from his chest, and I cannot help but do the same. This is good. Perhaps we can get along better than I thought.

CHAPTER 7

FREYJA

I'm surprised by how fast he can move as we trek across the snowy landscape. The heavy snowfall continues unabated, chilling me to the bone and obstructing my view, but Aurdyn seems unbothered. A human would definitely be unable to keep this sort of pace in this weather. Perhaps he's not entirely wrong about the disadvantages of my people compared to his, but I'll never admit that to him.

The muscles of his back flex and bunch beneath me as I hold tightly to him. His warm masculine scent surrounds me, and I find my attention fixed on his scales. Their silver-white color shimmering iridescent each time a stray patch of sunlight reaches us through the thick tree canopy overhead.

The forest is dense, and I wonder where we're going. I have no idea where we are, and I've not noticed any signs of civilization so far. "Do you know where we're going?"

"Of course, I do," he replies haughtily.

I refrain from rolling my eyes. "Care to share our destination with me?"

Aurdyn stops and his head whips back to me, his brow furrowed deeply. "Did you hit your head?"

"What?"

"We already discussed this. I am taking you to the Ice Mountains."

Pursing my lips, this time I do roll my eyes. "I *know* that," I state exaggeratedly. "But we certainly will not make it in one day, right?"

He nods.

"So, where are we staying tonight?"

"I will find a place for us to shelter before sundown."

His answer suggests he does not have a plan. He's just figuring it out as he goes along too. I would be worried, but he *is* a Dragon. And he's already shown that he wants to protect me, even if I still don't entirely understand why. And we haven't discussed his statement when he said I was his.

I want to ask, but I do not want to distract him. Not while he's trying to find somewhere for us to stay.

The Ice Mountains rise in the distance, their peaks disappearing in the thick cloud cover above. I shudder inwardly. As cold as it is here, I wonder how much more so it will be when we get there.

A line of smaller mountains looms before us. While not as tall as the ones he calls home, they still appear rather formidable. He points toward a yawning cave mouth ahead. "We will shelter there."

When we reach the cave, he stops just outside the entrance. Tipping his head up, he draws in a deep breath. "I do not scent anyone or anything else in this cavern. It should be safe."

He walks inside and sets me down near the wall while he arranges a series of stones in a large circle. I wonder what he's doing but assume he must be prepping the area for a fire.

"I saw some branches outside," I offer. "And a few smaller sticks we can use for kindling."

A slight smirk twists his lips as he steps back and then opens his mouth to blow fire on the rocks. It takes me a moment to realize what he's doing, but then I notice the glowing crystals embedded in the stone. "Are those l'sair crystals?"

"Yes. The Dwarves mine it from these mountains. It should keep us warm through the night."

It also provides a soft glow throughout the cavern, allowing me to see further inside. L'sair crystals are highly sought after as a safer alternative to fire. They can provide light and heat to a space for several hours. Because of this, almost everyone uses it in their home.

He moves back to my side and then hoists me to his chest, carrying me to the middle of the stone circle. It's deliciously warm and I'm no longer shivering. "Thank you."

Aurdyn sits across from me and reaches for my legs. I pull away and he leans back, cocking his head to the side. "Do you still think I mean to harm you?"

He's right. My fear of him is ridiculous at this point. Aurdyn has had any number of times he could have hurt me, but he didn't. I meet his gaze evenly. "I know you will not hurt me." He studies me and I feel compelled to explain. "It is simply instinct now, I think. I—" I start but stop as the words catch in my throat. The memory of my time in the dungeon is still fresh in my mind. "I was treated rather... roughly by the guards when I was imprisoned," I finally explain.

His expression hardens as I rub at the faded red marks left by the shackles they kept on my wrists. He pulls the salve from our pack. Cautiously, he wraps one large hand around my forearm and uses his other to apply the medicine to my skin. "I should have treated these earlier," he murmurs, taking great care to apply it gently and evenly.

"They do not hurt." His eyes flick up to mine, narrowing. "At least… not as much as the memory of how they got there," I amend.

Aurdyn dips his chin in an almost imperceptible nod and then carefully unwraps the bandages from my legs. I suck in a sharp breath at the sight of my fully healed skin. Tears sting my eyes at the faint scars that now mar my flesh. Swallowing against the lump in my throat, I force myself to straighten and brush away the lines of moisture that track down my cheeks. I should not be crying. If not for his salve, the scarring could have been much worse. And I would be dead right now if Aurdyn had not saved me.

Two claw-tipped fingers lift my chin as Aurdyn forces my gaze to his. A deep frown creases his brow. "Does it still hurt?"

How do I explain that my pain is not from my physical wounds, but from the ones that are scored across my very heart? I shake my head and then place my hand over my chest. "It only hurts here now."

I'm not sure why I said that out loud or why I felt comfortable enough to lay my feelings out before him—so raw and vulnerable. Perhaps it's because we are alone. I've heard forced proximity can bond two people very quickly.

But I rather suspect it is because he tended my physical injuries with such care that my heart has decided to instinctively trust him with the ones deep within—the ones that cannot be seen but are felt just as acutely.

"All that time in the dungeon, I could not understand why my uncle would treat me like that. Why he would allow his guards to hurt—" My voice catches, and I draw in a shaking breath. "I cannot stop seeing his face as he watched me up there on the platform, tied to the stake."

I swallow against the lump rising in my throat. I do not want to dissolve into a crying mess.

"How did you come to live with him?" Aurdyn asks. "What happened to your parents?"

"My father and mother were both warriors." A wistful smile crests my lips. "It is how they met. As brother to the King, my father was in charge of Ruhaen's army. I was just a child when we went to visit the fortress at Uslo, along our northern border. The kingdom of Morath attacked while we were there, and my parents rode off to defend our lands." I turn my gaze to the far wall, remembering the last time I saw them. "They never came back."

A maelstrom of emotions churns deep within, but I push down my sadness as I continue. "They managed to drive away the invaders in only two days. When it was over, and word returned of their deaths, my uncle came for me immediately. He has raised me as his own since then. He was as a father to me, Aurdyn. And I understand now that he was under Luria's spell, but it hurts just the same." My voice breaks on the last word. I bite my bottom lip to stop it from quivering, unable to speak through my sadness.

He studies me a moment before speaking. "The heart seldom ever heals as quickly as the flesh." Something about the way he says this, tells me he speaks from experience.

"What happened to you?" I ask softly.

He clenches his jaw, lowering his gaze as if trying to decide how best to answer. He is quiet for so long I cannot tell if I've angered him or if he is sad. After a moment, he lifts his emerald eyes to me. "My father's brother challenged me for the throne. I had just lost both of my parents. And my own flesh and blood... my uncle betrayed me when I needed him most." He sighs heavily. "It has been ten years, and although the pain has lessened with time, the scar"—he brings his palm to his chest, directly over his heart—"still remains."

It seems we are not as different as I'd thought we were. Each of us understands pain.

Silence settles in the space between us a moment before he changes the subject. "Are you hungry?"

"Just a bit," I murmur. "But... what about your wing? Is it feeling any better?"

He flexes his left wing experimentally, gritting his fangs as he tries to extend it fully before folding it back to his body. "It will heal," he says gruffly. "But I cannot fly or shift forms yet. Not without risking damaging it further."

I start to ask something else, but he pulls some of the meat from our pack and hands it to me. "Eat. You must maintain your strength. It will take at least half a day to reach the village of Arganth."

"Arganth?" I frown. "Isn't that a Dwarf mining village?"

He nods.

"Dwarves hate Dragons, do they not?" I ask, wondering if this is simply an unfounded rumor that has been repeated so often it's accepted as truth.

"Yes," he replies with a low growl.

I wait for him to say something else, but he remains silent, eating his food.

"Well, do we not need a plan then?" I press. "Or are we just going to show up at Arganth and hope that the Dwarves do not take issue with you being a Dragon?"

"If they know what's good for them, they will suffer my presence in peace and silence." His lips curl up in a snarl. "They should know better than to anger a Dragon."

Great. It seems there is no plan except to hope that his mere presence intimidates them enough that they leave us alone.

Not likely to happen.

"You are *one* Dragon," I point out. "And the village will be crawling with Dwarves."

"Yes," he grinds out. "But I will burn their pitiful village to ash if they—"

"Can you do that in this form?" I cut him off. "Or do you need to shift to cause that type of damage?"

His brows draw together, and I realize he has not thought this through.

"All right." I lean forward. "Unless you have a better idea, here is *my* plan."

He listens intently as I explain that he should hide in the forest while I find a place for us to stay. Then, he can simply crawl into the window or something to that effect. His expressions cycle between irritation, anger, and something else I cannot quite put my finger on, and I'm not entirely sure he is convinced it will work.

"You expect me to hide in the shadows, skulking around like some sort of thief in the night?" he asks incredulously.

"Yes. Do you have a better idea?"

When he doesn't answer, I nod. "I will take that as a no."

Aurdyn sits back, crossing his arms with a grumpy look on his face. It seems he is a Dragon of few words and even less smiles.

It's dark outside and I'm not sure what time it is, but I am exhausted. I lie down on my side. "I'm going to try to get some sleep."

He loops an arm around my waist, and I squeak in surprise as he pulls me against him. "What are you doing?"

With my back to his front, he drapes his good wing around me. Tucking his knees up under mine, he curls his much larger body around my own. "I am keeping you warm." He loosens his grip. "But if you wish to sleep apart and risk dying of the cold, that is your choice."

He slides back a bit, and I already miss the warmth of his body. "All right. All right," I concede, and grip his forearm, which is still draped lightly over my waist. "You have a point."

Aurdyn tugs me to him again. Heat creeps up my neck and face as my entire body hums in awareness of his. My hand rests lightly on his forearm, the thick cords of muscle wrapped in scales as soft and smooth as silk. We're so close his breath is warm against the shell of my ear as he whispers in a low growl. "Are you comfortable?"

A small shiver runs down my spine as my heart pounds in my chest. "Yes," I barely manage to breathe out the word.

Aurdyn tightens his wing around me, and I skim my fingers along the leathery folds, studying them in wonder.

He inhales sharply, and catches my wrist, pulling my hand away from his wing. I twist my head back to him. "Did I hurt you?"

"No." His voice is a low, rumbling growl. "A Dragon's wings are very sensitive."

I may be inexperienced, but I do not have to ask for any clarification of what he means. I recognize the hunger that burns in his eyes.

"I—I did not know," I whisper.

He draws in a deep breath, slowly exhaling it out as he releases his grip on my wrist and dips his chin.

I think again about his statement claiming that I'm his. I'm not exactly sure what that means, but I think I need to find out sooner rather than later or else things might get awkward between us rather quickly.

Clearing my throat, I steel myself and twist back to face him. "What did you mean when you said that I was yours?"

"You are mine—my responsibility," he states firmly. "Mine to protect."

"Is this some kind of Dragon code of honor?" I ask a bit cautiously. "Or is this more akin to slavery?"

He frowns. "Slavery is barbaric."

All right. Dragon code of honor it is then. This is good. My cheeks warm as I brace myself to ask my next question. "So… you're a gentleman, right?"

"No," he replies without hesitation, and a frisson of worry ripples down my spine. "I am a Dragon."

"A… gentle-Dragon then?"

"There is no such thing." He gives an indignant huff. "All Dragons are fierce warriors."

My mouth drifts open, but I quickly snap it shut. He has absolutely no idea what I'm talking about. It seems Dragons are very literal creatures, so I decide to be blunt. "You will not try to touch me when I sleep, right?"

"I am already touching you." He glances between us and then looks at me as though I've lost my mind. He studies me in concern. "Are you certain you do not have a head injury?"

"Oh, seven hells," I mutter, rolling my eyes. "I *know* you're touching me. What I mean is: you will not try to touch me inappropriately while we lie together like this, right?"

His face twists in disgust. "I would never take advantage of another in such a way. I am a *Dragon*, not a deviant Troll."

He is so obviously offended that I'm relieved, and I decide to tease him. "Met many deviant Trolls, have you?"

"Only the ones I have eaten," he quips, a smirk playing on his gorgeous mouth.

I laugh. "I would imagine Trolls must taste terrible."

"Worse than eating humans," he replies, and I laugh even harder.

After a moment, he tightens his wing around me, and I snuggle into his warmth. "Rest now, Freyja. I vow not to eat you or do anything else untoward. You are safe with me."

His words are only mildly reassuring though, because I know we're still being hunted. From the way his sharp gaze scans the cavern entrance, I'm sure it's at the forefront of his mind as well. "I will keep watch," he murmurs. "While you sleep."

Although I'm tired, my body is wide awake. I turn my back to him again and he molds his powerful form around mine. Aurdyn is handsome in an otherworldly way that human men could never be. And despite his strength, he is so very gentle with me. He saved me. Twice.

He is very different from what I'd imagined a Dragon would be like, and I wonder what else I do not know about him and his kind. We have at least a few more days before we reach the Ice Mountains, so I suppose I'll have plenty of time to find out.

"Wake me when you want to rest," I offer, and I feel him nod behind me.

Closing my eyes, I allow myself to fall away into sleep.

CHAPTER 8

AURDYN

It is less than a few hours until sunrise. Freyja lies asleep in my arms, and I curl my wings tighter around her against the chill in the cavern, mulling over the question she asked of me earlier.

Did she ask this because someone tried to touch her against her will before?

As I consider this, anger smolders in my chest. As long as I draw breath, if anyone so much as lays a hand on her without her permission, I will burn them to ash.

Part of the fated bond is protectiveness of one's mate, but I never thought it would be so strong. Even the mere thought of someone looking at her in a way that displeases her conjures murderous thoughts in my head.

"What time is it?" she murmurs against me.

"It is nearly dawn."

"Morning?" Her head jerks up. "Why did you not wake me so I could take watch?"

"You were sleeping."

"Yes, but... did you not need to rest as well?"

"I am a Dragon." I tip up my chin. "We do not require as much rest as humans seem to."

"Of course not." She breathes out an irritated sigh. "Because everyone knows Dragons are superior to all other beings," she says, a hint of sarcasm lacing her tone.

We may have only recently met, but I do enjoy the fire in her eyes when she is riled, so I decide to tease her. "This is truth. I am glad you are finally recognizing this."

"Are you serious?" she asks incredulously. "I was *being* sarcastic."

"It does not change the fact that it is true," I reply smugly.

Her mouth drifts open and her cheeks darken. "Well, one thing's for sure," she grumbles. "Dragons are definitely the most *arrogant* beings *I've* ever met."

"Met many Dragons, have you?" I arch a teasing brow.

She narrows her eyes. "One is enough."

I try but fail to suppress a smirk. She may not be a Dragon, but she is *val'nor* all the same—one who possesses a heart of fire.

* * *

WHEN WE LEAVE THE CAVE, Freyja insists upon walking herself. Now that her injuries are healed, she claims that she does not need help. I curl my hands into fists at my sides as I think on her injuries.

My temper boils and it certainly does not help that I've missed my morning tea for two days in a row, giving me a pounding headache. Savage thoughts churn in my head as I gaze down at her legs. The Mage will die a fiery death. I swear it to the fire god. Freyja could have died, and I never would have—

"Why are you looking at me like that?" Her question snaps me back from my dark musings.

"Like what?"

"Like you're angry."

I frown. "Why would you think this?"

"So… you are not mad?"

I was, but not at her. "No."

We walk a bit further in awkward silence before she stops and turns to me again. "So, is this your normal resting face then? A perpetual scowl?"

"I am *not* scowling."

Her gaze travels over my face and she raises a brow. "You could have fooled me."

"Believe me." I cross my arms over my chest. "When I am angered, you will know it."

Freyja mimics my stance, and purses her lips. "It would not hurt you to smile every now and then, Aurdyn."

"Dragons do not smile."

"Ever?"

I narrow my eyes.

"Are you just not a morning person, then?" she asks. "Is that it?"

When I do not answer, she continues. "My uncle was never a morning person… always a bit grouchy before he's had his morning tea, you know."

My eyes snap to her, and her brows shoot up toward her hairline. "That's it, isn't it?" She grins. "You're grumpy until you have had your morning cup."

Not wanting to admit weakness, I sniff disdainfully. "No."

I should have never allowed myself to become addicted to the stuff. *S'eleya* tea is one of the things we trade regularly with the Dark Elves. I curse King Varys for having introduced me to it. It was a smart move on his part to ensure peace between us. He knows I would never declare war upon his people now. Not with the threat of losing our supply of morning tea.

The teasing smile falls from Freyja's face, and she grunts as she struggles through a patch of thick snow. It is just above her knees and much more difficult for her to navigate than it is for me. I understand the desire to be independent and strong, but we are being hunted. It is important that we move swiftly. "You should let me carry you."

"I'm fine."

"No, you are not."

"Yes, I am," she insists.

I look pointedly at her legs. "The snow is too high for you. Your human body is ill equipped for this travel." She glares at me, but I continue. "Your kind are fragile and weaker than a—"

"Dragon?" she finishes my sentence. "Yes, you've pointed this out before."

"And?" I lean closer.

"And I am tired of hearing it," she snaps. "I can walk. Albeit a bit slower than you, but it is not impossible."

Clenching my jaw, I run a hand roughly through my hair as I turn to face her. "Why must you be so stubborn?"

"Stubborn?" She gives me an incredulous look. "I'm not being stubborn. We still have a long way to go. I'm *being* considerate."

"Considerate?" My head jerks back. "You—" A twig snaps behind us.

Freyja's wide eyes indicate she heard it as well. The forest is eerily silent. Something I had not noticed until now. I'd been so focused on my mate, I had not realized that I'd let down my guard.

A cool breeze blows through the trees, carrying wisps of snow that catch in Freyja's long red hair. Carefully, I spin toward the sound, making sure to place myself protectively in front of her as I scan the woods. The smell of death touches my nostrils, and my every instinct is on heightened alert.

"Something is here," I murmur. "Watching us. Stay behind me."

A low throaty laugh echoes through the forest.

"Show yourself," I growl. "Now."

Two glowing amber eyes blink in the distance as a dark shadow separates from one of the trees. The outline of a man, shrouded in smoke, prowls toward us and I spread my wings to shield Freyja from his line of sight.

A demon. But what powers he has, I do not know.

He stops less than ten steps from our position. "A Dragon protecting a human? I never thought I'd see such a thing. Luria claims she is your T'kara." Freyja gasps and my blood runs cold at the mention of the Mage that tried to end her life. "Tell me: Is it true?"

I bare my fangs in response.

"I've heard that nothing is more important to a Dragon than his mate." The shadows pull back just enough that I can make out the sinister curl of his gray lips. "And yet, a T'kara is infinitely more precious to your kind... or so I have heard."

The muscles ripple beneath my scales with want to shift and rend his limbs from his body. "I will burn you to ash if you dare try to harm her."

"Ah," he says. "So, it is truth. No wonder Luria believes she is one of the sanishon."

I narrow my eyes. The Mage said this word when I rescued my mate. She wanted her dead because of it. "What do you know of the sanishon?"

My knowledge of this prophecy is lacking. I'd always believed it was nothing more than myth. The Ancient Tomes of the Lythyrian state that the sanishon will be wielders of great power. Freyja is a human with the gift of foresight, not potent magic, so she cannot be what Luria believes. But none of this matters if the Mage is convinced she is one of those prophesied.

"Enough to know that others of my kind have been sent to hunt you," he replies darkly.

Freyja remains silent as a deep growl rises in my throat. "The Mage has sent you on a fool's errand. If you think you will win against a Dragon, you are wrong. There is nothing here for you but death."

"Tsk, tsk." He grins, revealing two sharp rows of gleaming white fangs. "We demons do not fear death, and Luria did not send me." He raises his hands in mock surrender. "I am not the one you should be worried about, Dragon King. I merely came to see if the rumor was true that a sanishon has been found."

"Who are you? And why would a demon care about such things?" I snarl, unwilling to let down my guard despite his statement that he is not here to harm Freyja. "Why are you really here?"

"Some call me shadow assassin, some refer to me as demon, and others call me monster." He gives me a mock bow. "But you may call me Tarak." He cocks his head to one side. "I came to warn you, Dragon King. It is not just one Mage that wants her dead. It is the entire Order. Above all else, they seek to destroy the sanishons."

"Why would they want them dead?"

"I cannot pretend to know the motives of the Order of Mages. All I know is that they will do anything to prevent the prophecy of the Lythyrian from coming to be."

"Why give me this warning?" I ask, still not convinced that this isn't a trap. "Since when does a creature of shadow offer help to another?"

The dark smoke that hides Tarak's form swirls around his

body in undulating waves as he steps closer. I growl low in warning, and he halts, his amber eyes locking with mine.

"I already told you. I am not the one you should be concerned with, King Aurdyn. Despite what you think, we creatures of darkness are not inherently evil. The dark magic of the Order may have created us, but many of us broke away from the Mages long ago."

Tarak's form seems to grow taller as he stands before us. "The Mages seek power, and I would not see them extend that power and influence to the other kingdoms. That is why I seek to thwart them every chance I have." His gaze shifts to Freyja, behind me. "If she is indeed one of the sanishon, the Ancient Tomes claim they will usher in an era of peace."

I understand we are in danger from Luria, but his claim that the entire Order of Mages want to prevent the prophecy from coming to be does not make sense. The Mages supposedly want peace between the realms.

They protect the humans by binding their lands so that no Otherworldly beings can use their magic in those territories. They do this to maintain the peace by creating an even balance between the humans, who possess no magic, and those who do.

If not for this, the Dark Elves could have conquered Florin long ago if they had access to their powers in the human kingdom.

"The Order of Mages wants peace," I counter. "Why would they want to kill the sanishons? Why would they want to prevent them from becoming the Great Uniters foretold in the prophecy?"

"The Mages do not want peace," he sneers. "They want power. And war is the best way for them to achieve it."

I've never trusted the Mages. They are powerful beings. But I am still not convinced what he speaks is truth.

Tarak cocks his head to one side. "You still doubt me."

I remain in my defensive stance, allowing my silence to confirm what he suspects.

"I desire peace as much as anyone else," he says.

"A demon—a creature of chaos and destruction—wants peace?" I ask, unconvinced.

"I met someone. It changed me." He gives a casual shrug. "I mean sure, chaos and destruction are fun, but it all becomes rather boring after a while, you know. Now, I just want to settle down and raise a family."

"You found another demon that feels this way too?" I fold my arms over my chest. "That certainly seems... rare for your kind," I pick my words carefully, unsure where this strange conversation is going. And one can never be too cautious with a demon.

"I am mated to a human." My mouth falls open, and he gives me a conspiratorial wink. He leans in and whispers. "Trust me. Your life is about to change for the better, my Dragon friend. My human mate... she is the best thing that ever happened to me."

"I... do not understand. What does that have to do with—"

A wide grin splits his face. "My mate and I are expecting twins. I want my family to be safe, to live in a world without the threat of war. And if your T'kara is truly a sanishon from the prophecy, she can bring about an era of peace."

I study him but say nothing.

Tarak rolls his eyes. "I can see you still doubt me. Here." He extends his arm. The faint outline of his hand reaches for me and then opens, revealing an obsidian stone on the end of a necklace. My eyes widen as a purple glow flashes across the glass-smooth finish and then fades away.

I rock back. It's a shade stone. They are extremely rare and highly valuable. Kingdoms have waged war for much less. "Where did you get this? And why are you offering it to me?" I ask, wondering if he is seeking some sort of bargain.

"Does it matter? I already told you: I am not a threat to you or your T'kara. I would see the Mages fall." His gaze shifts to Freyja. "And for that to happen, the sanishons must be protected."

He drops the necklace into my hand and then takes two steps back. Long tendrils of smoke coil and writhe over his form, obscuring all but his amber eyes as he slowly begins to fade back into the shadows of the forest. "Use it well," his voice echoes as he disappears into the woods.

As soon as I'm sure he is gone, I turn back to Freyja. Her small brow furrows softly as she studies the stone necklace in my palm. "What is that?"

"A shade stone."

She inhales sharply, telling me that she has heard of these before. They cast a glamour over the wearer. Many would kill for this prize.

"I thought they were myth." Her small brow furrows softly. "Are you sure it is real?"

I study her curiously. "Can you not feel the magic embedded in the rock?" Warmth spreads across my palm as the energy of the stone pulses through me. Even before touching it, I could feel its power, but she is human and I do not know if they are sensitive to such things.

Cautiously, I offer her the necklace, resting it in the center of her palm. She curls her fingers around it, tipping her head to one side. "It's strange," she murmurs. "Like a pulsing warmth, but very faint."

"Put it on," I urge her. "Let us see how well it works."

I've never been in possession of one of these. Shade stones are a highly coveted item, and I will not deny that I am eager to try it.

To my surprise she hands it back to me. I blink down at

the necklace, confused, before she turns her back to me, lifting her hair. "Would you?"

Her delectable scent fills my nostrils—lilac with a hint of jasmine. As I carefully position the chain around her neck, I realize that she trusts me. Completely. She slept in my arms and now this.

With great difficulty, I somehow suppress the low growl of approval that rumbles deep in my chest. It is rare for a female to trust a male so quickly. At least… among my kind it is.

When I fasten the clasp, I allow the tips of my fingers to graze her skin. It is petal-soft and warm beneath my touch. My eyes are drawn to the elegant curve of her neck, and I long to give her my mark. Everything inside me insists that I claim her now, as my instinct demands.

Allowing myself a momentary indulgence, I dip my head to the curve of her shoulder and inhale deeply, committing the scent of my mate to memory.

My sensitive ears pick up the quickening beat of her heart, and when she turns to face me, I drink in the delicate features of her face and the pink blush that spreads across her skin. There is no denying that my T'kara is lovely, her features soft instead of sharp-edged and hard like a Dragon's.

"Is it working?" Her question interrupts my errant thoughts.

"Not yet. You must touch it to activate it."

She clasps the stone in her hand and a faint shimmer of gold covers her body before fading away to reveal a stranger with long white hair and blue-gray eyes.

Her lips curve up in a soft smile, the skin crinkling at the corners of her eyes and mouth. "Did it work?"

"Yes. You must touch it again to remove the glamour. Use it sparingly, for I am uncertain how long it will last."

She touches the stone and the glamour falls away,

revealing her true form beneath. "How did I look?" She grins up at me. "Convincing?"

"And old."

Her face falls. "Well, at least no one will be able to recognize me then. What about you?" she asks. "Will you not need a disguise as well?"

"I am a Dragon." I frown. "No one would dare try to—"

"Yes, but you are an injured Dragon," she points out, gesturing to my left wing. "So, perhaps not as threatening as you usually appear."

I straighten, flaring my nostrils. "My injury does not make me weak."

Her lips form a tight thin line. "Must everything be about strength and weakness to you?"

"I am a Dragon," I state firmly. "Strength is power among my kind."

"Of course it is." She shakes her head.

"*You* are the one in danger," I counter. "Not me."

"And why exactly does a Dragon care about a human?" Her gaze travels over my face as if searching for something. "You've never quite explained that to me. And what is a T'kara?"

I have avoided speaking of this before now because I don't know how she'll take it. But now that the meddlesome Demon raised it, I cannot withhold the truth. She is my Fated One and I will not lie to her. "It means you are mine. My fated mate."

Her head jerks back. "What?"

I did not want to have this conversation. Not yet. "T'kara means *treasure* in the ancient tongue. It is a sacred word for 'Fated One.'"

"Fated One?" she asks. "I do not understand."

I meet her gaze steadily as I speak the truth that resonates deep within. "We are fated—bound to one another."

59

Her eyes widen, and she covers her mouth with her hand. "There has to be some mistake. This cannot be right. I cannot possibly be mated to a Dragon."

"The gods do not make mistakes," I state firmly. "We are bound. It is their will. You are mine."

"I belong to no one but myself." She levels an angry glare at me. "And I will not be forced into a marriage I do not want."

"*Forced?* I would never *force* you to do anything," I retort, completely offended by her accusation.

"This is ridiculous," she counters. "You cannot truly believe that we're fated by the gods. I'm human and you're a Dragon."

I cannot tell if her expression is one of disbelief or disgust. I may not be human, but I am far from ugly. At least… I'd always thought so until now…

"You think I was not upset when I first realized this as well?" I ask, remembering my initial thoughts of the terrible history between our two races. "Why would I wish to be mated to a human?"

"Well, you know what?" she asks, cheeks flushed dark red. "Why would I want to be married to a Dragon? And an arrogant one at that?"

"*Arrogant?*"

"Yes." She braces her hands on her hips. "I've lost count of how many times you've made it a point to remind me how superior Dragons are to all other races."

"How is that arrogance if I am speaking truth?" I ask, completely confused by her outrage. "You cannot help that you are human, and"—I pause, searching for the right words before finally settling on—"although it was difficult at first, I am resigned to accepting it."

Her lip curls, and fire burns in her eyes as she glares at me.

CHAPTER 9

FREYJA

I cannot believe his gall. "Well, I'm so sorry the gods have saddled you with a human mate," I say sarcastically. "I cannot imagine what a hardship that is for you."

"I am pleased you understand my predicament," he says in all seriousness.

I blink up at him in disbelief as he continues. "You have no idea how stressful it is to have a human T'kara. I mean... it is my duty to care for you and keep you safe." He paces back and forth, his nostrils flaring as he runs a hand roughly through his shoulder-length white hair. "With your paper-thin skin, blunt fangs, and pitiful excuse for claws... you have absolutely no natural defenses. The gods could have given you scales or at least some wings to fly away from danger, but they did not. And I don't understand why."

Rage boils in my veins and it takes everything within me to bite my tongue as he continues.

"And I fear I will never know a moment's peace from now

on. It is not your fault you are human. It is just very... stressful." His emerald eyes meet mine, sadness flashing across his face. "I will always worry for your safety, Freyja."

My anger dissipates with the last of his words. He may be an arrogant Dragon, but at least he cares... in his own strange and rather condescending way.

"I may be human, but I am far from helpless, you know." I stare hard at him. "I'm not one to normally brag, but I am well-trained in the use of a sword."

"This is good." Hope flares in his expression. "We must find one for you to carry at all times. Because you are my Fated One, the Mages believe you are one of the sanishon, and they want you dead."

"What is a sanishon?" My mind is still struggling to come to terms with the idea that I'm bound to a Dragon, but the fear of death overrides my concerns, and I force myself to focus. "And why would the Mages want me dead if I was one?"

He stops pacing and turns to me, something akin to guilt flitting briefly across his features. "I am not well-versed in the prophecy. I never had reason to study it because I thought it was merely the superstitious writings of a race that perished eons before I was born."

"Well, what *do you* know of it?" I ask, desperate for answers. "Tell me everything."

He lifts his gaze to the sky. The setting sun streaks the wintry landscape with vibrant orange fading to deep purple as it descends upon the horizon. "I will tell you, but we must keep moving." His eyes scan the forest around us. "It is too cold for you out here, and we are being hunted. We must find shelter before nightfall."

A cold wind whips through the woods and I shiver slightly. He clenches his jaw. "I will have to carry you, else we risk being caught out here in the open this night."

Anxious to get someplace warm and to also have answers, I nod.

He turns and I climb up onto his back, careful to avoid his left wing joint. The swelling has gone down quite a bit, but it is still there. "You're sure I am not hurting you?"

He turns back to me, pursing his lips, and I stop short of rolling my eyes, even as a smile curls my lips at his general grumpiness.

Aurdyn moves with a speed and grace that belies his much larger form as we make our way over the ice and snow. Despite the fur layers covering me, I'm still cold and I instinctively tighten my hold on him, reveling in his warmth. His masculine scent floods my senses. I suppose if I had to choose someone to be bound to, a Dragon is a good choice. Aurdyn is certainly very strong, and... there is a kindness about him even despite his arrogant manner. Right now, he is the only one in the world who actually cares about my well-being. It seems my fate is tied to his. At least for now. "Tell me about this prophecy."

"Sanishon is an ancient word, from a time when all of the Otherworldly races spoke a common tongue," he explains. "It means Outsider." He pauses. "The Lythyrian were rumored to be a race of seers. Some even believe all the otherworldly beings may have descended from them. A common ancestor among us."

"What about humans?"

"I do not know," he replies. "I only know that the Lythyrian and their kingdom are no more. They left behind a series of Ancient Tomes that preserved their knowledge and their history. The most prominent of their writings concerns the prophecy of the Great Uniters. Sanishons that will unite the various races. They will be heralds of peace. But first they will bring about the downfall of those who would seek to control the darkness."

"What is the darkness?"

"*That* I do not know." He pauses. "But I do know that you cannot be one of the sanishon."

"Why not?"

"Because they are rumored to possess great power, and you do not have magical abilities."

"What about my dreams of the Wraiths?" Dread settles deep in my gut. "It's the reason I was accused of witchcraft."

"The prophecy says the sanishon will have great powers of destructive magic. Being a seer is not quite the same. And your kind condemned you out of fear, Freyja. They had no proof. Just as we have none either. Your dreams of the Wraiths have not yet come to pass." He pauses. "Perhaps they were simply nightmares."

I open my mouth, about to tell him about my dreams of him before he saved me. But I hesitate, worried that it will only convince him even more that I'm meant to be his. And I'm still not sure how I feel about being bound to him.

Knowing that he believes I'm his T'kara, however, means he will do everything he can to protect me. Right now, Aurdyn is the only person who cares if I live or die. But I'm still not comfortable with his repeated assertions that I am his.

The fact remains, however, that we are being hunted. Luria and the Order of Mages want me dead. And right now, Aurdyn is my best chance at staying alive.

One problem at a time...

CHAPTER 10

FREYJA

I thought I knew what cold was, but as the wind lashes us and the falling snow pelts our bodies, I realize I had no idea what misery was before now. Unable to stop myself, I cling even tighter to Aurdyn, seeking the heat of his body.

Despite his warmth, I'm still shivering uncontrollably, and my teeth will probably break if I cannot stop them from chattering. I bury my face against the back of Aurdyn's neck, desperate to keep warm.

He stops and his large hands grip my legs and then my waist as he slides me from his back and around to his front, so I am facing him. Something flutters around me, and the wind suddenly dies down. "Freyja?"

Reluctant, I lift my head to his.

Aurdyn's arms and wings encircle me, shielding me from the blizzard in a lovely dark cocoon. It's quiet inside his embrace. "Is that better?" His voice echoes against the thick membrane of his wings as he studies me in concern.

Unable to speak through still chattering teeth, I nod.

"Your human body is not built for this weather; you will freeze. You cannot remain out in this storm." Anger flickers to life as he reminds me again how pitiful he thinks humans are, but it's instantly doused by the blast of cold air that hits my face when Aurdyn raises his head to scan our surroundings. "I will find us shelter."

"What about the mining village?"

I'm still wrapped around his front, with his wings folded over me. He threads his fingers through my hair and cups the back of my head, holding me against his warm, muscular body, protecting me from the full assault of the icy wind. "It is too far," his voice rumbles in his chest beneath my ear.

In the shelter of his wings, warmth slowly begins to seep back into me, heightening the sensation of each movement of Aurdyn's body against mine as he walks. His entire form is layers of thick, heavy muscle with not an ounce of fat. As if his powerful, muscular form were cut from marble—too perfect to be real.

Trying to distract myself from the terrible cold, I concentrate on the feel of his strong arms wrapped around me, one supporting my backside and the other banded across my back. I'm fascinated by the leathery texture of his wings, noting a few thick, jagged lines along one of the sails. I wonder if those are scars.

His heart beats a strong and steady rhythm beneath my left ear as I stay plastered against him. Closing my eyes, I focus on the sound, allowing it to crowd out any lingering discomfort from the blizzard swirling around us.

Aurdyn stops abruptly and I feel a shift beneath me as he balances on one foot while kicking out with the other. It connects with a hard thump against something, and I jerk my head up. "What are you doing?"

Instead of answering me, he bellows. "Open up or I will tear this door down."

"Aurdyn, you cannot just threaten to—"

A loud creak sounds behind me, cutting off my words, and I turn toward it. The door swings open, and a stocky man with blond curly hair, silver eyes, and pointed ears looks up at us, his expression furious before raw fear overtakes his features.

He's a Dwarf. If not for his pointed ears, I'd probably think he was human. Their kind are very similar to mine, and only a slight bit taller. Panicked, he tries to slam the door, but Aurdyn pushes through, causing the man to stumble back.

A woman screeches behind him. "Orin!" She rushes to his side, her curly chestnut hair falling like a curtain across her face as she leans over him.

"Get back, Moira!" he yells. "Run!"

Her gaze snaps to us and all the color drains from her face as she stares up at Aurdyn.

Orin twists and places himself between us and her. "Please, do not hurt my mate. I'll give you whatever you want, Dragon. But leave her alone."

Aurdyn kicks the door shut behind us and glares down at him. "I'm not going to harm you. Now get up, Dwarf," he growls. "And fetch whatever you have that is warm."

The man blinks several times in obvious shock.

"Now," Aurdyn commands.

A door creaks open across the way and two small children appear. "Mother?"

"Children." The woman jumps up and rushes to them. "Get back in your room," she says in a quiet but urgent voice. "Do as I say."

Instead of listening, they stare in wide-eyed fascination at the two of us. From the look of it, they appear to be twins—a boy and a girl. Each of them with brown, curling hair like their mother and bright silver eyes like their father, with cute, pointed ears.

Despite his trembling form, Orin stands staunchly between us and his family. "Please, don't hurt my family," he pleads.

"Then fetch something warm as I asked," Aurdyn snarls.

"Stop it!" I smack at his chest, and his head snaps to me. He blinks several times, as if he cannot believe I just did that. "Be nice, Aurdyn."

Before he can say anything, I turn toward the Dwarf and his wife. "You'll have to forgive my companion. My name is Freyja, and this is Aurdyn. We've been traveling all day, and he's just a bit grouchy." I lean in and whisper. "He also has not had his morning tea in a few days now, and that alone can lend itself to a short temper." They stare at me in shock as I continue. "If you would be so kind as to allow us to shelter here for the night, we would be very appreciative."

"You—you're not going to—to hurt us?" Orin's voice trembles as he stumbles over his words.

"No, we are not." I turn to Aurdyn. "Right?"

Aurdyn narrows his eyes but dips his chin in a subtle acknowledgement.

Moira bursts into a flurry of activity behind her husband, ushering the kids back into their room and closing the door before grabbing a thick quilt from a bed across the room. She holds it out to us, and Aurdyn huffs out a frustrated breath as he snatches it from her hands. "Do you not have any furs?" he grumbles. "Anything besides this pitiful, moth riddled—"

I press a finger to his lips, silencing him abruptly. I give him a pointed look before turning to the Dwarves. "Thank you so much. This will do nicely." I offer my best friendly grin. "Do you happen to have any tea?"

Moira nods and rushes to the small kitchen area on the other side of the cottage.

Obviously annoyed, a puff of black smoke curls out from Aurdyn's nostrils as he stalks toward the fireplace. He sets me down in a rickety chair near the hearth and wraps the blanket tight around my form before he turns back to our hosts. "She needs food and drink."

Orin goes to help his wife, and I sigh in frustration at Aurdyn's terrible manners.

He stands over me, head tipped up proudly and arms crossed with an imperious look on his face as he watches the two Dwarves practically falling all over themselves to serve us.

"Stop glaring at them," I whisper sharply. "You're making them nervous."

"They should be." He looks down his nose. "If they do not get me what you need, I will—"

"Stop it," I hiss between my teeth. "Now. We are guests here. Can you at least act like you are friendly?"

"Dragons are not—"

His words cut off at my sharp look of warning. Reluctantly, he uncrosses his arms and purses his lips. "Fine."

When they return with a plate of food and a glass of water, they hand it to me with shaking hands and then offer him some as well. Aurdyn wrinkles his nose as he stares down at the offering. A few chunks of meat and a small bit of cheese and bread. "Is this all you have?"

Moira's face falls. "We—"

"It's the cold season," Orin interrupts. "Food is hard to come by during this time of year. But what we have is yours, great Dragon." He holds up the plate to Aurdyn. "Please, accept our humble offering."

Aurdyn waves a dismissive hand. "I will hunt later. She"—

69

he points at me—"is the one who needs food and drink. I am fine."

"About that tea…" I look at Moira and she holds out a steaming cup for Aurdyn to take.

She's trembling so much the cup rattles on the saucer, spilling some of the liquid, but he takes it from her all the same, drinking the entire thing in one large gulp.

While it's nice to know he cares for my well-being, I hate seeing these Dwarves so terrified in their own home. It's obvious they are struggling and here they are, sharing what little they have with us.

Orin offers me Aurdyn's plate, but I shake my head. "I'm fine. Really. This"—I gesture to my food—"is plenty for me."

In truth, it's not. I am ravenous. But I cannot stomach the idea of taking any more from these people than we already are.

Aurdyn scowls as he scans the room, obviously displeased. He turns back to me, his green eyes searching mine in concern. "You need more food. I will hunt for you. Stay here until I return."

A teasing smile quirks my lips. "And just where exactly would I go if I wanted to leave?"

He narrows his eyes, but I notice the grin that tugs at his mouth. It falls away as soon as he stands and glowers at Orin. "I will return soon." He steps toward him, towering menacingly over the poor, trembling Dwarf as he points back to me. "She is mine. If you allow any harm to come to her, I will raze this pitiful hovel to the ground."

"Aurdyn," I hiss, but he ignores me.

"Do you understand, Dwarf?"

I sure hope that tea kicks in soon.

Shakily, Orin nods.

Aurdyn turns back to the hearth and throws another log

into the flames. He opens his mouth, releasing a stream of fire to make it catch, while the Dwarves watch agape.

After he's done, Aurdyn turns to me and tugs the blanket around my shoulders, wrapping it tight. "Better?" he asks, his eyes searching mine.

My heart melts at the concern in his gaze. "Better," I agree, offering him a faint smile.

If not for his arrogance and impatience with the Dwarves, I'd be inclined to think his attentiveness is so sweet. But when he flashes a warning glare at Orin again, I purse my lips.

"I will return soon," his voice rumbles through the house before he steps back outside into the raging blizzard.

The Dwarves turn toward me, eyes wide. Moira nudges her husband and instructs him to check on their children and then walks to my side. Her expression is one of pity. "Are—are you all right, dear?"

"Yes, I'm much more comfortable now." I give her a warm smile. "Thank you for allowing us to stay."

"Of course," she says, her voice strained, and I wince inwardly. It's not as if they really had a choice in the matter. "You are welcome to stay as long as you wish," she says, but her expression tells me otherwise.

She's afraid, and rightly so. After the way Aurdyn acted, I would probably be terrified if I were them too.

"He—" I start but stop, trying to think of something that might reassure her that they are safe. "Aurdyn is not as bad as he seems."

"He's a Dragon," she whispers. "They care not for any but their own."

"Aurdyn is… different," I reassure her. "I promise you, he will not harm you or your family."

She nods, but doubt is easily read in her features as she wrings her hands in her dress. She moves to the small bed in the corner and places a fur blanket on top, doing her best to fluff a very flat and pitiful pillow. "You are welcome to sleep in our bed," she says. "And we will stay with the children in the next room."

She gestures to a partition in the far corner. "There is a bath behind there if you'd like. It should still be warm. I'd meant to bathe the children this night, but they refused." She shakes her head in admonishment. "I'd scolded them and sent them to bed just before you arrived."

A bath sounds wonderful, so I do not argue. I make my way behind the partition and strip out of my clothes. When I enter the water, it is tepid at best, but better than nothing, so I bathe quickly. When I am done, she hands me a towel and an oversized tunic. "Wear this while I look for a sleep gown."

When I come out from behind the partition, she opens a small cabinet and pulls out a long sleeping gown. She also unfolds a thick leather, fur-lined dress tunic and pants, and a heavy fur cloak. She holds them up to me, eyeing me critically. "I think I can make some adjustments so these will fit you better."

"I cannot possibly accept these," I tell her. "It's too much."

"Nonsense." She waves a dismissive hand. "The cold is especially brutal this season. You'll need extra clothing for wherever you are going, my dear."

I open my mouth to protest, but the front door bursts open, slamming against the wall. Aurdyn's expression is fierce in the firelight as he steps inside, carrying a—I'm not exactly sure what it was as it's already been skinned and roasted, but it smells delicious. A strong wind gusts through the cottage, swirling thick flakes of snow before he kicks the door closed behind him.

Without a word, he stalks to the kitchen area and drops the thick slab of meat on the counter. "The rest of the stag is outside, buried in the snow to keep it cold and to cover the scent from predators."

The smell of roasted venison wafts through the air and my stomach growls. Aurdyn deftly carves several pieces off with his claws, arranges them on a plate, and brings it to me, along with a glass of water.

Moira and Orin stare in shock as he kneels at my side and pushes the plate into my hands. "Eat," he commands. "You need to keep up your strength."

The door to the children's bedroom opens again and two small but curious sets of eyes widen as they look at us. "Is he truly a—"

"Back to bed, children," Moira snaps.

"But we're hungry," a small voice says.

"Now," she says sternly. "I mean it."

My heart clenches for them. Judging from the food they offered us, who knows when they last had a good meal? "Perhaps they could have a bit before bed," I offer.

Orin's head swivels to us. "You would share?" he asks, a desperate edge in his voice.

Aurdyn's eyes narrow and a low growl rumbles in his chest, but I nudge him hard with my elbow, before I smile at Orin. "Of course."

His nervous gaze shifts to Aurdyn.

Aurdyn grumbles and I give him a pointed look.

He purses his lips. "Fine."

The twins burst through the door and rush to the table, excitement flashing in their little eyes as Moira arranges food on two plates for them.

They eat as though they've been starved, and my heart breaks again for this little family of Dwarves.

Aurdyn remains by the fire, his arms crossed and his tail flicking agitatedly as he stares at the flames. When everyone is finished, Moira, Orin, and the children retire to the other room, leaving us alone in this space.

The sound of something heavy being moved across the floor echoes throughout the cabin, and Aurdyn snorts. "Dwarves." He shakes his head. "If I wanted to break in, do they really think furniture braced at the door would stop me?"

"Can you really blame them for being afraid?"

"I told them I would not harm them," he grumbles. "What more assurances do they need beyond my word?"

"Perhaps if you didn't act like a fire-breathing Dragon, they would not be so scared."

"I cannot change what I am," he replies tersely.

Lowering my head, I pinch the bridge of my nose in exasperation. "My mother always said never to go to bed upset at someone," I mutter to myself. Sighing heavily, I lift my head and look at Aurdyn. "I know this is new to you, the idea of being…" I start to say 'friendly' but instead say, "not quite so intense around others who might be a bit skittish around Dragons. But perhaps you could smile a bit while we're here to… put them at ease."

He narrows his eyes at first, before his lips pull back in a terrifying grin, accentuating his sharp, white fangs. "Like this?"

If the Dwarves were not already terrified of him before, they certainly will be if he smiles at them like this.

I draw in a deep breath to calm myself. I do not want to spend the evening snipping at him for his manners or lack thereof. At least he's trying. Even if it is only for my sake. I sigh heavily. "We'll work on it later."

His expression falls a moment before he looks at my plate. "Are you certain you've had enough for this evening?" he asks, voice laced with concern.

"Yes. And I'm glad you shared the food with them."

"I did it because you asked," he reminds me.

I bite back a sigh of frustration. "Well… I'm glad all the same."

"You should sleep." He gestures to the bed. "You need to rest."

I glance down at the clothing next to my chair. "I need to dress for bed first."

I pick up the sleep gown, expecting him to turn around. Instead, he continues to stare at me. My cheeks flush and he cocks his head to one side. "What is wrong?"

"Aren't you going to turn around, so I can change?"

His brow furrows deeply. "Why?"

"Because I need to undress."

He frowns. "If you are worried that I will find you strange, I promise not to pass judgment upon your human form. I'm sure you are not terribly different from a female Dragon."

"You've seen other women—Dragon women," I correct, "naked before?" I blink several times.

"Of course," he answers matter-of-factly.

Jealousy sparks in my gut, but I do not understand why. I mean, it's not as if we are married or anything. And he is a king, after all. I'm sure he's probably had several lovers by now. My lip curls as I conjure an image of him lying in bed, surrounded by a harem.

"Is something wrong?" he asks, ripping me from my dark thoughts.

"While I'm sure you've probably had your fair share of lovers, it is improper for you to see *me* undressed."

"Dragons do not take lovers. When we mate, it is for life." I'm stunned by his statement, and I open my mouth to speak, but he continues. "Is nudity frowned upon by humans?"

"Yes," I reply, although I'm not quite sure if it's specific to just us, or if the Fae and the Elves are the same. "Most people… humans, I mean… we only undress in front of our partners."

"Partners?"

"Mates," I clarify, using a term he's familiar with.

My gaze travels down his form. "I'm guessing nudity is rather casual among Dragons?"

"Yes."

"If nakedness is not frowned upon in your culture, why do you wear pants?" Heat flares my cheeks, as the question escapes me unfiltered, but it's too late to take it back.

"Like Wolf Shifters, we conjure the image of clothing." He shrugs. "I suppose it is something that has carried over from a time when we all used to interact more regularly with each other—humans and Otherworldly beings."

My gaze drops to his pants. "Are you saying those are not real?"

He nods.

My jaw drops, but I quickly snap it shut, regaining my composure. "Well"—I place my hands on my hips—"if it's all the same to you, I would appreciate it if you would turn around while I change into my sleeping gown."

He turns away from me, his tail moving back and forth across the wooden floor as I change.

With his back to me, I take a moment to study him in a way I have not been able to before. There is no denying he is handsome. The firelight shimmers over his silver scales, accentuating the thick cords of muscle across his broad shoulders and back. My pulse quickens at the play of his muscles as he crosses his arms, flexing his very muscular biceps.

I never truly appreciated a male body before, but probably because I have seen none like his. Heat pools deep in my core as I allow my gaze to linger on his powerful form.

He tips back his head, scenting the air, and embarrassment floods my veins. With his keen sense of smell, he can probably detect my interest in him.

"Why is nudity frowned upon in your culture?" he asks. "Are you ashamed of your bodies?"

"Uh... no." His blunt question catches me off guard. "It's just something that is... intimate for us," I explain. "Something most people choose only to share with their mates."

I drop my old clothing on the ground, and his tail stops as he goes entirely still. It's as if the very air itself is charged. A shiver moves down my spine as I stand completely bare behind him, my entire body humming with the tension between us.

How is it that he makes me feel this way? It's not as if I have never seen a man partially unclothed before. My uncle's guards regularly practiced while dressed in the same manner as Aurdyn is now. And yet... I never felt drawn to any of them as I do to him.

Sighing heavily, I force myself to push down my desire, quickly pull the sleeping gown over my head. "You may turn around."

He spins back to me, and his vertically slit pupils expand. The threadbare sleep gown does almost nothing to cover me. Heat flushes my entire body under the intensity of his gaze, and my heart thunders in my chest.

Is it possible that he finds me attractive?

I thought Dragons hated humans and the only reason he is caring for me is because of this bond he insists we have between us... because he thinks it's his duty.

He moves toward me like a predator stalking his prey and I'm frozen in place as his gorgeous emerald-green gaze locks on mine. He's so close, the warmth of his body radiates to my own.

His nostrils flare and hunger flashes behind his eyes, and I find myself wondering if he's going to kiss me or kill me because, right now it looks as though it could go either way. As he stares down at me, all rational thought leaves my mind. I'm completely mesmerized.

He grasps the light fabric of my sleep gown between his thumb and forefinger, lifting it slightly as he leans in. My breath catches in my throat as I stare up at him, spellbound. "Wha—what are you—"

"This gown stinks of Dwarf." He wrinkles his nose. "And the material is so worn, I doubt you'll make it through the night without freezing to death."

And just like that, the spell is broken.

"We will have to sleep together." He motions for me to get into the bed, and then slips in behind me. "Do not worry," he says, looping an arm around my waist and hauling me back to his chest. "I will tolerate the stench to keep you warm."

"Well, that's certainly very magnanimous of you," I say, my voice dripping with sarcasm. "Very thoughtful indeed."

"Of course," he replies, and I cannot tell if he's being serious or not.

But it's late, and I'm tired, and we still have a long journey ahead of us. Drawing in a deep breath, I push down my irritation.

Despite the covers, and the fire burning in the hearth, it's still rather cold in here and I start shivering.

Aurdyn tightens his hold around my waist. My heart pounds as he wedges his knees behind mine and drapes a wing over me, cocooning me in his warmth and his delicious scent.

He shifts and a sharp hiss of pain escapes his lips. I turn to face him. As much as I enjoy his warmth, I do not want him to be in pain. "This is uncomfortable for your bad wing. I'll move over and—"

"You need to stay warm," he says, not loosening his arm around my middle. "I will be fine."

I start to argue, but he presses a finger to my lips, silencing me. A sly smirk twists his mouth. "Do not argue with me, Freyja. We should not go to bed upset. Remember?"

He removes his finger, and I narrow my eyes. "Clever Dragon," I murmur, trying but failing to hold back a grin of amusement as he uses my own words against me.

"Do not forget 'strong and handsome,'" he quips, and I laugh softly.

I roll onto my side, with my back to his front, nestling into his warmth.

A soft puff of air parts the hair on the back of my head as he sniffs me, and suddenly, I feel self-conscious about my smell. He pointed out that my clothes stink. Then there is the fact that he doesn't particularly like humans to begin with. With his sensitive Dragon nose, he probably thinks I reek.

"Your scent," he murmurs. "It is—"

"I know. I know," I blow out an irritated breath. "You do not have to say anything. I know I probably smell bad."

"You smell like spring." His voice is a deep rumble that vibrates against my back.

"I—*what?*"

"You smell of lilac with a hint of jasmine…" His voice trails off as he skims the tip of his nose along my neck, sending a small shiver of pleasure down my spine, and I have the strangest urge to lean back into him. Fortunately, I catch myself before I do.

What in the seven hells is wrong with me?

"Stop sniffing me and go to sleep," I grumble, making a show of fluffing the flattest pillow I've ever seen before lying back down again.

"I cannot rest," he murmurs.

"Why not?"

"The Dwarves are snoring," he grinds out.

I lift my head off the pillow, straining to hear, but I can't make out any noise on the other side of the door. I frown. "I cannot hear anything."

"My kind have exceptionally heightened senses compared to yours."

Of course, they do. Yet another example of 'Dragon superiority.' I glance over my shoulder, pursing my lips.

"And the Dwarves smell terrible." He gives me a grim look. "I doubt I will get any rest this night."

"Well, just close your eyes and try your best," I whisper, trying to hide my irritation. If he keeps complaining, I doubt I'll get any sleep tonight either.

He buries his nose in my neck, inhaling deeply, and warmth spreads through my body as desire ignites deep within.

His voice is a low rumbling purr as he whispers against my flesh. "This close, your scent is almost able to completely mask theirs."

The fires of my longing die a quick death. "Wait a minute." I frown. "Is that why you were sniffing my hair a moment ago? To cancel out the smell of the Dwarves?"

He nods, and heat floods my cheeks. I feel like such a fool. I thought we were having a moment, and that he was interested in me.

Awkward silence settles before I clear my throat. "Well... there's nothing we can do about the snoring or the... smell. Just try to ignore it. All right?"

Aurdyn sighs heavily. "Easier said than done."

I shake my head softly. Of all the things he could be worried about right now... He emits a tortured groan, and I bite my bottom lip to stifle a laugh.

"You find my suffering amusing?" he grumbles.

"I hardly call it suffering, Aurdyn."

"It is," he insists.

"I had no idea Dragons were so dramatic," I tease.

"Dramatic?" He scoffs. "You have not seen drama until you've spent time with the Fae."

"I've never met any Fae." I laugh softly. "But I've certainly learned that Dragons possess a flair for the dramatic."

He growls low in his throat.

"Oh stop," I lightly nudge him with my elbow. "I'm only teasing you."

"You truly do not fear me at all," he says, surprise tinging his voice.

I glance over my shoulder, arching a brow. "Should I?"

His emerald eyes stare deep into mine, and warmth unfurls from within. "Never."

My heart stutters, and I swallow hard as I turn away from him again. I do not understand how or why he has this effect on me. He's arrogant, frustrating, pompous... And yet, he can be gentle. The way he's so attentive to my needs is surprisingly tender.

Drawing in a deep breath, I remind myself that he's only doing these things because of the bond. If not for that, he'd probably want nothing to do with me. I'm a duty to him. Nothing more.

Aurdyn shifts closer and tightens his arm around my middle. With my back pressed to his front, I can feel his heart beating in a strong and steady rhythm.

Something brushes my lower leg, and I glance down as his tail coils loosely around my ankle. My heart flutters. This gesture feels oddly intimate, but I do not feel inclined to pull away.

My Dragon protector may be arrogant and overbearing, but he makes me feel safe in a way that I haven't in a very long time. And it doesn't hurt that he's the most handsome man or Dragon I've ever seen.

Sighing heavily, I push down my errant thoughts and close my eyes, drifting off into sleep.

CHAPTER 11

AURDYN

I t is impossible to sleep like this. Between the infernal snoring of the Dwarves, their terrible stench, and sharing the bed with Freyja... I will certainly not sleep this night.

Her nearness is affecting me in ways I did not think a human ever could. Freyja shivers slightly in her sleep and I tuck my wing tighter around her, pulling her back into my chest to keep her warm. She instinctively nestles further into me, and a low growl of arousal vibrates in my chest a moment before I force myself to stop.

Although my mind understands that Freyja and I are not yet mated, my body believes otherwise. I glance down her form to find that I've unconsciously wrapped my tail around her ankle. This is something only done with one's mate.

Since we are not truly mated, it would only be proper to remove it. And yet, I cannot force myself to do so.

My every sense is attuned to her as I watch the rise and

fall of her chest and listen to the soft sound of her breathing. The desire to protect her is an urge I cannot ignore and the need to possess her is a fire that simmers in my veins and would ignite if I let it.

I am completely fascinated with her and everything she does. When she touched her finger to my lips to silence me earlier, I was stunned. No one would dare do this to me, and not fear for their life. No one but her, that is.

My T'kara is brave.

I lean in just enough to run my nose through her hair again, breathing deep of her lovely scent. As much as I try to convince myself that I do this to drown out the smell of the Dwarves, I know it is more than that. It is instinct to memorize the scent of one's mate, and my heart rate quickens with the longing to claim her as mine.

My nostrils flare as her scent sours with fear. "No!" she cries out, thrashing against my hold in the throes of a nightmare. "Stop! Please!"

"Freyja," I speak calmly and evenly. "Wake up."

She stills and her eyelids flutter open, widening a moment before her gaze locks on to mine. "You were having a bad dream."

She pulls back the blanket and examines her feet, smoothing a hand over the light scarring along her calves and ankles as she breathes out a heavy sigh. "I thought I was there again… tied to a stake," she whispers, her vacant gaze fixed on the wall. "I was burning and—" She swallows hard. "No one came to save me."

"I came for you." I touch her face, drawing her attention back to me. "I saved you. And I vow I will allow no harm to come to you, Freyja."

"No one can make such a promise." Her eyes are glazed as if still trapped in the terrible memory. "Not even a Dragon."

Cupping her chin, I carefully lift her face to mine. "I can." I frown. "Or do you still doubt my strength, human?"

Despite the pain still etched in her features, the spark of defiance that I enjoy so much, returns to her eyes, chasing away her sadness and replacing it with fire. "It's *Freyja*. Not *'human.'* Remember? Or shall I refer to you as 'Dragon' for the rest of our journey?"

The fire in her gaze stirs something deep and primal within, and I force myself to bite back a low growl of desire. "Have you not heard?" I tease. "It is unwise to challenge a Dragon, especially a king."

"And it is unwise to provoke a woman, regardless of rank or species." A mischievous smile curves her mouth. "Surely even Dragons have learned this lesson by now, else your race would have ceased to exist long ago."

A deep rumbling laugh moves through me. "Clever and witty human," I murmur under my breath.

"Frustrating and arrogant Dragon." She narrows her eyes, but they sparkle with amusement.

Despite what she has been through, Freyja is brave and does not hesitate to speak her mind. This is something I'd not expected of a human. They have strength when in numbers, but alone... I've found them to be rather timid creatures.

All except for her—my T'kara... my fire heart.

After a while, her eyelids become heavy.

"Go back to sleep," I murmur, holding her close. "I have you. You are safe."

A faint smile tips her lips and she closes her eyes, resting in my arms so trustingly.

I listen as the sound of her breath becomes soft and even. Reverently, I lift a lock of her hair, balancing the silken strand on my claw as I study her sleeping form. She may look fragile, like those of her race, but I understand now that she is anything but.

Perhaps the gods knew what they were doing when they paired her soul with mine, after all.

My T'kara is a rare and fascinating treasure. And it is a compulsion of my kind to covet rare and precious things.

CHAPTER 12

AURDYN

When morning comes, I open my eyes to find Freyja turned toward me, her face tucked into my chest and her hands on my waist. As much as I would prefer to rest, especially holding her this way, I know we must get up. We have a long day ahead of us.

Slowly, I push the hair back from her face. "Freyja. It is morning. We should—"

"Just ten more minutes," she groans, snuggling into me. "Ten more..." Her voice trails off as her breathing evens out again.

Primal possessiveness floods my veins as I gaze down at her. I suppose ten minutes does not seem unreasonable. I try to convince myself that it will be better for her to be well-rested for our journey, but the truth is: I am loath to let her go. She fits so perfectly in my arms. I would hold her like this forever if she would let me.

The door across the room slowly creaks open, and that blasted Dwarf pokes his head into the room. I suppress a low growl of irritation as Orin tiptoes into the space. He darts a glance in our direction but doesn't notice I am awake.

Inwardly, I sigh. He thinks I still slumber. Dwarves are rather dense creatures, and it is difficult to suppress a huff of amusement as he takes great care to tiptoe past us. He turns back to the door, where Moira is waiting. He waves her through and whispers. "Quietly now, or you'll wake the Dragon."

"The Dragon is already awake," I say darkly, and they both freeze in place.

His head snaps to mine, eyes wide as his heart rate quickens. He gulps. "Forgive us, we—"

"Silence," I hiss, pinning him with a pointed look. If he continues talking, he'll wake Freyja, and she asked for ten more minutes.

"Oh, Aurdyn," Freyja yawns. "Do not be so grouchy."

Orin gasps at her unfiltered words, his entire face going deathly pale.

"I am *not* grouchy." I huff. "I was simply trying to get them to be quiet so you could sleep. I—"

The rest of my words get stuck in my throat as she stretches her lithe body against mine before sitting up and yawning loudly.

"Good morning," Freyja greets the stunned Dwarf and his wife, while I struggle to suppress a snarl at the fact that she chastised me for trying to keep them from awakening her.

Orin and his wife set the table and despite Moira trying to persuade their children to stay in their room, they sit on the bench across from me, their expressions gaping. When their mother sets their food before them with two strips each of the cooked meat from my kill last night, they quickly wolf it down. "Can we please have some more, Mother?" one of them asks.

"Yes, please," the other chimes in.

"Now, children," she gently chides. "This is not ours. It belongs to our guests. They are merely sharing it with us this morning."

Freyja gives me an expectant look and I frown, unsure why she is looking at me this way. After a moment, she rolls her eyes as if I have displeased her with my inability to read her mind, and then turns to the Dwarf and her husband. "Have as much as you like. There's more here than the two of us can eat."

It is obvious Freyja has no idea about the appetites of a Dragon. I could easily eat all of this in one sitting if I wanted to store enough food to last me for the next two weeks.

"Truly?" Moira asks.

Freyja nods.

I watch as the Dwarf and his wife give the children another two strips of meat each, but do not take any extra for themselves. In fact, they've hardly eaten anything at all this morning. As I study them more closely, I realize how thin they are, even their offspring.

An uncomfortable knot forms in my chest. They must not have enough food to last the season. This winter has been particularly brutal compared to the one prior.

I push back from the table and make my way to the door.

"Where are you going?" Freyja's voice calls out behind me.

"To hunt," I call over my shoulder as I step outside into the snowstorm.

Seven hells, this human will be the end of me. I cannot believe I feel bad for Dwarves, but I certainly know whose fault it is that I'm suddenly going soft.

CHAPTER 13

FREYJA

As soon as Aurdyn leaves, Moira looks to me, worry etched in her features. "Are you certain you are under no duress, my dear?"

I lean forward and rest my hand over hers. "I appreciate your concern, but it is unwarranted. Aurdyn is not a bad man."

"He's not a man," Orin says grimly. "He is a Dragon. Their sort are not known for their kindness."

One of the children looks at me, hope shining in her expression. "Then... the Dragon will not eat us if he gets angry?"

"Of course not, little one." I give her a warm smile. "He's just a bit grumpy because he misses his home."

"Why does he not simply fly back to the Ice Mountains then?" she asks.

"Why, indeed," Orin muses. He exchanges a glance with his wife and something unspoken passes between them before he turns back to me. "You're the one they're searching for, aren't you?"

Icy fingers run up my spine.

"The Order of Mages is hunting you for the crime of practicing witchcraft," Moira presses. "Are they not?"

Panic twists deep inside me, but I force it back down. "Yes." I straighten in my seat as I meet their eyes evenly. "I thought Dwarves and Otherworldly beings did not consider witchcraft a crime."

"It is not a crime among our kin," Moira says. "But that isn't the danger you face outside of your uncle's kingdom."

"It's the bounty on your head that's the problem," Orin interjects. "It's high enough that desperate folk might be tempted to turn you in."

I dart a glance at their children. It's easy to see from their appearance and the way they are eating now that they're near starving. "Some might say you and your family are in dire straits due to this cold season," I state flatly.

"Seven hells," Orin curses, rocking back in his chair. "If we were going to turn you in, we certainly wouldn't be alerting you to it."

"We're simply trying to warn you," Moira adds. "You seem like a nice human, and we didn't want you to leave here unaware, you see? There will be some who are searching for you, and if you can avoid them, all the better. They're looking for a human with red hair, traveling with a Dragon."

Growing up in the royal court, I learned long ago not to trust easily. And yet, I find myself wanting to believe these two.

"Is it the storm that keeps him from simply flying you to his mountains?" Moira asks. "Because I thought Dragons could fly in most any type of weather."

While I doubt they mean us any harm, I am unsure whether to divulge that Aurdyn's wing is injured. Before I can think up an answer, the door bursts open, slamming against the wall.

Aurdyn steps through the doorway, carrying a large, already-skinned animal. Flakes of snow shake off his silken, silver-white hair as he kicks the door shut behind him.

His footsteps reverberate on the wooden floor as he moves past us and into the small pantry near the back of the kitchen area, where he sets his kill on the carving block. He turns to Orin. "There is more outside by your barn."

Orin nods and then stands from his chair. He looks at his wife. "I'd best go out and see that it's stored properly."

As soon as he leaves, Aurdyn turns to me. "The storm is moving off. We should be able to leave in an hour or so."

I nod. As much as I hate the idea of going back out into the cold, I know we cannot stay here forever. Besides, I'm sure this family will be much more comfortable with us gone. Despite my reassurances that Aurdyn will not harm them, they still regard him warily.

I suppose I cannot blame them. I'd probably be the same way if I had not spent as much time with him alone as I have over the past few days.

Moira moves to the kitchen and begins packing strips of meat and even some cheese for our travels. She hands me a large fur cloak to wear over my borrowed dress tunic and pants and a pair of sturdy fur-lined boots to match. Each item is a definite improvement over what I arrived here with. "This is too much," I tell her, feeling guilty at the thought of leaving her without warm clothing.

"Orin can make me some more," she insists. "Besides, you've a long journey to the Ice Mountains from here."

She returns to the kitchen, while Aurdyn follows me to our small corner of the room near the bed. After I put on my new boots, I stand and take a few tentative steps as I test them.

"These are still a bit large on my feet, but much better than what I had. Besides, this is the least of our worries." He arches a questioning brow, and I continue. "While you were gone, Moira and Orin informed me that there is a bounty on our heads."

His expression darkens. "Why did they not say anything before now?" A thin curl of black smoke puffs out of his mouth as he glowers in their direction. "Why wait until—"

"Stop." I grip his forearm, drawing his attention back to me. "They are already afraid of you as it is. Is it really that shocking that they would wait to say something until after you were gone?" I shake my head softly. "They could have kept it a secret, but they did not, because they wanted to warn us."

Crossing his arms over his chest, he narrows his eyes. "Still. They could have said something earlier. I wasted the morning hunting for them when we could have already been on our way."

"But I thought you said the weather was still too bad to leave any earlier."

"It does not matter," he grumbles. "We've already wasted too much time. Hurry. We must leave at once."

I fasten the cloak around my shoulders and Moira hands me a satchel with supplies. The door opens and Orin rushes inside to his wife. He clasps her shoulders as he leans in, whispering in her ear.

A beaming smile lights her face. "We're saved," she exclaims. She turns to us, taking my hand as tears gather at the corners of her eyes. "Oh, thank you ever so much for your kindness."

I blink several times, wondering why she's so happy, but when I look up at Aurdyn, his face is a stern mask. "Tell no one we were here," he says in a low voice laced with irritation. "Do you understand?"

They both nod vigorously.

We turn to leave, but the children rush up to us. "Thank you for the food," one of them says. "And for not eating us, Mr. Dragon," the other adds, and I clap a hand over my mouth to stifle a laugh.

When we walk out into the snow, I turn to Aurdyn. "Why were they thanking you so profusely? What did you do?"

"Nothing," he replies absently as he focuses on scanning the woods around us, presumably searching for any sign we are not alone out here.

"It did not seem like nothing." I put a hand on his arm and his head snaps to mine. "Tell me."

"I left them extra meat."

I wait a moment for him to elaborate. When he does not, I ask, "How much?"

"Enough to last the winter."

I'm stunned. "I thought Dragons did not like Dwarves."

"Just because I dislike their kind does not mean I wish them to perish for lack of food." He frowns. "This winter has been harder than the last; I could see they were starving. And despite what you may believe, I am not a heartless monster."

CHAPTER 14

AURDYN

Why does it matter if she thinks I am unfeeling? I've never cared what anyone thought before, especially a human. But Freyja is not just anyone. She is... important to me. There is something about her that draws me in, but I do not understand why. I would think it is the bond that makes me so intrigued by her, but I am not sure I can entirely attribute it to that.

She is fascinating in the way she views the world. In a situation where I would normally be indifferent, she instead chooses to be kind. As she was to the Dwarves. And it makes me consider my own actions in a different light when I study them through her lens.

Before her, I doubt I would have given the Dwarves much thought, and I certainly would not have paid enough attention to recognize that they were struggling to survive.

Freyja seems pleased with what I did for the Dwarven family, but she also seems surprised. Then again, she does not know me. Not well, at least. Not yet. I would never wish starvation upon anyone. Even Dwarves.

"I do not think you are heartless, Aurdyn." Her voice cuts through my thoughts.

"You do not?"

"No. I mean… you may not possess an ounce of humility, but you are definitely not heartless."

I narrow my eyes, and she laughs. Freyja is fearless, and I admire her for it. No other human would dare say such a thing to a Dragon.

The snow is falling heavily around us, and I offer to carry her, but she refuses. I understand her wish to be independent, especially since her burns have healed, but her legs are shorter than mine. We could arrive at our destination much faster if she would only accept my help.

But it seems my T'kara is as stubborn as she is fierce.

Icy wind blows through the forest, catching the hood of Freyja's cloak and pulling it back from her head. She quickly puts it back on, but the next gust billows her cloak, and she gasps at the cold.

As she secures it back around her body, I turn to help her, but stop as she makes a low growl in her throat.

I straighten, instantly at attention as my blood heats and my entire body flushes with warmth. *Is she trying to initiate the mating ritual?*

Freyja's eyes meet mine and she frowns. "What's wrong? Why are you looking at me like that?"

"Were you…" I hesitate, unsure how to ask. Perhaps I was merely imagining it. "Were you… growling?"

"Yes."

I am momentarily stunned, but remind myself that she is human, and surely their ways must be different. "I suggest you not do that around any other Dragons when we get to my kingdom."

Her head jerks back. "Why? Is it bad?"

"That particular pitch of growling indicates you are interested in initiating a mating."

"What?"

"It is what a female Dragon does when she wishes to initiate the mating ritual and the *To'vara*."

"The... *To'v what?*" she asks, her voice rising in pitch.

"It is the mating battle," I explain. "The female will declare To'vara to a male she is interested in. If he accepts the challenge, he must then conquer her to claim her as his mate. She then accepts him into her body, sealing the bond between them."

Her jaw drops.

CHAPTER 15

A*mating battle?*

"Despite what you may think, it is not all romance," he explains casually.

I blink up at him in disbelief. *Romance* is certainly not what comes to my mind with the words 'mating battle.'

He continues. "It is very dangerous for males. One of my strongest warriors was nearly killed during the battle with his mate."

"What?" I sputter, unsure if I've heard him right.

Aurdyn turns to me. "Female Dragons are larger than males, and very fierce warriors. Males Dragons prepare for many years to be strong enough to battle a female."

"I... do not understand. Why do they battle in the first place?"

"A Dragon female will only accept a male who is strong enough to defeat her as her mate, proving he can protect and defend their nest and future fledglings at least as well as she can."

I stare up at him dumbfounded.

"Do humans not do something similar?" He cocks his head to the side to regard me. "I've heard of jousting, and I thought perhaps it was—"

"*Not* the same thing," I cut him off.

"Then… how do humans choose their mates?"

"Well, sometimes, as in the case of a political marriage, it is arranged for them. Like an agreement," I explain. "But sometimes it's through courting by spending time together… getting to know one another, and giving each other gifts."

"Gifts?" he asks, curious.

"Jewelry or flowers, or something you know that person may like. Sometimes people even give little notes to the person they're courting, letting them know that they are thinking of them."

His brow furrows deeply. "I should *hope* they are thinking of the person they are courting. If not, I would assume they are either unworthy or completely confused about what they are even doing in the first place." He shakes his head. "Your people are very odd."

"*My* people are odd?" I ask incredulously. "How can you say that when you literally just told me that Dragons fight each other? Courtship is supposed to be about wooing and romance. Since when is a battle romantic?"

He frowns. "Why do you believe it is not? Romance is fire and passion." He arches a brow. "And fighting can be a very passionate affair, do you not agree?"

A smile tugs at my lips. "You're impossible," I murmur.

He tips up his chin. "If you mean impossibly strong and handsome, you are correct."

I laugh, and a hint of a grin quirks his mouth.

Thunder rumbles in the distance, and Aurdyn lifts his gaze to the sky. Dark clouds gather overhead as snow falls steadily around us. The cold wind bites at my exposed skin and I tighten my cloak, trying my best to keep it out.

He narrows his eyes as he scans the area behind us. "That storm is moving fast. If you want to reach Arganth before it is upon us, you must let me carry you."

A rolling boom of thunder shakes the ground. I'm definitely not going to argue. He turns his back to me, and I carefully climb on, wrapping my arms and legs tightly around him. A small sigh escapes my lips as the warmth of his body radiates to mine.

"We will find you some warmer clothing when we reach the village," he says, as he begins to walk at a brisk pace. "You will need more layers as we climb higher up the mountains."

I do not point out that neither of us has any coin for clothing or a room because it will not matter anyway if we cannot stay ahead of this storm. If we are caught out here tonight, I worry we could freeze to death.

I would, at least. Aurdyn is a Dragon of the Ice Mountains, as he loves to point out. He would probably survive without any problems.

This is not the first time he has carried me, but I ask anyway. "Are you sure your wing is all right with me on your back, like this?"

"It is fine," he replies. "My wings have suffered far worse."

I think of the thick jagged lines on his right wing. "Did you injure them before?"

He dips his chin. I wait for him to expound on his answer, but he remains silent. So, I gently press. "How?"

"My cousin and I were very young and foolish." He shakes his head softly. "We knew nothing of the world and the way things worked."

Now, I'm definitely curious. "What happened?"

"Dragons normally begin flying around the age of three. But we do not develop the strength or the stamina for long distance until we are nineteen." He sighs. "Brovyn and I are the same age; we grew up together, like brothers. We were only seventeen when a plague swept through our kingdom. My mother fell very ill, and the healers told my father and me to be prepared to lose her. But I knew there was a plant, called *lysian*, that can break a fever. It grows north of the Great Wall. It is extremely rare and dangerous to obtain."

"Because of the Wraiths," I murmur, and he nods.

Everything north of the Great Wall is Wraith territory. Few have crossed into it and ever returned alive.

My brow furrows. "But I thought the Mages have lysian, do they not?" A memory returns of them treating my cousin, Inara, with it for fever when she was a child. She was well after only a few days. "Could you not have asked them for some?"

"My father begged," he says darkly. "And begging for a Dragon is no small thing. But they demanded something in return that they knew he could not give."

"What was that?"

"Our kingdom," he grits through his fangs. "They wanted us to bend the knee to their Order, but we could not. Not after they were the ones who aided the humans that betrayed my grandfather during the last Great War. Our people nearly lost everything because of them.

"So Brovyn and I took the risk and traveled over the Great Wall. We managed to retrieve an entire bag full of lysian leaves. But when we crossed back over, a Mage attacked us," he grinds out. "He was a High Mage assigned to guard the Wall. He thought we were spies and he used his magic to bring us down."

He shakes his head. "And because we were so young, we were already exhausted from the long journey, and we were unable to evade his attack." His entire body tenses. "He chained us and cut into my wings. I made sure his attention was on me, so that Brovyn could be spared."

I inhale sharply as he continues. "He denied me a healer, and my wings scarred as a result. It was very painful, but I eventually healed. I am fortunate that I did not lose the ability to fly from my injuries."

"How did you escape?"

"I cut out his heart, and Brovyn flew us both home."

The memory of him killing my attacker like this, at the cottage, returns.

"I had killed no one before him," he says solemnly, suggesting that there have been many others since then. "If I had not done it, Brovyn and I would probably have been murdered. And my mother would have died without the lysian. But we managed to get it to her in time, and she lived."

He sighs heavily. "At first, I hated my scars. Every time I looked at my wings, they were all I could see."

"They are very faint now," I offer. "I did not notice them until you had me wrapped up in your wings."

"They have faded with time," he admits. "But I no longer regret them. It was a small price to pay to save my mother's life."

"That was very brave," I tell him. "I'm sure your mother must have been proud."

He dips his chin in an almost imperceptible nod. He swallows hard, but he does not speak, and I understand it is because the loss of one's parents is a sadness that runs deep no matter how long it has been since they have passed. He sighs. "She used to regale the story of how Brovyn and I saved her to any Dragon that my father invited for dinner."

He chuckles softly. "My mother always had a flair for storytelling, even when we were children. She would tell us exciting tales about heroic Dragons of our past."

I think of my own mother. Even though my parents have been gone many years, I still miss them so much.

"My mother used to tell me stories too, when I was a child."

"What were they about?" he asks, curious.

I shrug. "Most were ones that almost all parents told, to teach their children lessons."

"What sort of lessons?"

"Lessons about loyalty, sacrifice, honesty, bravery..." I pause. "There was one about a guard who watched over a princess. He fell in love with her, even though it was forbidden. And one day she fell ill. Desperate to save her, the guard summoned a Blood Witch."

Aurdyn's eyes widen. "A Blood Witch is not something children should be taught to summon."

"Trust me." A smile quirks my lips. "Summoning is not the lesson, it is merely part of the story."

He arches a condescending brow, and I continue. "As the princess lay dying, the Blood Witch offered the guard a choice to sacrifice his heart for hers so that she might live."

"What did he do?" Aurdyn asks, and it's easy to see that despite his initial skepticism, he's now invested in the story.

"He did not hesitate, no matter that it meant certain death for him in return. He went to the princess's bedside and took her hand, placing it over his heart. As the Blood Witch wove her spell, he whispered to the princess: 'Here is my heart. Take it. It is yours. Use it to heal. I have no use for it if you are not in this world.'"

"And did he die?" Aurdyn asks, impatient. "Or did magic somehow save him at the end?"

"He died."

"What is the lesson of this tragic story?" He asks incredulously. "And how is it appropriate for fledglings?"

"I'll admit it is a bit dark," I agree. "But the lesson is this:

Sometimes to save what is important, you must be willing to sacrifice everything."

He shakes his head. "I still do not understand how the guard went straight to summoning a Blood Witch when the princess fell ill. Did he even *try* to enlist the aid of a healer first?"

"I am sure he did," I reassure him.

"Then, why is that not in the story?"

"It's implied."

"Is it?" He arches a condescending brow. "I think it should be mentioned," he murmurs. "A Blood Witch should *only* be summoned as a last resort. And even then... one must consider it very carefully." He turns back to me. "You think *my* people are strange, but *yours* are teaching children how to summon Blood Witches."

"Oh, Aurdyn." Laughter bubbles up in my throat. "It is just a story."

"One with a tragic ending," he grumbles, "and a rather dangerous message."

"And what sort of stories do your people tell their children?" I ask.

"They are mostly retellings of glorious conquests and battles."

"How is that any better?" I ask teasingly. "Battles are full of blood and death."

He purses his lips. "Even battle is much safer than bargaining with a Blood Witch."

I laugh some more, and a hint of a smile tugs at his mouth in return.

* * *

As we continue through the forest, a small shiver runs through me, not so much from the cold, but from the knowledge that I'll soon be surrounded by an entire kingdom of Dragons. From what Aurdyn has shared, his people seem to respect strength above all else.

What will they think when their king shows up with a human? Especially if they believe humans are weak.

For all his arrogance and grumpy manner, I *do* trust Aurdyn. After all, he has made it very clear that he is committed to keeping me safe. And we get along very well. But I grew up in a royal court and I know all rulers have enemies, and people who would do anything to take control of a throne.

I worry that his bond to me—an 'inferior human,' in the eyes of other Dragons—might be used as a weapon against him. And if enough of his people decide to turn against their own king... that leaves both of us in a very dangerous position. Especially him.

I glance up at him. His face set in his typical stern expression. Right now, he is the only person who actually cares about my well-being, and being labeled a witch by the Order of Mages has left me with few choices of places to go.

But it's more than this. The truth is, despite his gruff manner, I like Aurdyn... more than I want to admit. If I am being entirely honest with myself, I am starting to fall for my Dragon protector.

I know I'm safe with him, but I'm concerned that his connection to me could cost him everything. And that is something I do not want. Surely there must be a way to dissolve our bond.

Besides, I cannot simply live out the rest of my life in the Ice Mountains. I have to find a way to set my uncle free from Luria's clutches. Once we reach the safety of Aurdyn's kingdom, I plan to send a raven to my cousin, King Edmynd of Florin, asking for his help.

But I can do none of that if I am tied to Aurdyn by this

bond. And I certainly cannot ask him to help me retake Ruhaen. If anything, that would make his people turn on him even faster because of the bad history between Dragons and humans.

I need to ask Aurdyn if there is a way to sever this connection between us, but as I glance back at the gathering storm behind us, I know now is not the time. We need to reach Arganth and find shelter. Everything else can wait until then.

CHAPTER 16

FREYJA

When we finally reach the outskirts of Arganth, I'm exhausted and half-frozen. The last of the daylight leached from the sky over an hour ago, and I've been miserable ever since. Carefully, I peel myself away from Aurdyn's back and step down to the ground. I wrap my arms around my torso, already missing his warmth as the blistering, cold wind envelopes me, whipping through my hair and stinging my exposed skin.

We stand at the edge of the forest, studying the city for any signs of trouble. The snow has started again, blanketing the rooftops and streets in a thick layer of white. Walkways and paths lined with slush cut through the ice and snow where people carved paths toward their homes and places of work.

Rows of buildings and houses are stacked and crowded against each other, several leaning upon their neighboring structures for support. Golden light spills out from the windows and doorways as puffs of black smoke spiral up from crooked chimneys.

It's dark and cold out here. Only a few people hurry down the streets wearing heavy cloaks covered in snow, hiding their features from view.

"Dwarves." Aurdyn's emerald eyes track the closest one as he heads toward a tavern. His nostrils flare and he growls low in his throat. "Dozens of them."

I'm about to ask where, but stop as the man opens the door and bright light, raucous laughter, and a cacophony of voices and music spills out into the darkness. I notice a sign tacked to the door that reads 'vacancies.'

"A tavern with an inn." Hope sparks in my chest, and I am already imagining a soft, warm bed for the night. "They might have rooms."

His gaze slides to mine and he snorts out a huff of smoke, obviously not fond of the idea of going in there. "It is… loud. Perhaps there is another inn further down."

I place my hands on my hips. "And just where did you imagine we'd take shelter, if not in a place like that?" I gesture to the village. "This is a mining town, not a place people come for their leisure."

A woman shrieks and my head snaps toward the tavern as a man roughly grabs her and then pins her back against the outer wall. My heart rate spikes, and I gasp. "He's assaulting her." I push up to my feet. "We have to—"

Aurdyn grasps my forearm, pulling me back down. "Quiet," his voice is a hushed whisper.

Infuriated, I rip my arm from his grasp. "We have to help her. We cannot—"

I stop abruptly as the man captures her lips in a sloppy kiss. The woman releases a throaty moan and her partner grunts in response, hoisting her up as she wraps her legs around his waist, running her fingers through his hair.

Heat burns my cheeks and I quickly avert my gaze. Aurdyn scowls at the pair. "Dwarves," he grumbles again, disgust stamped on his normally stoic expression. "This tavern is little more than a brothel. We will *not* be staying there."

I'm shivering beside him, clenching my teeth, trying to keep them from chattering. He, on the other hand, seems fine out here. Not visibly bothered by the cold at all. "I do not think we have much choice right now. It's all fine and well for you to be picky about where we shelter, but I'll freeze to death if we don't find somewhere to stay soon."

He turns to me, and I think he means to argue, but instead he takes my hand and pulls me with him toward the village. I dig my heels into the snow, and he stops. "Wait," I hiss as he spins back to face me. "We cannot just walk in there like this."

Aurdyn's gaze flicks up and down my form before landing on my necklace. He frowns. "Then activate the glamour."

"What about *you?*" I ask incredulously. "You cannot go in like that."

"Like what?"

"Like a Dragon walking into a tavern full of Dwarves." I gesture exaggeratedly at him. "Orin and Moira said the reward is for a human woman with red hair traveling with a *Dragon*."

"Dwarves know better than to cross a Dragon," he snarls, smoke puffing out of his nostrils as he cracks his knuckles. "And if they dare try anything, I will end them."

"Yes." I huff out an irritated breath. "But perhaps it would be best if we try to avoid attention."

He makes it a point to look down at himself before turning his sharp eyes to me and lifting a brow. "And how would you suggest we do that? It's not as if I can hide what I am."

I study him a moment. "Since you are able to conjure clothing, could you make yourself appear human?"

He shakes his head. "Holding another shape that complex, outside of my Draken form, is too difficult to maintain. Even the appearance of clothing can be... taxing after a while."

I remove my necklace and offer it to him.

"That is for *you* to wear, Freyja."

"I know. But I'm less likely to stand out here than you are."

He examines me critically. "Even if you cover your rounded ears, you are too comely to pass as a Dwarf woman."

Was that a compliment? I blink several times as heat flares my cheeks. I clear my throat. "Yes, well... still... I believe a human would be less conspicuous here than a Dragon, don't you?"

He purses his lips and gives me a grudging nod.

Reluctantly, he takes the necklace and fastens it around his neck. I watch in wonder as he transforms into a tall, burly man with shoulder-length, silver-white hair and green eyes. A human. He straightens, tipping up his chin in that imperious way of his. "How do I look?"

"Like a king," I answer honestly. "A human one, but still..." He frowns as I bring my hand to my chin, studying him. "I think it's your stance. It's too proud for a simple worker."

I stretch up onto my toes and place a hand on either shoulder. "These need to slouch, just a bit."

"Why?" He bristles. "Do you wish me to appear weak, like some pitiful human male?"

"That is exactly how you need to look," I snap, unable to hide my irritation. "You need to look unassuming, like a man who has been working so hard all day that you're tired and worn out. Like someone who has lived a life of hard labor."

He compresses his lips as he allows his shoulders to sag forward, but he still holds his chin high, and I sigh heavily. This is not going to work. "All right. Maybe we need to try something else."

I remove my heavy cloak and wrap it around his shoulders, flipping the hood up to cover his head. "There."

If no one looks too hard under his heavy clothing, hopefully he'll look like just another person traveling through, searching for work in these parts. "If anyone asks, we are husband and wife and we're just traveling through."

He dips his chin in a subtle acknowledgment.

A chill shivers down my spine as I turn toward the tavern. Hopefully, we can buy a room for the night and be on our way as soon as possible in the morning. I doubt Aurdyn will be able to act 'human' for very long.

CHAPTER 17

FREYJA

As soon as we open the door, loud voices, even louder music, and boisterous laughter fills the space. The stale scent of sour beer, smoke, and sweat make my eyes water. The entire downstairs is a crowd of people, almost all of them with a tankard of mead in hand or on their tables.

When we reach the counter, a man leans forward on his elbows. Dark, curly hair frames his round face. His cheeks and rather bulbous nose are bright red, probably from the drink. If not for the pointed tips of his ears sticking up on the sides, one could easily mistake him for human.

His blue eyes meet mine and a wide grin splits his lips. "Why, hello there. My name is Garvin. What can I do for you, lovely lady?"

Aurdyn tenses beside me, but I step forward before he can say anything. "I'd like to inquire about a room for the evening. Do you have any vacancies?"

"Aye."

"How much?"

"Ten *shials* for the night. But you'll probably be wanting to stay here for at least two because of the storm." His gaze travels appraisingly up and down my body, pausing briefly at my rounded ears. "We don't get many humans around here. What's a pretty lady like you doing in these parts all alone?"

"I'm not—" My voice cuts off with a squeak of surprise as Aurdyn wraps a possessive arm around my waist and hauls me into his side.

"She is not alone," he growls, leveling an ice-cold glare at the Dwarf. "She is *my wife*. Mind where your eyes look, or I'll rip—"

I elbow Aurdyn, cutting off the rest of his sentence as Garvin takes a step back from the edge of the counter. "All right." He raises his palms in a placating gesture. "No need to get upset. I was merely asking a question. I meant no offense."

A snarl curls Aurdyn's lips and a wisp of smoke leaks from his nostrils, thankfully disappearing almost as soon as it appears. He pulls out a pouch and produces twenty shials, dropping them into the Dwarf's hand. "We'll be staying two nights," he says darkly. "And we expect to be left alone during that time."

I blink several times, wondering where in the world he got the coins from, but keep my mouth shut. Now is not the time to ask.

"Of course. Here at the Tipsy Dragon Inn, we value our customer's privacy." The Dwarf winks and pulls a key out from under the counter and offers it to him. "Second floor, last door on the right. And the room comes with a meal and a mead each night." He gestures to one of only a few empty tables in the corner. "Elsie or Olmar will serve you."

As much as I want to go to our room and lock ourselves inside until morning, I realize it would be wiser to have a meal. After all, we've been traveling all day. I slip my hand into Aurdyn's and lead him toward the table.

He sits across from me, eyes narrowed as he scans the room, no doubt searching for any signs of danger. "We should just go to our room," he grumbles. "We are completely exposed down here."

"I agree, but we need to eat something. We'll just have to be quick. All right?"

He makes a subtle grunt. I suppose that's a *yes*.

Crossing my arms on the table, I lean in. "Where did you get money?" I whisper. "I did not think you had any coin on you."

"With this necklace, my tail is invisible." A smirk plays on his lips. "Very useful for acquiring things unnoticed."

My jaw drops. "Who did you steal from?" I hiss, gaze sweeping the room. "What if they find out?"

He sits back in his chair and gives me an unbothered look. "Even if they do, what can they do to me? I am a—"

"Dear," I say loudly, cutting him off as a Dwarf walks up to us.

His face is strikingly similar to the man at the bar. He smiles widely. "Hi, I'm Olmar. My father says you're staying with us this evening." He must be the innkeeper's son. "Here you are, good sir and lovely lady," he says, giving me a wink.

Aurdyn growls low and the Dwarf takes a healthy step back.

I kick Aurdyn under the table and his head snaps to me. "What was that for?" He gives me an indignant look. "Why did you kick me?"

I stop short of facepalming myself and plaster a saccharine smile on my face. "Nothing, darling. My foot accidentally slipped."

He narrows his eyes, but remains silent.

I turn to the Dwarf and offer a polite grin. "I'm Mary and this is my husband, Jon."

Aurdyn huffs, but I do my best to ignore him.

"Lovely to meet you, fair Mary," Olmar flashes a winning smile. "We do not get many humans in these parts. And definitely not any as beautiful as you." He waggles his brows at Aurdyn. "You're a lucky man, Jon."

I wince inwardly. Apparently, Olmar loves flirting with danger.

Aurdyn glares at the Dwarf. If looks could kill, I'm certain Olmar would be dead a thousand times over by now.

The Dwarf's face pales as he sets two bowls of soup down before us, hands shaking as he does so. It seems he may have just realized how foolish it was to rile my "husband." When he sets the mead tankards on the table, I thank him for the meal and the mead, and he quickly disappears back into the crowd.

As soon as he's gone, I give Aurdyn a pointed look. "Could you please stop growling at everyone?"

"I will if they stop eyeing you like you're a tasty morsel," he grumbles.

"What do you care if they look at me?"

"What sort of male would not be upset about another gazing lustily upon his mate?"

While I appreciate him trying to protect me, it's going to draw attention. "We're not *actually* married," I counter.

"*They* do not know that, *Mary*," he emphasizes my fake name and gestures angrily toward the bar. "As far as they are concerned, *you* are my mate, and *they* are disrespecting both of us and the sanctity of our union by staring at you thus." He crosses his arms over his chest. "And what sort of name is Jon?"

"A human one," I say pointedly.

"It sounds like the name of a simpleton," he grumbles. "Not a warrior."

"My grandfather's name was Jon." I struggle to hide my annoyance. "And you're supposed to be a laborer, not a warrior, remember?"

He huffs out another wisp of smoke.

"And stop doing that?" I hiss. "You're going to give yourself away with all that smoke coming out of your nostrils."

Aurdyn leans in. "And just how do you expect me to do that? It's not as if I can control it."

"Maybe try acting happy instead of annoyed?" I say pointedly.

He growls low in his throat.

"All right, look." I draw in a deep breath to calm myself, and pick up my spoon. "Let's just eat and we can go to our room."

He nods and then turns his attention to his soup. His nostrils flare and he wrinkles his nose in disgust. "What is *this*?"

I'll admit, it looks far from pleasing, but we don't really have any other options here. "It's food. Now, eat it."

He straightens and pushes the bowl away from him. "I refuse to eat this slop. It is not even fit for swine."

I grab hold of my patience with both hands. "You need to eat."

Aurdyn peels his lips back from his teeth. "I will hunt tomorrow."

I could argue, but it's not worth it. It would only draw more attention to us than we are already getting. I swear every time someone even looks our way, Aurdyn shoots them an evil look, baring his teeth in aggression.

"Humans do *not* do that," I tell him.

"Do what?" he snarls at another patron, and I watch as the Dwarf's face pales and he lowers his eyes to his table.

"Bare their teeth like that to others." His head whips back to me, irritation shifting into his gaze. "Could you at least try to act a bit more human?"

"Fine," he grumbles. "But I refuse to smile at anyone."

I doubt he could smile if he wanted to, anyway.

Forcing myself to take a few spoonfuls of soup to keep my hunger at bay, I down each one with a drink of my mead, which is surprisingly good. I'm careful not to drink too much, however. I've seen the effects of honeyed mead on others, and I'd rather not get drunk.

Besides, I am starting to get a bit uncomfortable by the amount of attention we are receiving from some very inebriated Dwarves.

CHAPTER 18

AURDYN

It is difficult to be around all these insufferable Dwarves. The way they keep eyeing my mate makes my blood boil in my veins. And the more they drink, the bolder they become with their lusty stares.

Freyja chastised me for baring my teeth and growling, so I narrow my eyes at the closest one, hoping he can read the murderous intent in my gaze if he does not look away from my *wife*.

He quickly averts his eyes, and a satisfied smirk curls my lips.

"Aurdyn?" Freyja's voice draws my attention back to her as she stands from the table. "I'm going to speak with the innkeeper about having a bath prepared for our room."

I stand too. "I will—"

"I'll do it. You just wait here," she says pointedly. "And try not to glare at everyone, all right?"

I cross my arms over my chest. "Fine."

She turns and I watch as she weaves through the crowd.

It's much busier in here than it was when we first arrived. It seems this is the place where most of the miners come after their shifts. Many of them still wearing their dust-covered clothes as they sit around the tables with their friends, indulging in mead and beer.

Several scantily dressed Dwarf men and women move among the patrons. Out of the corner of my eye, I watch as one of them leans in and whispers to one of the miners before they make their way, together, upstairs to one of the rooms.

I grit my teeth in disgust. Dwarves are rather lusty creatures and I hate that I've brought my T'kara here, but we had no choice. It was either this, or another night in a cave.

When we reach my home, I will make sure she has everything she could possibly want for her comfort. The finest clothes, the softest bedding, the tastiest food...

I keep my gaze fixed on her as she walks toward the bar. Off to her left, a Dwarf watches her like a fox that has just seen a hare. He slides off his bench and slithers toward her like a snake as she leans on the bar, raising her arm to get the innkeeper's attention.

Primal possessiveness burns in my chest. I know she told me to wait here, but I do not like the way he is looking at her.

I'm ten steps away when he reaches down and grasps her backside with his grubby hand.

Fire builds in the back of my throat. I will kill him where he stands.

I push through the crowd to attack him, but she is quicker.

Lightning fast she spins and pulls the pickaxe from his belt. She grips his shoulder-length hair and jerks his head back, raising the axe to his throat.

"Wait, please!" he begs, but she keeps the blade pressed to his skin.

Everyone stops what they are doing to stare at her. The entire place completely silent except for the thudding of my boots on the floor, as I push my way toward her, and the howling of the wind outside the tavern.

"How dare you touch me," she grinds out.

"I—I'm sorry. It won't happen again," he pleads. "I swear."

I move to her side. "I've got this." She seethes as a trickle of blood slides down his throat.

Fire burns in her eyes as she glares at the Dwarf, and pride fills my chest. She is as fierce as a Dragon female, and I am completely and utterly obsessed with her.

She will be a fine mother to our fledglings.

"If you're going to murder Barlen, I'll ask that you please do it outside," Garvin says nervously.

Freyja looks at me. "Throw him out into the cold."

I crack my knuckles, but she puts a hand on my shoulder, and leans in to whisper. "Do not kill him."

Little does she know, he is already dead. His fate was sealed the moment he touched her against her will.

As if reading my murderous thoughts, she adds, "We do not need that kind of attention here. I've already drawn enough to us as it is."

Sweeping my gaze over the room, I realize that she is right. Reluctantly, I nod.

She steps back, and I wrap my hand around Barlen's throat and lift him into the air. He struggles as I tighten my grip, dragging him to the doors. I kick them open and launch him out into the snow as far as I can.

He hits the building across the way with a loud thud before sliding to the ground in a crumpled heap.

Everyone stares in silence as I return to her side. I narrow my eyes at the crowd as I loop my arm around Freyja's waist, leveling a dark glare at any who meet my gaze.

My threat is crystal clear: You touch her, and you die.

Garvin raises trembling hands, a nervous grin plastered on his face. "All right, everyone! Back to your business! There is nothing more to see here!"

Slowly, they turn back to their tables and the dull roar of conversation starts up again.

CHAPTER 19

FREYJA

With the pickaxe still in my hand, Aurdyn and I make our way toward the stairs. Several pairs of eyes track us. The weight of their stares is uncomfortable, and worry pricks the back of my neck. We're the only two humans here, and we just beat up one of their fellow Dwarves. Hopefully, no one is inclined to seek revenge on Barlen's behalf.

Aurdyn loops his brawny arm around my waist. His familiar scent calms me as I lean into him, thankful in this moment for the possessive gesture. Many look away, not wanting to be on the receiving end of his death glare or my blade.

"You have the heart of a Dragon," Aurdyn's voice rumbles in my ear. "As brave as you are fierce."

I cannot deny the swell of pride at his words. High praise indeed from my Dragon protector. Especially, given the fact that he thinks humans are pitiful creatures. I arch a brow.

"Does this mean you realize you were wrong about humans? That we are not weak?"

"I was wrong about *you*." His eyes meet mine evenly. "As for the rest of your kin... I've only ever dealt with the males, and from what I have seen, I believe they may be the weaker half of your species."

I smile brightly at him. "I agree."

We walk up the narrow staircase and into the hallway. Several rather loud and suggestive noises filter out from the doors as we pass, and my cheeks flare with heat. I believe I understand now why the innkeeper mentioned valuing customer's privacy. Aurdyn is right. This place is probably more of a brothel than an inn.

"Dwarves," Aurdyn grumbles again, lips curling in disgust. "They breed like rabbits."

When we reach our door, the key rattles loosely in the lock, telling me this has probably been forced several times. I grab the handle and push the door open. It swings in with a heavy creak, and we step inside.

A bed much too small for the both of us rests in the far corner. Across from it is a fireplace with a few burning embers and a stack of split wood beside the hearth.

Aurdyn takes off his necklace, returning to his two-legged Dragon form, dressed only in black pants while his upper half remains bare. Unable to stop myself, my gaze travels appreciatively over his powerful form, and the thick cords of muscle that wrap around his arms and his back. He is definitely more handsome in his Dragon form than he is as a human.

He throws a few logs on the fire, stirring the embers with the tip of his tail until flames begin to lick at the edges of the wood.

"The fire does not hurt you at all?" I ask. "Not even the slightest discomfort?"

He shakes his head. "We Dragons are creatures of fire. It cannot harm us."

On the opposite wall is another door, slightly ajar. "What is that?" I gesture toward it.

"A cleansing room."

My mind is already conjuring an image of a warm bath. "Truly?"

He nods and I make my way toward it. When I push the door open, I gasp. They have indoor plumbing in this place. I would not have thought to find such luxury here.

Although it is a bit small, the cleansing room has a toilet, a metal tub, and a sink. A bucket of lavender scented soap and some towels sit on the counter. When I test the water, it's not exactly warm, but it is not entirely cold either. Even so, the desire to bathe is stronger than my aversion to the undesirable temperature.

As I start to fill the tub, Aurdyn walks up beside me. "Hmph," he remarks. "I did not expect them to have this here."

"It's lukewarm"—I gesture to the water filling the tub —"but it's better than nothing."

His gaze slides to mine, a sly smirk on his lips. "Fortunately, you are traveling with a Dragon."

He opens his mouth, and a stream of flame hits the side of the metal tub, heating the water inside until a light mist of steam rises from the surface. When he's done, I cautiously test the temperature and find it pleasantly warm.

That was rather thoughtful of him. "Thank you."

"I am glad this is here," he remarks. "After sleeping in that bed last night, we both stink of Dwarf. Hurry, so I may bathe after you and rid myself of their stench."

Shaking my head, I stop short of rolling my eyes as he leaves the room. Despite Aurdyn's insistence otherwise, I am fully convinced Dragons are just as dramatic as the Fae.

Peeling out of my clothes, I step into the tub and sigh as the warm water envelopes my entire body, easing the tension in my muscles. I dip my head beneath the surface and run my fingers over my scalp to cleanse my hair.

I suspect this might be the last bit of relaxation I'll have for the evening. Given where we are, I'm almost certain Aurdyn will complain about the 'terrible smell' of the Dwarves again tonight.

A smile crests my lips. It is so hard sometimes to not laugh at all of his grumbling.

When I'm done, I dress in the sleep gown Moira packed for me. I'm sure Aurdyn will say it stinks as well, but he will just have to suffer through it. I am certainly not sleeping naked.

When I open the door to step back into the main room, my jaw drops as he turns to face me, completely nude. His black pants are gone. Before I can stop myself, my gaze travels from his strong, broad shoulders to the thickly carved muscles of his abdomen, forming a 'v' that goes down to his—

I blink, trying to hide my surprise that he does not seem to have what I thought was common amongst men—human and Otherworldly alike. Instead, he has a vertical line along the scales in his groin area.

He quickly conjures his pants once more.

Although he claims we are fated mates, it seems we may not be physically compatible. For some strange reason, a wave of disappointment moves through me, but I forcefully push it away. I remind myself that I should not even be looking in the first place, much less thinking about anything potentially happening between us.

Try as I might to avert my gaze, I'm so drawn to him, I cannot help but notice the way his 'conjured' pants now hang low on his hips.

I cut off the thought abruptly. I cannot be attracted to Aurdyn, I firmly tell myself. He's a Dragon and even despite his physical differences, it would never work between us. We're too different. Besides, he does not even like humans.

CHAPTER 20

AURDYN

Constantly having to maintain the appearance of clothing can be tiring. I had only meant to relax for a moment in my true form while she bathed, but because I am exhausted, I did not conjure my pants quickly enough when she emerged from the cleansing room.

My true appearance disappoints her. I can read it in her expression. Before her gaze traveled fully down my body, her scent had grown stronger, indicating an attraction to me.

But as soon as she saw the line of scales that conceals my *stav*—or 'manhood,' as her people call it—she froze. It seems I am very different from a human male, and this displeases her.

I cannot deny the blow to my vanity. I have always been considered attractive among my kind—highly sought after by many females.

Just last year, no fewer than three females tried to entice me into the mating battle, but I refused. I have always hoped to find my T'kara. Now that I have, she finds my appearance so displeasing she averts her gaze.

It seems I will die old and alone, without a mate or heirs.

Clenching my jaw, I push down my wounded pride and move past her to the cleansing room.

Determination fills me anew. Freyja is mine, and I will not give up so easily.

Grabbing one of the threadbare hand towels by the sink, I use it to buff my scales to a fine pearlescent sheen. Female Dragons appreciate a male who takes extra care with his appearance; I must simply hope that human females do too.

Once I am finished bathing, I study myself in the mirror. Flexing my arms, I twist first one way and then the other, appraising my appearance from various angles.

It was foolish to believe she would simply run into my arms because of the bond, especially when she does not feel its pull as I do. I have been expecting her to accept me, without making any efforts to entice her to become my mate.

I glance at my reflection once more, pleased at the polished finish of my scales. They practically glow beneath the soft lighting of the l'sair crystals that illuminate the room.

I extend my wings, but quickly wince at the slight twinge of pain still present in my left wing joint. The pain and swelling have lessened, but not enough. It is frustrating to be unable to fly or shift forms.

Before I leave the cleansing room, I conjure black pants to conceal my lower half. When I step back into the room, Freyja turns to me. I puff my chest out and tip my chin up with pride, casually flexing my muscles as I strut toward her. The light from the fire reflects off my scales, making them shimmer like finely polished silver.

Squinting her eyes, she blinks several times as I approach. "Your scales are very... shiny," she says a bit hesitantly.

Shiny. My chest deflates. I was hoping for *regal* or *hand-*

some. But as I move closer, it is easy to see her mind is preoccupied as she turns her attention to the window, watching the blizzard outside.

In the reflection of the glass pane, her gaze is fixed and unfocused as she rubs her hands over her arms, trying to warm herself against the slight chill seeping in through the windowsill.

I do not like the hollow look in her eyes. "Freyja," I speak her name softly, calling her back from whatever it is that troubles her.

She blinks as if coming back to herself.

"Everyone was curious about us downstairs. Even before my incident with the Dwarf." She runs a hand through her long, red locks. "This might as well be a beacon," she grumbles, turning to face me. "My hair has always been a curse."

"A curse?" I'm completely taken aback by her statement. Gently, I hook a stray tendril with one claw, allowing the silken strand to slide over my forefinger. "Why do you say this? I would think this rare physical trait would be revered, not frowned upon."

"I was the subject of relentless teasing when I was a child because of it. And these—" She gestures to the spots on her skin.

Humans are so strange. Her hair and her markings would be highly prized among my kind, not ridiculed.

"Our scales come in many colors, but red is the most desirable because of its scarcity." I touch her face, careful to retract my claws so that I do not scratch her petal-soft skin as I trace my first two fingers across her cheek, observing in wonder as a pink bloom highlights the many small spots that dot her flesh. "And those with more than one color are even more scarce, revered as treasures to behold."

I stare deep into her luminous eyes, the color of clear,

blue skies. "You are rare among your people, Freyja. And it is a compulsion of my kind to covet rare things."

Gently, I tuck a stray tendril of silken hair behind the curved shell of her ear, pleased when she does not pull away. I'd always believed no other race could rival the beauty of the Fae or the Elves, but as I study Freyja, I realize that I was wrong.

Witnessing her altercation with the Dwarf, I also realize she is much stronger than I thought. I was wrong to call her weak or fragile, when she is anything but.

She has a will of iron, a heart of fire, and the skills of a true warrior. I am completely and utterly enthralled. Freyja is mine, and I will do whatever it takes to conquer her heart and claim her as my mate and my queen.

CHAPTER 21

FREYJA

My heart hammers as his emerald eyes stare deep into mine. There is something fierce and intense in the way he looks at me. As if he means to possess me entirely: mind, body, heart, and soul.

He leans in, and I'm frozen in place as awareness hums along my skin. A maelstrom of emotions swirls deep within. Part of me wants to pull him in closer, while another wants to push him away. The smell of spice and ginger fills the air around us and I have the strange urge to press myself against him and breathe deeply of the heady mix, but I do not move.

It's as if he has a strange power over me, and I cannot force myself to look away from him. His face is sharp lines and hard angles, extremely handsome, but in an Other-worldly way that a human man could never be.

His powerful form towers over me, but I am not afraid. He could easily harm me if he wished, and yet he has been nothing but gentle.

His eyes search mine, their vertically-slit pupils expanded

so that only a thin rim of green is barely visible around the edges.

Completely mesmerized, I lift my hand to his face, wanting more than anything to touch him, to trace my fingers over the smooth scales of his cheek and down to his mouth.

I want to know if his lips are soft and pliable, or hard and unforgiving, like the stern expression he presents to the world. The one that hides the Dragon who is so gentle with me underneath.

Gently, I touch his cheek. Aurdyn's gaze holds mine as I stretch up on my toes until my face is nearly even with his. His warm breath is a soft whisper across my skin as I drift closer. He leans in, closing the small gap between us. I inhale sharply at the featherlight brush of his lips against my own as my heart hammers in my chest.

A loud moan echoes from the room next door, breaking the spell, and I quickly pull away.

"Forgive me." I smooth a hand down my gown and clear my throat. Embarrassment scalds my cheeks as I look anywhere but at his face. "I should not have done that. I don't know what got into me."

"Freyja." He reaches for me, but I take a small step back. "We should go to sleep, Aurdyn. We still have a long journey ahead of us."

He stands before me a moment before moving back to the fire to stoke the flames.

When I curl up beneath the thin comforter, I'm exhausted, but I cannot rest. Not like this. Despite the fire burning on the hearth, there is still a chill in the room, but that is not what keeps me awake. It's the thought of what might have happened if we had not been interrupted.

Am I truly falling for this Dragon who has appointed himself as my fiercely loyal protector?

The bed dips behind me as Aurdyn slips beneath the comforter. He drapes his strong arm over my waist and pulls me to him, his familiar warmth and ginger-spice scent enveloping me as he curls his wing around my form like a heavy blanket.

I breathe out a sigh, reveling in his warmth and reassuring presence at my back.

He tightens his hold on me and my heart pounds, not from fear but from something else entirely. "Are you warm enough?" His voice is a low rumble in my ear, sending a tiny frisson of delight down my spine.

"Yes," I whisper breathlessly. "Thank you."

Despite my previous exhaustion, I'm wide awake. My entire body is humming with longing at the press of his form against mine. Desperate to focus on something else, I change the subject. "How long do you think it will take to reach your home?"

"At least two days." He sighs heavily. "If not for my injury, we could fly and be there in a matter of hours."

"Must be nice. Being able to fly everywhere."

"It is. Walking everywhere is... tedious."

I laugh softly. "Well now you know what it's like for the rest of us."

"Indeed," he grumbles.

"What will happen when we reach your kingdom?" I ask both anxious and dreading his answer. "Will I be the only human there?"

"Yes."

"And will your people accept me? Being there, I mean."

"I am the king, and you are my T'kara—my Fated One," he says, an edge of menace in his tone. "To disrespect you in any way would be treason."

At least the bond will offer me protection in his realm, although it could still cause problems as well. Especially since he has expressed many times how low his people regard humans. Just because I'm his Fated One, does not mean everyone will simply accept me.

Severing our connection would be the easiest way to avoid problems for him *and* for me. I had not wanted to bring it up yet, but I suppose now is as good a time as any.

I want to simply ask outright, but the words get stuck in my throat. Instead, I try a different approach to ease him into the conversation.

"Were your parents fated to each other?"

"No," he replies. "There are very few among my kind who find their fated mates."

"Has anyone ever already been married to someone else and then found their T'kara after?"

"Yes."

My ears perk up. "What happened then?"

"They are given the choice to have a priest dissolve the bond." Hope flares inside me, before he adds, "But none have ever chosen this."

"Why not?"

"As I said, the bond is sacred. A gift from the gods."

I turn in his arms to face him. I rest my hands on his chest, pushing back just enough that I can tip my head up to his, acutely aware of the thick muscle beneath my fingers and the feel of his hands at the small of my back, holding me close against him. "What if we asked a priest to sever our bond?"

His head jerks back, but I continue. "You said it yourself— Dragons do not like humans. You don't want to be married to me anymore than I want to be married to you. So it's the obvious choice, is it not?"

His brow creases in a deep frown. "It would be sacrilege. The bond is a blessing of the highest order."

This is not going how I planned. I thought he'd be glad of

my suggestion, but it seems I was wrong. "What if the gods made a mistake?"

"The old gods do not make mistakes," he counters. "As for your new gods… I would not put it past them."

I purse my lips. "Just because I am human does not mean I worship the new gods. My family has always kept to the old ways."

"That is good news."

His statement baffles me. "Why?"

"I thought I would have to build a temple to the new gods in my kingdom, specifically for you. It is good to know I will not."

I huff out a frustrated breath. This is definitely not how I imagined this conversation would go. I thought he would want to be rid of me, but it seems I was wrong.

Despite his arrogant manner, Aurdyn is good to me. And while I can think of far worse situations to be in, than to find myself bound to him, I spent enough time in a cell to know that I'll never be trapped again. If I stay with him in his kingdom, it will be because it is *my* decision, and I have not come to one yet. I'll not have my choices taken from me ever again.

"What if I choose not to stay with you?" I ask the question I have dreaded bringing up most. "Will you try to force me?"

Anger darkens his features. "Do you truly believe that I have such little honor, that I would force you to do anything you do not wish?" He relinquishes his hold on me and stands from the bed, his expression hard. "Is this what you truly think of me?"

"I…" I hesitate as I sit up in the bed, considering my next words carefully. I had not meant to offend him, but that's what I've done. "I did not mean offense. I know you are honorable, but I—" I sigh heavily. "I had to ask."

He crosses his arms over his chest, waiting for me to continue as I stand and meet his gaze evenly. "I was betrayed by the only person I had left in this world after my parents died. And being locked away in a dungeon for weeks… it was —" My voice catches, but I swallow hard against the lump in my throat. "I take nothing for granted now, and I will not have my choices taken from me. Do you understand?"

His expression softens, and he dips his chin in a subtle nod. "Yes."

CHAPTER 22

AURDYN

I understand her reasoning. She was betrayed by the person she loved most. She was imprisoned, and she wants to make sure that I do not do the same. I will not keep her if she does not want to stay.

"When we reach my kingdom, if you still wish to dissolve our bond, we will go to the priests and ask for their help in severing it."

She blinks several times. "You... would do this even though it has never been done before among your people?"

"As King of the Ice Mountains, I give you my word," I state solemnly. "If that is your decision, I will honor it."

She lowers her gaze, her brows furrowed as if in deep contemplation before she lifts her eyes again to me. "Then, I must ask you: Do Dragons... love?"

"Dragons do not love." At least, not in the way I've heard humans do. "We are fiercely protective of our mates—especially Fated Ones." The desire to claim and possess is a primal instinct deeply embedded in our blood, passed down from our ancestors. "If you choose to remain with me, my people will accept you because they understand this."

"So… you would bind yourself to me simply because of the fate bond?"

"Yes. You are my T'kara. It is my duty to protect and care for you."

"Duty…" she murmurs, lowering her gaze.

She appears troubled by my answer, but I do not understand why.

"If not for our connection, would you still want to bind yourself to me?"

If she had asked me this when we first met, the answer would be no. Now, the answer is not so simple. I only know that the thought of losing her makes an uncomfortable knot form in the pit of my stomach. And I cannot determine if this is the bond making me feel this way or if it is something else. And I do not know how to explain this to her when I don't even understand it myself.

Instead, I give her the truth that I do understand. "We are bound by the will of the gods. That is all that matters to me."

Something akin to disappointment flashes in her eyes, but it is too brief for me to be sure. She moves to a chair by the fire, studying the dancing flames with a look of intense contemplation.

I want more than anything to convince her to stay with me, but I must give her time to weigh this decision. Freyja is human. Her people do not have fated bonds to each other. All of this is new to her, and now she is trying to reconcile it within herself.

After what feels like an eternity, she turns her gaze back to me. "I cannot sleep. I know they have plenty of mead, but do you think the dwarves have any tea here?"

* * *

Wearing the shade stone necklace to disguise my appearance, I make my way downstairs to the tavern. Many of the Dwarves have retired for the night, but there are still several gathered around the tables drinking.

I walk over to the bar and tap the counter to draw the innkeeper's attention. His head snaps in my direction and he comes directly over. He gives me a conspiratorial wink. "Having a bit of trouble with the missus?"

Before I can answer, he places a tankard of mead before me. "This should fix you right up."

I push it away and level a dark glare at him. "Tea," I growl. "Now."

He blinks several times. "Well, all right then." He motions to his son, and Olmar rushes to the back. "No need to get upset. I meant no offense."

"My wife needs new clothing as well. Sturdy and warm, and a pair of boots half this size." I hand him one of the ill-fitted boots from the Dwarves at the cottage. I drop a handful of coins onto the counter, watching with amusement as his beady eyes widen. "This should more than cover it."

He greedily gathers the coins, biting one to test it before smiling widely at me. "And when will you be needing these?"

"First thing in the morning."

I expect him to protest, but the coin I gave him must be worth far more than I realized because he doesn't bat an eyelash. When his son walks up with a pot of tea and two cups, he instructs, "Follow him up to his room with the tea and then come back down and wake the clothier. We've got an order that needs to be filled by morning."

Olmar trails me back up the stairs to our room. When I open the door, he moves past me to place the tea on the table. He gives Freyja a small bow, and when she smiles in return, his cheeks turn bright red.

With a low growl, I usher him back out the door, slamming it shut behind him.

Freyja gives me a pointed look as I remove the shade stone. "What did I say about growling at everyone?"

"How am I *supposed* to react when a Dwarf makes *eyes* at my *wife*?"

"We're not really married, Aurdyn."

I gesture angrily to the door. "He does not know that, now does he?"

She exhales an exasperated huff, but her expression soon changes as I pour her a cup of tea and hand it to her on a saucer.

I take a seat beside her, in front of the hearth. The firelight dances across her skin, casting her in an ethereal glow. She is truly magnificent to behold, and I cannot stop thinking of how fierce she was in dealing with the Dwarf in the tavern.

"I was wrong to call you weak or fragile, Freyja, when it is clear to see you are not." Her eyes snap to mine, and I continue. "You have the skills of a true warrior. I have always heard that humans do not allow their females to fight. But it seems this is merely a rumor."

"Most do not, but the kingdom of Ruhaen is not like the other human territories. All are taught to fight with a sword and shield. In battle, women take up arms alongside the men."

"Even a princess?" I ask.

She tips her chin up proudly. "I am a shield-maiden of Ruhaen, as was my mother and the line of strong women before me."

Before I met Freyja, I did not think human females were trained as warriors, but I am pleased to be wrong. It seems there is much I do not know about my human T'kara, and I am eager to learn more.

"I was fortunate to grow up in Ruhaen," she says. "It is a shame that most human kingdoms discourage or outright forbid women from learning to fight and defend themselves."

"It is a skill everyone needs," I agree. "In my kingdom, our fledglings begin training when they are seven years old. It is the hope that they never have to use their training, but we want them prepared in case we ever go to war."

"Tell me more about your home," she says. "I've only ever heard vague stories about the Ice Mountains."

"What do you want to know?"

She shrugs. "What is it like there?"

I study her a moment. "Unfortunately for you, this time of year is the brutal season."

"Brutal season?"

"Much colder than the average winters you are familiar with," I explain. "The people of the Moldani believe the desert teaches warriors the meaning of endurance, but they are wrong." I meet her gaze evenly. "It is the ice and snow that forges real strength."

She gives me a curious look. "I heard your people relocated to the Ice Mountains after the last Great War instead of rebuilding on your original lands."

I nod. "My grandfather knew that if our race were to survive, we would need to be strong. Stronger than we were before. And in the Ice Mountains we can hone our strength in a place that is also difficult for our enemies to attack us without warning."

"Dragons are said to have long lives that rival even that of the Fae and the Elves," she says. "Were you... alive during the last Great War?"

"No," I reply bitterly, cursing this fact. It is the reason my uncle had so much support for his claim to the crown. It was how he tried to undermine my rule when I first took the throne. "I was born in the Ice Mountains. In the capital city of Windhelm thirty years ago. Over two hundred years after the Great War."

"You're thirty years old?" She smiles. "We are closer in age than I thought."

"How old are you?"

"Twenty-five," she says. "But you'd think I was a spinster the way my uncle goes on about how I need to find a husband."

Her mouth turns down briefly before she lowers her gaze. "Despite what you witnessed, my uncle did love me... before Luria's spell. I have to find a way to free him from her enchantment."

I understand she is in pain, but she can never return. Surely, she sees this. "If you go back there, the Mages will have you executed."

"I cannot just give up on him, Aurdyn. He raised me; I love him."

"He would have burned you at the stake if I had not gotten there in time." I clench my jaw. "You would be dead now, Freyja and—"

"Stop," she snaps. "It was not his fault, and you know it. You saw it yourself."

"And just how do you intend to reach him?" I frown. "Do you have a plan that does not involve your death?"

She nods. "I will send word to the kingdom of Florin. King Edmynd is my cousin, and I believe he will help me."

"You were accused of witchcraft," I remind her. "Are you certain he will give you aid?"

Her silence speaks to her uncertainty.

As much as I want to protect her, I can see how important this is to her, and I want to help. Gently, I place two fingers under her chin, tipping her face back up to mine. "When we reach my kingdom, we will send word to your cousin—King Edmynd of Florin."

"Thank you," she whispers.

It has been many years since my kind have had any dealings with the Kingdom of Florin. I have heard they despise the Fae as much as we do, but I know little of their people, beyond that they are human. And as such, they are probably under the protection of the Order of Mages. If so, I doubt King Edmynd will be so eager to help even his own cousin.

"How exactly are you related to King Edmynd?" I ask, trying to assess the likelihood of him actually helping her.

"Our mothers were cousins," she replies. "I used to play with him when we were children, before…" Her voice trails off as she stares at the fire with a faraway look. "I was only nine when my parents rode off to battle and never came back."

Her eyes brighten with tears. "My uncle not only raised me as his own, but he also named me as his heir since he has no children." She pauses. "I was so happy when he found Luria. My uncle has never married before and I—" Her voice hitches.

"My uncle is a good man." Her expression hardens. "Luria betrayed us both, and I want her to pay for it."

"I understand the need for vengeance, but you must seek it carefully. For it rarely comes without a terrible price." I cup her chin, tilting her face up to mine. "Ten years ago, my mother was murdered by a rival Clan leader, who was as close to my father as a brother. And my father was so consumed with grief and the bitterness of his friend's betrayal that he left to hunt him without telling anyone… without me or any of our warriors."

"What happened?" she asks, her gaze searching mine. "Did he find him?"

"Yes." I clench my jaw as the painful memory returns. "But it was a trap. My father got his revenge by killing the Dragon who took my mother's life, but he was fatally wounded in the process."

I shift my gaze to the dancing flames in the hearth. "I know why my father did what he did… but I wish—" My voice catches as I struggle to speak around the knot in my throat, surprised at how acute the pain still is after so many years. "I thought I would have many more decades by my father's side to learn from him, but I was wrong. I am the youngest king to ever claim the throne of my people, and there are many who question my rule because of it."

The thoughts I leave unspoken are the ones that plague me most. There are many times that I have found myself wondering if perhaps they are right. That I *am* too young to bear the mantle of rule.

But I do not dare speak this aloud because it would only be construed as weakness, and there is nothing worse among my people than a Dragon that is weak.

"I am sorry, Aurdyn." Freyja reaches across and gently cups my cheek.

Sorrow shines in her eyes, but I do not want her pity. Dragons respect only strength, and females would never tolerate weakness in a potential mate.

"Why?"

"Because I know what it is to lose one's parents." Lowering her eyes, she shakes her head softly. "I've always thought that saying 'I'm sorry' is not quite adequate to encompass the acknowledgement of such terrible loss, but I… do not know what other words to replace them with." Her small brow furrows. "If I did, I would give them to you, for I heard them often enough after my own parents died to know they are not quite what they should be."

"*Mal'von*," I murmur, and she lifts her gaze to mine with a questioning look. "It is an old word in the archaic form.

Loosely translated, it means: I grieve with you for that which was lost and can never be replaced."

Her blue eyes meet mine evenly as she whispers in return. "Mal'von."

We talk for a few more hours by the fire as we drink our tea. After a while, her eyes grow heavy lidded as she struggles to stay awake.

Carefully, I carry her to the bed and then crawl in behind her, wrapping her up in my arms and my wing. I scent her neck, breathing in her lovely fragrance that reminds me of lilac and jasmine.

She is so much stronger than I first realized. Each of us has experienced great loss, and we both know the sting of betrayal at the hands of one who is supposed to be family. The difference is that her uncle is under a Mage's spell, while mine had no such excuse.

I understand Freyja wants to save her uncle, but the Order of Mages have him under their dark enchantment and they want my T'kara dead. And I will do everything in my power to keep her safe. Even if it means waging war on the Order.

CHAPTER 23

FREYJA

"**F**reyja, wake up," Aurdyn speaks softly in my ear. "We must leave soon."

Tired and groggy, I lift my head from his chest and squint up at him. It's still dark outside, the only light in the small room from the crackling blaze on the hearth. "What time is it?"

"We have a few hours before dawn. We must leave before everyone else is awake."

"What about the storm?" I glance at the window. A thick layer of snow lies on the sill and ice covers the pane. "I thought we were staying here for two days."

"I checked outside," he says, and I wonder when he managed to do that, because I never felt him leave the bed. "It is still snowing, but there is a break in the storm. We should leave before the weather turns bad again."

Aurdyn sits up, and I quickly pull the thin blanket over me like a cocoon. It's still cold in here despite the roaring fire across the way. Rolling onto my stomach, I bury my face in the bedding and groan. I hate waking up early.

"Are you all right?" he asks, voice laced with concern. "Do you feel ill?"

"No," I mumble into the pillow. "I've just never been a morning person."

He snorts with amusement. "You can sleep in all you want once we reach my kingdom. But until then,"—he rips the blanket from me, and I jerk up to sitting—"you need to get up."

"What are you doing?" I hiss. "It's freezing!"

He gives me a stern look. "We must go. The sooner we leave, the better. We are still being hunted, Freyja, or have you forgotten?"

"No, I have not." I glare as I stand from the bed. "I'll get ready quickly."

I know he's right, but I'm not looking forward to trudging through the ice and snow again today. I'm exhausted already just thinking about it.

With a heavy sigh, I turn to look for my clothes, but Aurdyn hands me a new set of fur-lined leather pants, a tunic, and a heavy cloak, along with a pair of boots that look like they might actually fit me properly. I blink up at him. "Where did you get this?"

"I ordered them last night and the Dwarves left them outside the room this morning."

That was thoughtful of him. "Thank you." I smile. "These look very warm."

"They had better be," he says gruffly. "I paid the Dwarf handsomely for these. If he used shoddy material, I will—"

"I'm sure it's fine." I rest a hand on his shoulder, trying to stop him before he gets all worked up and grumpy before we even start our day. I notice two cups of tea on the table, steam rising from the cups. He must have had them bring that for us as well. "Drink your tea. I would rather travel with a happy Dragon instead of a grumpy one today," I tease.

A faint smile twitches his mouth as he walks over to the table and takes a cup while I make my way to the cleansing room to change.

After I dress, we eat a few of the supplies Moira packed for us. Now that he's had his tea, Aurdyn seems to be in a much better mood. His lips curl up in a slight grin as he tells me another story about his cousin, Brovyn, and all the trouble they got into as children.

When we are done, Aurdyn gathers our supplies and ushers me to the door. With his hand on the latch, he turns to me and leans in. A warm puff of air hits the top of my head as he scents me, drawing in a deep breath.

I laugh. "You're so dramatic."

"The Dwarves smell terrible," he murmurs. "If your sense of smell was as acute as mine, you would understand why I do this."

He takes another long whiff, and I put a hand on his chest, playfully pushing him away with a grin. "You're being ridiculous. Now, let's go before you find something else to complain about."

He snorts with amusement before putting the necklace back on, morphing into his human disguise. We go downstairs, both of us pulling our hoods over our heads to hide our faces.

Fortunately, only a few people are in the tavern, but it's enough of a crowd for us to easily slip away unnoticed. I hope.

We're not even halfway across the room when the front doors burst open, and dozens of Dwarves come piling in. Dirt covers their clothing and skin. "Must be the night shift coming in straight from the mines," Aurdyn mutters, wrapping a protective arm around my waist and tugging me close.

I glance over at him and gasp at the flash of silver-white scales visible beneath his hood before tanned human skin replaces it again. "What is it?"

"Your disguise," I whisper. "It's failing."

His eyes widen as he looks at his hand, the white scales and black claws blurring in and out of sight. "This should not be happening." His head whips toward the door. "Unless—"

Six cloaked figures walk through the doorway. The first one lowers his hood, and I inhale sharply at his pale gray skin, raven-black eyes, pointed ears, and razor-sharp teeth. "A Mage," I whisper under my breath. "They've tracked us here."

Ice fills my veins as I recognize the insignia on the metal armor of the other five men. They push back their hoods as they scan the room. They are hunters—humans loyal to the Order of Mages.

One of them turns to a Dwarf behind him, dropping a small sack of coins in his palm. Anger tightens my chest when I recognize the Dwarf. It's Barlen. The one who touched me last night. He must have turned us in for the bounty. Whistling, he skips back out the front doors and into the snow.

The front entrance is blocked, but I notice a door off to one side. I take Aurdyn's hand and pull him toward it, weaving our way through the crowd. We push our way inside and find a long, poorly-lit hallway.

"We should have killed that Dwarf," Aurdyn snarls. He glances down at his necklace. "I suspect the Mage has cast a hunting spell. His magic is affecting the shade stone's power."

I turn back toward the door, pushing it open just enough to see the Mage walk toward the innkeeper.

The Dwarf pales as he approaches. "How—how may I help you, fine sir?" Garvin asks, unable to hide the tremor in his voice.

Everyone fears the Order of Mages. They are powerful beings with magic to rival that of the Dark Elves and the Fae.

"We are searching for a woman," the Mage says darkly. "A human with red hair. She is traveling with a Dragon."

"A Dragon, you say?" Garvin's brows shoot up toward his hairline. "We've not had a Dragon in these parts, thank the gods, for the past five years, at least."

"What about a human woman with red hair?" one of the other men asks.

I still, holding my breath as I wait for his answer while Aurdyn growls low behind me.

"Humans rarely come to these parts." He gestures to the tavern. "As you can see, we're mostly Dwarves here. But if I see a human woman, I'll be sure to alert you."

A relieved sigh leaves my mouth as I sag against Aurdyn.

The Mage glares at the innkeeper, and the Dwarf swallows hard. "Anything else I can help you with?" he chirps. A nervous smile quirks his lips. "Because if not, I've many things to do."

"How much for lodging?"

"Ten shials a night per room, no more than two occupants," he replies. "It includes an evening meal and a mead for each of you."

The Mage slaps a sack of coins on the counter, and then he and the others walk toward a table. Everyone in the room gives them a wide berth, falling silent as they watch them pass.

The Mage turns and faces the room, his dark eyes traveling over the occupants. "We are searching for a human woman with red hair and a Dragon," he announces. "Anyone who helps us find them will be paid handsomely for their efforts."

My heart hammers, and I hold my breath, sure that at any

moment one of the Dwarves will mention us. Barlen certainly did. That must be how they tracked us here.

A long minute passes, and they all remain silent. I'm surprised, but pleased beyond measure that none of them say anything when I know several saw me last night.

It seems even the Dwarves do not trust Mages.

Another Dwarf sidles up to the innkeeper, and I immediately recognize him as the one who served us yesterday evening. Olmar—the innkeeper's son. He leans in, whispering in his father's ear.

I glance back at Aurdyn. He's mentioned before that Dragons have good hearing. "Did you hear what he said with that superior Dragon hearing of yours?"

"He sent someone to our room to warn us the Mages seek a red-haired, human woman."

Another Dwarf rushes down the stairs to Olmar and his father, shaking his head. "She and that ugly husband of hers were not there," he says loud enough that I can just make out the words myself.

"Ugly?" Aurdyn practically snarls in my ear.

Despite my nerves, I cannot help but tease him. "To be fair"—I glance up and down his form—"you are a bit homely in this disguise."

Aurdyn narrows his eyes. "A good wife would never say such a thing to her husband."

"Good thing we are not married then." I flash a grin before sobering again. "Let's see if there's a way outside from this hallway without being seen."

He nods, and we start down the corridor.

Someone rounds the corner up ahead, and fear spikes through me. With nowhere else to hide, we need to look like we're in this hallway for an entirely different reason.

I grasp Aurdyn's cloak and push him back against the

wall, stretching up on my toes until my face is nearly level with his. "Quick," I whisper. "Pretend to kiss me."

Despite the darkness inside our hoods, his green eyes flash with surprise a moment before he wraps his arms around my waist.

I squeak as he spins us both, so my back is now to the wall instead. His fiery gaze searches mine a moment before he leans in and crushes his lips to my own.

His powerful form presses firmly against mine, his warm smell of ginger spice surrounding me in a heady mix. My heart pounds and I'm overwhelmed with sensation. I gasp as his sharp fangs brush lightly against my lips, and his tongue sweeps into my mouth, finding mine and curling around it.

This is everything I had wanted last night but was too afraid to ask for.

He tastes of warm spice, and I'm completely lost as the soft ridges along his tongue stroke against mine, both demanding and giving all at once. I've never been kissed before, and my pulse races as I fist my hands in his cloak, pulling him even closer.

Aurdyn pins me against the wall. He cups the back of my head with one hand while his other arm tightens around my back. A soft moan escapes me as he kisses me long and deep, as if branding me as his with his lips and his tongue.

A low growl vibrates his chest, and he curls his tail around my ankle.

Panic shoots through me when I hear a horrified gasp.

Aurdyn quickly pulls away, leaving me breathless and panting as he spins toward the source of the noise.

"You're a Dragon," a Dwarf breathes out beside us, all the color drained from his face. "What are you—"

"Silence, Dwarf!" Lightning fast, Aurdyn wraps a hand around his throat, baring his fangs. "If you so much as breathe another word, I'll end you. Do you understand?"

The Dwarf nods repeatedly, sweat already beading across his brow as he trembles in the grasp of my fierce Dragon protector.

"There you are," a voice whispers urgently behind us, and I spin to find Olmar. "Let Alfie go. He's not going to rat you out."

Aurdyn gives a low warning growl to the Dwarf before releasing him.

"This way." Olmar gestures down the hall. "Follow me. Hurry."

We rush down the corridor after Olmar. Outside is still dark, and only the small l'sair stones at the far end light the hallway. I hold tightly to Aurdyn's hand, trusting him to guide me since I can hardly see anything.

When we come to an abrupt halt, I recognize the hurried sound of bolts sliding open, followed by the loud creak of a heavy door swinging on rusted hinges. Faint light spills into the darkness and as we step out into the snow, the rising dawn is barely a thin line of soft orange and red over the mountains in the distance.

Olmar turns to face us, gesturing to the left. "This way to the mountain pass." He darts a glance around us. "Go! Before they find you!"

Instantly, Aurdyn gathers me up into his arms and breaks into a run, racing toward the mountain pass with inhuman speed. The buildings and trees are a blur all around us, and I close my eyes, swallowing against the bile threatening to rise in my throat.

Something hits Aurdyn's back with a heavy thud, and my eyes snap open as he stumbles forward and drops to his knees in the snow. "Aurdyn, what—"

The words die in my throat as a bolt of red magic races toward us. A deafening roar rips from his throat as it slams into his back in a powerful burst. Still holding me to his chest, he falls forward, twisting at the last moment to land on his back, so he doesn't crush me beneath him.

"Aurdyn!" I cry out, but his eyes are closed. Only the slight rise and fall of his chest tells me he's still alive.

"There you are," a voice calls ominously, and I scramble to my feet as the Mage stalks toward us. "I had a feeling you were here, and I was right," he sneers.

My limbs are shaky, but I muster all of my courage as I face the Mage. "Leave us alone!"

"The Order has sentenced you both to death, and now I will carry it out."

I dart a glance at Aurdyn, still lying on the ground, his eyelids fluttering. "Leave him be! I'm the one you want!"

"I'm afraid I cannot do that, Princess." The Mage raises his hands as the other five men gather around him, unsheathing their swords.

There is nowhere to run, and we cannot hide. A glowing red orb of magic gathers between the Mage's palms as he glares at me. Stealing myself, I push down my fear and place myself directly between him and Aurdyn.

"Freyja, run." Aurdyn groans as he struggles to stand. "Now."

"No." I state firmly. "We will either live or we will go to the gods together this day, but I *will not* leave you."

My chest tightens and everything slows as the Mage flings his arms, sending his destructive magic racing toward us like lightning.

Desperate, I raise my arms as if that will somehow stop it from reaching us. Intense heat sears my palms, and a ball of flame shoots out from my hands, arcing in front of us like a giant shield.

The red orb slams against it, disintegrating as soon as it touches the flames.

My heart thunders as I stare at my hands in shock. I don't

know how I'm doing this, but I pray to the gods to help me maintain it as the Mage casts another volley of destructive magic.

I stumble back at the impact, but my fire shield holds steady, weathering the assault without breaking.

My arms tremble and sweat beads across my brow as I concentrate on holding my position through another attack. Everything aches, and darkness gathers at the corners of my vision as I muster all of my strength to maintain our shield.

If I fall, the Mage will kill us both.

A rush of wind behind me parts my hair, followed by an ear-splitting roar. A stream of flame arcs over my head toward the Mage, but he throws up a glowing shield of magic at the last minute, halting his assault just as my own powers fail.

Without warning, his shield collapses, and he releases a feral cry as flames lick over his skin, completely engulfing him.

His men stare in shock at their leader as he writhes in pain.

Struggling to remain conscious, I'm vaguely aware of all the Dwarves gathered nearby, their eyes wide at the terrible scene that plays out before them.

The Mage drops to his knees and weakly waves a hand, dousing the flames, but it's too late. His skin is charred black, and his clothes are melted to his ruined flesh. Panting heavily, he grits his teeth. "She is a sanishon. And she must be killed."

"She is mine, and you will die for trying to harm her," Aurdyn's voice booms behind me. I twist my head back and my jaw drops at his massive Draken form.

His large wings are extended out to his sides, making him appear even larger than he already is. His lips are pulled back in an angry snarl, revealing two rows of fangs—each of them as long as my forearm. He moves over me protectively, lethal black talons digging into the snow on either side of my body as he glares at the Mage.

"She's a witch!" one of the hunters cries out, gesturing wildly at me. "She must die for her crimes!"

"She is *my* witch," Aurdyn growls. "And you *will not* touch her." He opens his mouth and sends another stream of fire toward them, burning the Mage and all but one of the hunters into a pile of charred remains.

Aurdyn snarls at the remaining man. "Return to your masters and tell the Order of Mages that if they send another assassin, I will rain down fire and destruction upon their kind and burn their sacred temple to ash."

He rakes his massive claws across the ground as he stalks toward the trembling hunter. "Tell them, I am the death that will come for them if they dare try to harm she who is mine."

The man stumbles back, barely catching himself before he falls. He scrambles to his feet and races away, disappearing into the forest.

Unable to fight it any longer, exhaustion hits me like a giant wave, and I drop to my knees.

"Freyja!" Aurdyn shifts in a whirl of snow and wind back into his two-legged form and wraps his arms around me, lifting me up. He brushes the hair back from my face, staring down at me with a panicked expression. "What is wrong?"

"I don't know. I'm so tired," I barely manage. "I..." My eyes close and my head falls back as I tumble away into oblivion.

CHAPTER 24

AURDYN

Panic twists deep inside me as Freyja goes limp in my arms. I snap my head toward Olmar. "She needs a healer! Now!"

"Follow me!" Olmar runs back to the tavern, barking out orders to the other Dwarves around him. "Find Healer Trilan! Bring her to the inn!"

When we reach the tavern, Olmar guides me to a room in the back of the main seating area. A large table sits in the middle of the space, surrounded by storage racks of wine and mead. Gingerly, I lay Freyja down and then lift my head back to him, my temper flaring. "Where is the healer?" I bellow. "Get them here! Now!"

The door opens, slamming against the wall as an elderly Dwarf woman rushes in, her chest heaving with exertion as she moves to Freyja's side. Her dark hair is streaked through with white and tied up in a series of twisted braids atop her head. Her amber eyes meet mine and narrow. "I'm Healer Trilan. What has happened here?"

"This human used magic and then she collapsed," Olmar answers before I can.

Trilan leans over Freyja, her hands hovering over her still form as she closes her eyes in concentration.

The healer's brow furrows deeply and my anxiety spikes, stripping away the last of my control. "What is wrong with her?"

"She is a human possessed of powerful magic," she murmurs, her eyelids squeezed shut as her hands move over Freyja's body. "But it comes at a great price."

"What are you talking about?" I snarl. "Speak plainly, Dwarf."

Her eyes snap open to meet mine steadily. "I have never seen a human with magic before. It is a different kind than that possessed by the other races."

"What do you mean?" I ask, not bothering to hide my impatience. "How is it any different from that of the Elves or the Fae?"

"They draw their power from the earth all around them. But her magic—" Trilan gestures at Freyja, "draws from her own life force, weakening her with its use." She rests a hand over Freyja's forehead and smooths the hair back from her face.

My heart clenches at how vulnerable my T'kara appears at this moment, and I can barely breathe, much less think.

"She will live. *This time*," Trilan says with a sobering look. "But if she is not careful—if she uses too much—it *will* kill her."

A vortex of emotion churns within me as I stare down at my T'kara. "But how is this possible? I do not understand. Her kind are not supposed to have magic."

Her amber eyes slide to mine, full of suspicion. "Since when does a Dragon care so much for a human? Tell me, what is she to you, Dragon King?"

The other Dwarves gasp, and I still. "You know who I am."

"Of course I do. You have the look of your father, King Aurdyn." She leans in, scrutinizing me with a piercing gaze. "Did you inherit his cruel nature as well?"

She refers to his handling of the Dwarves who dared cross our borders by tunneling beneath our mountain in search of treasure. He set fire to the tunnels, killing them all even after they had begged him for mercy. The memory of that terrible day will forever be burned in my mind.

"I am *not* my father," I state firmly. "Now, tell me what I want to know."

"First, *you tell me* what this human is to you," she counters.

I level a dark glare at her. I do not have time for these games. "She is my T'kara—my Fated One."

Trilan's eyes widen, and she blinks several times. "You are certain?"

"Of course I am," I grind out. "Now, tell me what you know."

She steps closer and holds up her hands. "Will you allow me?"

Dark smoke puffs from my nostrils as they flare. "What does this have to do with anything?"

"Please," she says. "I must confirm something."

Clenching my fists, I bite back my temper and give her a shallow nod.

Trilan closes her eyes as she waves her hands over me, assessing me as she did Freyja.

She inhales sharply and her gaze drops to my T'kara in wonder. "She is a sanishon—one of the Great Uniters from the prophecy of the Ancient Tomes of the Lythyrian."

"Sanishon," I repeat darkly, eyeing her with suspicion. "How do you know this term? And what does it have to do with anything?"

"All who wish for times of peace know of the prophecy," she explains. "It is said the sanishons will possess great powers, unlike anything seen among their kind before." She puts a hand to her chest, bowing slightly to my T'kara in sacred reverence. "And they will use it to conquer those who seek to control the darkness, ushering in an era of peace."

My stomach churns. The last thing I want is for rumors of Freyja's magic to spread, putting her in even more danger than she already is. "The prophecy is a story—a myth—nothing more."

"It is truth." Conviction burns in Trilan's eyes. "And *she* is a sanishon—an Outsider like the ones foretold, who will unite the other races and bring an end to the darkness that would lead us to war."

"Enough!" I snap, baring my fangs. "Your superstitious drivel will only place her in danger, Dwarf."

"Whether you believe it or not, it doesn't matter," she states firmly. "She is a sanishon of the prophecy. It is the only explanation for what I felt when I assessed her. As your fated mate, the gods have given her the ability to conjure your Dragon's fire—a power gifted to her through your bond." She pauses. "This is how the prophecy explains it."

I rub the back of my neck. "If she is what you say—a herald of an era of peace—why does the Order of Mages want her dead?"

"The Mages claim to protect the humans from the other races, but in truth, they control the human kingdoms with their powers. Magic like hers is dangerous to their rule."

"Why do the Mages care if humans possess magic, when almost all Otherworldly beings do as well?"

She shakes her head. "I do not know. I only know the Mages bind the human kingdoms so that no Otherworldly beings can access their powers in those lands. In return for this protection, the humans allow the Mages to enforce the laws of the Order, executing any humans discovered practicing magic."

I understand the Mages not wanting any humans to possess power in the lands they control, but why do they care about a human *outside* of the kingdoms they supposedly protect? And why would they want to murder one they believe is a sanishon, when the prophecy says their coming will herald in an age of peace?

"You wonder why the Mages want her dead for being a sanishon," the Dwarf healer's words echo my thoughts. "I do not have an answer for this."

"Are you reading my mind somehow, old woman?" I snarl.

"Calm yourself, Dragon King." A faint smirk twists her lips. "If I could read minds, I'd probably be half mad by now. But we Dwarves are not the simple creatures your kind imagine us to be. I am simply smarter than you think I am."

She steps closer and I bristle slightly at her bold manner. "Calm," she murmurs. "I need to assess your wing."

I suppress a wince at the dull ache in the main left joint, forgotten until just now. "I am fine."

"Can you fly?" She arches a brow.

When I do not answer, she sighs heavily. "I figured as much." She moves around behind me. "Probably injured yourself worse when you shifted to save her, did you not?"

I still. She was not there. Olmar had to retrieve her after Freyja fell. "How do you know that I changed forms?"

"You think I've gotten this old without learning a few things?" She shakes her head. "I would recognize the deafening roar of a fully shifted Dragon anywhere."

Her hands ghost over my sore left wing joint and I huff out a curl of black smoke.

"There it is," she mumbles, more to herself than to me. "Now, stay still and allow me to work."

Warmth blooms at the site. At first, it's painful, but then it slowly ebbs into a soothing heat. I knew some Dwarves possessed healing magic, but I did not know it would work on Dragons.

The pain fades away into nothing and when she steps back, I cautiously flex and extend my wings, testing the joint. I'm surprised when I feel nothing. Not even a hint of discomfort. Tucking my wings into my back, I turn to face her. "How did you do this?"

"I believe the words you're looking for are 'thank you.'" She crosses her arms over her chest. "You're welcome, by the way, Dragon King."

Now that I can shift forms and fly without pain, I must take Freyja to my kingdom immediately. I pull her into my arms and hug her to my chest as I turn for the door.

"Where are you going?" Trilan calls out even as the other Dwarves, including Olmar, move out of my way.

"To my kingdom."

"She needs to rest," the healer declares. "She should not be out in that cold until she's fully recovered."

I hate that this did not occur to me. Grimacing, I turn to Olmar. "Your best room. Where is it?" Now that they know who and what I am, I am done playing the part of a peasant.

He motions for me to follow him. Before I do, I look back at Trilan. "You will assess my T'kara first thing in the morning."

She bows her head in a subtle nod of acknowledgment.

As soon as I step through the door, I hear someone utter under their breath. "That poor girl... stuck with an arrogant Dragon like that."

"Aye," Trilan agrees in a hushed tone, oblivious to the fact that Dragons have sharp hearing. "But she'll never want for a better protector."

Fierce protectiveness swells my chest as her words ring

true in my heart. Freyja is my T'kara, and I will burn the entire Order to ash and raze their temples to the ground if they dare try to come for her.

CHAPTER 25

FREYJA

The sound of an argument startles me awake, followed by a low and menacing growl. My eyelids flutter open, and I turn my head to find Aurdyn snarling at an elderly Dwarf woman, his wings fully extended and his tail lashing agitatedly behind him. "You said she would be fine, but she has not awakened," he snaps. "What is wrong with her?"

"She has been through much," the woman replies. "You must let her rest and—"

"Aurdyn," I force the words past my lips despite my intense exhaustion, and he spins to face me, his angry expression softening instantly as he moves to my side.

"Thank the gods you're awake." He takes my hand, squeezing it gently as he stares down at me in concern. "How do you feel?"

I struggle to push myself up to sitting, but the world spins. "Help me sit up."

He places an arm around my back, pulling me up the rest of the way and bracing several pillows behind me.

"I'm Healer Trilan," the elderly Dwarf woman says. Her amber eyes are full of warmth as she moves to my bed, nudging Aurdyn aside as she leans over me.

He growls at her but stops when I give him a sharp look.

"How are you feeling, Princess?"

My mouth dries, but Aurdyn quickly adds, "She knows who we are. She is"—he glowers at her—"a friend," he grits through his fangs.

She gives him a wry look. "Oh, we're friends now, are we, Dragon King? Well, let me tell you, *friends* do *not* growl and snarl at one another."

He snarls, and I try but fail to stifle a weak laugh.

"Look at that," she tells Aurdyn, gesturing to me. "You've put her in good spirits. At least you're good for something, it seems."

He narrows his eyes, and I laugh again.

"Your color is returning." She touches my cheek. "Are you in any pain?"

I'm not sure pain is the right word. Whatever this is, it's something much deeper. "It's strange... almost like... being burned, but from inside." Aurdyn's eyes widen. "It's a hollow feeling... I cannot quite explain it. It is not pain exactly, but a dull, raw ache."

"Do you remember what happened?" Aurdyn asks.

"Some, but not all." Lifting my free hand, I study my palm as flits of memory return. "I conjured flame to shield us, but I —" I shake my head. "I'm not sure how. I've never done anything like that before."

"I believe it is an effect of our bond," he explains. "You can create my Dragon's fire. You inherited this from me, through our connection."

Myriad images flood my mind, and I gasp as I remember

him shifting forms. "Oh, Aurdyn, your wing." I glance over his shoulder. "Did you hurt it when you changed into a full Dragon?"

"Do not worry for me." Tenderly, he combs the hair back from my face with his fingers and then smirks. "My kind are strong. Concentrate on yourself. You need to rest and gather your strength, so we may leave for the Ice Mountains."

"But why did I fall unconscious in the first place? Why do I feel so weak?"

Healer Trilan steps forward. "You've inherited fire magic from your Fated One, but you must be careful how you use it."

"I—I'm not even sure how I did it," I say.

Trilan studies me. "And you've done nothing like it before? Never manifested any powers?"

Thinking of my visions, I exchange a quick glance with Aurdyn, and then shake my head 'no.' Trilan seems friendly enough, but the only person I trust entirely right now is my Dragon protector.

As if sensing this, she regards me steadily. "I am not your enemy and I do not wish you harm. I know your people condemn those who have magic, but our kind are not this way. And we have never aligned ourselves with the Mages, nor do we trust them."

That much was obvious when Garvin denied having seen me, and the others remained silent when the Mage offered a reward for information.

"If one of them found us, others will not be far behind," Aurdyn says darkly. "Now that I am able to fly, I will check the forest surrounding the village for any signs of danger while you rest. We should leave tomorrow at first light, if you are able."

"She should be well rested by then," Trilan chimes in.

"We could just leave now," I suggest, swinging my legs

over the side of the bed. But when I stand, the room lurches around me.

Aurdyn snags an arm around my waist and carefully sets me back down, his gaze full of disapproval. "Do not be stubborn. You cannot travel like this."

"I'm not being—" I start to say 'stubborn' but stop as he pins me with a hard stare.

"Do not try to deny it," he grumbles. "I already know how you are."

I gape at him.

He turns to Trilan. "I will return shortly. If anything happens to her while I am gone, I will raze your pitiful village to the ground. Do you understand?"

Her face loses all color as she nods.

"Rest." He points a stern finger at me. "I will be back in less than an hour."

As soon as he leaves, Trilan walks over to me. A faint smile tugs at her mouth. "Never thought I'd see the day a human tamed a Dragon."

"I've not *tamed* him," I deny. "We're—" I almost say 'friends,' but as the memory of our kiss returns, my cheeks heat, and I know it is more than this, so instead I say, "*bound* to each other. That is all."

"Is that what you're calling his obsession with you?" She shakes her head. "He was so worried, I thought he'd burn us all last night, blaming me for you not awakening."

My eyes widen as she continues. "I'm surprised he did not wake you with all of his raging. And every time you even slightly stirred in your sleep, he rushed to your side."

"He did?" I ask, even as faint memories of being held against a muscular chest and a silver-scaled hand brushing the hair back from my face return from last night. "But... Aurdyn doesn't even like humans," I mumble to myself.

"*You*, I believe, are an exception." She grins and then

smooths a hand down her tunic, yawning loudly. "I'll be off as soon as the Dragon King returns. I've not slept a wink all night and I'm eager to get to my bed." She rests a hand over mine. "Remember what I told you about your powers. Use them sparingly. Do you understand?"

"I do. I just... wish I knew how I even accessed them." I glance down at my palm. "I'm not sure if I could conjure fire again if I tried."

"We'll speak with a priest when we get to my kingdom," Aurdyn's voice drifts in as he steps through the doorway. "They understand the fated bond better than anyone else and the effects such a connection has upon those who have it."

Trilan gives me a warm smile. "I wish you well, Princess Freyja." She darts a glance at Aurdyn. "You and your Dragon."

I open my mouth to thank her, but Aurdyn cuts me off. "Where do you think you are going?" he asks, brow furrowed menacingly.

"Home," she says.

"My T'kara has only just awakened. You will stay here in case she needs a healer."

She goes rigid.

"Aurdyn," I hiss. "You cannot just order people around. She's tired. She needs to rest as well."

"Is this true?" His head snaps to her. "You are in need of rest?"

She nods.

"Then you will sleep in the next room," he says.

Before she can respond, he opens the door and bellows down the hallway. "Garvin!"

The sound of dishes crashing to the floor echoes from downstairs, followed by quick steps up the stairs and to our room. Garvin braces himself on the door, chest heaving and face red, as he stares wide-eyed at Aurdyn. "What is it?" He pants heavily. "Is something wrong?"

"Prepare the room next to ours for the healer," he says imperiously. "I want her nearby in case Freyja needs her before we leave."

"But—but that room has already been taken," he stumbles over his words. "They—"

"Then, assign them another," Aurdyn snaps. He turns back to Trilan. "Garvin will ready your room for you."

"I—of course I will," Garvin says. "Right away." He motions to Trilan. "Follow me."

As soon as they leave, Aurdyn closes the door.

"Aurdyn, you *cannot* treat people like that." I cross my arms over my chest. "They are *not* your servants."

He gives me a look as if what I've just said is preposterous. "I am *trying* to take care of you."

"By ordering people around?"

"By making sure they are available for whatever you may need, Freyja. When you collapsed, I—" He stops short and turns away, his gaze fixed on the window and the snow falling outside with a faraway look.

"What is it?" I ask softly. Whatever this is, it troubles him. That much is evident. "Tell me."

"I feared you might die," he says, his voice thick with emotion.

A smile tugs at my mouth. He was truly worried for me. Maybe he is falling for me, just as I am already falling for him. "I thought Dragons were not afraid of anything," I tease.

"So did I." His emerald eyes snap to mine, and he moves to my side. His expression is a strange mixture of worry and devotion as he gently smooths a stray lock of hair behind my ear. "You could have died trying to save me, Freyja. You do not feel the pull of the bond as I do. Why would you risk your life for me? I do not understand."

"Because I care for you, Aurdyn." I take his hand, threading my fingers through his.

A faint smile breaks through his normally stern expression. His eyes sparkle with amusement. "Even if I am an arrogant Dragon, as you claim?"

"Yes." I cannot help but grin in return.

His gaze travels over my face like a gentle caress, and he squeezes my hand. "I care for you as well, Freyja." His expression hardens. "And I forbid you to die."

A short huff of air escapes me in a laugh. "Well then, I will try my best to stay alive."

"See that you do."

A small shiver runs through me at the way his gaze holds mine—fierce and intense. "You are *val'nara,*" he says reverently.

"What is that?"

"The direct translation is 'one with a heart of fire,'" he says solemnly. "Fire heart. In the ancient tongue of my people."

High praise from a Dragon. Pride fills my chest. "Thank you for the compliment."

"It was not meant as a compliment. It is truth."

Well, now it's an even bigger compliment than it was before, and I cannot help the smile that curves my lips.

He lowers himself onto the bed beside me, and I feel the familiar tug around my waist as he pulls me into him. He drapes his wing over me like a blanket, cocooning me in his warmth and his scent. "Is that better?" his voice rumbles in my ear. "Are you warm enough now?"

Heat suffuses my entire body as I recall our kiss, and the way he pinned me against the wall and practically devoured me with his lips and his tongue. Desire pools deep in my belly as I whisper against his chest. "Yes."

He lowers his head, skimming the tip of his nose down my neck, and I inhale shakily, both nervous and excited at the thought of his touch. I hope he will kiss me again.

Instead, he draws in a deep breath, and I frown. "What are you doing?" I ask, although I'm fairly certain I already know, and a pang of disappointment spears me. I'd hoped we might repeat what happened between us in the hallway.

"This entire place reeks of Dwarf," he grumbles. "Your scent is the only pleasing one in this entire inn."

"Glad I can help you out like this," I say sarcastically, even as a smile tilts my lips at his dramatics.

"It's the least you could do," he replies matter-of-factly. "Especially after I stayed by your side all night while you were unconscious. The stench is terrible here. You have no idea how much I've suffered."

I swallow a laugh because I'm fairly sure he is serious. "I can only imagine."

Gently, he nuzzles my temple and my heart pounds as desire flares brightly within. "Your scent has changed," he murmurs into my hair. "It is much sweeter now."

He pulls back and cups my chin, tracing his thumb across my lower lip. "It is the same as when we kissed." His intense gaze holds mine. "Does this mean you desire me?"

His blunt question catches me off guard. Why does he fluster me so? "I'm not sure what you're talking about," I clear my throat. "Besides, that was a pretend kiss, anyway."

Aurdyn leans in and brushes his lips to mine. The featherlight touch is soft and unexpected, and my heart flutters in my chest. "Shall I give you a real kiss then?" he whispers.

My entire body flushes with heat, and I draw in a shaking breath, breathing in the warm scent of ginger spice —a potent and heady mix—as he drops a tender kiss to my jaw.

"Tell me you do not want me, and I will stop, Princess Freyja," he murmurs, pressing his lips to a sensitive spot just behind my ear. I tilt my head to one side as he kisses a trail down my neck. Small ripples of pleasure flow through me as a low growl vibrates in his chest. "Tell me to stop," he whispers. "Or I will kiss you again."

I draw in a shaking breath but remain silent. I'm nervous, but I want the feel of his lips on my own. He pulls back and his eyes search mine. "Tell me what you want."

Cautiously, I reach up and touch his face, studying the stern set of his features that soften as he studies me in return. He is a king, and a Dragon, no less. He is used to taking what he wants, and I love that he does not do this with me. Whatever happens between us, it is my choice.

"Kiss me," I whisper.

Fiery possession sparks in his gaze. "As you wish." He crushes his mouth to mine in a searing kiss, stealing the breath from my lungs.

His touch is fire as he skims his hand down the length of my body, the tips of his fingers trailing along my outer thigh. Cupping the back of my knee, he pulls it over his hip. He curls his tail around my ankle, holding me in place as his length presses against my core, hard and insistent.

He slides one hand in my hair, cupping the back of my head, while the other grips my hip, holding my body flush against his.

"You are mine," he breathes and then sweeps his tongue into my mouth, branding me with his fiery kiss.

He moves his hips into mine, and all rational thought falls away. His wings fold tightly around me, and nothing exists outside of the feel of his body against my own.

When he rolls me beneath him, I freeze, worried this may be happening too fast. His people mate for life, and while my heart may want him, my mind knows this is all still so new.

He pulls away, and I stare up at him, breathless and panting. "Aurdyn, I—"

"I can sense your hesitation," he says soothingly. "Know that I will never take that which you do not willingly give."

I didn't believe him to be the kind of man who would force me into anything I did not wish, but to hear him speak it aloud warms my heart. He cares, and whatever happens between us will always be my choice.

He leans in and skims the tip of his nose alongside mine, and a low rumble accompanies his words as he whispers against my skin. "Sleep, my fire heart. I will hold you."

As we lie in bed together, I think about Aurdyn's worry when I was unconscious. He was truly concerned about me. He warned me that Dragons do not love, but I'm falling in love with my Dragon protector, even if he never feels the same.

I rest my palm on his chest, directly over his beating heart. We are not as different as I thought we were, and perhaps he is wrong. Maybe his kind are capable of loving someone, but I suppose only time will tell.

CHAPTER 26

AURDYN

When morning comes, Healer Trilan assesses Freyja once more. As she examines the burn scars on my T'kara's legs and feet, a deep frown creases her brow. "I've heard the Fae have poultices that can lessen the appearance of scars."

Trilan is right. I don't know why this never occurred to me. I vaguely remember hearing that they treated the Dark Elf King Varys with a poultice to minimize the appearance of his many scars. The Fae are known for their vanity. It is no wonder their healers have developed such things. I turn to Freyja. "I will speak with King Kyven about this if you wish."

Hope sparks in her ice-blue eyes. As much as I loathe the idea of asking the Fae king for anything, I will do it for her.

I would do anything for her.

Crossing my arms, I lean against the doorway and study my T'kara. Soft morning light spills in through the window, highlighting the various shades of her long, scarlet hair and the many small spots that dot her skin. I stare transfixed as a stunning smile curves her lips and she laughs at something Trilan has said, the sound sparkling and bright like the sun on a warm summer day.

She mentioned speaking with a priest about dissolving our bond, but I do not want our connection severed. Even the mere thought is unbearable. Freyja is a rare and precious treasure. I will not force her to stay with me, but I do not know how I'm going to let her go if she chooses to leave.

"I've a favor to ask of you, Dragon King," Trilan's voice interrupts my depressing musings.

"I am not in the habit of granting favors to Dwarves." I narrow my eyes. "What would you ask for: gold, gems?" Dwarves are greedy, and more than one has been flamed trying to steal from a Dragon's hoard. "I'll not give you access to my holdings, but I will see that you are handsomely compensated for my T'kara's care."

Trilan purses her lips. "I'm not after your treasure."

"Oh?" My brows tick up in surprise. "What *are* you after, then?"

"Your destination is the Ice Mountains," she begins. "My cousin Kaila lives in Vangarn. She's expecting a child soon, and I want to check on her. I would ask that you take me there, on your way to your home."

I dart a glance over her shoulder at Freyja, watching our interaction intently. I want nothing more than to get her to my kingdom as soon as possible for her safety. I do not have time to drop a Dwarf off to visit her relations. "No."

"Aurdyn," Freyja says my name pointedly. "Vangarn is on the way, is it not?"

Drawing in a deep breath, I straighten. "It is. But that does not mean we need to stop."

"But—"

"Until we reach the capital city of Windhelm, and I have you secured in my fortress, you will not be safe," I cut her off.

"You are still being hunted. Just because we defeated one Mage and his pitiful band of humans, does not mean there won't be more."

Freyja crooks her first finger, summoning me to her side, and despite my pride, I go willingly for I can deny her almost nothing. She then turns to Trilan. "Would you mind waiting outside the door for a moment?"

Trilan nods and slips out, closing the door behind her.

Freyja turns to me, anger flashing in her eyes. "I cannot believe you," she admonishes. "After everything Trilan has done for us, you cannot be bothered to make one stop for her to visit her pregnant cousin, even though it's already on our way?"

"Your safety is more important," I counter. "I will not have it compromised for one Dwarf."

"She *treated* your wing, Aurdyn," she points out. "*She's* the reason you're even able to fly home right now, and you haven't thanked her for it yet. Nor have you thanked Garvin for giving us this room."

Clenching my jaw, I swallow back my pride and stalk toward the door. I jerk it open and Trilan and Garvin both jump back, startled by my sudden appearance. Irritation burns in my chest as I glare down at them both, hating what comes next. But it must be done, else Freyja will remain cross with me our entire trip. I am certain of it. "Thank you," I grit through my fangs. "For the rooms and for our care."

The ungrateful Dwarves both blink up at me, mouths gaping, and I wonder for a moment if they are both slower than I thought Dwarves to be.

I turn back to Freyja, arching a questioning brow. "There. Is that better?"

Shaking her head, she pushes past me to the Dwarves. "Garvin, thank you so much for the rooms and for your hospitality. And Trilan, we will take you to Vangarn." She turns back to me, tipping her chin up as if in challenge.

"Fine." A dark curl of smoke leaves my nostrils as I turn to the healer. "Pack your things. We leave in five minutes. If you are not ready by then, we will take off without you."

She rushes back to her room, and I'm surprised when I turn to Freyja and her lips curve up in a stunning smile. "Thank you, Aurdyn. Now, was that so hard to be nice?"

"Dragons are not supposed to be nice," I grumble. "Our mere presence is supposed to strike fear in our enemy's heart."

Freyja purses her lips. "Have you had your tea this morning?"

"What does that have to do with—"

"That's what I thought," she says. "Come on, my grumpy Dragon. Let's ask Garvin to brew some for you before we leave."

My first instinct is to protest that I am not... grumpy, but I stop because she called me hers, and I like the sound of that too much to argue my point. Maybe I am growing on her.

This is good. Perhaps after a few more days of my natural charm, she will become so attached she'll decide to stay with me, forgoing a conversation with a priest about our bond.

CHAPTER 27

FREYJA

Sure enough, tea is the answer. Aurdyn's grouchy demeanor dissolves into his normally gruff manner, which is the much more preferable side of him.

We walk outside and almost all the Dwarves follow us out into the snow, probably fascinated to watch Aurdyn shift form. Or perhaps they are just wanting to confirm that he's leaving so they can stop living in fear he'll make good on his threats to burn their village if they upset him.

He takes a few steps away from me and Trilan, and in a whirl of snow and wind, he transforms into a massive Dragon. I've seen him like this before, but I did not study him closely.

Flexing his large wings, the membranes shimmer beneath the sun, but not as brilliantly as his gorgeous, silver-white scales. Great horns sweep back from his head, and his fangs are as long as my forearm. He lowers his head, studying me briefly before he leans in. Warm air puffs through my hair as he breathes deep. He lightly rubs the left side of his jaw and then the right along my arms and shoulders, tickling me slightly. I laugh, playfully pushing at him. "What are you doing?"

"The Dwarves stink. I am masking their stench with your delicious scent." His voice rumbles in my mind, and I inhale sharply.

"I heard you in my mind."

"All Dragons can communicate in this way with their Fated Ones, in this form."

Closing my eyes, I concentrate and think the words to him. *"Can you hear me?"*

"Yes," he practically purrs in my mind. *"I can."*

He rubs his chin along my shoulder, careful not to place too much pressure on me. *"So... my scent is delicious now, is it?"*

"It has always been this way," he replies in my mind before speaking aloud. "You smell better than any human I have ever scented."

I decide to tease him for the odd compliment. "Smelled many humans, have you?"

"Only the ones I have eaten." His lips pull back, revealing two large rows of razor-sharp fangs in a feral grin as he jokes with me in return.

The Dwarves all jump back, eyes wide in terror, but they relax when I start to laugh. "All right," I lightly chide. "Let us leave before you give everyone another fright."

Aurdyn makes a low rumbling laugh and then gently picks me up in his massive front paw and Trilan in the other.

He flaps his colossal wings, the disturbed air nearly knocking over the gathered Dwarves as he takes to the sky. The ground falls away beneath us with dizzying speed as he continues his ascent. Cold wind howls around his form, but he holds me tight to his chest, his warmth completely enveloping me.

I look down at the wintry landscape in wonder. *"This is amazing,"* I project with my mind.

With a slight dip of his left wing, he catches the current, lifting us higher and up toward the gray clouds. I watch in awe as the dawning sun sets the snow-covered terrain on fire below us in brilliant shades of red, orange, and yellow.

In the distance, I notice a settlement carved into the side of the mountain.

"Vangarn," he speaks the word in my mind.

The Dwarf village sits on a series of plateaus, all of them connected by carved stairways and stone bridges. People move back and forth among the walkways and structures. The houses and buildings appear as though sculpted from the rock face and stacked close together. Gray smoke rises from the crooked chimneys along their roofs.

As we approach, sharp cries rend the air as the Dwarves scatter, terrified at the sight of a Dragon circling overhead.

"It's all right!" Trilan calls out, waving her arms. "The Dragon will not harm you. He's a—" she hesitates a beat before saying the word, "friend."

Aurdyn grumbles but remains silent as we land.

He touches down so gracefully, I'm not even sure we're on the ground until he carefully places my feet on the snow.

Several Dwarves surround us, each armed with axes and swords, despite Trilan's reassurances.

"What business do you have here, Dragon?" one of them yells.

"Lower your weapons," Aurdyn growls. "Before I breathe flame and melt them in your hands."

"Aurdyn," I chastise, and he stops growling. "Enough."

The Dwarves snap their attention to me, blinking in shock. "We merely came to drop off a friend." I gesture to Healer Trilan, and when she nods, their eyes widen even more.

"Since when are Dragons and Dwarves friends?" one of them mutters.

"I am King Aurdyn of the Ice Mountains," Aurdyn's voice booms above me, still in his Draken form. "Healer Trilan took care of my mate, and I repay her by bringing her here to visit her family."

Something about the way he says the word 'mate' makes my heart beat faster in my chest.

A Dwarf woman with a heavily rounded belly rushes forward. "Trilan! Oh, you've no idea how glad I am to see you! We've just had word there was a Wraith attack at Erabron, and I worried Arganth may have been attacked as well."

"A Wraith attack?" Aurdyn says, startling the poor Dwarf woman.

Another Dwarf rushes to her side, sword drawn. Trilan steps forward, holding out her hands in a placating gesture. "King Aurdyn will not harm you or your mate, Ferlin."

Reluctantly, he lowers his sword, but his gaze remains wary as he stares up at Aurdyn. "Yes. Several families have come here from Erabron, seeking shelter after their homes were destroyed. King Davin sent his army, and they pushed the Wraiths back, but he insisted that the families evacuate here in case they come again."

Aurdyn glances at me. *"Your visions,"* he speaks in my head, and I nod.

I've never met the Dwarf king, but my uncle always said that King Davin was a fierce fighter and his army was a force to be reckoned with. The Dwarves are master craftsmen in armor and weapons. They forge them from the strong metals they mine in the Erabron mountain.

"Wraith attacks are rare." Aurdyn meets Ferlin's gaze evenly. "It is difficult for them to cross the Great Wall in the North. How many were there?"

"Dozens," another Dwarf says, stepping forward. "My name is Maylin, and I've just come from there. They nearly overran our defenses, but King Davin and his army pushed them back."

"Since when do Wraiths make coordinated attacks? And why would they attack Erabron?" Aurdyn asks. "They've no use for weapons. They are creatures possessed of dark magic."

"Aye," Maylin says. "Why indeed? That is the question, now isn't it?"

"My uncle's armies purchase their weapons and armor from the Dwarves of Erabron," I speak in Aurdyn's mind. *"I know that Florin, and at least two other human kingdoms, do as well."*

"Erabron is also where they make black arrows to pierce Dragon scales," Aurdyn replies through our connection, his lips twisting in a snarl.

Aurdyn looks to the Dwarf. "Wraiths are supposed to be feral, mindless creatures. And yet, they attacked a city known to produce weapons for most of the seven realms."

"Either they've learned to think for themselves, or someone is controlling them," Maylin replies. "And if that is true, they may go to Arganth next to cut off the l'sair crystal mines during the brutal season."

"We must warn Arganth," Trilan says.

"We've already sent a raven," Ferlin interjects. "It should reach them today. And we've had word that King Davin is sending some of his army to defend it as well."

"Do not worry," Aurdyn speaks in my mind. *"The Wraiths will not come to my kingdom. It is too remote."*

"I'm not just worried about us," I stress through the bond. *"I'm worried about the people of Arganth—Garvin and Olmar. They were good to us, Aurdyn. Do you not care what happens to them?"*

He frowns. *"The Dwarves are fierce fighters, and they have excellent armor and weapons. King Davin, for all his blustering ways, is a good strategist when it comes to battle. They will be fine."*

"I hope you are right," I reply, disappointed at how little he seems to care about the Dwarves, even after they helped us and refused to betray us to the Mage and his hunters.

"Besides," he adds. *"We do not even know if they speak truth."*

"Why would they lie?"

"Why do Dwarves do anything?" he grumbles. *"They are not to be trusted. I will send a scout to confirm their reports as soon as we reach Windhelm."*

Trilan turns back to us. "Thank you for bringing me here." She lifts her gaze to Aurdyn. "My people gave you shelter and care when you needed it. If our king calls for aid, will you answer?"

I look at Aurdyn expectantly, waiting for his response. He huffs, and a line of black smoke curls from his mouth. "King Davin is a proud Dwarf. I believe he would rather walk through the seven hells than ask for aid from a Dragon."

"Perhaps you are right." She nods. "Still… I wish to know. Would you answer?"

Aurdyn stands tall, spreading his massive wings behind him, as he stares down imperiously. "It depends upon how he asks."

A smile tugs at my mouth. It seems he may care more for the Dwarves than he's let on. Although I suspect if King Davin were to ask for aid, it would probably have to involve a lot of groveling.

When we leave, I watch as Vangarn disappears in the distance and pray to the gods to protect the city of Arganth, as well as my uncle and our kingdom.

CHAPTER 28

AURDYN

Freyja has a tender heart. In this form, I am able to catch wisps of her thoughts, and I can sense her growing worry at the thought of the Dwarves in danger. She worries for her uncle and his kingdom as well, even though they would have burned her.

A low growl vibrates my chest. As far as I am concerned, I would see her uncle's kingdom fall. They do not deserve her worry and her pity. Not after what they tried to do.

"Are you all right?" she speaks to my mind.

"Yes."

"Then why are you growling?"

That she has to ask tells me she cannot sense as much of my thoughts as I can hers. It occurs to me that I could lie, but I do not wish to conceal things from her. *"You are too forgiving."*

"What are you talking about?"

"I can sense much of your thoughts while I'm in this form," I

explain. *"You worry for those who tried to end your life, but they do not deserve your pity."*

"Have you forgotten that they were under Luria's spell? And why are you in my head, anyway? I did not give you permission to read my thoughts," she says, anger punctuating her response.

"You are my T'kara," I remind her. *"We share a bond. I cannot control how it manifests between us."*

My answer seems to settle her because now she worries, not just about our connection, but also about how my people will receive her.

"They will respect you," I reassure her.

"How do you know?" she asks, unable to hide her concern.

"Because I am their king, and I will make them," I state firmly. *"Anyone who does not will be unwelcome in my court."*

"I... do not want to cause any trouble between you and your people."

Her concern is valid. I have considered many times the problems that may arise from bringing her to my kingdom. But I have no choice. She is mine—my T'kara. And even though she is human, my people will surely understand this. I will not tolerate dissent. *"It will not be an issue."* I try to assuage her concerns. *"I've told you Dragons revere the fated bond, so it will not matter that you are different."*

"It mattered to you when we first met," she reminds me, and I curse myself for having voiced my thoughts aloud to her then. *"You did not want to be bound to me, remember?"*

Her words shame me. I should never have even thought that, much less said it to her. The fated bond is one of the highest blessings one can receive from the gods, and instead of treating her as such, I lamented that she was human, instead of Dragon.

But much has changed between us since then, and I recognize that we are not as different as I once thought we were.

We are close to Windhelm, but I must settle this between us before we reach my fortress. She must know, without doubt, that my devotion to her is absolute.

There is a temple to the old gods not far from here. It is inside the castle grounds, and upon returning to my kingdom, I always visit it first. It is also where I go to be alone with my thoughts and ask for the guidance of the old gods. Now, I will take Freyja there and give her my most solemn vow. I will not have her doubt my regard for her.

CHAPTER 29

FREYJA

Dark clouds hide the mountain peaks, and the air grows colder the higher we ascend. Moisture clings to my skin, and I shiver as we move through the mist. The moment Aurdyn breaks through, I squint against the bright sunlight as my eyes adjust.

In the far distance lies the city of Windhelm. Dozens of homes and buildings are carved directly into the ivory stone walls of the Ice Mountains, surrounded by a sea of green trees, heavily laden with snow, that stand tall and majestic.

Cascading waterfalls spill down the mountain's face, many of them landing in elegant collecting pools before continuing their descent. I stare in wonder at the Dragons in both two-legged and four-legged form that fill the skies. Their colors vary from silver-white, like Aurdyn, to green, black, gold, and even a few red.

As we draw closer, a castle comes into view. Carved into a sheer cliff wall, sunlight gilds the ivory fortress, making it shine like gold. Surrounded by formidable towers with gold-capped domes and built-out terraces, it seems to have been built as much for defense as it was for aesthetics.

The bottom level of the castle has a large garden area around it. A waterfall splashes down the side of the mountain into a pool that branches into several winding streams. They carve a series of paths through the dense vegetation before collecting in a basin and then running down the rock face below.

A temple stands on the far side of the garden area. The proud stone structure comprises a ring of tall columns of ivory stone, wrapped with thick, leafy, green vines.

I gasp when I notice the heart tree in the center. It's beautiful; I've never seen one this big. Completely covered with tear-drop shaped white petals, these trees are sacred and very rare.

Their roots are infused with old magic; their branches constantly shed their leaves and replace them almost instantly. The fragile silver-white petals dance on the wind, swirling around the temple as if dancing through the air.

Aurdyn lands just outside the structure. As soon as he sets down, he lowers me to the ground and shifts into his two-legged form, dressed in black pants but nothing else.

The small white leaves from the heart tree whirl around us on the cool breeze. Several catch in my hair and my clothing like flakes of snow. A quick glance reveals no one nearby. Although it is lovely, I wonder why he has brought me here instead of straight to the castle.

"Every time I return from a long journey, I stop here to pay my respects," he says, answering my unspoken question. "This is the first temple my people built to the old gods. It is older than the line of our rulers."

He extends his hand to me, and I take it without hesitation. His palm is warm against mine as he leads me up the stone steps and into the center of the temple ring until we are standing beneath the heart tree.

"I thought your people only moved to the Ice Mountains —to Windhelm—after the last Great War."

"Before the Great War, our priests came to worship at Windhelm." His gaze travels over the temple before he looks up at the sky. "A remote mountain with ice-blue skies… it was a place of reflection." He pauses. "It is why we chose this sacred place to relocate our people, seeking the shelter and protection of the gods to guide us through what was, at the time, an uncertain future."

I stare at the heart tree and the ancient temple in wonder. "It's beautiful."

"My ancestors were all crowned here when they assumed the throne, as was I."

He rests his hand on the heart tree, whispering words in a foreign tongue that I do not understand. But these words need no translation to be understood. The solemn reverence with which they are spoken fills the temple around us. A stillness settles in the air, as if the gods themselves are here listening.

"Of all the ones who have ruled before me, none were ever blessed to find their Fated One." He turns his emerald gaze to me. "I tell you this so that you understand. Some may object to our connection because you are human, but I believe there will be more who accept you because of what you are to me."

"And… what exactly is that?" I ask. Before he can answer, I continue. "I know I am your T'kara, but you referred to me as your 'mate' to the Dwarves."

I hold his gaze, leaving the question unspoken between us as I wait for his answer.

"If you were a Dragon, you would be both," he replies evenly. "There would be no question of this."

"But I'm not," I counter. We have kissed and there is an attraction between us, and definitely something more than friendship, but beyond that... everything else is uncertain. He claims his kind do not love and I don't know if I can love someone who could not love me in return. And the fact that I am human could have devastating consequences upon his rule. So whatever happens between us, it must be navigated very carefully.

"We're very different, Aurdyn. You said so yourself. You did not choose this any more than I did." Drawing in a deep breath, I steel myself to speak the truth I fear most. "And I cannot help but wonder how much the bond influences what you feel."

"In the beginning? All of it." His gaze holds mine. "But now? I know you. I want you. I desire you to be mine. Why does it matter if the bond influenced me?"

"It *matters* to me." Tears sting my eyes, but I blink them back. Before I allow my sentiments to deepen any further, I must know that his feelings are real. "Why did you bring me here, Aurdyn?"

"Because I want you to understand how important you are. To bring you to the most sacred place, not only for my people, but for me." He points to the heart tree. "To show you the place where I have knelt at least a hundred times, praying that I would find someone I cherished. Someone I treasured. Someone I would want by my side until the end of my days."

His voice grows thick with emotion. "The spirit of this tree is a messenger of the gods themselves. She is the one who told me to go to Ruhaen, and I listened. She said I would find my greatest treasure there, and I did. I found you, Freyja."

My heart clenches as he continues. "She told me that my Fated One would doubt the bond and that when that day came, I would bring her here, and she would know the truth." He takes both my hands in his own as his eyes search mine. "Although I could not see your face, I dreamed of your eyes." My mouth drifts open in shock as he cups my cheek. "She told me that you dreamed of mine in return. Fate was guiding us to each other, Freyja. All this time," he whispers. "I have waited for you. Tell me you saw this too."

Unable to speak through my emotions, I nod. Aurdyn leans in and presses his lips to my own in a tender kiss. He drops his forehead gently to mine. "Tell me you will stay with me, my T'kara."

I want so much to wrap my arms around him and never let him go. Fate drew us together, but I must know that it is more than this. It is for me, but I must know that it is for him too.

"Aurdyn, I—"

"You have finally returned to us, my King," a deep voice draws our attention to the front of the temple.

A Dragon with obsidian scales walks toward us. His silver eyes widen slightly as they land upon me before his face returns to a stoic mask. "You have… a guest?"

"Freyja, this is High Priest Arkon," he gestures to the Dragon. "Arkon, this is my T'kara, the Princess Freyja of Ruhaen."

The High Priest's eyes widen but he quickly schools his features and bows low. "It is an honor to meet you, T'kara of King Aurdyn, and blessing from the gods."

I had not expected immediate acceptance, but Aurdyn had told me that many would respond this way. Evidently he is right, and the bond is revered among his people. So much so that even a High Priest is willing to overlook the fact that I am human.

Years living at my uncle's royal court have trained me well, and I easily slip back into the practiced role that I remember. "It is pleasing to meet you as well, High Priest Arkon."

Another Dragon with silver-white scales approaches. He looks so much like Aurdyn, I would think they are brothers, but I know he has no siblings. This one's face is set in a stern expression and his golden eyes flash with anger as he rounds the column and stalks toward Aurdyn.

"Where have you been?" he snaps. "We sent out warriors to—" the words die in his throat as he stares at me in shock. "You've captured a human female? Have you gone mad?"

Aurdyn moves to my side and hooks his arm around my waist, curling his left wing possessively around my shoulder. "Princess Freyja is not my captive." He tips up his chin. "She is my T'kara."

His jaw drops.

Aurdyn ignores his stunned expression and introduces us as if everything were perfectly normal. "Freyja, this is my cousin Brovyn. Brovyn, this is Freyja." He gestures to the still gaping Dragon. "Brovyn is not just my cousin; he is my advisor."

His words seem to snap Brovyn out of his stupor because he turns to Aurdyn, blinking several times. "You found your T'kara." His words are full of awe-filled reverence. He looks again at me and bows low. "It is an honor to meet you, Princess Freyja."

A smile quirks his mouth, and he claps a hand on Aurdyn's shoulder. "This is wonderful, cousin. We should make an announcement at once." He looks between us both. "There is much to prepare. We will need to inform the court so that we can plan the bonding ceremony and the coronation and—"

"My T'kara needs rest," Aurdyn cuts him off. "We can address all of that at a later time. We will meet you for dinner."

"Of course." Brovyn dips his chin, and then turns his attention to me. "I am sure you must be tired from your journey." His lips quirk up at the edges. "I look forward to speaking with you this evening."

"That will be lovely," I reply, offering him a warm smile.

As soon as Brovyn leaves, Aurdyn's gaze slides to mine. Something akin to sadness flashes behind his eyes. He knows I have not yet decided to stay with him. "Come, Freyja." He offers me his arm, and I loop mine through his. "I will show you the castle and our rooms."

Our rooms? I wonder if I've heard him wrong, but I do not ask. Not while we have an audience. The way the High Priest and his cousin reacted to the news of what I am, I wonder how bad it will reflect upon Aurdyn if I choose to have the bond removed.

I also wonder how damaging it would be to his rule if we leave it intact, and I choose to stay.

Only two people know about me, thus far. But they are both close to him, and their sentiments regarding me and our connection may not be echoed throughout the rest of his kingdom.

Several of Aurdyn's guards bow low to their king as we pass, but they lock their eyes on me with thunderstruck expressions.

My stomach feels queasy as we walk toward the castle, but I hold my head high. Dragons respect strength above all else. I am the T'kara of their king, and I will make sure they know I am strong.

CHAPTER 30

FREYJA

As we walk through the palace gardens on our way to the castle, I'm surprised by how wild and untamed it appears, as if we were in an actual forest, instead of carefully manicured grounds outside the fortress.

Tall trees with needle-like leaves are scattered throughout, their thick branches heavily laden with ice and snow. Bubbling streams of ice-blue water wind along curving paths, cutting through the thick layer of white that blankets the ground before collecting in a large pool near the cliff edge and spilling over the side to continue down the mountain.

The sun shines brightly on the smooth, pale stone of the palace, making it shimmer like gold. We approach the main doors and I have to tilt my head back to study the intricate design etched into the golden metal of beautifully curved, and interlocking patterns, with a large flying Dragon in the center.

Two guards push them open, and we step into a large entryway with polished stone floors and walls covered in tapestries. I grimace when I realize they portray Dragons in battle against Elves, Fae, and humans. This does not bode well, but I hide my concern behind a confident mask as we walk farther inside.

Our footsteps echo loudly as we proceed toward an enormous staircase that takes up nearly half of the far wall. Aurdyn takes my hand as we ascend to the next level, and I trace my free hand over the elegantly carved stone along the banister. Similar winding patterns to those on the front doors.

Aurdyn guides me down a long hallway to another set of double doors. A green Dragon at the end pushes them open for us, bowing low. Aurdyn turns to him as we enter. "Send for a seamstress and have them return to the castle first thing in the morning."

He bows low and then disappears down the hallway.

Aurdyn closes the door behind us, and I allow my gaze to travel over the room. A large bed made of rich, dark wood, with a canopy of silken green drapes, is covered with a blanket of white fur.

Against the far wall, and across from the bed, is a fireplace with a large, white fur rug in front of the hearth. Several stacked l'sair crystals provide soft light and heat in the space. A large wooden desk and chair sit in the far corner.

Aurdyn gestures to a door on the left. "That is the cleansing room."

He leads me to another door along the opposite wall, near the bed. When he pushes it open, sunlight spills into the room so bright I raise a hand to my forehead, shielding my eyes as they adjust. "How is this possible?" I gape up at open sky overhead and a lovely, enclosed garden with a water fountain in the center and a wooden bench beside it. "I thought we were deep in the mountain."

"We are," Aurdyn replies. He points to the obsidian stone wall that surrounds the garden. "This has been carved out to make this private space. This was a gift from the Dark Elves to my grandfather. They used their magic to spell this place so that it is like a perpetual spring garden, protected from the elements, and yet enchanted so that I can fly through the barrier without issue."

I observe in wonder as snow falls from above, disappearing the moment it hits the invisible barrier that shields this space from the elements. Thick bushes and vibrant, flowering plants are spread throughout, and the temperature is pleasantly warm.

"Your people were friends with the Dark Elves?" I'd always thought they were enemies.

"We both lost many people during the war. We were allies then."

"Are you still on good terms with the Dark Elves?"

"Sometimes."

I wait for him to expand on his answer, but he does not. As I study the space, my attention is drawn to a door directly across the garden. "Where does that lead?"

A smile tugs at his mouth. "I will show you."

When he pushes open the door, a room even larger and more opulent than the first awaits us. Large tapestries of nature scenes decorate the walls, and thick fur carpets cover the floor. A massive bed, even bigger than the one in the first room, sits against the far wall. It's made of the same dark wood, but the curtains are white instead of green, matching the many furs piled atop the mattress. Two sofas sit before a large hearth with l'sair crystals. The cushions are dark green and appear luxurious.

"That door"—he points to one along the right wall —"leads to another cleansing room."

He guides me toward it, and I gasp at the sunken, crystal-clear pool in the center of the vast room. Delicate plumes of steam drift up from the surface. Beside it is a long counter with folded towels and another door conceals a sink and a toilet area.

"This is a mirror image of the cleansing room attached to my bedroom."

As I take it all in, it occurs to me that this room is only accessible from the garden, which can only be reached by going through the first bedroom we entered. "What is this place?"

"The first bedroom is where I sleep and this one is yours," he replies, eyes shining with pride. "I have had this place prepared ever since I came of age, waiting for the day I would find a mate."

"Aurdyn, I—"

"I know you have not decided to stay here yet," he interjects before I can protest. "Even so, this nest is yours for as long as you wish to remain."

"Nest?"

He nods. "It is the most secure room in the entire castle."

"I… don't understand."

"All males prepare a room like this when they come of age. It must be ready because it is not unusual for an egg to be conceived during the mating battle, and the female will tolerate nothing less than a well-protected nest for her and their eventual fledglings."

"Is that why this room can only be accessed by going through yours first?"

"Yes."

Understanding dawns. "You said the mating battle is so that a female Dragon can find a mate who is at least as strong or stronger than she is. Because it is his job to defend the nest when she is vulnerable… like when she is guarding an egg or their fledglings."

He nods again. "Dragon females are larger and stronger than most males. However, there are times, such as when they are nesting, that they are vulnerable and require protection."

"What about the males?" I ask. "Do they ever sit with eggs? Or is it always the females?"

"We revere our mates and do whatever they ask of us. Often, the male stays with and guards the egg. Many females prefer to hunt during that time."

It's nice to know that responsibilities seem to be shared equally. But I cannot stop thinking about how different his culture is compared to mine.

Nesting. Eggs. The words swirl through my mind, reminding me of just how dissimilar we are. Aurdyn is a king. And most rulers desire heirs above all else. Even if I stayed with him, I doubt we'd be able to have any children, and I wonder if he has considered this at all.

I do not, however, want to bring it up. Especially since I am undecided about whether to stay. I'm falling for Aurdyn, but I cannot give him my heart. Not when I have no idea if he can even love me in return.

CHAPTER 31

FREYJA

Word of my arrival has spread quickly among Aurdyn's warriors. As we make our way through the castle to the main dining hall, I try to push down my unease when his guards openly stare as we pass. Their gazes are full of awe-filled reverence and their whispered words echo down the corridor after us.

T'kara. Sanishon. Human.

It seems many of his people believe in the prophecy foretold in the Ancient Tomes of the Lythyrian.

Aurdyn ushers me down the stairs and along a wide corridor. At the end is a double set of doors, almost as beautiful as the ones at the entrance of the castle. They are solid gold etched with intricate patterns depicting Dragons flying amongst the clouds.

The doors open into a great dining hall. An immense heating pit at the center is full of l'sair crystals that cast a soft light making the room feel intimate and cozy. Surrounding it are several long tables made of dark wood decorated with scrolling carvings. I imagine this room could fit at least a hundred people, but right now it is just us and Brovyn, Aurdyn's cousin.

We take a seat across from him at one of the tables in the center of the room. Three platters of food are already set out, along with goblets and pitchers of wine and water. Aurdyn lifts one silver platter of meat, balancing it on one hand while he breathes fire over it, roasting it for me.

I smile as he sets it back down on the table, while his cousin frowns. "You just ruined that, you know," he tells Aurdyn.

"Humans can become ill if they consume raw meat," Aurdyn explains.

"That is terrible," Brovyn says. Shaking his head softly, he gives me a pitying look. "Absolutely ruins the taste."

A smile quirks my lips as I bite back a laugh.

Two guards stand post at the doors, but Aurdyn's cousin dismisses them to stand out in the hallway. As soon as they leave, he turns to Aurdyn. "While you were gone, a raven came with word that the Order of Mages is offering a reward for the capture of Princess Freyja of Ruhaen and King Aurdyn of the Ice Mountains." He arches a brow. "Care to explain what you did to cross the Order?"

Brovyn's eyes widen as Aurdyn explains everything that has happened, including how my uncle and his kingdom are under the dark spell of a Mage.

When he's finished, Brovyn shakes his head. "It makes no sense. Why would the Mages want her dead if she is a sanishon? The prophecy says their coming heralds a time of great peace among all the races. Is that not what they want? Is that not why they protect the humans with their magic?"

"I don't understand it either," Aurdyn replies, his brow creased in a deep frown. "I do not trust the Mages, and I've never understood why the human kingdoms agreed to ally themselves with those foul creatures."

Brovyn turns to me, his gaze searching mine. "Is it true, then? Are you a witch? Do you have magic?"

I glance at Aurdyn, unsure how much to share. As if sensing my hesitation, he takes my hand beneath the table, squeezing it gently before giving me an affirmative nod.

I turn my attention back to Brovyn. "I had a vision of the Wraiths invading my uncle's kingdom. I told him of this, and I was accused of witchcraft, which is a crime punishable by burning at the stake." Brovyn's brow furrows deeply as I continue. "But when we were in Arganth, I was able to conjure a shield of fire to protect us from the Mage's destructive magic."

Aurdyn leans in. "The Dwarf healer that tended her claimed she could tell that Freyja had inherited the ability to conjure fire from me, through our bond." He looks at me again. "And I would like High Priest Arkon to assess you as well," he says softly. "He is wise, and I trust him. And he is very familiar with the fated bond and how it manifests between couples."

"All right," I agree. "If you trust him, so do I."

Aurdyn's expression softens, and his tail curls loosely around my ankle.

"You mentioned the Wraiths." Brovyn leans in. "We've received reports of a Wraith attack on the Dwarf city of Erabron but were unsure of its veracity."

"We heard of this attack from a Dwarf who was there," I reply. "She said a large number of Wraiths attacked, but King Davin managed to push them back. He is fortifying their defenses at Erabron and Arganth, fearing another attack soon."

"How did that many Wraiths manage to pass through the Great Wall in the North undetected?" he asks. "The wall is heavily guarded, and the Order of Mages uses its dark powers to enforce the barrier."

"It does not make sense." Aurdyn frowns. "Someone had to have helped them."

Brovyn looks between the two of us. "But why would anyone do this? Everyone knows how dangerous the Wraiths are. It is the one thing the seven High Realms can all agree upon, despite our differences with each other."

"That, I do not know," Aurdyn says grimly. "But until we have more answers, I want to double the number of patrols along our borders."

"I believe that is wise." Brovyn dips his chin. "I'll relay your order to our warriors."

"And send scouts to Ruhaen." Aurdyn darts a glance at me before turning his attention back to Brovyn. "The Order of Mages has put a price on our heads. Ruhaen shares a border with us, and their king—Freyja's uncle—is under the influence of their dark powers. I want to know what they are doing there. If they are planning an attack on our home, we must be prepared."

Brovyn nods. "Agreed."

Aurdyn's cousin continues to fill him in on various things that happened while he was gone, as we eat.

None of the foods are unfamiliar to me, but the sweet and savory spices used to flavor the meat are something I've never tasted before. Everything is wonderful. It's been so long since we've had a decent meal, I close my eyes and a low hum of appreciation escapes me as I take another bite.

When I finish one plate of food, Aurdyn pushes another full one toward me. Normally, it would be too much, but I'm still hungry. I suspect it has something to do with the use of my magic yesterday.

I look at Brovyn. "Aurdyn says you two grew up together."

"We did," Brovyn says. A smirk crests his lips. "But did he tell you about all the trouble he used to get us in?"

"Me?" Aurdyn huffs. *"You* were the one who was always getting us in trouble."

Brovyn crosses his arms. "What about that time you insisted we go clear out that griffin's nest near the northern peak?"

"Griffin's nest?" I ask incredulously. "How old were you?"

I've never seen one, but I have heard that Griffins are terrifying creatures. They have the body of a lion, but several times larger, and the head and wings of an eagle, and razor-sharp talons that can rip a person to shreds.

Aurdyn shrugs. "Fifteen."

"Fifteen?" I blink at him. "You could have been killed."

"We almost were," Brovyn says. "We were sneaking up on the nest when someone"—he gives Aurdyn a pointed look —"just had to sneeze and wake it up."

"How was I supposed to know I was allergic to its fur?" Aurdyn counters. "I'd never been that close to one before."

"You and your sensitive nose." Brovyn rolls his eyes.

"Speaking of his sensitive nose… You should have seen him when we stayed with the Dwarves." I laugh softly. "He complained almost the entire time about their smell."

"Do not get me started on the Dwarves." Brovyn laughs. "That's why Aurdyn always sends me to deal with their King Davin whenever we need to discuss something."

"Their stench does not bother you as much as it does me," Aurdyn says.

"Yes, it does." Brovyn narrows his eyes. "I'm just not as vocal about it as you are." He turns to me. "You should have seen his face when I told him King Davin wanted to betroth his daughter to Aurdyn to forge an alliance between us."

I laugh half-heartedly as jealousy rears its ugly head at the thought of Aurdyn married to someone else.

"I was only playing a prank on him." Brovyn laughs. "King Davin would *never* marry off one of his daughters to a Dragon. Especially a moody one."

"I am *not* moody." Aurdyn narrows his eyes.

Brovyn gives me a pointed look, as if he wants me to agree with him.

I take Aurdyn's hand and entwine our fingers. "He's just a bit grumpy sometimes, but it's cute."

Brovyn snorts in amusement.

"Cute?" Aurdyn's head jerks back. "Dragons are *not* cute."

"Handsome, then?" I tease. "Is that better?"

His eyes darken and a low rumbling growl vibrates his chest as he loops his wing around my side, pulling me closer to him. "Better," he agrees.

They continue teasing each other as we sit at the table. It warms my heart to see how close Aurdyn is to his cousin.

The wine is exceptional, so I decide to have two glasses. I've never been one to partake too much. I've seen what excess alcohol can do to a person, but this is so delicious I cannot resist. After the second glass, warmth spreads across my entire body, seeming to seep into my very bones. I relax into Aurdyn's side as we continue to laugh and joke with Brovyn.

When we're finished, I stand from the table and the world tilts and spins around me. Unable to keep my balance, I stumble back, but Aurdyn's strong hands catch my waist and he hoists me into his arms as if I weigh nothing.

"Are you all right?" he asks, concern lacing his voice. "What is wrong?"

"I feel warm." When I lift my head to his, everything spins again, and I groan, dropping my forehead to his chest. "And a bit dizzy."

"Fetch the healer," Aurdyn's voice rumbles above me. "Now. Have her meet us in our chambers."

"I don't need a healer. I'm fine." I swallow against a wave of nausea that threatens. "I think it's the wine."

"We'll have the healer check you, just to be sure," he says, trying not to jostle me too much as he carries me back to our rooms. "I will not take a chance with your health."

I feel too bad to argue, so instead, I simply nod against his chest.

Carefully, he lays me down in his bed, beneath the thick comforter and furs. A Dragon with golden scales leans over me. Her violet eyes study me intently as her hands hover above my head and then move down my body as she performs her assessment. "Interesting," she hums.

"What is it?" Aurdyn demands. "What have you found?"

"Nothing. I was merely musing on how similar human anatomy is to our people. She is fine, my King." A faint smile quirks her lips. "I am Healer Tala. Our wine, it seems, is a bit too strong for you, but nothing a cup of tea cannot remedy."

She disappears, only to return shortly with a cup on a small saucer.

"Leave us," Aurdyn's voice rumbles overhead.

"Of course, my King."

The bed dips beside me, and his strong arms gently pull me up to sitting. The room spins a moment before settling. "Here," he murmurs softly, pressing the rim of the cup to my lips. "Drink some of this."

I take a careful sip of the warm liquid. The delicious flavor of berries and spice rolls across my tongue. "This is delicious." I drink the rest in three gulps, surprised by how much better I already feel. "What is it?"

"A unique blend of tea from the kingdom of Ithylian. It is infused with a bit of healing magic. It works rapidly, but it will make you sleep as well."

"The Dark Elves make this?"

"Yes," he grouses. "They also make an orange-and-spice

blend that I drink every morning. I blame them for my addiction to tea."

"Well, there are worse things to become addicted to, you know." I yawn, surprised at how quickly I'm tiring. "One of the men who sought my hand had a problem with pipe weed. Lord Gile's breath was terrible." I grimace at the memory. "He tried to kiss me, but I refused and pushed him away."

"What was his full name and title?" Aurdyn growls. "Tell me, and I will make certain he never—"

"I already took care of it." I manage a faint smile as I struggle to stay awake. "I pushed him over the balcony railing and into the castle moat." A booming laugh escapes Aurdyn as I continue. "He withdrew his proposal rather promptly after that."

My eyelids blink open and closed as I fight against the sleep trying to claim me. I want to finish the conversation we had earlier, when we were interrupted at the temple. I need to know if there is something between us besides just the bond.

I know there is for me, but for him... I am uncertain. And even though I could ask now, I'm afraid... knowing that his answer could shatter my heart.

I scrutinize my hand, remembering the fire that erupted from my palm as I conjured flame to shield us from the Mage's attack. The bond gave me this ability, and I wonder, if it is severed, will it go away entirely? I'm not even sure how I called it forth, and that worries me because I do not know how to control it.

Aurdyn cups my chin, smoothing his thumb across my cheek. "What is wrong?"

"I still do not know how I could use fire magic," I whisper. "And I worry it might happen again, and I will not be able to control it."

"Perhaps High Priest Arkon can help you understand it better."

"And if he cannot?" I ask, giving voice to my fear. "What if I accidentally hurt someone?"

"We are Dragons—creatures of fire." Aurdyn huffs out a laugh and a thin line of smoke curls around his nostrils as if to emphasize his point. "There is no safer place for you to learn how to wield it, than here, among my kind."

I'm relieved, but also sad because my powers mean that I am what they accused me of… what they would have burned me at the stake for. I glance down at my open palm again. "Now, I truly am what they said I was: a witch. Even if we free my uncle from Luria's spell, my people will never accept me now."

"Perhaps you are right," Aurdyn murmurs as he wraps a hand around my wrist and lifts it to his mouth. He presses a tender kiss to the center of my palm before his gaze locks on to mine, full of fire and possession. "But you are *my* witch. And if anyone dares try to harm you, I will incinerate them."

A smile crests my lips. I am falling hard for my dragon protector.

My pulse quickens as he leans in, his warm breath fanning across my skin before his lips brush mine in a tender kiss.

A sharp knock at the door startles me and I quickly pull away as the healer returns.

"I brought another cup." Her eyes shine with kindness as she holds the cup out to me. "One more should be enough to chase the alcohol from your system."

"Thank you," Aurdyn says, taking the cup before I can grab it and pressing it to my lips again for me to drink.

"Remain nearby," he tells her. "In case we have need of you."

"I will take the room down the hall." She bobs her head and then leaves.

He offers me the cup, and I finish the last of my tea.

He is a Dragon—a race feared by many for their fierce strength and devastating fire. And yet, he is so gentle with me. A maelstrom of emotion swirls deep within. But exhaustion steals through me, and I struggle to keep my eyes open.

"Shall I carry you to your room?" he asks. "So you may sleep."

"I'm fine right here," I whisper, resting my head on his shoulder as I lean against him, my back still propped against the headboard. "I'm too tired to move."

Gently, he guides me to lie down, then pulls the blankets and furs over me. Closing my eyes, I'm just starting to drift away when I feel a puff of warm air part the hair on top of my head.

His excuse each time he did this before was to overcome the smell of the Dwarves. Already half asleep, I mumble. "There are not any Dwarves here now. Why are you scenting me?"

"Because you are mine," his voice rumbles, and warmth floods my system as I slip away into the peaceful oblivion of sleep.

CHAPTER 32

AURDYN

When morning comes, a seamstress arrives to fit Freyja for new clothing. I am glad she will no longer have to wear the items given to her by the Dwarves. Now, there will be nothing masking her distinct scent that calls to the primal part of me that longs to claim her.

When she emerges from her rooms, my breath catches in my throat. Her new emerald-green tunic dress and pants, and matching gray boots set off the fiery color of her vibrant red hair. As her ice-blue eyes meet mine, a low growl builds deep within.

The desire to challenge her in the mating battle roars through my veins. Clenching my jaw, my nostrils flare as need burns through me like liquid fire. She is mine even if she does not realize it yet. I will conquer her, claim her as my mate, and make her my queen.

I have gifted her a nest that any Dragon female would envy and now I will prove that I am worthy of being hers.

* * *

After we eat breakfast, I lead Freyja back to the temple. High Priest Arkon is already waiting for us. He bows low as we approach. "Greetings, my King." He turns to my T'kara. "It is agreeable to see you again so soon, Princess Freyja."

"And you as well," she replies formally.

I do not ask how he knew we were coming because I learned long ago not to question such things. He is as mysterious as he is wise.

"Come." He motions for us to follow him to the center of the temple. "I am eager to assess your bond."

We stand beneath the tree. Its silver-white leaves fall steadily all around us, dancing and whirling on the cool breeze, tangling in Freyja's flowing, lustrous hair.

Arkon places his hand on the trunk, and Freyja's jaw drops as the wood glows with a soft silver light. "Magic," she whispers.

The High Priest nods. "This tree grew from a seed of the very first heart tree created by the Fae and their magic. Their king gifted it to our very first king. A token and a reminder of the peace they each promised to uphold among our people."

I clench my jaw as I think of the Fae. King Kyven grates on my nerves to no end. If not for the blood promise, first bound in this tree by our ancestors, I would have been tempted to make good on my threat to singe his perfect, silver-white hair and burn his castle to the ground the last time we met.

"Each of you must rest one hand on the tree," Arkon instructs, pulling me back from my thoughts. "It will help me assess the bond between you."

As soon as we touch the tree, there is a loud rush of sound, like water spilling violently over a fall, before everything goes silent. The world disappears, fading away into bright light. Suddenly, we are standing in a temple, similar to this one, but much larger, with a heart tree in the center.

Silver light spirals up through the branches and into the veins of the delicate leaves. It is so beautiful, it is almost blinding. I turn my head and find Freyja beside me, wearing a crown. She takes my hand and the same fire that burns in my chest flows through her veins.

A faintly glowing thread of light winds around our joined hands, binding us together. Her eyes meet mine, and I can see my entire future in their mesmerizing depths.

A fledgling appears before us. He has silver-white scales and hair like mine, but when he turns to me, my breath catches when I see his eyes are ice blue, like Freyja's.

The vision fades and then morphs into a fully grown Dragon with the same blue eyes, but muted crimson scales cover his back and the top of his head. When he spreads his wings, the underside, just like his face, chest, and abdomen, are silver-white.

"Who are you?" I ask, stepping toward him. "Tell me your name."

But he doesn't respond. It is as if he is frozen in place. I move closer, but a voice stops me in my tracks. "He is your son," a voice whispers, and I immediately recognize the spirit of the heart tree. "The one born of the sanishon—your T'kara. Tell no one of your vision, Dragon King."

"Why?"

"This is but a glimpse of what could be," she replies. "The future is not set, and you would risk losing that which you desire above all else."

"Why show this to me, then?"

"You came to me for answers, and I have given you what you need to guide your path." She pauses. "Now, go back. Go back and fight for the future I have shown you."

"My son," I murmur in disbelief as I turn back to the image of the red and white Dragon.

A son. A smile breaks across my face as joy brighter than a thousand stars explodes within me. *We will have a son.*

CHAPTER 33

FREYJA

As soon as I rest my hand on the tree, everything falls away and goes silent. After what feels like an eternity, bright light floods my vision and I raise my free arm to shield my face before it dims.

I'm standing in the middle of a field. Dark smoke billows all around me, and the smell of smoke and ash is heavy on the wind. The glowing, blood-red eyes of dozens of Wraiths glare at me from their skeletal faces, lips pulled back to bare their razor-sharp fangs. Their tattered black cloaks wave in the wind, covering their twisted, grotesque forms as they hover over the ground.

The vision changes and I'm still standing on the field, but it is covered in blood and littered with bodies. Amongst the chaos, I notice a flash of silver-white scales. "Aurdyn!" I race across the field, dropping to my knees before his bloodied and broken form.

I cup his cheek, but he does not respond. Tears sting my

eyes and flow down my cheeks. "No!" I cry out. "I don't understand. How did this—"

"Will you sacrifice yourself for him?" A woman's voice whispers in my mind, and I still.

"Who is this?"

"Will you sacrifice your life for his?" the voice asks, this time more insistent. "Answer me."

"Yes," I reply without hesitation. "I will. What do I have to do? Tell me how to bring him back. Now!"

"Learn to wield your powers and trust your heart, Freyja. You will know when the moment arrives," she replies. "Tell no one what you saw here."

"We share a bond," I point out. "He can read many of my thoughts when he is in Draken form."

The image of a wall being built fills my mind. "I will help you shield this knowledge from him so he cannot discover it."

That solves one problem, but there is still another. "You want me to use my magic, but I do not even know how to bring it to the surface. How then can I wield it if—"

A surge of warmth rushes through me, burning from the inside as heat sears my palms. I sway slightly as the knowledge of how to call forth my fire fills my mind.

The vision fades and my eyes blink open to find that I'm still standing with my hand resting on the heart tree. I rip my hand away from it as if scalded, staring at my shaking palm in disbelief. I whip my head toward High Priest Arkon. His wide eyes meet mine and I take a stumbling step forward before falling to the ground.

"Freyja!" Aurdyn's voice cries out as if from a faraway place as everything goes dark.

CHAPTER 34

AURDYN

Scooping her limp form up into my arms, I rush Freyja toward the back of the temple, where the caretakers reside. A priestess guides me to lay her down on a sofa. "What is wrong with her?" My voice echoes through the cavernous space, bouncing off the glass dome overhead and the ivory stone walls.

Arkon moves to my side. "The spirit of the heart tree, did it speak to you?"

I open my mouth to reply yes but remember what it said about telling no one of my vision.

Arkon dips his chin in a nod. "I understand."

"It spoke to me as well," Arkon says as the priestess and several others gather around us, listening eagerly to his words. "She is a sanishon. One of those foretold in the prophecy of the Great Uniters."

"You are certain?" I ask, and he gives me a solemn nod.

Freyja stirs on the sofa and then opens her eyes. They

widen slightly when she notices the crowd of priestesses and priests gathered around her.

"Give her space," I command. "Now."

She pushes herself up to sitting. "What happened?"

"You passed out." I take her hand. "As soon as you stepped away from the heart tree."

"It spoke to me." Her eyes sweep to Arkon. "But it told me not to speak of what was said."

His gaze darts briefly to me before returning to her. "Whatever was spoken was between you and the great spirit, and was given to you to help guide your path."

Freyja's brow furrows deeply. "I understand," she murmurs. "Did it speak to you as well?"

We both nod. "You are the sanishon foretold in the ancient prophecy," Arkon says. "I suspected this when we met, but it has now been confirmed. The spirit of the heart tree would not have spoken to you if you were not the destined one.

"It also confirmed that your fire magic is because of your connection to King Aurdyn," he adds. He rubs his chin thoughtfully. "It is an unusual manifestation of the fate bond, but you are the first Outsider to be fated to one of our kind." He cocks his head to the side. "Can you speak to each other in your minds when the King is in his Draken form?"

"Yes," she answers.

He nods before he continues. "The Dark Elves are able to gift some of their life force to their fated mates, to heal them if they are injured. But they do this with the aid of their magic, and our people do not possess these abilities as far as I know. We have fire, not magic."

"How did I inherit this power if Aurdyn has none?" she asks.

"I am uncertain," he replies. "Fated mates usually strengthen each other's fire. Perhaps the bond granted this

215

ability to you, in this way, because you cannot breathe fire like we can."

Freyja swings her legs over the side of the sofa and then stands. I move close to her side, ready to help her balance if necessary. "Are you all right?"

Instead of answering, she raises her upturned palms out before her and balances twin flames on her hands. She turns them toward each other, combining the fire and expanding it into a fiery orb of magic while everyone in the temple stares in awe.

"The spirit taught me how to bring my magic to the surface." She lifts her gaze to mine. "I'll need to practice though."

I nod. "We will find a place for you to train."

Closing her hands, she snuffs out the flame. I take her arm to guide her back to the castle, and everyone around us bows low as we pass.

I am certain word of her abilities will spread like wildfire now that it has been witnessed by so many. Part of me had worried about the possibility that some might use the fact that she is human to question her right to rule as my queen. But now anyone who may have doubted that she is my T'kara, will be unable to deny the truth of our bond.

An image of our son flashes through my mind again, and I can barely contain my joy. A glorious future awaits us. Freyja will be mine, and I will be hers.

CHAPTER 35

FREYJA

Aurdyn leads me through the castle, and I recognize the path back to our rooms. He probably thinks I need rest after what happened earlier, but I do not. I stop and turn to him. "If you are taking me back to rest, I'm fine, Aurdyn. I'm not tired in the least."

"It is not that," he replies. "There is something I wish to show you."

"What is it?"

"Something important."

Now my interest is more than piqued. "Can you give me a hint?" I ask, smiling.

"I could. But I prefer to surprise you."

His cryptic answer only makes me even more impatient to find out what it is, as we walk through the corridors and toward our rooms.

As soon as we reach them, he leads me into the enchanted garden. We walk along one of the small paths to the wall on the left. He stops directly in front of it, and I watch curiously as he places a hand on the wall, smoothing it over the cream-colored stone as if searching for something. After a moment, he applies pressure and with a scraping of rock, the stone pushes in, revealing the faint outline of a hidden door.

He turns back and takes my hand, lifting it to the sunken stone. He places his palm over the back of my hand and the stone glows a faint blue before fading. "The magic that protects this door is now tied to you as well," he says.

"Where does it lead?" I ask, peering around him to try to see what is within.

"To my treasure hoard."

My jaw drops as I step inside, gaping at the large mound of gold and gemstones piled high in the center of the immense room. Several hanging tapestries decorate the space, depicting various nature scenes and images of Dragons in battle. L'sair crystals line the walls, their soft light reflecting off the treasure and scattering beautiful colors from the precious gems onto the ceiling.

He walks around the gigantic pile to a wooden table off to one side. Various weapons—daggers, long and short swords, a bow, an axe, and a shield—are neatly arranged on top.

I run my hand over the sword, tracing the intricately carved symbols that start on the pommel and travel down the length of the steel blade. I lift the sword from the table, getting a feel for its weight and balance before I move through a few of the stances I learned during my training.

"What do you think?" Aurdyn asks.

It's perfect. "I've never seen such a fine weapon," I admit. "Even the sword that was crafted for me by the royal black-smith cannot compare."

"It's yours," Aurdyn says.

My eyes snap up to his, and I set the sword back on the table. "I—It's too much. I cannot possibly accept such a lavish gift."

"All of this is yours." He raises his arm in a sweeping gesture toward the mountain of treasure. "Everything in here."

I'm speechless as he takes my hand. "All that I have is yours, Freyja."

"But it's your Dragon's hoard. I always heard such things were sacred... precious to your kind."

"This used to be my most prized possession... before I met you."

As much as his words touch me, they are also a bit troubling. "I am not a possession, and I belong to no one but myself, Aurdyn. I—"

He cups my chin, tipping my face up to his. "It is not an insult, my T'kara. I am as much yours as you are mine. I told you before that my kind do not love as yours do. We are Dragons. We claim and possess."

His eyes flare with heat as he wraps his other arm around my back, pulling me flush against him. My heart pounds at the intensity of his emerald gaze. "And above all else"—a low growl vibrates in his chest—"we covet rare and precious things."

Aurdyn's expression is full of hunger as he leans in and brushes his lips to mine. "Tell me to stop, and I will."

Desire pools deep within as he slowly walks me back toward the mound of treasure. His muscular form towers over mine, making my heart quicken as fire sparks in his gaze.

He runs his hand through my hair, gripping the long strands between his fingers and gently tilting my head to one side. He dips his head to the curve of my neck and shoulder. The tip of his nose skims across my already sensitive skin, and heat flushes my entire body. Inhaling deeply, he growls low in his throat. His sharp fangs graze the pulsing artery of my neck. "Your scent is intoxicating," he rasps. "Tell me to stop and I will leave you be."

My pulse pounds in my ears and I draw in a shaking breath as his eyes search mine, waiting for me to speak, but I remain silent.

Before we went to the heart tree, I wanted to know that he truly loved me. That his desire was about more than our bond. Now that I know how it will end, I find it no longer matters because he already has my heart. And my love will be enough for both of us. I want this. I want him… before I am gone.

I stretch up on my toes and wrap my arms around his neck. Our eyes lock a moment before I crush my lips to his. Aurdyn opens his mouth and deepens our kiss, claiming me with each stroke of his tongue against mine.

I moan and it's as if something snaps inside him. He rips a thick tapestry from the wall and spreads it out beneath me as he bears me to the ground, laying me down on a bed of gold and precious gems as he crawls over me, his large, muscular form caging me beneath him.

"You are mine," he rasps, his words both a command and a plea. "Tell me you want me in return."

I want so much to be his, but how can I give myself over to him when I know I will die? There is no future for us, and I cannot bind him to me knowing this. Instead of answering, I pull his lips down to mine and kiss him with the passion of a person who knows that their time is fleeting.

Every moment that passes brings me closer to our end, and I cannot bear the thought of leaving, even though I know it must be done. When the time comes, one of us will die, and I must make sure it isn't him.

His hand dips beneath the hemline of my tunic dress and finds my bare skin. I gasp and then moan into his mouth as he cups my breast, gently squeezing the soft globe before rolling the stiff peak between his thumb and forefinger.

"Do you wish me to stop?" he asks, his voice husky with longing.

"No." I barely manage to breathe out the word.

He removes my tunic, and his lips are urgent against mine as he slides the waistband of my leggings down past my hips and removes them entirely.

Aurdyn kisses a trail down my neck to my chest, closing his mouth over my left breast. He swirls his tongue expertly over the peak, sending a pulse of heat straight to my core. He turns his attention to the other breast, sending my desire spiraling even higher.

"If you do not want this," he murmurs as his hand moves up my thigh. "Tell me to stop, and I will."

I know we should, but I don't want to. "Aurdyn, please," I whisper, and he stills. He starts to pull away, mistaking my plea, believing I wish him to stop when the opposite is true. I cup his cheek and trace my thumb across his lower lip. "Touch me."

Fierce possessiveness burns in his eyes, and his gaze holds mine as he slowly drags his fingers through my already slick folds, careful to retract his claws so they do not harm me.

"Gods," he groans. "You are perfect, Freyja."

A strangled cry escapes me when his fingers brush the small bundle of nerves at the apex of my thighs. He rumbles in arousal as he concentrates his touch on that small pearl of flesh and I grip his arm, arching into his touch. "Don't stop." My breath comes in quick, shallow pants as desire winds tightly within.

Something hard bumps against my inner thigh. I glance down to see his length protruding from the line in his groin until it is hard and erect against my skin. A bead of liquid gathers on the end, leaving a wet trail against my quivering flesh.

We are not so different as I imagined, and I've never wanted anything as much as I want him.

Pleasure pools deep inside me as he continues his ministrations, holding me on the precipice of need and desire that I've never known before.

I reach down and carefully wrap my fingers around him, but he is so large I cannot completely encircle his length or the slight bulge at the base. He groans as I trace the ridges that run up and down his length, converging together in a tapered tip.

Aurdyn growls as my exploration unleashes something within him. He concentrates his touch on my sensitive pearl of flesh, pulling me over the edge and into blissful oblivion. I cry out his name as waves of pleasure wash over and through me.

My release triggers his own and my name leaves his lips on a strangled groan as his length pulses in my hand, warm liquid erupting from the tip and onto my body, completely covering my abdomen and pelvis with his essence.

He smooths his hand over my body, spreading his release over my breasts and down my thighs. He leans in and his breath is warm across my skin as he scents me. A deep growl rumbles in his throat. "You are mine, Freyja."

He lifts me to his chest and carries me back to his room. Gently, he lays me down beneath the furs and then crawls in beside me. I turn into him, snuggling against his chest as he wraps his powerful arms and wings solidly around me, holding me close.

Aurdyn runs his fingers through my hair as he tenderly nuzzles my temple. "Rest, my T'kara," he murmurs against my skin. "I have you, and I will never let you go."

A flash of worry shoots through me at his words, but I'm

too tired to speak. I shouldn't have let things go this far, but I could not deny my desire for him. But I cannot bind myself to him. His people mate for life.

I will die soon, and I do not want to become his mate only to leave him with no hope of a future with someone else. As much as I hate the thought of him with another, I would see him happy and with a wife and family. I love him enough to want these things for him, even if it means sacrificing my own happiness in return.

CHAPTER 36

AURDYN

With the door open that leads into the enchanted garden, sunlight filters into the room, highlighting the sleek strands of Freyja's red hair and her lovely face. Long red lashes fan soft pink cheeks, and I know that I have never seen anyone as beautiful as her.

I nuzzle her hair and a low hum escapes me as I breathe in our combined scent. She stirs in my arms and when her eyelids flutter open, her lips curve in a stunning smile as she gazes up at me.

My desire flares anew, and I capture her lips in a passionate kiss. When I pull back, she's breathless beneath me. "You are mine, Freyja," I murmur. "And now I will claim you completely, my fire heart."

Gently, I roll her onto her stomach. Gripping her hips, I pull her up onto her knees and hands before me and then cover her body with mine. My crown bumps against the entrance to her core, and I drop my head to the curve of her neck, grazing her skin with my fangs as the desire to give her my mark thrums in my chest.

"Wait," she says breathlessly, and I immediately still and then pull away.

She turns onto her back to face me. "I—we cannot do this, Aurdyn."

Confused, I study her a moment and then stroke her cheek. Perhaps she is afraid. After all, this is as new for her as it is for me, and I will not pressure her to do this. "We can wait however long you need, my T'kara. We do not have to mate until you are ready."

She moves out from under me and sits up, pulling her knees to her chest. "I—" she starts, but breaks off, catching her lower lip between her teeth as if trying to decide what to say.

"What is it, Freyja?" I ask gently. "Whatever it is, you can tell me."

She lifts her eyes, full of unshed tears. "I do not want to hurt you."

"Hurt me?" I blink several times. "What are you talking about? I am a Dragon. If you are worried about your fire magic, it is not a concern. I am—"

"That's not what I mean," she says, voice thick with emotion. "I mean I cannot bind myself to you. I cannot become your mate."

Her words make no sense. "Do you worry that my people will not accept you? I do not believe that is true. They know what you are to me. That you are my T'kara and—"

"No," she cuts me off. "That's not it. I—I'm human, Aurdyn. Your people mate for life. What would happen to you if I died?"

My head jerks back. "Why are you worried about death? You are safe here, Freyja. I will protect you. No one will ever harm you again."

"You cannot know that," she counters. "You cannot promise such things."

"After all we have been through, you still doubt my strength." I bristle slightly. "You do not believe I can protect you or that I would be a worthy mate to you."

"Why must everything be about strength with you?" she says, exasperated.

"Because I am a Dragon." I puff out my chest. "Strength is everything to my people. It is the measure of our worth to our mates. And I vow that I am strong enough to protect and defend you from harm. You and any fledglings we might have, Freyja. What have I done to make you doubt me?"

CHAPTER 37

FREYJA

The raw pain in his eyes is too much to bear. I hate that I'm hurting him like this, but I don't have a choice. I take both his hands in mine. "I do not doubt you, Aurdyn. Not for a single moment." Hope flits across his face and it nearly breaks me. "But I cannot marry you. I will not bind myself to you. As much as I want to, I cannot."

His expression darkens. "Cannot or will not?"

I swallow against the lump in my throat. "Both."

"I do not understand, Freyja." His gaze holds mine, full of confusion and pain. "Why do you reject me?"

Because I cannot tell him what the heart tree showed me, there is no truthful answer I can give that he will understand. So I lie. "Can you not see that we are both trapped in this, Aurdyn? It is the bond that draws us to each other, nothing more."

"You feel trapped?" he asks, voice tinged with sadness and disbelief.

"Don't you?"

"No." His posture slumps, and he stares down at his hands. "I did, at first… but not anymore. Not now that I know you, Freyja." He stands from the bed. Features pinched, he turns away from me.

I hate this. I hate lying and causing him pain, but I have to. I will not bind him to me, knowing that I will die. "You told me that because I am your T'kara, it is your duty to care for and protect me. But I am strong enough to protect myself, Aurdyn. It does not have to be your burden." I pause. "Do you not see? Dragons mate for life. If not for the bond, you would never choose a human. I know this because you've said repeatedly that my kind are weak. We do not even live half of your lifespan. And yet, the bond would compel you to bind yourself to me, regardless."

"You are not a burden," he says in a low, raspy voice. "You never were. But I will not force you to choose me when I am not what you want."

"I will write to my cousin Edmynd. Perhaps he will not care about the crime I was accused of, and will allow me to—"

"You do not have to leave. You will always have a place here, even if it is not by my side."

Tears sting my eyes, and I wince when he adds. "I cannot stay here. I…" He shakes his head and then moves to the door, disappearing through before shutting it behind him, leaving me alone with my lies and regrets.

I drop my head into my hands as a storm of emotions rages deep within. "What have I done?" I murmur to myself. "I just hurt the only person who truly cares about me."

He claims his people do not love, but the anguish in his eyes as I lied to him suggests otherwise.

Drawing in a shaky breath, I tamp down my sadness, reminding myself that I'm doing this for him. I tried to protect my heart, but I failed. I've fallen for this grumpy and arrogant Dragon and even if he does not understand it now, he will know when the time comes that this is how I prove my love for him.

* * *

I COULD SIT in my room all day and brood over things I cannot change, but if I am to save Aurdyn, I must learn to wield my powers so that I can call upon them when they are needed.

When I enter the secret room where Aurdyn keeps his treasure, I force myself to look away from his mound of gold and the place where we nearly made love the other day. I walk around it to the table and grip the longsword firmly in hand. As I turn back to the door, I notice a shield leaning against the wall. Whoever made this carved an ancient Dragon rune across the front in gorgeous detail. Picking up the shield, I leave the room and head to the garden to practice.

CHAPTER 38

AURDYN

Freyja does not want me. Her rejection pierces my heart like a sharp blade. I may not be who she would have pictured for a mate, any more than she is who I had envisioned. But I thought my devotion to her care and safety would prove I am worthy to stand by her side.

Curling my hands into fists, I roar my pain to the sky. I am a Dragon. I am not supposed to love. And yet... I can find no other excuse for the agony that twists deep within.

"Cousin!" Brovyn's voice draws my attention as he flies up beside me. "What is wrong? Where is Freyja?"

"I left her in the castle." The blade turns deeper in my chest. "She does not want me."

He rubs the back of his neck. "I was so sure that she—" He stops abruptly. "She seemed just as taken with you as you are with her." He shifts his gaze to mine. "Did something happen?"

"She said we are trapped by the bond." I exhale heavily. "That our connection is the reason I want her as my mate."

"You've always had little regard for her kind before now." Brovyn studies me intently. "Is there not some validity to her concerns?"

Anger flares brightly within. "No. She has a heart of fire. Any Dragon would be proud to be hers."

"Does she know this?"

The fire of my anger dies down to mere embers. "In truth, I do not know. I thought I had made it clear, but… maybe I have not."

"Then, perhaps you should tell her."

"She also asked me last night about love."

"Humans place great emphasis on this word, as do the Elves and the Fae."

"It is a weak term to describe the emotions of a Dragon," I grumble.

"But it is one she is familiar with," Brovyn offers. "So, perhaps you should learn to use it."

Reluctantly, I nod. Drawing in a deep breath, I head back to the castle. I'm halfway there when I come upon two of my warriors. "My King, we were just on our way to report to you."

"What is it?"

"There are reports along the southern border of Wraith sightings."

I straighten my spine. "Double the guards patrolling our boundaries," I command.

They each bow low and then leave to carry out my orders.

The mountain has always been a deterrent to most, but to the Wraiths, I am not certain. It has been a long time since I've asked anything of the Fae or the Dark Elves, but I believe I will have to remind them of the friendship our people used to share.

Although I do not doubt that my warriors and I could

defend the kingdom against attack, it would be an extra protection to have a magical barrier erected around our lands. The Fae are much closer than the Dark Elves and could be here straightaway if we reach an agreement.

A snarl twists my lips. King Kyven and I did not part amicably last time we met, but if it means keeping Freyja safe, I will do what I must to make that happen.

But first, I must find her.

CHAPTER 39

FREYJA

The palace gardens are vast and untamed. They are so different from the carefully manicured spaces that surrounded my uncle's castle. As my boots crunch over the snow and ice, I would think myself lost in a forest if not for the worn path, winding through the trees.

Wisps of snow dance and twirl on the cool breeze. The air is crisp and clean, and the ground is covered in a thin layer of white. The woods are so thick I can barely make out the castle behind me and the columns of the temple up ahead. Somewhere between here and there, I hope to find a secluded space to train.

If I want to save Aurdyn, I must learn to wield my newly acquired powers.

Off to the left, I notice a clearing. On the opposite side of it is the cliff face wall. The ivory rock will provide the perfect target to test my magic.

But first, I will begin with the familiar.

Remembering my training, I step through various defensive positions with my sword and shield. My movements are smooth and efficient from many years of practice. My teacher, Sir Vorgen, was deadly with any weapon, but even more so with a longsword, and he taught me well. The sun tracks across the sky overhead as I lose myself to the motion, becoming one with the weapon in my hand.

Clarity pierces the doubt in my mind as I imagine my fire is a blade to be wielded against my enemies. I sheathe my sword and close my eyes, remembering the battle with the Mage.

When he attacked, I sent a silent prayer to the gods, begging them for a weapon. Something sparked deep within, building into a roaring fire that traveled through my body and gathered in my hands, allowing me to wield it as a shield to protect us.

I focus on that memory, using it to call forth my fire. Heat flares across my palms, and when I open my eyes an orb of fire hovers between my hands. Sweat beads across my brow as I force myself to concentrate.

Raising my arms, I throw the fireball to the cliff wall, watching in triumph as it explodes against the rock in a devastating display of power.

Breathing deeply, I lift my hands and stare at my palms, trying to will my magic to the surface again, but it is no use.

I clench my jaw and pick up my sword. Clearing my mind, I begin moving through the motions once again, hoping this intense focus will rekindle the fire in my veins.

"I heard that human males do not allow their females to fight," a voice calls from one side, startling me. I turn to find Brovyn strolling toward me. "But it seems those rumors were inaccurate."

"Most men do not approve, but my uncle's kingdom is different," I explain. "In Ruhaen, everyone is trained to fight and defend themselves, for anyone can be felled by a blade whether they wield one or not." Sadness tightens my chest as I think of my parents. "The kingdom of Morath has long been our enemy, invading our lands to try and expand their territory. Our people have fought many battles with them over the past three hundred years."

"Your people are warriors then," he says. "Like ours."

I tip up my chin with pride. "Yes."

"Perhaps that is why the gods fated you to my cousin."

"What do you mean?"

"Aurdyn was very young when his father died and he took up the mantle of rule. It is a heavy burden to bear, but he has carried it well." He pauses. "His uncle—my father—challenged him, but Aurdyn put a swift end to the division by defeating him publicly."

I inhale sharply. I knew his uncle betrayed him, but I never knew the details.

Brovyn continues. "My father was a warrior with little tolerance for politics. But Dragons revere strength, even if it is destructive. I grew up with Aurdyn. He is much like his father before him—both a strong warrior and a great leader. I knew he was the better choice for our kingdom, and I was right.

"He has managed to maintain peace among the seven Great Houses. His strength kept us together when our people would have fractured, leaving us vulnerable to our enemies. It makes sense that the gods would have fated him, not only to a warrior, but a sanishon."

Instead of addressing his statement about the prophecy, I study him curiously. "You chose Aurdyn over your own father."

"I am loyal to him. If that is what you are asking."

"You refer to his father as a great leader, but the Dwarves speak of a king that was cruel. One who murdered their people without cause."

"Of course they would say this." Brovyn clenches his jaw. "Their greed led them to dig tunnels beneath our mountains, searching for riches. He told them to seal them up, but they did not listen. It was those same tunnels that his father's enemy then used to abduct his mother—the queen. It led to her death. That is why he burned them to ash." He shakes his head softly. "It was the act of a grieving Dragon seeking vengeance."

Sadness tightens my chest at all Aurdyn has been through. I cannot imagine how hard it must have been for him to have to take on the crown, not only while he was so young, but also while he was still grieving the loss of his parents. Thank the gods he had Brovyn, at least.

"He considers you as a brother to him. I am glad he has you, Brovyn. All rulers need someone they can trust."

"And what of you?" He regards me closely. "Would you leave him simply because you begrudge the bond that first drew you together?"

I blink several times at his blunt question and then look at my feet. "It's… not that simple."

"Then what is it?" Aurdyn's voice calls out from behind me, and I spin to face him. "Tell me, so that I may prove that I am worthy of being your mate."

Brovyn abruptly vanishes down one of the garden paths as Aurdyn stalks closer, his gaze locked onto mine. "When I first recognized what you were to me, I was resentful because you are human, and humans are weak."

I bristle. "Is this supposed to be an apology of some sort? Because if it is—"

"It is not," he cuts me off. "I would be lying if I said I thought your people are strong. But you—" He tips my face up to his with a finger under my chin, "are not weak, like the males of your species so often are. And yet… without the bond, I would never have bothered to learn this about you."

I nod tightly. I was right all along. It's the bond that makes him want me.

"Yes, the bond initially drew me to you, but I can tell you now, without doubt, that my desire for you is not because you are my T'kara, but because of who you are, Freyja." His eyes search mine. "You are strong. You are val'nara—one who possesses a heart of pure fire."

His words touch something deep inside, but I cannot allow them to sway me.

He leans in and his lips brush gently to mine. My heart pounds in my chest. The memory of what we did last night sends a thrill of heat straight to my center. But I keep my mouth closed, refusing him the entrance that he seeks. I must remain strong. I cannot bind myself to him, knowing I will die soon.

His eyes snap open and he pulls back, his nostrils flaring. "I can scent your desire. Why do you hold back?"

"I already told you, Aurdyn." I force my voice to remain even despite my sadness. "I cannot bind myself to you. I'm human. You're a Dragon. We're too—"

"Do not say we are different," he snarls. "Fate crossed our paths for a reason, Freyja. I found you because I know the fire that burns in your heart. And I know this because it is the same one that burns in my veins as well."

My resolve nearly breaks beneath the intensity of his gaze. But I cannot give in to my longing, even though I want nothing more than to fall into his arms and bind myself to him. "You don't understand, Aurdyn."

"Then, at least tell me why."

"I cannot."

His eyes grow cold. "Fine. If that is what you truly want, then—"

"Aurdyn!" Brovyn's voice cuts through the trees. Something about the urgency in his tone fills me with dread.

"What is it?" Aurdyn asks, not bothering to hide his irritation.

"The Dark Elf king—Varys—has requested you meet with him."

My chest constricts. Everyone fears the Dark Elves and their king. Varys is a fierce and lethal warrior, capable of terrifying and devastating magic. Why would he want to meet with Aurdyn?

Aurdyn stills. "Did he say why?"

"No," Brovyn says gravely. "But his message said it was important that you come right away."

"I am not his subject to command or to summon," Aurdyn says severely. "Did he give a good reason for not coming to me instead?"

Brovyn crosses his arms. "Perhaps it has to do with the incident that occurred with the last ambassador they sent."

"What incident?" Aurdyn huffs. "It was an uneventful visit, and a waste of my time, if I remember correctly."

"You threatened to set him on fire because he made you angry." Brovyn purses his lips. "And when he continued to argue, you singed his hair."

I slap a hand over my mouth to smother a gasp.

"He was fine," Aurdyn grumbles, waving a dismissive hand. "Besides, surely it has grown back by now."

"That's not the point." Brovyn glowers at him. "Knowing how his last ambassador was treated, I'm sure that's why King Varys has requested you go to him instead."

"Fine," Aurdyn grumbles. "I will leave at once for Ithylian and see what is so urgent."

"I insist you take three guards to accompany you this time."

Aurdyn bristles, fire burning in his eyes. "Do you suggest I am weak, cousin?"

"No." Brovyn squints at him. "But the Dark Elves have powerful magic."

"Yes, but I have fire," Aurdyn says menacingly. "King Varys and his people know better than to cross a Dragon."

I'm worried for Aurdyn, and although I risk wounding his pride, I cannot remain silent. "Would it not be wiser to take a few guards with you?" I ask. "Why risk going alone? Besides… arriving with your warriors would be a show of strength, would it not?"

"Humans believe there is strength in numbers, but among my kind, it is a sign that one is not strong enough to stand alone."

Dragons are overly proud beings, but this is extreme. Is he really going to place a show of strength above his own safety?

"I am a Dragon, not some pitiful human male." He puffs his chest out with pride. "Varys is too smart to challenge me."

"Even so, it would be wise to have another person with you," I press. "Surely you can admit this, can you not?"

He narrows his eyes, his tail flicking agitatedly behind him.

"Take me with you." His brows shoot up to his forehead. "I shielded you from the Mage's attack in Arganth. If the Dark Elves try to—"

"No." He cuts me off. "You will remain here, where it is safe."

"But what about you?"

"Do not worry for me," he says gruffly. "My kind are not easily killed."

"Aurdyn, I don't want you to go alone. I—"

"The Mages want you dead, Freyja." He spins to face me, eyes blazing with frustration. "Do you think they have stopped hunting you?"

"They tried to kill you as well. We defeated them together before, Aurdyn."

"And you nearly died because you used too much of your power," he snaps. "I will take no chances with your safety."

"You will *not* leave me here." Frustration burns in my chest. "I demand that you take me with you. I will not stay behind while you are in danger."

"Why do you care so much about what happens to me?" he challenges. "You do not want me, and yet you act as if you were my mate, ready to protect and defend me. Why?"

My frustration wars with anger, and I bite back the words that I so desperately want to speak. But I know I cannot.

His gaze holds mine, fire burning in his eyes as he stares down at me. "You are holding something back. I know you are. Why will you not yield to me, Freyja? Tell me," he demands. "Now."

"I cannot." I hide my sadness behind a mask of outrage at his demanding tone. "I already told you this."

Scowling, he steps back away from me. In a gust of wind and leaves, he transforms into a massive Dragon. Thick, black smoke puffs out from his nostrils as he surveys me, obviously upset by my answer, before he spreads his wings and lifts into the sky.

"Aurdyn, wait!"

He releases a series of thunderous roars as he disappears into the clouds.

I turn to Brovyn. "What did he say?"

The scales on his cheeks darken. "You are sure you wish to know?"

I nod.

"He was wondering why he is cursed to love such a stubbornly infuriating female."

My heart stutters and stops. "Love? He… said that?"

Brovyn nods.

"But I thought Dragons do not love. That you claim and possess."

"This is true," Brovyn replies, and a deep ache settles in my chest. "Or so I have been told."

My brows go up in surprise. "What do you mean?"

"Our mates are our treasures, and we hoard and covet them above all else."

"Some would say that is a form of love," I suggest.

"It is... different. Our obsession with our mates is all-consuming and powerful, bordering on madness, even." He runs a hand through his hair. "Many would argue that love is not a strong enough word for what a Dragon feels for their mate."

"Then why would he use it?" I frown. "Why would he say this word as he is leaving?"

"Because, as his advisor, I may have pointed out that it is a term familiar to your kind." A smile curves his mouth. "One you cannot mistake for anything else in regard to his feelings for you. And one he should learn to use from now on."

CHAPTER 40

AURDYN

Cursed sky and seven hells! Why have I been cursed to love such a stubborn, infuriating female! I release a stream of flame into the air, bellowing out another roar of frustration as I descend through the clouds.

Freyja will be the end of me. I just know it.

I do not understand why she refuses to become my mate. The vision gifted to me by the heart tree spirit revealed our son. Surely, she must have seen this as well.

My heart stops. Perhaps she did, and that is why she refuses me now. Maybe the idea of becoming my mate and bearing my child is not something she wants. And yet... if that were true, why did she allow me to touch her after our visit to the temple?

I must have done something to upset her. But what? That is the only explanation that makes sense. She has often referred to me as arrogant, and has never had issue speaking her mind before, so why does she not simply tell me what is wrong now?

Movement in the distance distracts me. Swooping down lower, I glide toward it to investigate. As I dip in and out of the clouds, the image comes into sharper focus.

It is an army of men carrying the banner of the Kingdom of Kolstrad. They march along the main road toward Florin —the kingdom where Freyja's cousin, King Edmynd reigns.

With my superior vision, I can stay far enough away that their pitiful human eyes cannot see me and yet close enough that I can study them further, and perhaps even determine their intent.

I've seen armies march to the aid of neighboring kingdoms, and perhaps that is what this is. Maybe the Dark Elves have finally decided to invade Florin and take it for themselves, and Florin has called upon the other human kingdoms to help defend their lands.

Kolstrad is the logical choice for this, since their kingdom is so close to Florin. If Florin were to fall to the Elves, it would only be a matter of time before they entered Kolstrad as well.

King Varys is a young king, like me, but I thought he was more evenly tempered. If he is indeed behind a Dark Elf invasion, the humans must have done something truly unforgivable.

As I draw closer, something darts off to one side. My gaze zeroes in and worry tightens my chest when I notice over a dozen Wraiths trailing behind Kolstrad's army.

I blink several times, wondering if my eyes are deceiving me. Dark hooded capes that blow in the wind cover the twisted, grotesque forms as they hover above the ground. Their eerie red eyes glow like sinister beacons behind the soldiers.

Brovyn informed me there had been sightings of Wraiths,

and so had the Dwarves, but I did not think it was this serious. Until now.

This does not make any sense. Wraiths are a cursed form of life—a deadly foe for any they encounter. As far as I know, they are more animalistic in nature than they are sentient; they cannot be controlled.

A booming voice echoes through the throng of footsteps, and the Wraiths line up in straight formation behind the army. Off to the side, I notice a Mage. The sickly gray pallor that marks his species is visible beneath his black robes. Judging by the decorative metal armor of the male on the horse beside him, he rides next to a human of importance. The standard draped across the back of the human's horse marks him as one of the royal family of Kolstrad. A closer look reveals it to be the Crown Prince Aegryn.

Whatever this is, it is ominous. That the Mages are behind it, only confirms what I've always suspected of them. They are power-hungry creatures, and their claim that they defend and protect the human realms is merely a way for them to take control and grab more power.

I could warn Florin, if they are not already aware of this. But I am a Dragon and my people have not dealt with their kingdom for many years. If I showed up, they would likely think I am there to attack their kingdom, and I'd rather avoid any black arrows.

I make a wide arc around the army to avoid detection and continue on toward Ithylian. As their kingdom comes into view, I notice the banner of the king flying high over the old ruins of Elysarin castle. It seems King Varys is not in the capital of Cyridil, beneath his mountain.

The Dark Elves suffered devastating losses, just as we did, in the last Great War. They abandoned their castle in Elysarin and made their home deep in the mountains, creating a new capital city for their people.

As I fly toward the banner, I wonder if they have decided to rebuild the ruined castle and move the capital back to Elysarin.

I drop down low, scanning the overgrown castle gardens, and spot King Varys and his entourage waiting below. The blue gray of their skin stands out in sharp contrast to the greenery that surrounds them. I narrow my eyes as I notice a female with long blond hair and pale skin standing beside Varys. I don't know who she is or why she is here. Perhaps he has taken a High Elf as his mate.

Dipping my left wing, I make a slow circle above them before touching down. I remain in my four-legged form, ready to breathe flame upon them if this is some sort of trap.

Deep down, I doubt Varys would try to harm me, but one can never be too sure. Especially when dealing with the Elves and the Fae.

Folding my wings tight to my back, I lower my head to study the female beside Varys and am shocked when I realize her ears are rounded. She is human then, and not High Elf.

My nostrils flare and my head jerks back slightly in surprise when I realize they carry each other's scent. Seven hells! "A human?" My gaze snaps to Varys in disbelief. "Since when does your kind mate with them?"

"Queen Inara is my bondmate." He growls, baring his fangs. "You will show your respect."

In a whirl of wind and debris, I transform into my two-legged form, conjuring a pair of black pants to cover my lower half, and cautiously move toward them.

Everyone knows Dark Elves are just as protective of their mates as Dragons, and I watch King Varys warily as I approach.

CHAPTER 41

AURDYN

Varys's human queen wears a long, silken blue dress that highlights the strange color of her eyes—a combination of light brown and green. Her blonde hair hangs down her back and over her shoulders, in sharp contrast to the black and white hair of the Dark Elves all around her.

The guards behind her and Varys slowly begin to form a tight formation at their backs, no doubt readying to defend them both if necessary.

With great difficulty, I manage to not roll my eyes. Do they not realize that if I'd wanted to harm Varys or his queen, I could have easily done so from the air in my full Draken form?

Varys stands beside her, his feet spread slightly apart in a defensive stance and his lethal, black claws extended, ready to protect her. His pointed ears stick up through his short, black hair and his glowing blue eyes scan me from head to toe.

"I called you here to speak of the Wraiths," Varys says. "They discovered a way to cross the Great Wall."

A thin curl of smoke puffs out from my nostrils as I reply. "The Mages have finally made their move."

"What do you mean?" Varys asks.

"They have always hungered for power. Now, they have found a way to acquire it."

"How?" Queen Inara asks.

My eyes narrow as I reflect on the army I just saw marching to Florin with a Mage and the Wraiths. "You should know, *human*. It is your kind who have helped them." She frowns, appearing confused by my words before I turn my attention back to Varys. "Prince Aegryn is marching even now across the land with an army of Wraiths toward the kingdom of Florin."

"How do you know this?" Queen Inara asks.

"I saw them," I grind out.

"How are the Wraiths being controlled?" Varys asks. "I thought it was impossible."

"The Mages seem able to enslave them with magic. There are reports that a few Wraiths have escaped. Those are the ones now wandering across the lands unchecked."

"But why would the Mages do this?" Queen Inara asks. "They *know* how dangerous the Wraiths are."

"Why does anyone want power?" I reply grimly. "All I know is that they are controlling the Wraiths, and they have allied themselves with Prince Aegryn of Kolstrad to march upon Florin."

"If this is true, we must stand against them," Varys says.

We? Since when do me or my people answer to his? "I will not drag my kind into a war they need not fight," I state firmly. "Kolstrad and Florin are both human kingdoms. Long ago, they aligned themselves with the Order of Mages to protect them from Otherworldly beings, such as ourselves. If the Mages are now turning their human pets against each other, that is their problem, not ours."

Queen Inara levels an icy glare as she steps toward me. "Do you truly believe that Prince Aegryn and the Mages will not come for your people too? What will stop them from attacking you after they finish with the rest of us, Dragon King?"

I doubt this would happen. We are safe in our mountains. It is why we chose to make our homes there. "That time may not even come."

"It will, if they are successful," she counters.

I'm surprised by her boldness as she stands before me, appearing unafraid.

Perhaps it is only human males that are weak, for the females I've met seem to be possessed of as much fire as any female Dragon.

I turn to Varys. "I have no quarrel with the Dark Elves. I came to this meeting to share what I know. That is all."

CHAPTER 42

AURDYN

"If my brother's kingdom falls, yours could be next." Queen Inara's eyes flash with anger.

Brother? If she is speaking of King Edmynd, then that means she is...

My thoughts are interrupted as she continues. "How can you not see this?"

"I doubt that would happen," I scoff. "My people are strong. Humans are weak."

"And I heard Dragons were brave," she retorts. "But it seems I was wrong. You are a coward who would hide in his mountain while the rest of the world burns."

One of Varys's guards sucks in a sharp breath, as shocked as I am that she would speak to me in this way.

Heat flushes through me, and my nostrils flare. "You *dare* to insult me?"

"If I am wrong, then I will gladly apologize. But I suspect I am not."

A deep growl rises in my throat as Varys's guards look on,

stunned by the boldness of their queen. Puffing out my chest, I step closer to her, glaring as her gaze locks with mine.

Instead of stepping back, she stands her ground like a true warrior, fierce and unafraid, reminding me of Freyja.

Varys pulls her behind him, baring his fangs in a feral snarl. "Do *not* threaten my queen, for it will be the last thing you do."

He is challenging me? My muscles ripple beneath my scales, readying to shift into my Draken form. A flash of light catches my eye over his shoulder, and I halt abruptly, staring in shock at his human mate.

Power arcs between her fingers, crackling like blue lightning across her skin. She is like my T'kara. "You have magic." I gape at her in disbelief. "How is this possible? I thought there was only one."

"Only one what?" she asks.

"One human who possessed magic. Princess Freyja," I explain. "I saved her from the Mages. Her uncle—the king—would have let them burn her for witchcraft because of her power. Before her, I did not know humans possessed such a thing."

Inara stills, her magic dissipating immediately as she lowers her hands.

"You know her." It is not a question; I can see it in her eyes.

"Our mothers were cousins. We used to play together when we were children. Tell me, where is she now?"

"In my kingdom, where she is safe."

Her brow creases into a small frown. "You speak of humans as if we were nothing, Dragon King, but you saved my cousin. Why?"

Her boldness is both irritating and, at the same time, admirable. She is as strong as my T'kara. "My reasons are my own."

"And I should simply take your word that she is safe with you?" Inara challenges.

"Yes," I state flatly, my patience for her doubt wearing thin. "She is under my protection. I will allow no one to harm her ever again."

Varys studies me keenly. "You protect *her*, but you would let her kind fall to the Wraiths while you hide in your mountains?"

"Her kind would have killed her if not for me," I growl. "They do not deserve our protection."

"You cannot judge an entire race by the actions of only a few," Inara says. "If you do not help us, Florin may well fall. If it does, then Ithylian could be next. Eventually, the Wraiths will come for your people, King Aurdyn, and I believe you know this."

"I have considered it, yes." But I do not think it is as certain as she seems to believe. We lost so many during the last Great War, and I will not allow such a thing to happen under my rule. "My grandfather trusted the words of a human king long ago; it led to his doom and nearly cost my people everything. We were hunted mercilessly, and it almost caused our end.

"We survived only because we made our homes in the Ice Mountains, where most others would perish. So, you will understand why I hesitate to repeat the same mistakes as my ancestor."

"And what of Ithylian?" Varys asks, reminding me of the aid the Dark Elves gave my people in the past. "If you refuse to help the humans fight for Florin if they stand against the Wraiths... My people have helped you before. If I call upon you, will you honor the history between us?"

I narrow my eyes. "*You*, I will help. The humans, I will not."

"Fine," he replies in a clipped tone, obviously unsatisfied

by my answer. "Then, you'd best hope the humans do not fall to the Wraiths, because if they do, only *we* will be left to face them, when there could have been more."

"I will take that chance," I reply solemnly. "If this is the only reason you wished to meet, I have said what I came to say."

I'm eager to return to my T'kara, but as I regard Varys's human queen, I recognize an opportunity to obtain insight from another Otherworldly being on how to convince a human to become my mate.

"But I would speak with you alone a moment before I go."

He dips his chin and turns to his queen. "I will return shortly."

I'm shocked when she kisses him before he leaves with me. Dark Elves are often rather cold in their interactions with others, and yet... it is promising to see the obvious affection his human mate has for him.

It seems he has not only claimed her hand, he has won her heart as well. And I am eager to learn how he did this.

I follow him toward the ruined castle. Even in its ruined and crumbling state, it is still an impressive structure. It is a shame they never restored it after the last Great War. Now they make their homes so deep in their mountain, I wonder how often they ever see the sunlight.

"Your ancestors created things of not only beauty but strength." I run a hand over the gray stone wall and tiny sparks of energy ripple across my skin. "Even the magic of these stones still lingers. If I remember correctly, this was the last building left standing, sheltering your citizens during the last Great War."

"That is true," he replies, a hint of sadness in his tone.

"If anything had been spared of my grandfather's king-dom, we never would have left," I say soberly. "We would have rebuilt to honor the memory of those lost and to preserve the culture of our people."

Varys peers at me. "What is it you are so cryptically trying to tell me?"

"You should not hide inside the mountain. Your people are not Orcs. If you stay too long in that place, you could end up buried in it, like they were."

He flinches slightly at the reminder of the Orc stronghold of Grundyn. Unlike our home in the Ice Mountains, the Orcs lived like Varys's people do now. They had no easy access to the outside, not even any windows.

When the Orcs were overrun by their enemies, their only means of escaping the mountain were cut off. Nearly half of their people died, and the survivors are now scattered throughout the seven kingdoms, struggling to rebuild.

Varys studies the ruins before him critically. "Perhaps you are right."

My head snaps around in shock. In all the years I've known him, he has conceded this to me less than a handful of times.

"But that is not what you wanted to speak to me about, is it?" Varys says curtly. "So, tell me what it is you wish to discuss."

As reluctant as I am to ask a Dark Elf for help, I do not have a choice. Varys is my last hope. "Your human mate… How do I win a human's heart?"

"Win?" His eyebrows climb up his forehead. "I thought Dragons were conquerors."

I laugh derisively. "My female is strong of will and exceedingly stubborn. She will not be conquered."

"*Your* female?"

He is right. She isn't mine. Not yet. I drag a hand roughly through my hair, shaking my head in frustration. "She is my

T'kara—my Fated One. I saved her, yet she will not yield to me. And I do not understand why."

"That is where you are going wrong, Aurdyn." Amusement dances behind Varys's eyes. "You cannot treat her as you would another Dragon. You must woo a human to win her heart, not fight her until she yields it to you... because I guarantee you, she never will. They are stronger than they appear."

"I know this," I grumble. "But how do I... *woo* her?"

"Spend time with her. Talk to her. Make sure she knows how important she is to you."

"How could she not already know what she means to me?" I ask, completely exasperated. "I saved her. I protect her. I have provided her a nest any Dragon female would envy. I made her stay behind when she wanted to come with me because she needs to remain in our home where she is safe."

His mouth drifts open, but then he gives me a commiserating look as he claps a hand on my shoulder. "That was a mistake you will pay for dearly when you return. Humans are stubborn creatures, used to having their way. I have not told you the circumstances of how I met my bondmate. Even her own brother—the king—could not convince her to obey him when it came to her safety."

Varys explains how they met and how they wed while I listen in rapt fascination. Apparently, he captured her when she snuck into his camp the night before he was to go to war with her brother, King Edmynd.

He recognized immediately that she was his Fated One and proposed a marriage to create an alliance between their people. "So, now you understand," he finishes his story. "You cannot force a human to do anything she does not wish, including remaining out of danger. The best thing you can do is teach her to defend herself and keep her close by your side."

"You do this with your mate?" I ask dubiously.

"Why do you think she is here?" Varys says, referring to his queen being present at our meeting.

"There is no danger here." I'm completely insulted. "I would *never* harm a female."

"Yes, but she is human, and I know how much anger you have toward their kind." He sighs heavily. "And do not think I have forgotten how you set fire to my last ambassador."

Must he bring this up again? "He was *fine*, Varys. I only flamed his hair. I knew it would grow back."

"You *terrified* him," Varys counters. "Now, you have a reputation among my kind for your temper."

"Dragons are not sprites," I grind out, frustrated that he cannot seem to get over this minor incident. "We are not supposed to be known for our friendliness, but for our fierce strength."

"Trust me." He sneers. "No one will *ever* confuse your kind with sprites."

I throw up my hands. "I must return home." I am eager to see Freyja. And after speaking with Varys, I am concerned that if I do not return soon, she will be even angrier with me than she is already. I sigh heavily. He is right. I probably should not have left her behind when she demanded to come. "If I stay away for much longer, I fear I will incur more wrath from my human."

"She is not quite *your* human yet, though. Remember that," he says brusquely. "You are to court, not conquer."

I scrub my hand roughly across my face. Why do humans have such complicated courtship rituals?

A mating battle is a much more efficient way to choose a mate. And while it is often dangerous for males, it is also over rather quickly either way. Whereas, wooing one's

JESSICA GRAYSON

potential mate seems to be a very drawn-out affair. But if this is what I must do to win Freyja's human heart, so be it. "I shall remember your counsel."

Varys says bluntly, "A bit of humility would probably go a long way, as well, with your... human."

I scoff at the suggestion. I am a Dragon. Surely, he jests.

"Never mind." Varys shakes his head. "*That* would be an impossible feat for a Dragon."

I cross my arms in mock irritation, it seems his human's bold manner of speaking is rubbing off on him. I think of Freyja and Varys's queen. From what I have witnessed, human females appear to be much braver than the males.

I take a step back and then shift in a whirl of dust and wind back into my Draken form. "Goodbye, Varys. Perhaps, when this is over, you can bring your queen to see mine. After all, they are distantly related."

A hint of a grin curves Varys's mouth. "Be sure to invite us to your bonding ceremony."

I tip up my chin. "I will do that."

Flexing my wings, I lift into the sky and climb high into the clouds. Now that I have spoken to Varys, I cannot get back to my T'kara fast enough. The sooner I successfully woo her, the quicker I can have her in my arms again.

By the wind and the sky, I vow that I will make her my queen before the next moon.

CHAPTER 43

FREYJA

Aurdyn has been gone for hours, and I'm anxious for his return. My nerves are a wreck.

Although Brovyn has assured me many times that the Dark Elves are not a danger to Aurdyn, I cannot stop worrying about him. My entire life, I've heard terrifying things about the Elves and their powerful magic.

Dark clouds gather overhead, and the snow is coming down harder, but I do not want to go back to the castle. Not yet. Hoping to distract myself, I keep practicing wielding my fire magic.

After Aurdyn left, Brovyn led me to the far edge of the training fields. They are near the temple and yet far enough away that we are unlikely to be disturbed. Several warriors spar across the way, but thankfully they seem more concerned with their own training instead of observing mine.

I still feel a bit self-conscious though, and I keep glancing in their direction.

Brovyn follows my line of gaze. "Do not worry about them. They know better than to stare at you."

"What do you mean?" I frown. "Why?"

"You are the T'kara of their king, but you do not yet carry his mark. Until you do, they will take great care to avoid observing you closely, not wanting Aurdyn to see them as potential rivals for the one he desires as his mate."

While this all seems so primitive, I understand that Dragons are not humans. They have their own culture, and much of it is driven by pure instinct, especially when a potential mate is involved.

I probably should not ask, but I need to know. "What sort of mark do Dragons give their mates when they claim them?"

"Dragons mark each other with a bite upon the first mating. It is a claiming mark."

I blink several times as I think back on all the times Aurdyn has bared his fangs. They are razor-sharp. "Is it painful?" I ask, hoping he'll say no.

He shrugs. "I do not know. I have not found a mate yet. But if I do, I will let you know."

Not very helpful right now, but at least he is thoughtful.

Snow falls softly all around us, but my new clothes are warm, and the exertion of practicing with my powers makes me forget the cold.

The memory of Aurdyn leaving floats to the surface of my mind, and I shudder. What if that was the last time I'll ever see him? I force myself to concentrate my fire magic on the painted rock target Brovyn points to.

"I can see the worry in your eyes, Freyja," Brovyn says. "But you have no need to fret. Trust me. Elves know better than to cross a Dragon."

"Dragons and their arrogant natures," I mutter to myself.

Brovyn eyes me speculatively. "Your concern for Aurdyn's safety is like that of a Dragon for her mate."

Before I can respond, he points to another target. Concentrating my powers, I send a ball of fire to the painted rock, watching in triumph as it explodes with a brilliant display.

"Excellent." A faint grin tilts his mouth.

Exhaustion seeps into my bones. I know I should be careful how much magic I use at one time, but I let myself get carried away. "I think I'll practice a bit with my sword and then head back inside. Care to spar?"

He inclines his head. "I will go to the armory and procure a sword."

He leaves, and I begin the precise movements of my practice stances. The first time I saw my instructor demonstrate these, I was mesmerized. It is almost like a dance. Elegant, but lethal.

Focusing on a fixed point before me, I concentrate on the feel of the sword in my hand. The weight and the balance as I move through the practiced motions center me, until my sword is no longer a weapon, but an extension of myself.

Closing my eyes, I gather my power. When I open them, fire licks along the blade.

As I study the dancing flame on the steel, my thoughts turn to my vision, and my impending demise. *Death.* The word weighs heavy on my mind. A risk for anyone that wields a sword or goes to battle. My parents rode off to war and never returned. There are so many things I never got to say to them... things we never got a chance to do.

By concentrating on these memories and my worry for Aurdyn, it somehow helps me to access my magic. Perhaps it is an instinctual response—the desire to protect and defend those I love is the catalyst that sparks the flame deep within. My fear of losing Aurdyn overrides my fear of failure, and it is as if my power senses this, allowing me to bend it to my will.

Despite Brovyn's words earlier, about the other warriors trying to avoid me, I notice dozens of eyes observing me now. It seems my ability to conjure flame upon my sword is too much of a distraction for them to ignore.

As the Princess of Ruhaen, I had to get used to people staring when I would go through my training lessons. As heir to the kingdom, the guards wanted to see their future queen and her skills as a warrior. I suppose it is not any different now, here. Because of the bond, Aurdyn's warriors already consider me their future queen.

If I were not so worried about my arrogant Dragon, I would probably be more nervous about their curious stares.

My heart clenches as I think of him. I pushed Aurdyn away when all I want to do is wrap myself up in his arms and wings. I hurt him and he doesn't know why. There so much left unsaid between us. So much I want to tell him, but I cannot.

The High Priest said we are only given what we need to guide our path, but maybe there is another way. All I know is that I am desperate for him to return. Despite Brovyn's reassurances, the Dark Elves possess dangerous magic, and I will not be happy until I see my grumpy, arrogant Dragon protector again.

And when I do, I will make sure he knows never to leave me behind again.

CHAPTER 44

AURDYN

As soon as I reach the castle, I find Brovyn flying toward the gardens, so I fly up beside him. "Where is Freyja?"

"Nice to see you too." He purses his lips.

I am not in the mood for teasing right now. "Have you seen her?"

"She has been practicing with her fire magic. And now she wishes to spar."

I cannot suppress a growl. "With you?" When he nods, jealous anger grips my chest like an iron vise. Sparring is too similar to the mating battle. I dislike the idea of her training with him.

She should practice with *me*.

"Give me that." I pull the sword from his grip. "If she is going to spar with someone, it will be me. Not you."

He sighs dramatically. "I am not trying to lure her away from you, cousin."

Deep down, I know he would never do this. But I cannot

push down the fierce possessiveness that roars through my veins. Freyja is mine. Even if she does not know it yet.

He leads me through the gardens and toward the back of the training area. What should be a secluded location is full of at least a dozen warriors. Each is observing intently as she moves with lethal grace, wielding a sword with flame licking the blade.

She is truly magnificent and stunning to behold. Primal instincts surge through me, and I growl in warning at my warriors as I pass them to reach her. They all bow in deference. "Leave us," I command, and they all fly away immediately, including Brovyn.

I start toward her, my heart pounding as I approach. She is so lovely it nearly breaks me.

"Freyja," I call her name and her head snaps to me.

She drops her sword and rushes to me, launching herself into my arms. I catch her around the waist and hold her close, reveling in the feel of her body pressed to mine.

"Thank the gods you're all right." She wraps her arms around my neck, hugging me with a strength I'd not thought her people possessed. "I was so worried about you."

I pull back just enough to meet her gaze, frowning. "Do you think me so weak that I could not handle a few pitiful Elves?"

She purses her lips. "I know you are strong. I've never doubted that, Aurdyn."

"Good." I puff up with pride at her words. "And I cannot have my future queen thinking I am weak."

"Aurdyn, I—" she starts, but I put a finger to her lips.

"I will prove myself to you, Freyja." I stare deep into her eyes. "I will show you that I am worthy of you. But until then, there are things I have learned that we must discuss."

Worry mars her features. "What is it? What did you discover?"

"On my way to Ithylian, I saw Prince Aegryn of Kolstrad marching his army to Florin. They were traveling with a Mage and at least a dozen Wraiths in their formation. I believe he was controlling them."

She inhales sharply. "Why would the Mages do this? I don't understand."

"They want power and now they've found a way to take more." I give her a grim look. "I believe they seek to turn the human kingdoms on each other. And once they have conquered and united all the human lands under their absolute rule, they will turn their gaze to the rest of us."

"We must warn my cousin—King Edmynd—before they reach Florin."

"I am sure he is being informed even now as we speak." If Varys wishes to foster his alliance with his new brother-in-law, he probably sent a raven to Florin as soon as I left.

"How do you know this?"

"King Varys has recently taken King Edmynd's sister—your cousin, Inara—as his mate and queen." Her eyes widen. "She is his Fated One, just as you are mine."

"Inara is married to the Dark Elf king?" she asks, distress evident in her features. "How could Edmynd give her over to that monster?" She takes my hand. "Aurdyn, we have to save her. We cannot leave her with him. He'll—"

"Varys is not a monster, and they appear quite taken with each other." Her mouth drifts open, and I cup her cheek. "She was just as worried for you when I told her about us as you are for her right now."

"That's ridiculous." She frowns. "You would *never* hurt me."

Pride fills my chest at her complete trust. "And I can assure you that Varys will not harm her either. She is just as precious to him as you are to me." A pink bloom spreads across her cheeks, and I drop my forehead gently to hers. "I would not have left her with him if I thought otherwise. I told them about Prince Aegryn's army, and I am sure they have already sent a raven to Florin to warn them."

"Thank goodness," she murmurs.

"I also told them about... how we met."

She lowers her gaze, swallowing hard. "Inara... did she know I had been imprisoned? That I'd been accused of witchcraft?"

"She was shocked when I told her."

The tense set of Freyja's shoulders relaxes a bit, telling me she was worried that her cousins may have known of her imprisonment and death sentence. Known and not cared. I am glad to remove that doubt from her.

"There is more." I place two fingers up under her chin, studying her luminous eyes. "Queen Inara has powers similar to your fire magic. It was the same type of magic I've seen Varys wield before. I suspect it results from her fated bond to him, just as your fire magic came from our bond."

"Do the Mages know of Inara's powers?" she asks.

"If they do, neither of them said."

"Will the Dark Elves go to Ithylian's aid?"

"I believe they will. Varys's marriage to Inara was made to broker peace between their kingdoms and foster an alliance."

Her blue eyes meet mine evenly. "Would you help Florin if they asked for your aid?"

It was only a matter of time before she asked this question, and I have been dreading it the entire journey back home. "King Varys and Queen Inara asked me this as well." I rub my temples. "I told them it was not worth risking the lives of my people. My grandfather once trusted a human king, and it nearly led to our ruin. I have always told myself I would never make the same mistake.

"If you had no intention of helping humans, why send

scouts to my uncle's kingdom?" she asks. "Why bother if you never intended to get involved in the first place?"

"That is different." Frustration burns through me as she levels an accusatory gaze at me. Does she not realize that all I have done has been to protect her? In truth, I care not if her uncle's kingdom falls. I only care that she would be upset by it. "We share a border with Ruhaen. I sent scouts to make sure the Order of Mages were not a threat to you, Freyja."

"What about my uncle?" Her eyes search mine. "What about the people of Ruhaen?"

"I will not lie to you, Freyja." I speak slowly. "I will not pretend that any of that matters to me when all I care about is you and this kingdom."

"Are you saying you will not help Ruhaen or Florin if they ask you for aid?" Disappointment flashes in her eyes. "Even when you know that the Mages and Wraiths are not just a threat to them, but to everyone?"

"The entire journey home, all I could think of was you, Freyja. I will do anything to protect you from harm." I take her hand and bring it to my chest. "You are my heart, my T'kara. And I realized you will never be safe so long as the Order of Mages remains." I bare my teeth. "They tried to end you, and now they will know the terrifying horrors of a Dragon's wrath. I will set their bodies ablaze and demolish their temples. And I will not stop until all of them are dead."

CHAPTER 45

FREYJA

Our boot steps echo loudly across the polished stone floor as we enter the throne room. Aurdyn and I are alone. Brovyn is supposed to meet us, but he has yet to arrive.

This is such a large, cavernous space that I wonder if the size is to accommodate the massive four-legged form of Aurdyn's people. Two rows of long stone benches, presumably for people of importance, line either side of the room. Sunlight filters in from a large, glass dome overhead, gilding the two thrones at the far end of the room. The brilliant light glitters on Aurdyn's silver-white scales, lending him an ethereal glow.

We walk toward the thrones, and I marvel at the gorgeous, scrolling design chiseled into the stone, similar to the intertwining patterns that embellish the doors. Each of these elegant lines and images is highlighted with gold that should make the throne appear gaudy, but does not.

The thrones are perfect mirror images of each other in

size, shape, and design. The space between them is perfectly aligned with the main doors so that neither one is more centered than the other. I study it curiously. In Ruhaen, my uncle's throne is much larger and more lavishly decorated than the one beside it, meant for a queen consort when he chooses to wed.

"Which one is yours?" I ask.

Aurdyn leans close and a teasing smirk twists his lips. "If you become my queen, you may have your pick. I do not favor one over the other."

I blink up at him. "Then... whoever you take as your mate would be your equal?"

"Yes." His eyes search mine. "Why does this surprise you?"

"I—I thought it would be like Ruhaen or Florin. Whomever is the ruler, their mate becomes the queen's or king's consort. And in some human kingdoms, only males can inherit the crown."

Aurdyn's head jerks back. "Why only males?"

"There are many, among my kind, who consider men superior to women."

"Why would they believe this? In my experience, human females are far braver, and thus superior to human males."

I cannot help the swell of pride that fills me at his words. A smile tugs at my lips as I think about his meeting with Inara. She's always been very outspoken. "I'm guessing from your statement that Inara was not afraid of you."

"On the contrary. The sour smell of her fear was potent when I first arrived, and yet... if not for this scent, I would never have imagined she was afraid." He gives me a thoughtful look. "She masked it well, and did not hesitate to speak her mind. She reminded me very much of you in this way. Despite what many believe, bravery is not the absence of fear. It is having courage in spite of one's fear."

Behind the throne dais, I notice a long, rectangular stone table. "What is that?"

"Where I hold my council," he says. "It comprises Brovyn —my cousin and advisor—and a representative from each of the seven Great Houses of our people."

"There are seven Great Houses?"

"Ours is the eighth," he replies. I flinch inwardly at how he includes me in this, already considering me part of his Great House, even though I have still not accepted him as my mate.

The sound of the doors swinging open draws our attention as Brovyn walks in. Two guards seal them shut behind him as he walks toward us. He gives us a quick greeting, but doesn't bother with any small chat before getting straight to the business of what he has learned.

"I've spoken with members of each Great House. Three of them strongly agree that we should do whatever we can to stop the Mages, especially if they are using Wraiths as weapons of war." His gaze sweeps to mine. "And they would not be opposed to aiding the human kingdoms in quelling this threat."

"This is good," Aurdyn says, but a deep line of worry still creases his forehead. "But what of the others?"

"They are, as yet, undecided," he replies grimly.

With the others still left to declare where they fall on the issue, Aurdyn might not gain the support he would need to aid Florin or Ruhaen.

"Any word from our scouts in Ruhaen, or from Florin?" Aurdyn asks. "Surely, the raven with Freyja's message has reached King Edmynd by now?"

"Perhaps it has, and he is suspicious," Brovyn opines.

I hate that he's right. But Edmynd would definitely be wary, believing that I am under some sort of distress when I wrote it. "Hopefully, he understood the personal line I wrote at the top of the letter," I offer. "It was a sort of code we all used when we were children."

Brovyn arches a brow. "Which reminds me... I meant to ask, what exactly is a *narwick* mouse?"

I can't stop a laugh. "It's a tiny mouse-like creature that makes a distinct and rather cute cry when it signals its people."

"How did this sound become a code for you?" Aurdyn asks.

"When I'd visit, we would often sneak out of the castle and go on adventures in the gardens and the forests at night." A wistful smile curves my lips at the memories. "We were children, and we would pretend we were in search of gold or treasure, or"—I stop short of saying 'slaying a Dragon,' and instead offer—"riding unicorns.

"Whoever snuck out first would watch for the guards to leave and then they would signal the rest, making a sound like a narwick mouse. That was the all clear to sneak out of the castle so we would not get caught. Like this." I demonstrate the soft sound, and Aurdyn and Brovyn each grin.

"Simple, yet effective. Rather ingenious, to be honest," Brovyn says, and I bask in the praise. "As for our scouts in Ruhaen," he says, his expression falling. "They reported the arrival of at least a dozen Mages, but no Wraiths thus far."

"And my uncle?" I ask. "How is he? Did they see him?"

The look in his eyes makes my stomach drop. "He has fallen ill."

"What?" I ask, unable to hide my panic. "How? What kind of illness?"

"He is too weak to leave his bed most days," he replies. "At least, that is what they've overheard from a few of the castle workers.

I look between the two of them. "They're going to kill him, Aurdyn. We have to do something."

"We will," he reassures me. "I am meeting with the council tomorrow to discuss it." He takes my hands. "In the meantime, I do not believe the Mages will kill him. Not yet, anyway. They need him to act as the figurehead ruler while they work behind the scenes to slowly transition his power to them."

I hope he's right. And I pray the council will agree to drive out the Mages in Ruhaen.

"How do you think the council will vote?" I ask.

Brovyn turns to me. "I'll admit it will be difficult to convince them."

"Why?" I ask. "Ruhaen shares a border with you. If the Mages control the Wraiths, why would they not wish to expel them from my uncle's kingdom?"

"Because they consider it a 'human' problem, not a Dragon one," he points out. "Regardless of the fact that Ruhaen is a neighboring kingdom. Then, there is the matter of your mating, or… absence of it," he says bluntly. "You are not yet queen, and therefore the topic of battling for your people will have to be presented very carefully if we are to gain their support. You are T'kara to our king, but you have not taken him as your mate. If you were a Dragon—"

"Brovyn," Aurdyn issues a warning growl, but Brovyn only scowls at him. "She must hear the truth of things so that she understands the workings of the council and your people."

Aurdyn curls his lip, but I put a hand on his arm, drawing his attention back to me. "Brovyn's right. I need to know this, Aurdyn." I look at Brovyn. "Continue."

He gives me a quick nod. "Many do not understand why you have not taken Aurdyn as your mate. Among our kind, any who find their T'kara take them immediately and without question. They usually issue the challenge of the mating battle within an hour of this discovery." He pauses. "Thus… they do not understand your hesitation."

From the look Aurdyn gives me, he obviously does not understand either. I hate that I cannot tell him the truth. No matter how much I may wish to.

* * *

WHEN WE RETURN to our rooms, Aurdyn leads me into the enchanted garden. He takes my hands as soon as we're inside. He studies me momentarily before sighing heavily. "My aid for your family does not come with the condition that you must be my mate and my queen. I will make sure my council understands this tomorrow, when they make their decision."

Tears sting my eyes as I realize he is not just saying this to make sure I'm not pressured, but because he worries that I might choose him, thinking it's the only way to save my people.

Gently, I squeeze his hands in return. "And I would never use you as a means to an end, Aurdyn. I—" I start but stop to clear my throat. "You are so very important to me, and I…" My voice quavers softly. "I am so afraid I will lose you."

His brow furrows deeply and his gaze holds mine, full of confusion. "You desire me as yours. I know you do. And yet… you deny this to both yourself and to me," he whispers. "Why? What have I done wrong?"

"Nothing."

"Then what is it?" Frustration laces his tone. "Tell me."

"I cannot," I state firmly.

"Why?"

Emotions lodge in my throat, but I somehow speak around them. "Do not ask me again."

He stiffens and then, without warning, spins around and

lifts into the air, flying through the magical barrier above, and into the night sky.

"Aurdyn!" I call, but he is already gone.

Anger wars with sadness, and I dig my nails into my palms as I make my decision. I must return to the heart tree. I need to know why I cannot speak the truth to Aurdyn. And it had better give me a bloody good answer, because I'm tired of hurting him.

Wrapping my fur cloak tightly around me, I pull my hood up and stalk through the castle and out into the gardens, following the long path to the temple nearby.

I do not care how late it is. I need answers, and I need them tonight.

CHAPTER 46

FREYJA

The full moon shines brightly overhead, casting a silver glow over the temple. The heart tree stands tall and proud in the center. The wind catches the delicate leaves as they fall, swirling and dancing around the columns before gently landing on the snowy ground below.

My boots crunch quietly over the light layer of snow blanketing the earth as I walk up the steps to the tree. Standing before it, I gaze up at the long, bending branches that hang down as if to shelter me from the outside world.

Cautiously, I place my hand on the dark trunk, and soft light begins to glow beneath the bark, tracing a pattern around my hand before twining its way up, spreading out over the branches and leaves. Warmth fills my body like a soothing balm.

I blink and a woman comes into focus, standing before me. Her long white hair flows down her back in soft waves. White lashes frame lavender eyes as she studies me. Her skin glimmers an unnatural shade of silver that is almost too bright to look at.

"Who are you?" I ask.

"I am the spirit of the heart tree," her voice whispers in my mind, as her lips remain unmoving. *"Why have you come to me?"*

"I wish to ask about the vision you showed me." She watches me in silence, and I continue. "What did you show King Aurdyn? Because he could not have seen the same future I did. If he had... he would understand why I push him away."

"I showed him what he needed to guide his path, just as I showed you," she replies cryptically.

"But why can I not speak of it? Why must I keep it secret?" A tear slides down my cheek, but I brush it away impatiently. "I love Aurdyn, and my silence is hurting him because he does not know why I cannot—" my voice breaks. My throat is thick as I draw in a shaking breath. "If I told him what I saw, maybe we could avoid it entirely. And both of us could live."

Her expression softens into pity. *"Each of the sanishon in the prophecy of the Great Uniters will be called upon to make an enormous sacrifice."* She reaches out and delicately lifts a long tendril of my hair, allowing it to slip through her fingers. *"I thought allowing you to see the sacrifice you will make was a kindness, not so that you could push away your Fated One, but so that you could hold him close and draw upon the strength of your union when the time comes for you to make that choice."* She pauses. *"If he knew what was to come, he would do everything in his power to keep it from unfolding, and in doing so, he could unravel the very fate of your world."*

"But how can I give myself to him and take him as my mate, knowing that I will die? How would that be fair to him?"

"All mortal creatures die," she replies impassively. *"It is the way of things. I am not mortal, but I understand how upsetting death is to your kind. The last king,"* she says, and I realize she is speaking of Aurdyn's father, *"came to me after the death of his mate. He lamented all the things he would have said to her, had he known what was coming."*

I blink several times. "Are you saying you gave me this knowledge so that I could face my fate with no regrets?"

She gives a subtle nod. *"Of the two of you, I knew you would accept your fate, whereas Aurdyn would rage against it."* A faint smile tilts her lips. *"It is his... arrogant nature, as you call it."*

Despite my sadness, a short puff of laughter escapes me. She's right. That is who he is. My wonderful, arrogant Dragon.

"May I ask one more thing?"

She gestures for me to continue.

"Will my death be painful?"

"I do not know," she says, and I'm completely taken aback.

"How can you not—"

"The thread of fate that is woven through each mortal life is part of a complicated tapestry of every life that it touches and is touched by in return. I am not the weaver. I am merely one of the few allowed to view the pattern on the loom." She touches my face, brushing away a stray tear. *"Return to your Dragon and live a life with no regret."*

I blink and I'm still standing by the tree, with my hand on the trunk. Tears continue to flow down my cheeks as I pull away, staring down at the snow.

I've wasted so much time pushing Aurdyn away. I've hurt him and I hate myself for it. Balling my hands into fists, I draw in a shaking breath. I don't want to waste another precious moment with him, for I do not know how many I have left.

CHAPTER 47

AURDYN

nger and frustration battle within me as I soar above the castle in my Draken form. The deep stretch of my wings as I ride the current, catching the wind in the large sails, is a welcome distraction.

There is something about this form that calls to me. It is always ready just beneath the surface, like a dark and primal thing waiting to be freed. I dip my left wing and make a slow arc over the sleeping city below.

A few guards circle the outskirts, scanning the area for any sign of danger. They are one of many patrols that I have ordered to guard our city and our borders. If the Mages try to invade, they will not catch us unprepared.

Cringing slightly, I think back on my conversation with Freyja. I should not have left as I did. She is hiding something from me, but in this form, I am able to read some of her thoughts. Perhaps if I were close enough, I could...

I force myself to stop this line of thinking. She has expressed her discomfort with this ability. Before, it was an accident, but to do this now, deliberately, would be a violation of her mind. And that is something I will not do. I will not force her to share her secrets, whatever they may be.

My thoughts return to the vision of our son, given to me by the heart tree. That is the only thing I cannot speak of. When I saw our future, I have never felt so much joy. But what if she saw something different?

The High Priest said the visions we receive are a guide from the heart tree to direct our path.

Suddenly, all of the pieces fall into place. How could I have been such a fool? The answers I seek lie with the heart tree. I am sure of it.

I flap my wings furiously as I veer toward the temple. It is late, but I care not. I will wait no more for my answers.

When I get closer to the temple, I shift into my two-legged form. I do not want to wake the priests and priestesses by landing in my larger Draken form. Quietly, I descend through the trees just outside the temple.

A cool breeze blows through the structure, and I freeze when I detect Freyja's distinct scent. My nostrils flare when I pick up the subtle, saline scent of her tears. My cheeks burn when I realize that I have caused her such pain.

Inwardly cursing myself, I climb the steps of the temple and see her standing by the heart tree. Her back is to me, and as I approach, she spins and gasps when her eyes meet mine.

Upset that I startled her, I start to apologize. "Freyja, I—"

My words are cut off as she rushes forward and launches herself into my arms. I catch her, wrapping my arms solidly around her form. "Aurdyn," she breathes against my neck as she holds me tight.

"What are you doing here?" I pull back just enough to study her face. I cup her chin and brush away her tears with my thumb. "Why are you crying?"

"I needed answers," her voice quavers. "I came to speak with the heart tree."

My gaze shifts to the tree, and my body tenses. I was right. "What did you see in your vision the other day?"

"You know I cannot speak of it, just as you cannot tell me either."

This confirms my suspicions. The problem between us is this gods-forsaken tree. Not me.

Instead of asking again what she saw, I pose a different question. "Do you want a future with me?"

Her tear-filled gaze holds mine as she cups my cheek. "More than anything."

Happiness brighter than the very sun itself fills my chest, and I crush my lips to hers, kissing her deeply. When I finally draw back, her entire face is flushed, and she is breathless and panting.

The desire to claim her is a fire deep within, and I am desperate to make her mine. I pull her tight to my chest and lift off into the sky, flying us back to the castle. She gives a sharp cry of surprise as I drop toward the barrier over the enchanted garden, extending my wings at the last moment to halt our descent before I carefully land and then carry her to my bed.

Need inflames my senses as I lay her down on the furs and crawl over her. I wrap my tail around her ankle and gently guide her legs apart as I settle between them. She gasps as I roll my hips against hers, my stav fully extended and painfully erect with the desire to join our bodies as one.

I push up on my elbows and stare down at her as I pull at her clothing, but she places a hand on my chest, and I still. "What is wrong?" I ask, worried that perhaps I am moving too fast. Maybe she is not ready to fully mate just yet.

"What about the mating battle?" she asks breathlessly. "Is

that not what we are supposed to do, according to your traditions?"

This wonderfully perfect female beneath me. How did I ever become so blessed?

"I cannot fight you in the mating battle, Freyja."

"Why not?" Pain and rejection flash briefly across her features, so I rush to explain.

"I cannot fight you because I have already lost." I reach down and touch her lovely face, staring deep into her luminous gaze. "You have conquered me, my T'kara. My heart surrendered to yours long before now."

"My heart is yours, Aurdyn." Her eyes fill with emotion. "I love you. More than anything."

"Tell me," I whisper against her skin as I press a series of kisses down her neck to her chest. Using my claws, I slice a line down her clothing, leaving her bare to my touch and my gaze. "Tell me you are mine." I trace my tongue along the soft mound of her breast. Her entire body is so soft and giving.

She sucks in a sharp breath as I swipe my tongue over the stiffened peak, and my eyes flick up to meet hers. "Are you mine to claim?"

"Yes," she breathes.

Holding her gaze, I close my mouth over her breast and lave my tongue over the sensitive tip as she arches up into me. I did not give this part of her the proper attention the last time I pleasured her, and now I will remedy that.

I cup my other hand over the opposite breast, tenderly kneading her soft flesh as she moans beneath me.

As I move down her body, I worship her with my lips and my tongue, tasting the sweet salt of her skin. When I reach the juncture of her legs, I slide my hand up her inner thigh, opening her to me.

I dip my head between her thighs and when my tongue

touches her, she gasps and tries to close her legs around my head. "What are you doing?"

I lift my head, frowning. "Pleasuring you with my tongue."

"I—I've never done any of this before." A pink bloom spreads across her cheeks as she stumbles over her words. "I have heard many things about coupling, but I did not know that this was something men did."

Pleased at the reminder that no man has ever touched her, I want to roar with possessiveness. "I am not a man." A deep growl builds in the back of my throat. "I am a Dragon. And Dragons always pleasure their mates."

"Always?" she asks, a faint teasing grin on her lips despite her shyness.

I move my tail up from her ankle to her knee and gently open her legs a bit more. I guide first one and then the other over my shoulders. "Always," I growl. Her gaze holds mine as I drop my head between her legs and drag my tongue through her slick folds.

A low moan escapes her as I concentrate on the small pearl of flesh at the apex, softly applying pressure with my lips and my tongue.

"Right there." She digs her heels into my shoulders as she writhes beneath me.

I band an arm across her waist, holding her in place as I continue my ministrations. I am desperate to be inside her, but her taste is exquisite, and I love all the small sounds she makes as I give her pleasure, so I am not ready to stop. Not until she cries out my name as she finds her pleasure.

"This feels so good," she breathes.

I bask in the knowledge that I am pleasing my mate. I want her addicted to this—to my touch—because I plan to take her every night for the rest of our lives.

Her entire body tenses a moment before my name rips

from her throat and she floods my tongue with the sweet nectar of her release.

I slide up her body, sealing my lips over hers. When I lean back, her eyes are wide with desire. Desperate to fully claim her, I start to roll her onto her stomach, but she puts a hand on my chest to stop me.

Worry fills me, and I wonder if she has changed her mind. Perhaps she does not want me as her mate after all.

"I want to stay like this," she whispers. "I want to see your face while we make love the first time."

Although I have never mated before, when we learn about coupling, we are taught that the proper position is from behind. But perhaps that is because the mating battle is usually violent. As I stare down at my T'kara, I am glad we did not battle. I dislike the idea of trying to conquer her when all I want to do is worship her body.

"As you wish, my beautiful fire heart."

I lean down and press my lips to hers, and she opens herself even more to me, cradling my hips between her thighs.

I notch the tip of my stav at her entrance and stare deep into her eyes as I slowly push inside her.

CHAPTER 48

FREYJA

Tight heat blooms in my core as Aurdyn slowly enters me. I bite back a gasp as he pushes through my barrier. With each roll of his hips, my body relaxes at the invasion as he carefully advances.

"You're so tight," he rasps.

I wince slightly and he stills, gritting his teeth as if it is taking every bit of his concentration to maintain his control.

"Are you all right?"

"I just need a moment to adjust," I whisper.

He drops a series of tender kisses on my lips, cheeks, and brow as my body adjusts to the fullness inside me.

A small burst of warmth deep in my core turns my discomfort to pleasure. "What was that?"

"It is some of my essence to soften your womb so your body will accept my seed."

I do not point out that it is unlikely we can even have children because we are different species. Instead, I simply allow myself to dream of a future with my Dragon.

I arch up into him, and he begins to stroke deep inside me. Shivers wash over me as the ridges of his length create a delicious friction in my channel.

I run my hands down his back, feeling the muscles of his powerful form beneath the tips of my fingers with each flex of his hips into mine. I'm completely lost in sensation, and it's all I can do to hold on as he quickens his pace and each stroke becomes deeper and more intense. The world falls away until nothing exists outside of the joining of our bodies.

Aurdyn growls as another burst of warmth blooms inside me, and I moan at the delicious sensation.

He presses my hands to the mattress on either side of my head, lacing our fingers together as his eyes remain locked on mine and he continues to move deep inside me. He wraps his wings around me, holding me close.

It's too much and not enough all at once, and I thrust up into each stroke of his body against mine as we balance on the edge of a precipice.

The fullness inside me expands almost to the point of pain, but not quite. "What's happening?" I whisper.

"My knot," he rasps.

The fullness turns to pleasure as it locks him in place. Each movement of his hips to mine is so intense I can barely catch my breath. I feel another small burst of warmth that makes my channel quiver and flex around his length.

My entire body goes taut and then I'm coming so hard I see stars behind my vision as waves of pleasure crash through me, and I cry out his name.

I'm so lost in my pleasure, I barely feel the sharp sting of his fangs against my neck as he marks me as his mate. I cling to him as a deep growl vibrates his chest, and he pulses strongly in my channel.

"Mine!" he cries out as intense heat floods my core. His

release triggers another orgasm deep inside me, this one even more intense than the last, and we fall over the edge together as he fills me with his seed.

He rolls us onto our sides as he nuzzles my face and my neck, leaving soft kisses along my skin as we remained joined by his knot.

My entire body is tingling and when he begins to rock his hips into mine again, pleasure builds once more. He kisses me passionately. "I will take you many times this night," he whispers against my skin, and I smile as he rolls me beneath him.

CHAPTER 49

AURDYN

Freyja is asleep against my chest. My tail is still curled around her ankle, and I tighten my wings around her body, holding her close. I breathe deeply of our combined scent. I love that she smells so strongly of me.

A rumbling growl reverberates in my chest as I study her face. She is so lovely and soft; I am already addicted to touching her. I smooth a hand down her body, resting it lightly over her abdomen, wondering if my seed is already quickening in her womb.

She is perfect, my beautiful mate.

Her eyelids flutter open, and she looks up at me with a soft smile. She shifts against me, wincing slightly. Worry fills me, and I rub her back. "Did I hurt you?"

"No," she whispers, pulling my lips to hers in a tender kiss. "I'm just a bit sore." She gives me another sleepy smile. "After all, I was thoroughly claimed and pleasured by my Dragon husband."

Masculine pride fills me at her words, and I run my

fingers through her thick red hair and tip her face up to mine, sealing my mouth over hers.

"Make love to me again, Aurdyn," she whispers as she pulls me over her.

Desire flares inside me, and I notch my stav at the entrance to her core, desperate to be inside her again. But a loud knock at the door startles us both.

"What is it?" I snarl, angered by the interruption.

"I would not have disturbed you, cousin." Brovyn's muffled voice floats through the door. "But the Dwarf King Davin is here."

I instantly stand from the bed. "Our guards captured him?" I call through the door.

Brovyn hesitates a beat before answering. "No."

Alarm ripples down my spine, along with fierce protectiveness, as I look at Freyja, staring up at me with wide eyes. I pull up two large furs to cover her body. "Wait here."

I stalk to the door and yank it open, glaring at Brovyn. "What do you mean, he was not captured?" I growl. "How did he get here?"

"He tunneled."

Blood pounds in my ears. "Where exactly are these tunnels?" I grit through my fangs. I will burn that miserable Dwarf for daring to invade my kingdom. His tunnels could put my T'kara's safety in jeopardy.

Brovyn opens his mouth to answer, but his nostrils flare and he jerks his head back slightly. "You are mated now?"

I straighten, tipping up my chin. "Freyja has accepted me as hers."

He claps a hand on my shoulder. "Congratulations. I will arrange for the mating celebration at once."

"Good." I crack my knuckles. "We will start by setting fire to the Dwarf."

CHAPTER 50

FREYJA

"**H**ave King Davin dragged to the throne room," Aurdyn grinds out. "I will be there shortly."

He slams the door shut and spins back to me. "Wait here, where it is safe, while I deal with this Dwarf." His lips curl up in distaste as he practically spits out the words. He crosses the room in five steps and sits on the edge of the bed. Cupping my chin, he rests his forehead on mine. "I will return to you as soon as I have dealt with this."

"I'm going with you," I state firmly.

"You heard Brovyn. The Dwarves tunneled here. And until we seal those tunnels, the safety of our city is compromised. For all we know, he could be working with the Mages to—"

"King Davin would no sooner work with the Mages than you or I would." Of all the ridiculous conclusions he could jump to, this one is beyond belief. "If the Dwarf king came here, there must be another reason."

Aurdyn narrows his eyes. "He could have sent a raven or

287

alerted one of our guards at the border that he wished an audience, but instead he tunneled through our mountain, creating a vulnerability in our defenses."

I understand why Aurdyn is upset. When this happened before, his father's enemy used the tunnels to steal his mother, and she was murdered shortly after. Knowing how his father responded, I doubt the Dwarves would risk tunneling again without good reason. "Perhaps what the king has to say, he needs to say in person," I offer.

"Then he could ask for a meeting."

"Has he done that before?"

"Yes, but I... refused," he reluctantly admits, and I purse my lips.

"Well, now you have your answer. He is desperate to speak with you. Desperate enough that he risked your wrath to gain an audience with you."

"Maybe," Aurdyn grumbles. "Still... he should know better. It is no small thing to jeopardize the safety of a Dragon's mate."

He tugs me to him and nuzzles my hair.

"Does this mean you will not set him on fire?"

"I make no promises," he grumbles.

I suppose that's better than nothing.

* * *

WHEN WE REACH the throne room, Aurdyn motions for me to sit beside him. When I hesitate, he frowns. "Do you prefer this chair instead?"

"No, I just... are you sure you wish me to sit beside you?" We may be mated, but it is recent, and I'm not sure what his people's protocol is for crowning a new monarch. "I have not been officially crowned."

"I will always want you by my side, Freyja. You have

chosen me as your mate." Male satisfaction shines in his eyes. "And when our people see you on the throne, they will know that you are my queen."

As I take the seat on the left, his gaze holds mine, full of pride and devotion. We sit side by side as the large double doors open. Indignant shouts of profanity laced with venom and ice echo throughout the space as two Dragon guards drag King Davin, kicking and cursing, to the throne and dump him unceremoniously at the bottom of the raised dais.

Davin springs to his feet, slapping at his clothes to brush them off before pulling at the edge of his tunic to straighten it. His entire face is beet red, from the tips of his pointed ears to his slightly bulbous nose, as he looks daggers at Aurdyn. Baring his teeth, he points a stern finger. "Never in all our history together have I ever been treated like this!" he snarls. "I am king of the Dwarves, and I have been insulted and mistreated at the hands of those brutes you call guards. If this is how you treat your guests, it's no wonder nobody likes Dragons! I—"

"Enough!" Aurdyn's ferocious roar fills the chamber. His eyes burn with rage as he slowly stands from his chair and prowls toward King Davin like a predator stalking its prey.

And King Davin, despite all his previous bluster, gapes up at Aurdyn like a hare about to be eaten by a wolf.

"You tunneled through my mountain, invading my territory," Aurdyn seethes. "And you expect me to welcome you as an honored guest? I should torch you where you stand."

All the color drains from Davin's face. "I—I can always sing the stones back into place and refill the tunnels. But I needed to speak with you. I—"

"Then you should have sent a raven." He plants his feet wide as dark smoke puffs from his nostrils.

"You ignored my last one," Davin retorts. "And I couldn't risk my message not reaching your ears."

"And just what exactly was so important that you would risk your life by incurring my wrath?"

"The Mages are behind the Wraith attacks on my people," he says. "They are controlling them somehow… using them to wage war."

"I know," Aurdyn replies harshly.

"You—you know?" Davin asks incredulously.

"Yes, the Mages ride with Wraiths and an army from Kolstrad. They are marching toward Florin as we speak."

"Florin?" the king blinks several times. "If what you say is true, then we've got bigger troubles than I thought."

"Why?" Aurdyn asks.

"Ruhaen has declared war on my kingdom. They have allied with the Mages who are controlling the Wraiths," he explains. "They are marching to Arganth right now."

"What of my uncle?" I ask, since we've had little word from Aurdyn's scouts. "Is he—"

"The king of Ruhaen is under a dark spell, Princess." My throat tightens as King Davin gives me a pitying look. "I do not believe he realizes they are using him to wage war."

"You will address her as queen," Aurdyn corrects him, and Davin's eyes widen.

"You—you've taken a human as your—"

"Freyja is my mate and my queen, and you will address her as such," he snarls.

Davin practically stumbles forward, bowing hastily before me. "Forgive me, Queen Freyja." He swallows thickly. "I—I meant no offense."

I give Aurdyn a pointed look, letting him know he is being much too hard on the Dwarf, and his lips curl up in a slight smirk.

I turn my attention back to King Davin. "None taken, King Davin," I reassure him. "You could not have known the change in my status, as you have only just arrived."

His eyes shine, probably relieved that the chances of Aurdyn actually setting him on fire are much less now. "Thank you, Queen Freyja."

"I came to ask for your aid, King Aurdyn," Davin adds. "Their army will arrive in Arganth in less than a week."

I turn to Aurdyn. "The Mages are trying to divide us. That's why they are attacking both Florin and Arganth now with their armies."

Aurdyn exchanges a worried glance with me. He knows I am right. We cannot help both kingdoms; we can only choose one. And Aurdyn has not yet even had a chance to speak with the council.

King Davin looks up at Aurdyn. "You know how proud we Dwarves are." He slowly lowers himself to one knee. "But I will bend the knee if that's what it takes to gain your help, Dragon King. I am not ashamed to bow before you and beg for the sake of my people."

"Rise," Aurdyn says, and the king slowly gets to his feet. "Our people are not friends, but neither are we enemies. Besides, why would I care to rule over a kingdom of unruly Dwarves?"

One of the guards snorts before quickly clearing his throat and standing to attention at his post.

King Davin looks up at Aurdyn, a gleam in his eyes. "What would you say to an alliance, then?" He pauses. "If you do not help us, and my kingdom falls, King Aurdyn, I am certain the Mages will set their eye on you next."

"I will speak with my council, and you will have my decision before the end of the day."

A wide grin splits Davin's face, but Aurdyn jabs a finger at him, and his expression falls again. "But you will sing those stones back into place immediately, sealing off the tunnel you carved out to get here."

Davin dips his chin in a quick nod.

"And the next time you need to speak with me, either send a raven or alert one of my guards at the border," he demands. "Do you understand?"

"Completely," Davin responds. "I will get to work on the stones right away." He pauses. "But I'll need your guards to release the Dwarves that came with me."

Aurdyn's gaze sweeps to the guards. "Release them, but watch them closely. See to it that no trace of the tunnel remains when they're done."

The guards start to guide King Davin out of the throne room, but halt when I call out his name. "King Davin?"

He turns back to face me, bowing again. "Yes, Queen Freyja?"

"Have you already evacuated the families from Arganth?"

His expression softens. "I thank you for your concern, my lady. The children are being evacuated even now."

The moment he leaves, Aurdyn turns to Brovyn. "Contact the council. Get them here immediately."

CHAPTER 51

FREYJA

I sit at the head of the table beside Aurdyn as we wait for his council. Brovyn sits on his left. The doors open and High Priest Arkon, along with seven other Dragons, walks in.

Arkon bows low before taking the seat closest to mine, and the other Dragons do as well.

Their scales range from green and obsidian to silver, gray, and red.

"We congratulate you on your new mating," the one with green scales and lavender eyes says.

"Thank you, Lord Straikyn," Aurdyn replies before introducing me to each of them.

I make a note of each name, along with which of the seven other Great Houses they belong to, repeating them in my mind to commit them to memory.

I am surprised there is no malice or disgust in their eyes, even though I am human. I worried they would resist having me as their queen, but it seems I was wrong.

Aurdyn explains the situation as we know it from King Davin, as well as what he witnessed with the Wraiths accompanying Prince Aegryn's army as it marched toward Florin.

When he proposes that we not only aid the Dwarves, but help my uncle to retake Ruhaen, Straikyn looks to me. "Your uncle tried to burn you at the stake, my Queen. His own flesh and blood."

I return his gaze steadily. "I can assure you, Lord Straikyn, my uncle would never have done this on his own. The Mages have my uncle under a dark enchantment. He knows not what he does. And if we allow them to keep a foothold in Ruhaen, they will only gather strength along our shared border."

"She is right," Aurdyn adds. "Ruhaen and the Dwarf kingdom both border ours. If we do not stop them now and expel them from both kingdoms, it is only a matter of time before they launch another attack. The Mages want power. And the way they seek to achieve it is through war."

One of the other Dragons—Lady Mathryn—leans in, her eyes blazing as she surveys everyone seated. "And let us not forget that they sent assassins to kill our king and queen." She turns to me and Aurdyn. "Our House stands with yours, King Aurdyn, and Queen Freyja—T'kara of our leader and sanishon of the Ancient Tomes of the Lythyrian."

High Priest Arkon looks at Lord Straikyn and the rest. "If any here doubt that this path is the right course, know that the heart tree confirmed that our queen is indeed one of the sanishons of the prophecy."

Brovyn stands and addresses the ladies and lords of the seven other Great Houses. "Is there any House that will not stand with our king and queen to take down the Order of Mages?"

Everyone remains silent.

Aurdyn stands beside him. "Gather your warriors. We go to war."

CHAPTER 52

AURDYN

Freyja went with Brovyn to send another raven to
Florin, informing her cousin of the situation here. I
know she wishes we could send aid to their kingdom, but we cannot split our forces. Fighting a war on two
fronts would leave us too vulnerable.

I descend into the tunnel dug by the Dwarves and stalk
toward King Davin. The other Dwarves immediately drop
what they are doing to form a tight semi-circle behind him, as
if they would be any match for my fire if I meant to harm him.

"How soon will this be done?" I ask, gesturing to the area
they've already begun to close.

"A few hours," he replies warily. "Any faster and we risk
the stones not fusing together properly."

I've heard stories of how the Dwarves sing to stones to
move them, but I have never seen it done. I motion with my
hand, telling them to continue.

He turns and instructs his people to begin. Their voices

are low and deep as they sing in their language. And I observe in awe as the stones begin to move and pack tightly together.

After a few minutes, Davin turns to me. "Will you help us?"

"On two conditions."

"Ah." He paces a few steps. "I knew I shouldn't have offered you my kingdom. You've changed your mind now, haven't you?"

"I meant it when I said I have no desire to preside over unruly Dwarves."

His shoulders sag as if in relief. "Thank the gods for that," he murmurs. "I was not looking forward to leading a rebellion to take it all back."

I take a threatening step closer, and he holds out his hands in mock surrender. "Forgive me." He grins. "It was a poorly made joke."

I do not find it funny, and I doubt he was joking.

"What are the conditions?" he asks a bit warily.

"You will make no more black arrows," I state firmly. "I will not aid you only to have you turn around and mine the ore that will be used against my people."

He grits his teeth, then nods. "Fine. You have my word. And the second condition?"

"I need armor."

His head jerks back. "Why on earth would a Dragon need armor when you have scales?"

"Not for me, for my mate."

A line creases his brow. "You mean to take her to war?"

"I may not have a choice."

"What do you mean?" He looks confused. "Why would you not have a choice?"

"My mate is very… stubborn," I finally admit. "I will try to convince her to remain behind, but I already know her. She will insist upon going into battle."

"Sounds like you've found a good one then." A mischievous grin lights his face. "Just like my Elsie. There is nothing I can deny that woman. That's why I married her, you know." He winks at me. "The stubborn ones are the best. All that fire and passion... it makes for an interesting life."

He claps a hand on my shoulder. "When this is all over, I think we should get together for a dinner. It sounds like the two of us have more in common than I thought."

I enunciate each word carefully. "Remove your hand from my shoulder or I'll remove it from your arm."

"All right," he harrumphs. "No need to be touchy. I was just trying to be friendly, you know."

Before I can respond, Freyja walks up. "There you are." She smiles at me and it as if the very sun itself is present in this tunnel. She loops her arm through mine and turns to Davin. "How soon do you think you'll be done?"

Davin's cheeks flush red at her smile, and I want to rip out his eyes for even looking at her.

Noticing my glare, he puts his hands out again. "Calm yourself. I'm not making eyes at your mate, Dragon King. I have a mate of my own, remember?" He clears his throat and speaks to Freyja. "Which reminds me... Aurdyn was telling me about you, and it sounds like you and my Elsie would get along well. I thought we might have you over for a dinner when this is all over."

"We'd be delighted," Freyja says. When I growl low in my throat, she elbows me and gives me a hard look. "Wouldn't we, Aurdyn?"

I huff out a frustrated breath and deliberately bare my fangs when I smile. "Indeed."

"You said you were already moving the children to safety,"

Freyja changes the subject as she addresses Davin. "Will you be able to get them all away in time?"

"That is my hope," he says.

She turns to me. "What if we sent some of our warriors to help? Surely, they could get all the children out in time."

My mate has such a tender heart. "Of course." I turn to a guard behind me. "Assemble twenty of our warriors to go to Arganth and help relocate the Dwarf children to safety."

"Yes, my King." He bows low and then leaves to relay my order.

Davin gawks at me in disbelief, but I ignore him as Freyja stretches up on her toes and wraps her arms around my neck. She presses her lips to mine in a tender kiss.

"Seven hells," King Davin mutters and looks at Freyja. "You've managed to thaw the ice-cold heart of a Dragon."

"Leave us," I hiss. "Before I change my mind and set fire to your hair."

"Just my hair?" He grins and winks at me again. "You are a changed Dragon indeed, King Aurdyn."

* * *

WHEN THE DWARVES finish resealing the tunnel, Freyja and I return to our rooms. We barely make it inside the door before I push her against the wall and fuse my lips to hers.

She wraps her arms around my neck and her legs around my waist as I breathe between kisses. "I have longed for you all day, my T'kara."

Desperate to be inside her, I swiftly remove her boots and leggings. I push her tunic dress up around her waist and then line myself up with her entrance.

She moans as I sink deep into her warm, wet heat, reveling in the tight clasp of her channel around my length. Supporting her backside with one hand, I tuck my wings around her to provide a cushion against the wall as I tangle my free hand in her luxuriant hair and tilt her head up to mine.

I stare deep into her half-lidded eyes as I thrust up into her. A deep growl vibrates in my chest as she breathes my name out like a prayer.

She clutches me, and I quicken my pace as I move deep inside her. A tingling sensation begins in my lower back as my knot expands, locking us together. Her channel ripples around my length before clamping down hard. She cries out and a loud roar rips from my throat as I erupt deep inside her, flooding her with my seed.

We're still knotted together as she relaxes against me, and I carefully carry her to the bed and lay us both down beneath the furs.

As she lies in my arms, I gently nuzzle her hair, breathing in her lovely scent. I want so much for her to stay here, where she is safe, but I doubt she will agree. Still… I must try.

"Freyja?" I whisper, and she opens her eyes and gives me a sleepy smile.

"Yes, my Dragon?"

"Your Dragon?"

She grins. "Yes, my wonderful, arrogant Dragon king." She presses her lips to my own and whispers against them. "You are mine."

I cannot deny how much her words please me to no end. I smile smugly at her claiming of me, and I have to have her again. But first…

"I want you to stay here."

Her expression falls. "No. My place is by your side, Aurdyn. I will not be left behind."

"Freyja, please. I—"

"I was a shield-maiden of Ruhaen before I became your wife. I am a warrior in my own right," she states firmly. "And

I believe the gods gifted me fire magic for a reason, and it was not to stay behind while you fight." She frowns. "My parents left me behind and they never returned, Aurdyn. It will not happen again. I want to fight by your side and protect you." Her eyes blaze. "Is that not my right as your queen? If I were a Dragon, it would not even be a discussion. It would be understood that—"

I seal my mouth over hers, cutting off the rest of her sentence. When I pull back, I drop my forehead gently to her own. "I do not wish to argue with you, Freyja. I will not force you to remain behind, my fire heart, but I would ask one thing."

"What is it?"

"That you remain close to me during the battle. I will not be able to concentrate if I do not know where you are."

She nods against me. "All right, my Dragon. I will do that."

I pull her to my chest, wrapping my arms and wings tightly around her as she drifts off to sleep. Although I hate the idea of taking Freyja to war, I trust the vision I received from the heart tree. And as I close my eyes, I imagine our future together before falling asleep.

CHAPTER 53

FREYJA

When I wake in the morning, I'm still wrapped up in Aurdyn's arms and wings. His tail is curled around my thigh and as I shift slightly, he tugs me close to his chest, nuzzling my hair in his sleep.

As I nestle into him, I sigh and imagine mornings like this one. A future stretched out before us of love and laughter and quiet moments like these.

A life that will not be.

I bite my lip and blink to hold back tears. I'm not ready yet. I want more time with my Dragon king.

His eyes snap open and meet mine. Worry flashes behind them as he hugs me close. "What is wrong?"

"I—" I hate lying to him, but if I tell him the truth, he'll find a way to keep me here, far away from the battle when he needs me. "I was just thinking of my uncle." It's not a complete lie. In truth, I was, but not right at this moment. "I worry for him."

"We will free him from the Mages, Freyja."

He sounds so confident it gives me hope. I just pray to the gods that I live long enough to see him freed of their dark enchantment. My uncle is a good man, and he deserves so much better than this.

I dress in my warm leggings and fur-lined tunic dress and boots. I sheathe my sword at my side and move to grasp my shield, but Aurdyn takes it for me. We move to the door, and I turn, casting one more glance around our room, committing it to memory.

I know I will not return here. Swallowing the lump in my throat, I turn around and step into the hallway. I loop my arm through Aurdyn's and we stride through the castle and down to the gardens.

Dozens of warriors line up in formation before us, each in their massive Draken form as they await our arrival.

Aurdyn releases my arm and steps away, transforming in a whirlwind of snow into his four-legged form. He stands behind me, his two front legs on either side as he looms overhead. His large claws dig into the snow as he addresses his people.

"We offer no mercy to the Mages," his voice booms above me. "They tried to assassinate myself and your queen. We will rid Arganth and Ruhaen of their foul presence, and we will not rest until they are exterminated."

The warriors' loud battle cries echo through the gardens.

Aurdyn's giant front paw wraps around me, and he carries me against his chest. Snow dances on the frigid wind as he extends his wings and leaps into the air.

The ground disappears below us, and the others follow in formation.

"Are you warm enough?" His voice rumbles in my mind.

My heart stutters. With all that has happened, I forgot he can read some of my thoughts. I know the heart tree created a barrier so that he cannot see my vision, but I still worry.

Concentrating, I partition my mind, closing off the things I do not wish to share. It is difficult, but the technique is taught to every shield-maiden of Ruhaen.

To fight, one must be able to focus, banishing any thoughts that do not serve them. I am grateful for these lessons. Without them, I would have no way of keeping Aurdyn from reading all of my thoughts.

"You are quiet," his voice rumbles in my mind. *"Are you worried?"*

It would do me no good to lie about this. Only a fool has no concerns on the eve of battle. *"Yes."*

"Only use your fire magic if you absolutely must," he says. *"Remember that to use it, you take from yourself. You could—"*

"I will be careful, my love. I promise."

My vow seems to calm him, because he does not bring it up again.

When we finally reach Arganth, I cannot believe how different it looks from when we left. There are several tents along the outskirts of the city at the edge of the woods. I suppose King Davin's army is much too large for Arganth to provide housing for them all.

They have erected a stone wall around the entire city, adding a layer of protection in case of attack.

Aurdyn circles above the inn we stayed at when we were here. He touches down so lightly, I'm not even sure we've landed until he carefully sets me on my feet. He shifts into his two-legged form and hooks a possessive arm around my waist.

King Davin rushes toward us, his eyes popping as our warriors begin to land in the snow before us. He turns to Aurdyn. "You've not brought any tents?"

"You sing to stone to build your structures," Aurdyn says roughly. "I expect you to make accommodations for your people."

"My people?" Davin's head jerks back. "What are you talking about? We've got the inn and the tents."

Aurdyn places his hands on his hips. "We will take the inn *and* the tents. While you and your kind sing to the stones to build your new shelters."

Davin steps back as if struck, face turning red. I half expect him to argue, but instead he spins on his heels, muttering about insufferable Dragons before barking a series of orders at his men.

Placing my hands on my hips, I turn to Aurdyn. "Was that necessary?"

A slight smirk twists his lips. "No. But it was amusing." He tucks me in close to his side. "And it got you a warm bed and plumbing, did it not?"

Try as I might to be cross with him, I cannot help my snort of amusement as I nod. "Yes, it did."

CHAPTER 54

FREYJA

Aurdyn instructs our warriors to take rooms at the inn and in the tents before we enter the tavern. Garvin's face pales as we approach the bar. "I—I'm sorry, but we are full up. There are no rooms to let. We—"

He halts as a line of Dwarves files down the stairs with their belongings in hand. He frowns and Aurdyn leans on the bar. "The Dwarf king promised us these rooms." He smiles, flashing his dangerous white fangs. "He even offered to cover our accommodations and our tab while we're here."

My head whips to Aurdyn. His eyes dance with barely restrained amusement, and although I know the right thing would be to demand he give the Dwarves back their accommodations, I have little time left.

Selfishly, I'd rather spend it as comfortable as possible rather than sleeping out in the elements.

As we make our way up the stairs, I turn to Aurdyn with a sigh. "It's one thing to force the Dwarves from their beds, but another to have King Davin pay for our warriors to sleep comfortably while his men are out in the cold."

Aurdyn pulls me into his arms. "Do not worry, my T'kara. I will compensate him once this is over. And I've instructed our warriors to hunt this night, to procure enough meat for ourselves and the Dwarves." A smile quirks his mouth. "But I do hope that I am nearby when Davin receives the bill for our stay."

Despite trying to keep it in, laughter escapes me, and secretly, I hope I'm around as well to see Davin's face when he finds out he is paying for our warriors.

Just as we step into our room, a voice calls from down the hall. "King Aurdyn, wait!"

We both turn to find Olmar huffing and puffing as he rushes toward us, a thick comforter, furs, and towels balanced in his arms. His face is beet red as he pushes past us, changing out the towels and the bedding.

When he's done, he walks over and gives a shallow bow.

"Thank you, Olmar," I tell him. He nods eagerly, smiling even as he wheezes, trying to catch his breath. "Are you all right?"

He lifts his hand, extending his forefinger in a silent bid to give him a moment as he steadies his breathing before answering. "My father told me you and your warriors were going to be taking the rooms. So, we rushed to bring you new bedding and towels." He pauses. "As for food, it's very scarce right now." He gives me a worried look. "We've been rationing since the army got here and the soup is more water than... anything else, but I will have someone bring you up—"

"No need," Aurdyn cuts him off. "Several of my warriors are out hunting right now. Fire up the kitchen and be ready to receive the meat they bring back. There will be enough for everyone, including Davin's army."

Olmar's eyes fill with hope as Aurdyn continues. "I will expect the first two servings to be brought to us immediately. Do you understand?"

"Of—of course," he replies, bowing again. "I'll let the cook know."

He quickly turns and sprints back down the hallway, his voice echoing up the stairs. "We're saved, Father! The Dragons are bringing back food!"

Pride fills me and I turn to Aurdyn, only to catch him rolling his eyes. "Dwarves," he grumbles.

I smile and pull him close. "I get the feeling they're growing on you."

"I certainly hope not. If they are, it is your fault."

Laughter bubbles up at the scowl on his face, but I notice the slight twitch of his lips as he holds back a grin.

"They're good people," I murmur.

"They helped you when I feared you would die after you collapsed." His expression sobers. "King Davin does not know this, but because of that, I would have helped them even if he hadn't begged."

His words melt my heart even as sadness spears through me. I wish we had more time, but I intend to make the most of each moment.

I stretch up on my toes and drape my arms around his neck as I whisper in his ear. "Do you have any idea how much I love you, my wonderful, arrogant Dragon king?"

He captures my mouth with his own, branding me with his kiss as he walks us toward the bed.

CHAPTER 55

AURDYN

When I wake in the morning, Freyja is still asleep. Quietly, I stand from the bed and tuck the blankets and furs around her body to keep her warm. I stoke the fire, and then carefully close the door behind me before heading downstairs.

For all their grumbling about having to build their own shelters, the Dwarves now openly thank me for the bounty of food as I pass them on my way to King Davin's tent.

As soon as I push through the flap, he jumps up from his chair, face red as a beacon, and angrily waves a scrolled parchment at me. "What is the meaning of this?" he barks. "The innkeeper just delivered this to me. He said you told him *I* was covering the bill for you and your warriors after you kicked *my* men out."

"And my men are feeding your people," I snap. "Besides, I will not have my mate sleeping outside in a pitiful tent in this weather." I cross my arms over my chest. "She is the one who convinced me to aid you, or have you forgotten that?"

He peers at me. "The gods certainly blessed you with that one, didn't they?" He arches a teasing brow. "Or did you call upon some dark entity to help you ensnare her?"

"Choose your words carefully, Dwarf King, or they may be your last."

"No need to get upset." He raises his hands in mock surrender. "I was merely teasing you, you know."

I try but fail to hide a smirk. It is amusing to tease King Davin. I sweep my gaze around his tent. "Did you get what I asked you for?"

"Aye." He walks toward a trunk next to his bed. Opening it, he pulls out a suit of armor fit for a queen. For all my dislike of them, there is at least one good thing about the Dwarves. They certainly know how to craft weapons and armor.

He holds it out to me, and I take it, shocked by how light it is. "Is this L'omhara?"

"Yes." He hooks his thumbs into his belt loops. "Light as a feather, yet strong enough to repel any blade or arrow."

A kingly gift, indeed, and perfect for my queen. "This will do."

"*This will do?*" he sputters. "I just gave you a set of armor that costs more than the worth of this entire village, including the mines, and all you have to say is, 'this will do?'"

I level an irritated glare at him.

"Far be it for me to expect something so simple as a 'thank you,' but I suppose the seven hells would sooner freeze over before a Dragon ever thanked anyone," he grumbles to himself, and a faint smirk curls my lip as I leave his tent.

I call over my shoulder as I leave. "Have it delivered to my room at the inn."

I'm halfway back to my T'kara when Brovyn walks up to me. "Our scouts have just returned."

"What did they find?"

"The Mages are leading Ruhaen's army this way." He gestures to the woods. "There is a clearing in the middle of the forest that lies in their path. Perhaps it would be best to meet them there instead of waiting for them in Arganth."

His advice is sound. It would mean less destruction here and fewer civilian casualties if we met them away from the hamlet.

"Show me this place."

He dips his chin, and I spread my wings, readying to take off, but stop at the sound of Freyja's voice. "Where are you going?"

I explain what Brovyn found, and she nods. "It's a good strategy. Arganth can remain undisturbed by the battle." She looks between the two of us. "I want to go with you to see it."

I would argue, but I can already see the determined look in her eyes, so I think better of it. Sighing heavily, I shift into my Draken form and carefully grasp her smaller form in my left front paw, holding her close to my chest as we ascend into the sky and head out over the forest.

CHAPTER 56

AURDYN

The cold wind claws at my scales as we circle over the clearing a few times before landing. It is strange to find such a wide-open space in the middle of the dense forest, but Brovyn is right. This is where we should meet the Mages and the army of Ruhaen in battle.

A mountain stands to the left. The cliff face wall is full of caverns, overlooking the battlefield. It would be a good location to position some of our warriors, while we wait for their army to arrive.

Carefully, I set Freyja down in the snow, waiting until she is secure in her footing before stepping back and shifting into my two-legged form.

Awareness prickles my flesh when I detect a small vibration in the ground beneath my feet. I eye the snow cautiously. "There is something beneath this."

Freyja's brow furrows as she scans the clearing. Tall trees, their branches heavily laden with snow line either side. Without warning, she drops to her knees in the snow and digs away the top layer until she hits something solid. "It's ice." She looks up. "There is a river under here."

I peer at the ice, noticing slight movement as water flows underneath it. It is very thick, however, so I am not concerned about falling through.

"This is perfect." She looks between me and Brovyn. "We can lure the Mages onto this and then use fire to melt it beneath them."

"How will that take care of the Wraiths?" Brovyn asks. "They can fly."

"Yes, but if we drown the Mages, there will be no one to control the Wraiths."

A smile tugs at my mouth. My T'kara is very clever. "Without someone to control them and coordinate their attacks, they will be easier to pick off."

"And Ruhaen's army will no longer be under their enchantment," Freyja adds. "So, we'd only need to worry about destroying the Wraiths."

"But what will we use for bait?" Brovyn asks. "How will we get the Mages into the clearing?"

Freyja's eyes light up. "Let's go back to camp. We need to speak with King Davin. I have an idea."

CHAPTER 57

AURDYN

When we return to Arganth, we go straight to King Davin's tent. Two of his generals stand on either side of him as they stare down at a detailed map spread out on the table before them. I notice the line they've drawn next to Arganth to symbolize the newly constructed rock wall that separates the city from the forest.

Several carved figurines sit on the map. Some look like a shield bearing King Davin's banner and others a Dragon, representing the Dwarf and Dragon warriors.

He lifts his head to look at us. "Ah, I'm glad you are here. We were just going over where to fortify our defenses along the wall. We—"

"The battle will not take place here," I state firmly. "We will intercept them here." I point to the clear space on the map, where we just came from. "This clearing is where we will meet them in battle."

One of Davin's generals studies the area thoughtfully before returning his attention to us. "According to our scouts, their army will be there tomorrow, around mid-day."

"Good." Freyja studies the map. "That gives us plenty of time."

"For what?" Davin asks.

She pulls the shade stone necklace from her tunic pocket. I had no idea she brought it with her, and I eye it warily as everyone else gapes in wonder, recognizing the precious stone immediately.

"Is that what I think it is?" King Davin asks, licking his lips as if eyeing a tasty meal. "Is that truly a shade stone?"

"Yes," Freyja replies. "And we're going to use it to trick the Mages, but first I need to know if you can manipulate the stone's magic with your singing."

He frowns. "What do you mean?"

She puts the necklace on and her image changes to that of an older human female. Brovyn gasps, as do the Dwarves. When she removes it, she hands it to Davin. "Do you think you can make it take on my form, as I am now? So that whoever wears it will appear like me?"

"I can try." He holds the stone in his palm, forehead pinched in concentration, as he begins to sing in the ancient language of his people.

The shade stone glows purple as he weaves his magic through the rock. When he finishes, he places it around his neck, and we watch in triumph as his image shimmers briefly before being replaced by one of Freyja.

He looks down at his hands in wonder. "How did you know that would work?"

"I didn't," she replies. "I only hoped."

My tail snakes around her ankle. My T'kara is as clever as she is beautiful, and I cannot stop the surge of pride that fills me as I pull her close and plant an affectionate kiss to her temple. "What next, my clever queen?"

She beams and then turns her attention to the spot I pointed out on the map. "This clearing is actually a layer of ice over a river," she explains. "It's concealed by a thick layer of snow."

Freyja draws a line on one side of the clearing. She looks at King Davin. "Your forces will be here." She makes a similar line on the opposite side. "And we will arrive early enough to be waiting for Ruhaen's army when they arrive."

"Then, what?" King Davin asks, eyeing the map critically.

"The Mages do not know that you've allied yourself with us. So, our Dragon warriors will be the element of surprise."

He frowns, and she continues. "There is a cliff face wall here." She marks a spot on the map to the right and slightly behind the line where Ruhaen's army will be. "The Dragons will wait in the caves there, while you pretend to hand me over to the Mages in exchange for a truce."

"I will not risk you," I growl. "You will not be anywhere near—"

She puts a finger to my lips, silencing me.

Davin and his men gape at her as if she has lost her mind.

Freyja turns to me. "I will be in the cave with you, my Dragon." She looks back at King Davin. "One of our warriors will use the shade stone to appear as me, and you will walk with him to meet the Mages in the middle of the clearing, directly over the ice."

Davin's eyes light with anticipation. "Ah, I think I know where you're going with this."

"As soon as the Mages walk out onto the ice to meet you for the exchange, the Dragon—pretending to be me—will shift and carry you away to safety while the others will swoop in from the caves. They will set fire to the area around the Mages, melting it beneath them."

I look at Davin and his generals. "Once the Mages are drowned, Ruhaen's army will no longer be under their spell, and the Wraiths will be easier to kill."

King Davin nods. "I'll inform my warriors."

CHAPTER 58

FREYJA

When we're finished laying out our plans, Aurdyn and I return to the inn. Olmar chases after us, panting as he races up the stairs with two steaming-hot plates of food. The venison is cooked to perfection, and the mead is better than I remember, but I'm having trouble eating.

Tomorrow weighs heavily on my mind, and I cannot stop dwelling on my vision. If all goes according to my plan, both of us will survive this battle. But if it does not, there is no question. I will be the one to die, not Aurdyn. I love him and I want him to live.

"Is the food not to your liking?" Aurdyn's voice snaps me back from my dismal thoughts. His brow furrows. "I'll call Olmar back and have him find you a finer piece of meat."

Before I can say anything, he's already bellowing for Olmar.

"Aurdyn, it's fine," I tell him, and he subsides.

It's too late, however, as Olmar is already knocking at our door. "What seems to be the problem?"

"It's nothing," I say. I shift my gaze to Aurdyn. "I'm just a little nervous about tomorrow, and it's affecting my appetite."

"I could bring you up some tea if you'd like?" Olmar offers.

I give him a warm smile, and his cheeks flush dark red. "That would be lovely, Olmar, thank you."

As soon as he leaves, Aurdyn begins growling, and I already know why. I pat his arm. "He's just nervous too, Aurdyn."

"He likes you," Aurdyn grumbles. "More than he should," he adds balefully. "All the Dwarves do."

I laugh. "Well, it's a good thing I have no interest in anyone else but my arrogant Dragon, then, isn't it?"

He curls his tail around my calf as he studies me hungrily. "Good." His chest rumbles with arousal. "Because you are my most precious treasure, my beautiful, clever mate. And Dragons do not share."

I stand and walk over to him, sitting on his lap. He wraps his arms and wings around me, nuzzling my temple. "Well, this human doesn't either," I tease lightly. "I want you all to myself."

He pulls back, his gaze full of devotion. "I am yours, Freyja. Now and always. There will never be another for me but you."

Emotions lodge in my throat, but I push out the words. "If things do not go as planned tomorrow, I want you to know that I—"

He presses a finger to my lips to silence me, as I've done to him before. "Do not speak of death." His expression is sober. "I will not let it claim you."

"No one can promise such a thing, Aurdyn."

"I can," he insists, and he sounds so confident that I almost believe him. "I would fight the gods themselves if they tried to take you from me."

Instead of answering, I entwine my arms around his neck, and he tightens his hold on me. After a moment, he stills.

He cups my chin, studying me intently. "Did you have a vision you have not told me about? A dream about tomorrow?"

"No." The lie burns my tongue, even as I brush my lips against his in a lingering kiss. I drop my head to his shoulder as I rest my palm on his muscular chest, mapping the thick, corded muscle with the tips of my fingers.

He makes a rumbling sound in response, and his gaze is full of molten possession as he tightens his arms around my waist.

"I'm tired of being worried about tomorrow, my Dragon," I whisper against his lips as I take his hand and place it on my thigh. "Help me to forget for a while."

He seals his lips over mine in a claiming kiss and then carries me to the bed.

CHAPTER 59

AURDYN

My eyes snap open as Freyja stirs in my arms. She buries her head in my chest and my nostrils flare as I detect the saline scent of tears. I run my hand through her hair, brushing it back from her face as I cuddle her.

"Freyja, wake up," I speak softly, not wanting to startle her. "You are having a nightmare, my T'kara."

She lifts her head, blinking several times as if slowly realizing where she is. Her cheeks are stained with tears, and her eyelids are puffy and red. "It is all right," I murmur, folding my wings tighter around her. "I am here." I cup her face, brushing away her tears with my thumbs. "What were you dreaming?"

"I don't remember," she murmurs. "It's gone now."

My mouth goes dry. Freyja has had visions before. Surely, if the gods gave her a warning, she would have remembered it. I smooth a hand down her back in a soothing gesture as she snuggles against me. Perhaps it was truly only a night-mare, and nothing more.

"Are you sure you remember nothing?"

She nods and then settles back into sleep.

Try as I might, I cannot rest. Not now. Not knowing the danger we face tomorrow. I am not worried for myself, but I am worried for her. She is everything to me. I could probably sneak away undetected, leaving her here where she'd be safer. But I know that she would never forgive me if I did.

Sighing heavily, I go over the plan in my head. It is sound and, more importantly, she will be by my side the entire time, so I will easily be able to protect her.

In truth, if not for the vision of our son—our future—that the heart tree gave me, I would find a way to keep her from the battle. But knowing that she will live has given me the assurance to acquiesce to her demand to fight the Mages.

I have no reason to deny her this when I already know how it will turn out.

Closing my eyes, I fall into a light sleep. Morning is only a few hours away and I am eager for the day to be done.

CHAPTER 60

FREYJA

The early rays of the sun stream in through the small window across the way. Aurdyn is not in the bed. Sitting up, I scan the room, but he is not here. Perhaps he is downstairs.

Wrapping the heavy furs around me, I pad to the cleansing room and ready myself for the day. I change into my thick brown leggings and fur-line leather tunic and boots. I am about to leave, but the door opens and Aurdyn steps in.

"I have brought breakfast," he says proudly.

I glance down at his hands, but he is carrying a trunk. Not plates or...

Olmar steps around him, carrying a tray with our breakfast and morning tea. He sets our table, trying his best to please a rather grumpy Dragon. It's hard to keep the wry smile from my face as I look over at Aurdyn—so pleased with himself.

"Technically, Olmar has brought us breakfast," I say dryly.

Aurdyn waves a dismissive hand at him. "Yes, but I instructed him to."

I shake my head in admonishment as Aurdyn grins.

Not that long ago, he barely ever cracked a smile. I swallow down the lump in my throat as I study him, trying to take in every detail of his face as he talks to me over breakfast.

I do my best to eat, but my stomach is in knots, and I can barely finish half my plate.

"You need to eat more," he insists, pushing my plate closer to me. "You need your strength."

He's right. I'll need every bit of strength if I am going to save him today. My nerves are running rampant as I think about the shade stone, praying its magic will hold long enough to do what we need. It failed Aurdyn before, but I comfort myself with the fact that he had it on for at least half an hour before its magic faded, revealing his true form.

When we're finished eating, I gesture to the trunk. I've been so nervous about the day, I completely forgot about it until now. "What is that?"

"Open it."

His eyes shine with anticipation as I stand from the table and walk toward it. Carefully, I open the trunk and my mouth drifts open when I see the brand new set of armor packed inside.

Sunlight glints on the polished silver metal as I pull it from the trunk. I study the scrolling patterns etched into the plating, complete with an image of a Dragon in the middle. It's the most beautiful set of armor I've ever seen.

"Where did you get this?" I ask.

"I asked the Dwarf king to make it for you," he explains. "It is pure L'omhara."

I inhale sharply. This set of armor is worth more than the

entire treasury of Ruhaen. "It's too much," I whisper. "I cannot—"

"I would have you safe," he says. "Besides, if you are worried about cost… it was one of the things I demanded from the Dwarf king for our alliance."

"What was the other?"

"I made him promise to never make another black arrow. I'll not have his kind making weapons that can kill Dragons."

I'm glad he did this. At least I know no more arrows will be made that could hurt him after I'm gone.

Aurdyn helps me into the armor, and I marvel at how light it is. Most armor feels bulky, making it awkward to wield a weapon as efficiently as one could without it. But this is so comfortable, I barely notice I'm wearing it.

Quickly, I braid my hair, twisting it up and tucking it in at the nape of my neck so it will not show beneath my helmet. When I'm finished, I stand before the floor-length mirror and my heart swells with pride.

I wish my mother were alive to see me right now, for I am sure she would be proud to know her daughter followed in her steps and became a shield-maiden.

Emotions swirl deep within, but I push them back down, knowing that if I die in battle today, my ancestors will welcome me into their great halls with honor.

CHAPTER 61

FREYJA

I t is early, but we must reach our position at least a few hours before the Mages and the army of Ruhaen arrive.

Our warriors gather outside the inn, near the tents. Each is in their Draken form and standing in formation before us. King Davin's army lines up on either side. They appear strong in their own right, but next to an army of Dragons, they pale in comparison.

Davin walks up beside us as Aurdyn addresses our warriors.

"Today, we will show the Order of Mages what it means to provoke a Dragon's wrath," he yells. "We are the death that comes for them! The last thing they will see is Dragon fire as we burn them all to ash!"

His men release a battle cry that echoes loudly through the city.

I notice Olmar and his father are standing near the front of one of the Dwarf lines, dressed and ready for battle. It seems there are no civilians, only warriors here today.

King Davin gives a rallying speech and his army cheers. When he is done, he gives the order to march and then he turns to Aurdyn. "Are you ready?"

"We are Dragons. We are always ready for battle." Aurdyn's gaze slides to his, and he gives him the arrogant look that I know so well. "Try to stay out of our way."

King Davin's jaw drops, but Aurdyn ignores him. He scoops me up in his front left paw and lifts off. I watch as the ground spirals away beneath us.

Aurdyn flies over the forest to a cave that overlooks the battlefield. The rest of our warriors conceal themselves in the many caverns along the cliff face wall around us.

The wind howls and bites at my exposed skin, and despite my many layers, I shiver. We're downwind from the battle-field, so the horses, Mages, and Wraiths should not be able to scent us, but I am so cold I am miserable.

Still in his Draken form, Aurdyn wraps his tail around me and pulls me to his side before curling his wing over me, sheltering me from the ice-cold wind.

I snuggle against him, grateful for his warmth as we watch the Dwarf army take up their position on the opposite side of the clearing. They stand in formation, shields, axes, and swords at the ready as they wait for our enemies to arrive.

If all goes according to plan, we will attack the Mages from behind, cutting them off from the rest of Ruhaen's army.

The Dwarves should be enough of a distraction in front of them that they won't think to guard their backs. Aurdyn's people and the Dwarves have been at odds for so long, I doubt the Mages suspect that the Dwarves have allied with the Dragons.

I force my focus to remain on the battle and our plan,

partitioning away the part of my mind that I do not want Aurdyn to see.

As if sensing this, he gently prods me with his snout. *"Do not worry, my T'kara,"* he speaks in my thoughts. *"I will keep you safe."*

"I know you will," I reply in kind. Guilt fills me and despite the risk of alerting him to my true fears, I add, *"But know that if anything goes wrong, it is not your fault."*

"The gods are with us, my T'kara. I know they are."

I still at his words. He sounds so certain.

The High Priest told us the heart tree gives us the visions we need to guide our path. Is this what she showed him? That we would live?

The question slips through the barrier I've erected in my mind, and Aurdyn's gaze meets mine composedly, and the truth falls into place.

This is why I am here. He would not have allowed me to come otherwise. If he thought I would die, he would have kept me from the battle.

His eyes search mine, and I reach out, smoothing a hand along his massive jaw. He leans into my palm, as if reveling in my touch, and I fear my heart will break. *"I love you, Aurdyn. More than anything."*

"And I love you, my T'kara. Do not be afraid. All will be well, my beautiful and clever fire heart."

A horn sounds in the distance, echoing through the forest. *"It's Ruhaen."* I catch sight of my uncle's banners through the trees as the marching cadence of hundreds of boots fills the air. Movement flits through the forest and my heart pounds at the sight of nearly two dozen Wraiths hovering on either side of the men.

Even one Wraith is dangerous, and I am glad we are downwind and high above them. They should not be able to detect us up here. They are able to scent magic and hunt beings that wield power, drinking of their life force to replenish their own. Because of my new fire magic, I'm sure if I were on the ground, they'd be on me in less than a minute.

The hooded figures fly among the trees with their glowing red eyes illuminating their skeletal faces and razor-sharp teeth. Their attention is entirely fixed on the Dwarf army up ahead. Dwarves may not have as much magic as the Elves and Fae, but it seems it's enough to entice the Wraiths.

Five Mages holding staffs ride at the back of the army. Their obsidian eyes scan the forest and their pale gray skin is easily visible beneath their cloaks.

One of the Mages pulls her hood back from her face, and anger flares in my chest when I realize it is Luria. Her long blonde hair replaces the silver strands as her glamour flickers into place over her body.

My uncle is nowhere to be seen, and I pray she has not already gotten rid of him. Hopefully, he is simply back at the castle, locked away where he cannot escape her enchantment.

The army of Ruhaen marches proudly at the front, facing the Dwarves. Dressed from head to toe Ruhaen's obsidian armor and wielding heavy swords and axes, they are a terrifying sight to behold. I feel sorry for these brave men, under the same dark enchantment that has enslaved my uncle's mind.

If this goes wrong, many, if not all, of them will die. Drawing in a deep breath, I ready myself to draw upon my magic. I will do whatever it takes to spare as many lives as possible here today.

Ruhaen's army stops at the edge of the clearing, glaring at the Dwarves.

King Davin holds up a white flag, indicating he wishes to talk. "I want to speak with the ones in charge."

The Mages and Luria ride to the front of the line. Such hubris, as if certain their victory is assured.

"Have you decided to surrender, Dwarf King?" one of them yells.

"I came to ask if you'd take a trade," he replies. "I have something you want, and I'll give it to you on the condition that you leave my kingdom in peace."

"What is it?" another asks.

King Davin motions to his men and one of them drags forward a bound and struggling version of me.

It's Brovyn. His tunic conceals the shade stone necklace, but the Wraiths must be able to sense its powerful magic because they gather at the front lines, a swarming mass of evil practically foaming at the mouth to reach him.

Three of the Mages aim their staffs at them, the stones at the top glowing brightly as they use their powers. This is good. Only the control of the Mages holds them back. Without them, they will be feral, mindless beings, easier to pick off.

"Is this the one you were looking for?" King Davin asks. "The Princess Freyja of Ruhaen?"

"Give her to us," Luria hisses. "Now."

"I will, but you must meet me halfway and no tricks, you understand? Each of you must make and abide by this agreement," he says, casting a wary glance at them. "Once you have her, you leave my kingdom and you do not come back. Do we have a deal?"

The Mages turn to each other. I'm sure they will say anything just so he'll hand me over. And once it's done, they'll unleash Ruhaen's army and the Wraiths to attack.

Aurdyn was not sure it would work, but King Davin said he was certain they'd fall for this trick. He said everyone underestimates Dwarves, much to their detriment.

Davin's words repeat in my mind. *They believe we are*

slow," he'd said. "But we are good fighters, and we are cleverer than most."

"We accept this bargain," one of them answers. They look at each other once more and then steer their horses toward the middle of the clearing as King Davin drags Brovyn toward them.

Brovyn fights against his bindings, shouting at the Dwarves and cursing them to the seven hells for their betrayal. I just pray the magic of the shade stone holds long enough for this to work. If it doesn't, he'll have little time to get King Davin out of there so they can escape.

The Mages and Luria are nearly at the halfway mark when the false image of me flickers.

"What is this treachery?" one cries out, raising his staff to attack.

In one swift motion, Brovyn explodes into his Draken form and grabs King Davin. He releases a stream of flame at the Mages, beating his wings furiously as he lifts off from the ice.

They repel his attack easily and I watch in horror as one waves his staff at the Wraiths, and they rush toward Brovyn.

Lightning fast, Aurdyn's tail grips my waist, setting me on his back, and we dive toward the clearing below, coming up behind the Mages, along with the rest of our warriors.

Aurdyn breathes a jet of flame between the Mages and Ruhaen's army, cutting them off from each other.

But that does little to stop the Wraiths as they fly amongst the Dwarves, ripping into them with fangs and claws. I watch in horror as their axes and swords bounce harmlessly off the Wraiths, and I realize the Mages have shielded them with magic.

Three of the Mages focus their powers on the Dragons flying overhead, sending lightning bolts of devastating power to our warriors. One falls, slamming hard on the snow and ice. Three others go to his aid, gathering him up and flying him behind the Dwarf lines where a healer awaits.

Aurdyn and several of our warriors concentrate their fire on the Mages, but they surround themselves with powerful shields that deflect the flames before sending out more destructive power and hitting a dozen more Dragons. Luria is directly in the middle, as if creating a shield around herself with her own brethren. It's despicable.

She has no honor. And today she will die a coward's death.

The Dragons make several low passes over the ice, trying to melt it, but the Mages realize their plan and cast a shield to repel the fire.

It's chaos beneath us as the Dwarves fight like demons against the Wraiths and the Dragons roar in anger as they focus on attacking the Mages and Wraiths.

Arrows whistle through the air, as Ruhaen's archers try to weaken our defenses.

These arrows do nothing against Dragons, but as they fly toward the Dwarves, I realize they are completely vulnerable, most of them unaware of what is coming as they struggle to fight off the Wraiths.

Instantly, I call upon my magic and send a shield of fire above the dwarven army. It arcs across the sky in a brilliant display, incinerating the arrows before they land.

Several of the Dwarves, as well as the Mages, turn toward Aurdyn and me. A chill runs down my spine as three of the Mages aim their staffs and send bolts of red magic flying toward us so fast, I'm barely able to raise my shield in time. The devastating power bounces harmlessly off the fire shield, and I struggle to hold it in place as they attack again.

Trilan's warning echoes in my mind. *If I use too much power, I will die.*

Aurdyn lets loose a battle cry in the language of his

people and several break off and head for the Mages. The Dragons rain down streams of heavy fire, forcing them to shield themselves and halt their attacks on me.

When the Mages shield themselves, the Dwarves cry out in triumph as they cut down three of the Wraiths.

"Look!" I yell. "The Wraiths are vulnerable when the Mages raise their shields."

"Concentrate all of your fire on the Mages!" Aurdyn yells to our warriors.

Another volley of arrows sails toward the Dwarves, but I send out another shield of fire, demolishing them in midair. Next, I adjust my shield to protect the Dragons as they fly low over the Mages, releasing a stream of flame and forcing them to repel their attacks.

My pulse pounds in my ears, and my arms shake as I struggle to focus my powers, calling forth all of my reserves to shield our armies from attack.

"Freyja!" Aurdyn's voice is muffled in my ears as my energy begins to wane.

I'm not sure how much longer I can hold out.

A flash of red catches the corner of my eye, and I turn, but too late, as a bolt of devastating magic hits Aurdyn's side. He bellows in pain, and we spiral toward the ground with dizzying speed.

Without warning, he wraps his tail around my waist, ripping me from between his shoulders and cradling me to his chest. He twists at the last second, slamming onto his back on the ice, cradling me from the impact of the fall.

"Aurdyn!" I scream, but he doesn't move.

My head is spinning, but I slide out from his now loosened grasp and crouch on the ice beside him, placing my body between him and the Mages.

"To the king! To the queen!" one of our warriors cries out,

but the Mages shoot spiraling bolts of their devastating magic, keeping them at bay.

The wall of fire keeping Ruhaen's soldiers from the clearing collapses, and they rush through. I raise a shield of fire around myself and Aurdyn, but two of the soldiers are trapped inside as well.

Knowing their swords will be unable to penetrate a Dragon's scales, they set their sights on me and rush forward, swords raised to attack.

Fighting on pure instinct, my mind goes blank and all I can see and hear is the battle before me, while vaguely aware that my shield is still in place.

I muster the last of my strength, calling forth more of my fire. Flame licks along the blade of my sword as we battle. I swing in a wide arc, slashing the first one across the chest before twisting to avoid the other knight's sword.

They have me between them, but if they think I will be easy prey, they are sorely mistaken. I feint left, and then twist in the opposite direction, swinging my sword and cutting a gash across the back of my opponent's leg.

He drops to his knees, and I spin toward the other, launching flame from one hand as I lunge with my sword in the other, dragging my blade across his torso and knocking him to the ground. With a blow from the pommel of my sword, I make sure he stays down.

Everything hurts, and I can barely keep my eyes open as I force one foot in front of the other to face Luria and the rest of the Mages.

Their concentrated powers begin to break through my weakening shield. A pain filled cry rips from my throat as agony sears through my veins.

Luria glares at me, baring her sharp fangs as she concentrates her devastating magic on her attack. "You should have died that day," she grinds out, referring to the day Aurdyn rescued me. "You escaped the fire then, but you will not escape it now."

Anger flares bright in my chest as sweat beads across my brow. "Neither will you," I grind out.

"Freyja!" Aurdyn's voice calls out from behind me, but I cannot turn around. I know what I must do.

The barrier in my mind falls away, and everything is laid bare before my Dragon. I need Aurdyn to know the truth. *"I love you, Aurdyn,"* I whisper through the connection.

His raw fear and panic claw at my mind as he desperately tries to reach me. "Freyja, no!"

Focusing the last of my energy, I level a dark glare at Luria and the Mages as I grit through my teeth. "If this is my end, we will all burn together."

CHAPTER 62

AURDYN

Shouts and battle cries reverberate through the clearing as Dwarves and Dragons try to rally to us. "To the king! To the queen!" Streams of flame scatter across the Mages' shields, and the Dwarves try to break them with axe and sword, but to no avail.

Freyja's mind is open before me, revealing the terrible truth. My T'kara will give her life for mine. The heart tree gave her this vision. Agony spears my chest and I scramble to my feet, desperate to reach her. "Freyja, no!"

She raises her arms, creating a circle of flame around her and the Mages.

Terror mars their faces as they realize she is inside their own shields. Like the lighting of a match, a massive orb of fire catches between her palms. In one swift motion, she drops to one knee, slamming the orb to the ground and propelling a ruinous wave of flame at the Mages.

Their agonized cries fill the air as the skin melts from their bones and they disintegrate.

The ice breaks beneath them and I cannot breathe as Freyja collapses and then falls into the freezing water below.

I dive into the icy torrent, panicking when I do not see her. Everything is dark, and I can hardly think through the fear that claws at my chest. I have to find her. I cannot lose my T'kara.

A flash of red catches my eye as a ray of sunlight spears through the water, lighting the crimson strands like a beacon in the ice-cold darkness.

I wrap my arms around her, kicking my legs and beating my wings furiously to reach the surface. I brace myself against the stabbing pain of my wing joint, injured when we fell to the ground. As soon as we break through, Brovyn flies up behind me, gripping my arms and taking us to the healer on the opposite side of the clearing.

With the Mages dead, the Dwarves already slaughtered all the Wraiths.

King Davin lays his heavy woolen cloak down on the ground and I place Freyja atop it. The Dwarves turn their backs as the healer removes her armor and slices away her wet clothing, but someone else immediately covers her with a cloak.

Freyja's face is deathly pale and her normally pink lips are tinged blue. She lies with an unnatural stillness that shreds my heart as the healer moves her hands over her in assessment.

A tear slips down her cheek as she lifts her gaze to me. "She is beyond my abilities."

"You are wrong," I say, refusing to believe it. "She will live. I know she will."

She exchanges a look with the Dwarf healer beside her, who tilts her head to me. "Perhaps her own people... maybe their healers could—"

"Ruhaen is chaos." King Davin gestures to the human

soldiers, each walking around as if in a daze. It is an effect of lifting an enchantment that enthralled them for too long. "It will be that way in the rest of their kingdom. Your best hope is the human kingdom of Florin."

"Stand back!" I yell.

Despite the searing pain in my wing, I transform into my Draken form and scoop Freyja's limp form up with my front paw.

"The humans will likely attack you if you show up in their kingdom," Brovyn says. "If they have black arrows—"

"I will have to chance it," I grind out.

"Then I'm coming with you," he replies. He signals to five others. "With us!" he commands, and we take to the skies.

* * *

THE FLIGHT to Florin feels as if it takes forever, although I know it is little more than a few hours since we cut through the mountains. I cradle Freyja to my chest, holding her close so she can warm with the heat from my body.

Desperate to hear her voice, I reach for her through the bond. *"Freyja, please. Say something, my T'kara."*

The silence that echoes in reply is deafening.

The moment we cross the border into the kingdom of Florin, alarm bells ring throughout the countryside, alerting their people of danger.

Soldiers scramble to nock arrows, but we fly past before they can hit their mark. Not that it would matter, since none thus far have been the type that can pierce Dragon scales.

I suspect they keep those at the castle, and although we are likely to be in danger when we reach it, I cannot turn back. Not now. Freyja's life depends upon it.

As we fly over the city, panicked cries and shouts fill the

air. People scatter, fleeing for shelter, afraid they're being attacked by Dragons.

It's been at least three generations since my people visited these lands, but I'm sure the stories have survived the long years. I have heard rumors of the terrifying tales that sprung up from the ashes of the cities my kind razed to the ground.

When we reach the capital city, I'm vaguely aware of colorful banners and decorations spread throughout. The streets are lined with carts full of food and wares, as if they are in the middle of a celebration of some sort. A festival perhaps.

The guards along the wall shoot their pitiful arrows, but they bounce harmlessly off my scales. My heart rate quickens when I notice the prodigious bows on four of the castle turrets.

Four black arrows sail toward us, but we manage to dodge them. As they nock more on the string, I emit a thunderous roar.

"Stop!" I bellow. "I have come with the king's cousin! The Princess Freyja! She needs a healer!"

Ignoring my statements, they loose off another volley of black arrows. I swerve to the left, but too late, and an arrow sinks deep into my right shoulder.

Brovyn roars in anger and aims a tongue of flame at the nearest turret. As fire races toward the bow, the archer dives down the stairwell and out of harm's way. Brovyn turns his attention to another bow, but a glowing shield slides over it instantly.

"What is—"

"Stop!" a voice calls out, and I turn to find King Kyven of the Fae and three of his warriors flying toward us. His purple Dragonfly wings flutter furiously as his lavender eyes flash with ire. He runs a hand through his short, silver-white hair and bares his fangs. "Why are you here?"

I start to answer, but pain lances through my shoulder and I grit my teeth. What is it with these humans and their damned poisoned arrows?

I land in the center of the courtyard, shaking the ground beneath us. My warriors gather in a circle around me and their queen. Fire licks at the back of my throat as Kyven and his guards surround us in return.

King Varys of the Dark Elves appears in the courtyard a moment later. "What are you doing here, Aurdyn? What have you done?"

Carefully, I lay my T'kara on the grass at my feet.

Everyone stares at us, gaping.

Using the last of my strength, I shift into my two-legged form and then scoop her limp body up into my arms, cradling her to my chest. I can barely breathe as I glance down at her still and pale form. "My queen needs help!" I roar my anguish to the sky. "Bring us a healer!" I demand. "Now!"

A heavily armed guard with short, dark hair and brown eyes approaches. "Give her to us, Dragon, and we will spare you and your warriors."

This brave fool is about to be burned to ash. "She is mine," I growl. "You will not touch her."

"Raiden?" A human male, wearing a gold crown, with short, blond hair and striking green eyes, walks toward us. This must be King Edmynd. "What is the meaning of this, brother?" he asks the man. "What are you—"

King Edmynd halts abruptly at the sight of Freyja. "What happened?" His eyes are wide. "What have you done to her?"

"She is my mate and my queen, and your cousin," I rasp, fighting against the poison coursing through my veins. "I brought her here to save her. Stop wasting time and fetch a healer," I thunder. "Now!"

A sharp howl pierces the air, and the stench of wolf

reaches my nostrils. I turn my head and see five wolves approaching, but these are no regular dire wolves. "Let her go!" The closest one growls.

They are Wolf shifters.

With dark russet fur, his golden eyes glare at me, full of rage. "What have you done to her?"

"Lukas, stop!" Varys calls out, and I realize who this Wolf shifter is. He is Prince Lukas—the Wolf Shifter Prince of Valren.

I have only met him a few times before, but I have never seen him in his Wolf form.

"She is mine," I snarl. "I am trying to save her."

Kyven and Varys walk toward me. Varys moves to take her from my arms, but I growl. "Do *not* touch her."

He exchanges a glance with Kyven and then motions for me to follow him. "Come! Hurry!"

In the back of my mind, I wonder why they are here. Varys is married to King Edmynd's sister, but Kyven... I do not understand why he would be present as well. And yet, none of these questions matter. The only thing I care about is finding a way to save my T'kara.

I follow Varys and King Edmynd through the castle. It feels like an eternity before we reach their healer. I stop short, and a vicious growl rips from my throat when I see a Mage standing on the other side of the entrance. His pale gray skin is easily visible beneath his dark robes. His raven-black eyes are twin pools of darkness as he stares at me with an unflinching gaze. I bare my fangs. "Why is he here?"

"This is High Mage Ylari," Varys quickly says. "He fought against the Order when they attacked Florin, less than a week ago, with their Wraiths and the army of Kolstrad. He is not with them. He's with us."

Us? I give him a questioning look before I push past the Mage and into the room. A human woman with long, braided brown hair, streaked with gray, moves to my side and motions to the empty bed. "Place her there."

Gently, I lay Freyja atop the stark white sheets, watching anxiously as the healer moves her hands over her. "What is the nature of her injury?" she asks. "What—" she sucks in a sharp breath and stumbles forward, catching the edge of the bed before she falls. Her eyes are wide as she stares down at Freyja.

"What is it?" King Edmynd asks.

"She is too close to death. I almost got pulled in with her. I—" She shakes her head, fear marring her features. "There is nothing I can do. She is beyond my help."

"Get away from her!" I flash my fangs, watching as she pales and collapses into the chair behind her. "Get her out of my sight!" I growl and then spin to Edmynd, unable to contain my frustration and fury. "Fetch another healer!"

Edmynd nods to one of his guards and the man sprints down the hallway, presumably to find someone else.

High Mage Ylari moves to her side. "Back away from her," I grind out. "Or I will torch you where you stand."

"Let me try, Aurdyn." Kyven steps between us, his lavender eyes full of concern. "My people are skilled in the art of healing. I may be able to help her."

As much as I dislike the Fae, I hate the Mages even more. A snarl curls my lip, rage coursing through me. "Save her, Kyven, or I'll—"

"*Do not* threaten him!" A feminine voice calls from the doorway, and I turn to find a woman with long brown hair and hazel eyes, a gold circlet crown across her forehead. Six Fae guards surround her.

"Grayce!" Kyven rushes to her, taking her hand in his own. "You should not be here. Go back to the room where it is safe."

She levels a dark glare at me, and I blow out a frustrated

sigh. "I'm not going to harm him," I growl. "But I need him to save my mate."

She blinks several times, shock easily read in her features. "You are married to our cousin?"

"She is my Fated One," I rasp, barely managing to contain the maelstrom of emotions that whirl deep within. "She will die without help."

Another woman with blond hair and hazel eyes comes up behind her, gasping at the sight of my T'kara. I recognize her immediately as Queen Inara—Varys's mate. "What has happened?"

"We fought against the Mages that came to invade Arganth," I explain. "Freyja used too much of her power to save us."

Varys glances at his mate. "This happened with Inara too, when she used her powers, but I was able to share my life force with her. It saved her." He steps closer. "Freyja is your Fated One. Use your life force to—"

"If I knew how, I would," I snap, unable to hide the desperation in my voice. "My kind possess fire, not magic like yours."

"I believe I can help you," Kyven says.

"How?"

"Before I was king, I was a second son," he says, reminding me of his father and his older brother's unexpected deaths not long ago. "I trained to be a healer. I may be able to create a link between you, so you can give some of your life force to her through the connection."

"Do it!" I command.

"There is risk," he says a bit hesitantly. "Both of you could perish."

"I would rather chance it than live without her." Emotions lodge in my throat, but I choke out, "If the goddess of death takes her this night, she will have to take us

343

both, for I will not let my T'kara go to those dark shores alone."

"Very well," Kyven says soberly. "Let us begin."

He places three fingers on Freyja's forehead and three on mine. *"Follow my voice and let it guide you to your mate."* The words flow through me like water as his voice echoes in my mind.

I blink and Freyja is standing next to the heart tree. The wind blows through her hair, tussling her long scarlet locks as silver-white leaves whirl around her, catching on the soft strands. Dressed in her green tunic dress, her back is to me. "Freyja," I call softly.

She turns and a brilliant smile lights her features. I rush toward her, gathering her to my chest.

She twines her arms around my neck and whispers against my skin. "I thought I would never see you again." Her voice quavers. "Forgive me."

Tears sting my eyes. "Why did you not tell me what you saw?"

"If I had, you would have left me behind, and you would have died, Aurdyn." A tear slips down her cheek. "My wonderful, arrogant Dragon king. I love you too much to let you die." She presses a loving kiss to my lips, and I taste the salt of her tears. "I'm sorry we did not have more time, Aurdyn."

I cup her cheek. "You're not going to die, Freyja. You cannot die, my T'kara."

"Aurdyn." Sadness shines in her eyes. "I—"

"I saw our future," I tell her. "I saw our son." Her luminous eyes search mine as I continue. "So, I know you will not die. I saw it, my fire heart. He was perfect and he was ours."

As her gaze holds mine, I remember the story of the guard and the princess. I understand now what it truly meant. To save what is most important, I am willing to sacrifice everything. My life is no longer my own. It is hers. I do not want it without her.

I take her hand in mine and bring it to my chest, resting our joined hands directly over my beating heart. Gently, I drop my forehead to hers and whisper the truth that resides in my soul. "Here is my heart, Freyja. My love is in here. Take it. It is yours, my T'kara." A tear slides down my cheek. "I have no use for it if you are not in this world."

Intense heat surges through me, flooding my veins like liquid fire. I shudder against the pain. It feels as though my very soul is being ripped in two and then sewn back together as my life force feeds into hers.

Agony sings through my very bones, and I release a booming roar as I fight against the death that seeks to claim us before falling away into peaceful oblivion.

CHAPTER 63

FREYJA

Aurdyn releases an anguished roar, and I feel myself slipping away, tumbling through darkness. The last moments of the battle replay in my mind and I'm back in the water, sinking into the dark and icy depths. The cold stabs at my flesh like hundreds of needles. Everything hurts. And as my heart rate slows, I understand now that I am floating in the in-between.

The void between this world and the next.

Every instinct tells me to swim for the surface, but my limbs remain still, unable to respond. An image of Aurdyn fills my mind. The first time I saw him flying toward me. His emerald-green eyes wide as they met mine for the first time, full of unbridled panic and anger. "I will save you, my T'kara," his voice is a low and deep rumble. "You are mine, my fire heart. Come back to me."

The vision changes and I'm standing at the heart tree. Her voice is a soft whisper on the wind as a child appears in the distance, with red and white scales. He lifts his head, and I recognize my own blue eyes staring back at me.

"Our son," Aurdyn's voice fills my mind as I stare at the child in wonder.

The vision fades and I find myself in the temple again. The silver-white leaves of the sacred tree catching in my hair as they drift all around me. "Come back to me, Freyja," Aurdyn whispers. "You are my fire heart, and I cannot live without you."

Drawing in a deep breath, I close my eyes. In the back of my mind, I understand that I have a choice. But as I think of my wonderful, arrogant Dragon, clarity pierces the darkness, parting the veil of the void, and showing me the way back home.

* * *

WHEN I WAKE, I'm in a large, fluffy bed. The gray stone walls are vaguely familiar, but my mind cannot yet place them as I climb through a murky fog to the surface as I slowly awaken.

"I am fine." I recognize Aurdyn's voice immediately, and a smile crests my lips. "Do not touch me," he growls. "It will heal."

"Stop being stubborn, and let me check it," an unfamiliar man's voice says.

"Aurdyn." I whisper, turning my head toward the sound of his voice. "Where are we?"

"Freyja." He moves to my side and takes my hand. "We are in Florin."

"Florin?"

"You almost died." I turn toward a woman's voice and recognize my cousin Grayce right away.

"Grayce." I smile. "It's been so long."

"Too long, cousin." A warm smile lights her face as her hazel eyes search mine. "How are you feeling?"

"You interrupted her wedding, you know," a man's voice calls out. I turn toward the sound and find my cousin Raiden standing in the doorway. His short, dark hair is slightly ruffled, and his brown eyes study my Dragon husband with a wary look before he walks toward me.

He takes my hand. "How on earth did you end up married to a fire breathing Dragon?" he teases. "First Inara weds a bloody Dark Elf, and now this." He darts a glance at Grayce. "And she would be married to the Fae King already if you had not shown up when you did."

"Oh, Grayce." I give her a pitying look. "I'm so sorry for ruining your wedding."

"Nonsense." She smiles warmly. "This just means you can attend the ceremony now as well, once you are better."

As I study her, I notice she does not look very thrilled about her upcoming marriage, but I know better than to ask her in a room full of others.

She gives Aurdyn a pointed look. "But *you* must be on your best behavior," she says. "No more threatening to burn everyone that makes you upset."

"He doesn't mean it." I laugh softly. "He's just a bit moody sometimes."

Aurdyn narrows his eyes, even as a smile quirks his gorgeous lips. "I am *not* moody."

"Of course not, my grumpy Dragon," I tease lightly.

Memories rush in and I inhale sharply. "My uncle? Is he safe?"

"I am here, Freyja," he says, and my breath catches in my throat as he walks into the room.

His blue eyes meet mine, guilt and shame burning in their depths. He moves to my side, and swallows thickly. "Freyja, forgive me." His voice quavers. "I did not—"

"I know," I barely manage, blinking back tears. "I know it was not you, Uncle Harald."

He gently rests his hand over mine, and then looks at Aurdyn. "If not for you," he says to my husband, "I would have lost the most important person in my life. I can never thank you enough, Dragon King."

Aurdyn dips his chin in subtle acknowledgement.

He turns his attention back to me, squeezing my hand gently. "You saved me, Freyja. You saved all of Ruhaen, my darling niece. Your parents would be so proud to see the person you have become." He shakes his head softly. "Forgive me."

"There is nothing to forgive," I whisper.

He presses a kiss to my forehead, and then steps back as my cousin Edmynd walks up beside him.

Edmynd smiles down at me. "How are you feeling?"

"Better," I speak softly. "Still a bit tired, though."

"When were you going to tell us you married a Dragon?" He flashes a grin.

"We tried to get word to you," I tell him. "We wanted to help when we discovered the Wraiths were coming to Florin, but then they attacked Arganth, and—"

"It is all right," he says. "The Dark Elves and the Fae helped us defeat them when they tried to invade with Kolstrad's army." He lifts his gaze to Aurdyn. "But I do not believe they have given up. I believe they will try again."

Aurdyn nods. "I agree."

Another man walks up behind him, and I gasp when I see the flash of his beautiful purple wings. Sunlight catches on his silver hair and highlights the lavender color of his eyes. He is Fae. "I am King Kyven," he says. "I helped treat you. I would like to assess you now, if I may."

I smile warmly at him. "You are the one who will marry my cousin, Grayce."

"Yes."

I dart a glance at Grayce. She smiles at Kyven, but there is something in her eyes that is distant, but I cannot explain it.

"I… understand that I interrupted your wedding. I am sorry."

"It is all right. We are just glad you are well." He lifts his hands to me. "May I?"

"Of course."

Aurdyn practically glares at everyone in the room. "Give him space," he demands. "Leave the room so he can work."

Kyven's lips quirk up and his eyes flash with barely restrained amusement. "Your Dragon can be quite demanding," he teases. "But I am certain you already know this."

Aurdyn curls his lip at him.

"Stop it," I say weakly. "He helped us. You should be nice to him."

Aurdyn narrows his eyes at Kyven. "Very well," he grumbles.

Kyven's hands hover over me as he assesses my condition. When he reaches my abdomen, his brows tick up toward his forehead. "This is interesting," he muses.

"What is?" Aurdyn is instantly on alert. "Tell me," he growls. "Now."

"She is carrying your fledgling." Kyven smiles, and Aurdyn's mouth falls open. "It is a—"

"Son," I finish his sentence.

He cocks his head to one side. "Yes, how did you know that?"

I reach a trembling hand up to Aurdyn and touch his face. Tears shine in his eyes. "Because my protective Dragon told me when he came to save my life."

Aurdyn turns his face into my hand, brushing a devoted kiss to my palm. "You remembered."

"Yes," I speak softly. "You gave me your heart, just like the guard and the princess."

He drops to his knees and kisses my abdomen reverently as I run my fingers through his silver-white hair. "Everything I am is yours, my fire heart."

I cup his cheek. "Do you think he'll have wings?" I ask, a bit worried that our son will be born wingless because of me.

"Of course, he will," Aurdyn says proudly. "His father is a Dragon, not some pitiful human male."

I laugh at his arrogance. "Yes, but—"

"I have seen it, my T'kara." His expression softens as he cups my cheek. "It was the vision the heart tree gave me."

A tear escapes my lashes, but he brushes it away. "I remember now," I whisper. "I saw it when you saved me."

Kyven clears his throat, and Aurdyn snarls. "Leave us before I set fire to your perfect hair, Fae King."

I give him an exasperated look, even as a smile threatens to break out across my face. "You cannot go around threatening everyone who upsets you, Aurdyn."

"It is instinct," he says, narrowing his eyes again at Kyven. "Especially when one's mate is nesting."

He crawls into the bed with me, slipping beneath the covers, completely uncaring that Kyven has not even fully left the room yet.

Aurdyn loops an arm around my back and pulls me to him, wrapping me up in his arms and wings. "Besides, I want to be alone with you," he whispers. "I thought I'd go mad waiting for you to awaken. I was so afraid," he admits. "You are my heart, Freyja."

I cup his cheek, studying his handsome face. "And you are mine."

EPILOGUE

FREYJA

I rest one hand on the slight swell of my abdomen as Aurdyn guides me to the heart tree in the center of the temple. Silver leaves twirl on the breeze, snagging on my dress and my hair as the cold wind blows around the columns.

Everyone is gathered around us, watching as the High Priest approaches.

Dragon warriors and several families have come to observe the official crowning of their queen.

My uncle stands beside my cousins, King Edmynd and Prince Raiden. While my cousin Inara stands beside her Dark Elf King mate, and Grayce is next to King Kyven.

Brovyn walks toward us, carrying a gold circlet crown. He smiles as he hands it to my husband.

Aurdyn raises it overhead, and then gently places it on my brow. "Heart of my heart. Blood of my blood," he speaks loud enough for all to hear. "My queen, forever and always."

Everyone erupts into cheers as he gathers me to his chest, pulling me close and wrapping his wings around me.

* * *

AFTER THE FESTIVITIES, he carries me back to our room. Ever since he found out I am carrying our fledgling, he has become even more protective than before. I barely yawned at the celebration, and he insisted upon taking me back to our room so I can rest.

But when we reach the bed, his eyes darken with a familiar hunger that I know so well.

Gently, he lays me down beneath the furs and then crawls over me. He kisses a heated trail from my lips, across my jaw, and down my neck. He pauses at my claiming mark, tracing his tongue lightly over the spot.

"Mine," he growls.

"Yours," I whisper, and he lifts his head. His emerald-green eyes stare deep into mine, full of devotion.

I thread my fingers through his silver-white hair and cup his face, pulling his lips back down to me.

"You are perfect," he breathes between kisses.

A whisper of fabric reaches my ears, and I glance down as he carefully slices a line down my dress, parting it and leaving me bare beneath him.

I laugh softly. "You destroy all my best clothing."

"Then, perhaps you should not wear anything," he teases as he kisses the spot just below my ear that drives me mad.

"You want everyone to see your mate, fully unclothed?" I arch a teasing brow.

"No," he snarls. "You are mine, and I will tear their eyes out if they so much as look at you like those blasted Dwarves always do when they visit."

353

"They are not trying to steal me away." I grin. "They know better than to even try."

He growls, and then cups my breast. I arch into his touch as he moves down my form, brushing his tongue over the already stiffened peak.

"Aurdyn, please," I dig my nails into his shoulders.

He moves back up my body, and I inhale sharply as the crown of his stav bumps lightly against my entrance.

His gaze holds mine as he slowly sinks into me. A low moan escapes me as I feel each and every delicious ridge of his length, deep in my channel.

I wrap my legs around his hips, holding tightly to him as he begins a slow and steady rhythm.

He folds his wings around me, pulling me so close there is no space between us as each stroke becomes longer and deeper. I'm lost in sensation at the delicious friction of our bodies as he moves deep inside me. His knot expands in my core. And when we reach the peak, we fall over the edge together.

I call out his name as I find my release and his roar echoes throughout our chamber as he cries out. "Mine!"

Aurdyn rolls us to one side and skims his nose alongside my own before claiming my mouth in a searing kiss.

He rests his hand on my abdomen and drops his forehead gently to mine. "I know why the gods fated you to me, Freyja."

"Why?" I run a hand through his silken hair.

"Because you are my heart," he whispers. "My T'kara. My treasure. My fire heart. My queen."

I brush my lips to his and smile against them. "And you are mine, my wonderful, arrogant, Dragon King."

ALSO BY JESSICA GRAYSON

Next book in the series - *Taken by the Fae King*

If you enjoyed this book please leave a review on Amazon and/or Goodreads.

Jessica Grayson

Of Fate and Kings Series

Bound to the Dark Elf King

Claimed by the Dragon King

Taken by the Fae King

Stolen by the Wolf King

Captured by the Orc King

Check out some of my other books while you're here.

Do you like Fairy Tale Retellings?

Fairy Tale Retellings (Once Upon a Fairy Tale Romance Series)

Taken by the Dragon: A Beauty and the Beast Retelling

Captivated by the Fae: A Cinderella Retelling

Rescued By The Merman: A Little Mermaid Retelling

Bound To The Elf Prince: A Snow White Retelling

Claimed By The Bear King: A Snow Queen Retelling

Protected By The Wolf Prince: A Red Riding Hood Retelling

Of Gods and Fate (Greek God Romance Series)

Claimed By Hades

Bound to Ares

Orc Claimed Series

Claimed by the Orc

Of Dragons and Elves Series (Fantasy Romance)

The Elf Knight

Scarred Dragon Prince Series

Shadow Guard: Dragon Shifter Romance

To Love a Monster Book Series (Fantasy Romance)

Claimed by the Monster: A Monster Romance

Ice World Warrior Series (Scifi Romance)

Claimed: Dragon Shifter Romance

Bound: Vampire Alien Romance

Rescued: Fae Alien Romance

Stolen: Werewolf Romance

Taken: Vampire Alien Romance

Fated: Dragon Shifter Romance

Protected: Dragon Shifter Romance

Want Dragon Shifters? You can dive into their world with this completed Duology.

Mosauran Series (Dragon Shifter Alien Romance)

The Edge of it All

Shape of the Wind

V'loryn Series (Vampire Alien Romance)

Lost in the Deep End

Beneath a Different Sky

Under a Silver Moon

V'loryn Holiday Series (A Marek and Elizabeth Holiday novella takes place prior to their bonding)

The Thing We Choose

V'loryn Fated Ones (Vampire Alien Romance)
Where the Light Begins (Vanek's Story)

For information about upcoming releases Like me on

Facebook at Jessica Grayson

http://facebook.com/JessicaGraysonBooks.

OR

sign up for upcoming release alerts at my website:
Jessicagraysonauthor.com

Made in United States
Troutdale, OR
03/23/2025

29979248R00210